Humanizing Ballet Pedagogies

In *Humanizing Ballet Pedagogies*, Jessica Zeller offers a new take on the ballet pedagogy manual, examining how and why ballet pedagogies develop, considering their implications for students and teachers, and proposing processes by which readers can enact humanizing, equitable approaches.

This book supports pedagogical thinking and development in ballet. Across three parts, it reflects how pedagogies come to be: through rationales, dialogues, and practices. Part 1, Philosophies, offers a contextual reading of ballet pedagogy's historic relationship to ideals, and it describes an alternative approach that takes its meaningful purpose from the embodied knowledge of participants in the ballet class. Part 2, Perspectives, looks at how the teacher's person shapes the ballet class. It draws from a new survey of ballet students that illuminates the direct effects of pedagogies and proposes future directions. Praxis, Part 3, includes three theoretically based approaches that can be applied directly or adjusted to readers' contexts for teaching ballet: yielding to student agency and autonomy, ungrading graded ballet classes in higher education, and practicing reflection for growth. Grounded in the wide range of people who participate in ballet, themes of equity, ethics, and humanity are at the heart of this book.

Humanizing Ballet Pedagogies is a valuable resource for those teaching or developing a teaching approach in ballet. It addresses important issues for school owners, administrators, or anyone responsible for supporting ballet teachers or students in the twenty-first century.

Jessica Zeller, PhD, MFA, is an Associate Professor of Dance in the TCU School for Classical & Contemporary Dance, USA, where she teaches courses across the ballet curriculum and in dance histories, theories, and pedagogies. Her first book, *Shapes of American Ballet: Teachers and Training before Balanchine* (2016), unearths the teachings of lesser-known European and Russian ballet pedagogues and situates them in the context of early twentieth-century American Capitalism, and her research on ballet pedagogies appears in *(Re:) Claiming Ballet* (2021), *Dance on Its Own Terms: Histories and Methodologies* (2013), *Dance Chronicle*, and the *Journal of Dance Education*. Zeller is a past president of CORPS de Ballet, International.

Humanizing Ballet Pedagogies
Philosophies, Perspectives, and Praxis for Teaching Ballet

Jessica Zeller

LONDON AND NEW YORK

Designed cover image: Brock Kingsley

First published 2025
by Routledge
4 Park Square, Milton Park, Abingdon, Oxon OX14 4RN

and by Routledge
605 Third Avenue, New York, NY 10158

Routledge is an imprint of the Taylor & Francis Group, an informa business

© 2025 Jessica Zeller

The right of Jessica Zeller to be identified as author of this work has been asserted in accordance with sections 77 and 78 of the Copyright, Designs and Patents Act 1988.

All rights reserved. No part of this book may be reprinted or reproduced or utilised in any form or by any electronic, mechanical, or other means, now known or hereafter invented, including photocopying and recording, or in any information storage or retrieval system, without permission in writing from the publishers.

Trademark notice: Product or corporate names may be trademarks or registered trademarks, and are used only for identification and explanation without intent to infringe.

British Library Cataloguing-in-Publication Data
A catalogue record for this book is available from the British Library

ISBN: 978-1-032-36575-6 (hbk)
ISBN: 978-1-032-36574-9 (pbk)
ISBN: 978-1-003-33271-8 (ebk)

DOI: 10.4324/9781003332718

Typeset in Galliard
by codeMantra

For my mother, a rather magical person, who believed me when at age three I told her I wanted to be a ballerina.

Contents

Acknowledgments: A Révérence		ix
Introduction		1

PART 1
Philosophies — 13

1. Ideal-Driven Pedagogies — 15
2. Student-Driven Pedagogies — 42

PART 2
Perspectives — 67

3. Teacher Presence and Behavior — 69
4. Student Voices — 91

PART 3
Praxis — 117

5. Student Agency and Autonomy — 119
6. Evaluation and (Un)Grading — 135
7. Reflective Practices — 158
   Conclusion: Reflections on Becoming — 176

Selected Bibliography — *183*
Index — *191*

Acknowledgments: A Révérence

This book owes its existence to scores of remarkably intelligent, thoughtful, generous people. To the editorial staff at Routledge—Claire Margerison, Lucia Accorsi, Steph Hines, and Ben Piggott—thank you for your thoughtful guidance and support of this project. To Kate Mattingly, Courtney Harris, Steven Ha, Lauren Huynh, and Fen Kennedy, who shared considerable insight into this manuscript in its preliminary stages, I am appreciative beyond measure—your keen and compassionate perspectives have elevated this book. My deep acknowledgment as well to those who generously offered their thoughts on the journal articles that became this manuscript: editors Sanja Andus L'Hotellier and Doug Risner, as well as Betsy Miller, Jenai Cutcher, Ashley Thorndike-Youssef, and Brian Devine. To Brock Kingsley, thank you for challenging my thinking and writing about pedagogy for 20 years; you encouraged me to "just fucking write it" when I needed to hear that most. I'm lucky to have your singular perspective behind this work. And to those who took the time to respond to a public survey: your perspectives matter. Thank you for sharing them. I hope I've done you justice.

Despite my efforts, it's quite impossible to acknowledge all that my ballet teachers have contributed to my pedagogical thinking, so I offer my heart-forward thanks for these bits of their wisdom and so much more: To Sondra Forsyth, who knew how to communicate with children and insisted that dancers were smart when that was not the prevailing attitude. To Jan Hanniford Goetz, who saw something in me and nurtured it, and whose luminous movement sensibilities have been a constant inspiration. To Maggie Black, who understood simplicity and took young people seriously. To Rochelle Zide-Booth, whose pragmatism makes everything possible, somehow, and who made me feel legitimate when I was at my most insecure. To Karen Eliot, who mentored my research with incisive generosity and who, between Maggie impressions, gently reminded me that I had rotators and hamstrings when I thought they were lost forever.

There are others, too, whose perspectives stayed with me: Helen Scott, beyond the ballet studio, helped me believe that I could. Michelle

Jarvis, Cynthia Pratt, Marek Cholewa, Rosanna Ruffo, and Stephan Laurent taught me to show up ready and read the room. Melanie Bales and Susan Dromisky both managed that magic pedagogical trick of making me laugh, hard, while I was sweating out their beautiful classes. There are too many more to mention here, and a few—thankfully just—who I've omitted. I am, reluctantly in these latter cases, grateful to all of them.

I am filled with appreciation for the robust communities of students who have indelibly shaped the perspectives in this book. It is only a mild exaggeration to suggest that every student I have ever worked with has contributed in some way to my ongoing education as a ballet educator, so I extend my heartfelt appreciation to every one of them. They've taught me the value of being in daily dialogue, and they give meaningful purpose to every ballet class.

To my TCU colleagues over the past several years, I am grateful every day for your collaborative and deeply thoughtful efforts. A big purple thank you to Keith Saunders, Kellye Saunders, Laura Barbee, Adam McKinney, Nina Martin, Suki John, Sarah Newton, Brad Garner, Annika Sheaff, Will Labossiere, Chad Jung, Susan Douglas Roberts, Larisa Cherkasov, Carrie Hickman, Angelique Hall, Heather McCreless, Lindsay Puente, Deborah Vogel, Najwa Seyedmorteza, Laura West Strawser, Roma Flowers, John Hopkins, Susan Austin, and Lori Schneider. I owe a tremendous debt of gratitude to Elizabeth Gillaspy, in particular, who supported me at a foundational level by making programmatic space for me to develop this work in practice and research. Thank you, Elizabeth, for your advocacy and for more than a decade of office doorway ballet pedagogy chats. Many thanks as well to Dean Amy Tully and the staff in the TCU College of Fine Arts for your consistent support of faculty. This book was supported by TCU's merited leave policy and research funding, which thankfully still exist for some of us, but which should be made available to all of us. I especially wish to thank my contingent faculty colleagues, whose institutionally undervalued work props up the system that enabled this book. The academy would be a far richer place if your expertise, dedication, and care were appropriately compensated.

I am fortunate beyond measure to have a personal support system of people who have always believed in me and taken my interests seriously at every turn. Mom, you're a wonder and a most extraordinary role model—thank you for being my champion and making me feel like I can do anything. Josh, you are an inspiration. Gabriel, after enduring the plight of the ballet sibling, shuttling back and forth to classes and sitting through umpteen-thousand *Nutcrackers*, you'll still go to the ballet with me. I'm so lucky I get to be your sister. To my dearest framily, Monserrat, Rachel, Cory, and Courtney, thank you for keeping me grounded and connected. And to my beloved late grandparents, I carry you with me—your strong beliefs in the arts and education are the ground beneath this book.

To my Brandon, your partnership throughout this process has been profound. With great care and good cheer, you've supported my unending and only occasionally successful search for balance while writing. You've made me feel completely rational and reasonable—sage, even—as I've prattled on for three years about all manner of book-related minutiae. Frankly, love, I'm not sure which of us that says more about, but I adore you for it.

Lastly, to Sam, my goofy and charming elder pup, for your big heart, your loving eyes, and your leadership on walks. Thank you for teaching me about humanity. May the treats always be plenty.

Introduction

Ballet teachers are role models and mentors, nurturers, and advocates. They support dancers through their formative stages of study and guide them throughout their performing careers. Bearing witness to extraordinary moments of humanity and skill in the studio, they facilitate students' relationships to technique and artistry, contribute to student maturation and development, and kindle the flame beneath students' love of ballet. They can become like family. Ballet teachers serve as sources of historical knowledge and wisdom. As embodied archives who enliven ballet's lineages, they connect students to ballet's past. Every day in the ballet class, teachers and students, together, spin the threads that tie ballet's histories to its futures.

As stewards of ballet and its pedagogies, ballet teachers are also some of the field's most ardent gatekeepers. They hold the authority to pass down ballet's traditions and determine how far students go while under their tutelage. While these responsibilities are often carried out with great compassion and care, far too many teachers abuse the power in these positions. They prioritize The Preservation Of Tradition and The Expectations Of The Profession over the dignity of the people they're charged with teaching. They tarnish the field with unethical, often inequitable approaches, as they demonstrate what amounts to a poverty of humanity in the teaching of ballet.

Ballet pedagogies are similarly complex; developed through this advocate-arbiter paradox that underscores teachers' roles. Ballet's pedagogies are embodied and lived, intellectualized and philosophically reconciled, and contextualized inside histories and experiences. They change over time, as do people. The study of ballet—a beloved system of movement and mode of expression—has the capacity to provide dancers with a connection to generations of ancestors, a sense of home and place, a purpose and set of values, and a lens through which to understand themselves and the world. Well into the twenty-first century, ballet's pedagogical emphases are shifting, from preserving tradition via gatekeeping and propping up hierarchies via exclusion, to critically examining and celebrating ballet's heterogeneous forms, aesthetics, lineages, and histories. Ballet pedagogies, today, have become an ongoing negotiation of the tensions between historical traditions, power dynamics, and contemporary contexts and people. When these dialogues are enacted as pedagogical praxis, they support the holistic development of ballet's students and dancers, as well as the growth of teachers and ballet's pedagogic profession at large.

To this end, this book is a thinking through—a process. It is about the possibilities that emerge when pedagogical inquiry supersedes pedagogical power, when curiosity and care become more valuable than exerting control or wielding status. It believes that ballet's heterogeneity is its greatest strength, and it trusts ballet's capacity to absorb and reflect multitudes. Necessarily messy and full of gray areas, this book revels in the complexities that echo the fascinating humanness of everyone who engages with ballet pedagogies.

While pedagogies are the purview of teachers, ballet's students are the embodied reflection of pedagogic work. They are its *why*. As both individuals and groups in the ballet class, they are collaborators and innovators. They bring fortitude and insight to their work through bodily knowledge and lived experience. They are people in and of the world who exist in and beyond ballet. When I teach, it is always the students who remind me that dancing, learning, and working in dialogue can generate immense joy. Students are at the heart of the pedagogic project, and they are the heart of this book.

Humanizing Pedagogies

Derived from the critical pedagogy of Brazilian educator, activist, and thinker Paulo Freire, humanizing pedagogies feature *becoming* as a key element.[1] Teachers and students, together, *become* through the study of ballet: more self-actualized, more aware of themselves and others, and more capable of recognizing their relationships to ballet's systems, histories, and institutions. They become more reflexively engaged as members of a collective and participants in dialogue, and they become more metacognitively adept. Learning is central to becoming; becoming happens when worldviews expand. In the study of ballet, becoming is also made evident through the body, as teachers and students deepen their embodied relationships to ballet's forms, styles, and histories—becoming more fluent in the languages of their field. Elizabeth McPherson, Doug Risner, and Karen Schupp note that "a dance classroom that is constantly *becoming* in the Freirian sense, models humanizing pedagogy, balances relations of power, openly examines tensions, and welcomes complex problems to solve communally."[2] Such environments function in direct contrast to ballet's authoritarian pedagogies, which have subjugated people beneath traditions, maintained hierarchies and invoked tensions, and dismissed problems as individual deficiencies for individuals to solve in isolation.

The process of teachers and students engaging in dialogues as "critical co-investigators" is central to humanizing pedagogies.[3] The dialogical component of education is ongoing—not reducible to a simple method— as Donaldo Macedo suggests: "the fundamental goal of dialogical teaching is to create a process of learning and knowing that invariably involves theorizing about the experiences shared in the dialogue process."[4] To this end, McPherson, Risner, and Schupp point out that "Freirian-influenced dance education scholars often interpret his pedagogical vision as a way of living in *the world* rather than a set of technical best practices or teaching methods."[5] Freire himself famously writes in *Pedagogy of the Oppressed*, "Knowledge emerges only through invention and re-invention, through the restless, impatient, continuing, hopeful inquiry human beings pursue in the world, with the world, and with each other."[6] It is the dialogues at the core of humanizing pedagogies—which happen in specific contexts with particular groups of people during given moments in time—that are the wellspring of becoming. This book, then, supports teachers in working with students as "critical co-investigators." It understands that teachers do their own pedagogical theorizing based on their dialogues with students in their unique contexts for teaching ballet. As such, I share my own experiences with these processes throughout this book, which range from little victories to humble attempts and cautionary tales.

Beyond its basis in Freire's critical pedagogy, I consider humanizing ballet pedagogies from a few additional perspectives. As an entity—a gerund—I propose that humanizing pedagogies recognize teachers' and students' whole humanness. The humanizing pedagogies I theorize here understand every person—teachers and students—to possess a fullness of being and humanity that, by virtue of their existence, deserves due regard. From an ethical perspective, Naomi Jackson contends that "regardless of specific circumstances... [human beings] have basic rights that guarantee a baseline treatment of respect and that they are treated with dignity."[7] Humanizing pedagogies, then, assume everyone is wholly human from the start, regardless of their level or quality of education or experience; their histories, heritages, or identities.

The actions that enable humanizing pedagogies—the verb form—ask teachers to actively acknowledge and genuinely believe in each student's full humanity, and to do the same with their own. It asks them to foster and bring their own sense of human wholeness to their work with students. Critical and feminist pedagogue bell hooks describes this as part of her "Engaged Pedagogy," saying: "Professors who embrace the challenge of self-actualization will be better able to create pedagogical practices that engage students, providing them with ways of knowing that enhance their capacity to live fully and deeply."[8] It asks ballet teachers to make their recognition of everyone's wholeness apparent and legible through their presence and behaviors in the ballet class. When teachers perceive of and interact with students as whole people, rather than as deficient charges to be molded or fixed; and when they work to develop as whole people themselves, ballet's hierarchies lose some of their power. The study of ballet, then, becomes focused on how dialogues between whole people, around ballet, can support everyone in their process of becoming.

It is important to note a departure from Freire's concept of becoming in my application of this theory to ballet pedagogies. Freire suggests that through dialogical education, students and teachers can, together, take as their joint purpose "becoming more fully human."[9] His suggestion that people can be "less human" or "more human" is linked to their degree of oppression; those "less human" constitute the oppressed, and thus "becoming more fully human" is the liberated objective.[10] A deeply political figure who taught literacy to people facing poverty, and who was imprisoned by Brazil's military junta for his radical approach, Freire's context was one in which the educator and the oppressor were two distinct entities with radically opposing agendas.

In twenty-first-century ballet pedagogies, however, Freire's divergent roles of educator and oppressor are one and the same: most often merged within the single entity of the ballet school and further consolidated within the sole person of each ballet teacher. It stands to reason that the majority of teaching positions in public and private ballet schools come with responsibilities for upholding those schools' policies and expectations.[11] Having been designed to maintain institutional control, uphold hierarchical power dynamics that allow for gatekeeping, and ensure economic profit or viability under neoliberalism (as in ballet programs in academia) or outright capitalism (as in private sector ballet schools), these policies and expectations tend to be inequitable at best, if not outright exclusionary. That ballet teachers are required to adhere to such institutional blueprints as a fixed condition of employment, then, establishes them as representatives of those institutions and their ethos. Teachers are educators, and perhaps even liberatory educators, but they are also oppressors who serve the institution.

Critiques of critical pedagogy suggest that students and teachers can never attain equivalent power inside of education's hierarchical structures, despite the hope that they could subvert the system collectively.[12] More broadly, they point out that the aim of subverting inequitable systems in and of itself becomes controversial when those same systems are the very contexts for that subversion.[13] While I hold a more hopeful view, perhaps, it is indisputable that capitalist and neoliberal teaching contexts make an indelible and too often authoritarian imprint on even the most liberatory pedagogies. To deny these realities is to work from a place of cognitive dissonance; charmed, perhaps, by philosophy out of context. Believing that I could be a ballet educator in most U.S.-based ballet institutions in the twenty-first century without also being an oppressor to some extent would be deliberately ignoring systemic factors in both educational settings and in the ballet field at large. There is a chasm between the feeling of the ballet teacher's role as a gatekeeper with institutional responsibilities and the feeling of the teacher's concurrent role as an educator with liberatory intentions. Yet, in most contexts, today's ballet teachers are functionally and simultaneously both.

This reality has ramifications when considering the purpose and language of "becoming more human" in ballet pedagogies, as the meaning of the phrase shifts when an oppressor—even a reluctant one—says it.[14] In the context of the dual role of the ballet teacher, "becoming more human" as a purpose gives me pause. In my position as a representative of my institution, for example, I am charged with instructing, assessing, evaluating, and contributing to determinations of how students advance through the program. As a white woman with such authority, if my pedagogical objective or a class learning objective were "becoming more human," then with Students of Color in particular, I would problematically be assuming a savior-esque role while simultaneously being responsible for judging these students' humanity within a racialized power dynamic. It would ask me to assume that students were "less human" at the start of our work together, and it would propose that I could then legitimately teach and, further, evaluate people in their own humanness—based on my perception of whether or how they allowed my teaching to shape their very humanity. Ethically, this is troubling to me, so I never consider the development of humanness to be a pedagogical element under my authority unless that humanness is my own. However antithetical it might seem given the origins of this work, and however important it may be to acknowledge the dehumanizing experiences students choose to share, I do not consider "becoming more human" an objective of humanizing ballet pedagogies. Rather, I conceive and describe humanizing ballet pedagogies throughout this book as rooted in the acknowledgment of students' and teachers' complete humanness as the assumed starting point. This work is based on a belief in people as fundamentally whole, which serves as the foundation for their becoming in a broader sense—for their capacity for learning and growth as people and dance artists.

No pedagogy can be humanizing without challenging how racism, sexism, ableism, ageism, gender bias, and a range of other prejudices have and continue to injure people in their attempts to educate and be educated. It is anathema for those in positions of power to claim interest in humanizing pedagogies while not acknowledging the full humanity of—and thereby actively harming—those with different identities from their own. The work to identify and disrupt individual bias, and to develop anti-biased pedagogical approaches is ongoing, uncomfortable, and necessary. It is also, however, joyful and inspiring; to feel traditionally exclusionary environments begin to open, and to experience the richness that diversity of all kinds brings to ballet's spaces. Humanizing pedagogies expect that teachers—particularly those who affiliate with dominant identity groups—actively work to identify and disrupt their own biases; that they educate themselves about approaches to pedagogy that foster equity, inclusion, diversity, belonging, and justice.

Expectations for humanizing action extend up the pedagogical hierarchy as well, with Jackson further noting the "obligation on behalf of those in authority at schools and companies to develop policies and procedures to protect [human] rights."[15] Both students and teachers should be able to feel secure in the knowledge that those above them in administrative or managerial positions, or those who design programs and oversee employment, will serve as stewards of their rights through the development of humanizing policies and procedures. The acknowledgment of humanity moves up and down these traditional hierarchies, with those higher up always holding the onus for extending recognition of humanity by default to those with less autonomy or control over their circumstances.

In addition to its footing in critical pedagogy, this book draws from theories that have been applied "in humanizing ways" to dance education and more recently to ballet, including but not limited to feminist pedagogy, Engaged Pedagogy, democratic education, culturally relevant pedagogy, and antiracist pedagogy.[16] While these philosophies are comprised of discrete elements and defining rationales that emerge from particular movements and struggles, they contribute to humanizing praxis. This book is thus in dialogue with several of these paradigms, while focusing on the work of humanizing and becoming through praxis-based teaching in ballet.

A brief note regarding the book's use of terminology: I've relinquished the term *training*, replacing it instead with the concept of *study*. The implications of training have begun to feel removed from work toward humanizing pedagogies; training so often implies extrinsic motivators, rote practices, and several varieties of force. A teacher can provide training, or a student can choose to train; but study suggests a fully student-driven action and an intentionally holistic approach to learning. Study might indeed include external pressures or even skills learned by rote, but it suggests student agency at its core—that the student opts in to the action. It's an only partially semantic shift that has changed my perception of my responsibilities and invigorated my approach.

Background and Context

The subjectivities innate to bodies and identities make it important to consider who is teaching ballet and who is speaking about it. My pedagogical development in ballet serves as the primary lens for this book; this includes my background with and knowledge of the form, as well as my physical self through whom I experience ballet. The content has therefore been filtered through my body, my experiences, and my identities. As lineage is part of experience in ballet, I offer here a brief map of my own pedagogical family tree. I describe the identities I hold and some additional contexts that are impressed upon this book.

My most significant early influences in ballet were co-directors of my ballet school in Long Island, New York: Jan Hanniford Goetz of the Joffrey Ballet and the Netherlands Dance Theatre and Sondra Forsyth of the Thalia Mara company. Maggie Black joined the faculty when I was 16; she had by then retired from teaching some of the most significant dancers of the twentieth century in her dance-boom era classes in New York City.[17] At Butler University, I was fortunate to work closely with Rochelle Zide-Booth of the Ballet Russe de Monte Carlo and the Joffrey Ballet.[18] I also worked with Vaganova-specific teachers there, and while I didn't embrace the style easily having come from a heterogeneous American ballet background, this period supported my later research into and teaching about various syllabus-based, national schools of ballet.

Currently, I am a tenured professor in the School for Classical & Contemporary Dance at Texas Christian University, a large private predominantly white institution with a secular curricular sensibility despite its religious affiliation. Since 2012, I've taught ballet, pointe, and repertoire in the BFA Ballet program, as well as courses in dance histories, theories, and pedagogies. The ballet classes I teach are populated almost entirely with dance majors who were admitted by audition; more than half of those major in ballet, and I get to know nearly all of them over four years across both classroom and studio courses. These classes have fewer than 20 students in them and are most often graced with the presence and skill of a musician. Because I've worked for more than a decade in the same institution where professor lore is passed down from cohort to cohort of students, my reputation often precedes me when I walk into a studio—I surmise that I am sometimes granted the benefit of the doubt before I can even introduce myself. I am conscious of these contextual privileges daily. This hasn't always been my lens for teaching, but this environment is the backdrop for many of the pedagogical examples in these pages.

My views on pedagogy are also grounded in seven years of teaching ballet to people mostly affiliated with modern and postmodern dance during my graduate work in the Department of Dance at The Ohio State University, where undergraduate majors and non-majors, my grad student peers, and sometimes dance faculty took ballet classes together. The thrilling diversity and eclecticism of people in that public education setting are unmatched in my current institution, although the range of people and perspectives I encountered during that time have shaped my work indelibly. While in graduate school, I taught in the trainee program at BalletMet and in their affiliated academy, prior to which I worked for nearly a decade in private sector studios and academies with teenagers on pre-professional tracks. As a teenager myself, I assisted my teachers and learned to teach pre-ballet. All told, I value what I've learned from four-year-olds and adult beginners just as much as my postmodern colleagues and the aspirant pre-professional ballet dancers I work with now.

The personal lens through which I interpret all things pedagogical comes from my lived experience and privileges in largely dominant identity groups as a white, cisgender, heterosexual, middle class, able-bodied woman. I most often feel represented in ballet—in the themes, stories, and roles that exist across the field—and I can navigate with relative ease in ballet's spaces. Not physically imposing, I am five feet tall with proportions that do not adhere to ballet's traditional ideals. This proved limiting when it came to professional possibilities with ballet companies, but it allowed me ample opportunities to perform in featured, often partnered, roles during my studies. I possess a few of ballet's idealized structural attributes in small amounts, which with age have decreased a bit in range and scope. My bodily privilege, however, is such that in my mid-40s I can still demonstrate the details of ballet's vocabulary clearly when I teach.

As a U.S.-based American professor, my research has considered how American Capitalism and pluralism have shaped the development of ballet and its pedagogies.[19] More recently, with this text as evidence, it has begun pushing upward against dehumanizing and inequitable structures in which ballet pedagogies exist. Contemporary American culture is full of people actively defying harmful traditions; protest and the challenging of authority are socio-cultural norms and part of the American national identity. I do not suggest here, then, that this work will translate globally or apply across the range of contexts in which ballet is taught outside the United States. Especially in cultures where reverence for authority and tradition is foregrounded, this work might be interpreted as deeply objectionable.

I continue to situate relevant elements of my position and privileges throughout the book as they relate to the contents of each chapter. Considering how books are so often read online in parts and how the assigning of chapters in academic coursework makes this book more likely to be read in excerpts than from cover to cover, the re-stating of my identities and my positionality serves to emphasize that humanizing pedagogical work in ballet is fundamentally subjective, and in my case at least, predicated on the privileges I hold. Lastly, I include examples of my teaching throughout this text for readers to draw from or push against as they consider their teaching in their contexts; mine is one approach among many, and it may not apply to all people or circumstances. I put it forward here for illustrative purposes, and not as a standard or exemplar.

About This Book

This book's first section, *Philosophies*, describes two contrasting rationales for the development of ballet pedagogies. Chapter 1 looks at the history and implications of pedagogies that are motivated by and focused on the achievement of ballet's ideals; from ideals for execution and performance, to idealized ways of being, to idealized bodies. This chapter considers the effects of such pedagogies on people, and it addresses issues of accountability when these pedagogies result in harm. Chapter 2, in contrast, examines how the subjective and embodied nature of ballet pedagogy's development serves to fundamentally humanize it. When students as whole people become the driving rationales behind the pedagogy, and when teachers embrace the heterogeneity of students' perspectives and persons in dialogue with their own, I propose that more equitable teaching in ballet is possible.

Part 2, *Perspectives*, considers how teachers and students understand ballet pedagogies. Chapter 3 is an examination of how the teacher's person shapes their pedagogy. Drawing from my own experience, I wade into the complexities of the teacher's ways of being and doing in the ballet class. The student's perspective is central to Chapter 4, which is based on anonymous public survey responses of students 18 years of age and older. As students have motivated the pedagogies I describe in this book, this chapter features their voices; it highlights students' interpretations of pedagogies in ballet classes, and their visions for the future of ballet pedagogies.

The remaining chapters make up Part 3 of the book, *Praxis*. Chapter 5 describes an approach to yielding pedagogical power to make space for student agency and autonomy. As the tipping of the traditional hierarchy has notoriously resulted in accusations of diminished "rigor," I address "rigor" and its implications here as well. Issues of evaluation and grading in the higher education ballet class comprise Chapter 6. Considering the nested hierarchies of ballet in academia, I focus on how ungrading practices can promote equity and support student preparation for a career in ballet or beyond. Reflective pedagogical practices are the subject of Chapter 7, which offers strategies for both teachers and students that can be applied or adapted to fit numerous ballet pedagogy contexts. The praxis-based themes in Part 3 are always in process in my work; by the time this book has been published, I'll already have made revisions.

I submit the ideas in this book as possibilities for teaching ballet as a form and field that thrives on heterogeneity. I aim to establish a stark contrast to those extant single-author books on ballet pedagogies that moralize and "should" around a homogenized—white supremacist, classist, misogynist, fatphobic, heteronormative—perception of ballet. I issue pedagogical imperatives when human rights and dignity are at stake: when ethics suggests a need. Some readers, for example, may find redundant my continued calls for educators in dominant identity groups to examine and disrupt implicit biases, or my persistent references to institutional contexts that shape pedagogical possibilities, yet these calls are warranted from a humanizing perspective and worth revisiting in different chapters for different reasons.

This book will be useful for ballet teachers in any range of ballet schools or educational environments. It covers a range of pedagogical ground, and I surmise that teachers working in higher education, or with teens and adult dancers in schools, or with professionals in ballet companies, will find the most possibilities in it. For those who teach young children, several ideas here could be creatively adapted to make them developmentally appropriate. This book will also serve ballet students seeking to understand the process of pedagogical inquiry; as well as administrators, owners, or those in leadership positions responsible for supporting teachers and students alike.

While the development of ballet pedagogies as humanizing praxis is well under way; there is much further to go. In support of this ongoing work, I consider ballet pedagogies here as subjective and malleable, despite the field's historical tendency to promote philosophies as objective and traditions as static. I spend time working through these mires in the text that follows. I filter theoretical paradigms from ballet, dance studies, education, and psychology through the embodied work in the ballet class, eschewing homogeneity and embracing a range of possibilities and perspectives.

Ultimately, this book acknowledges the balance between ballet pedagogy's problems and its potential through what Henry A. Giroux describes as the "language of critique" and the "language of hope and possibility."[20] Critical pedagogy, with its liberatory objectives, calls on educators to examine and critique the power structures and institutions in which they operate while maintaining a fundamental belief in the promise of change. To this end, Freire suggests that participants in education "must perceive their state not as fated and unalterable, but merely as limiting—and therefore challenging."[21] I accept this charge, and I thereby interrogate some of ballet pedagogy's historic problems while proposing humanizing possibilities for its future. Too much of the joy to be found in teaching ballet has been squandered at the joint altars of power and tradition. Writing this book has allowed me to reify my love for this art form and my commitment to those who participate in it—to develop a greater sense of curiosity in teaching. It is my hope that readers can find similar depth of meaning for themselves in these pages.

Notes

1 Paulo Freire, *Pedagogy of the Oppressed* (New York: Herder and Herder, 1970), 79–86.
2 Elizabeth McPherson, Doug Risner, and Karen Schupp, "Why Grade Inflation and Teacher Dispositions Don't Mix," in *Ethical Dilemmas in Dance*

Educations: Case Studies on Humanizing Dance Pedagogy, eds. Doug Risner and Karen Schupp (Jefferson, NC: McFarland, 2020), 172.
3 Paulo Freire, *Pedagogy of the Oppressed* (New York: Herder and Herder, 1970), 81.
4 Elizabeth McPherson, Doug Risner, and Karen Schupp, "Why Grade Inflation and Teacher Dispositions Don't Mix," in *Ethical Dilemmas in Dance Educations: Case Studies on Humanizing Dance Pedagogy*, eds. Doug Risner and Karen Schupp (Jefferson, NC: McFarland, 2020), 172; Donaldo Macedo, introduction to *Pedagogy of the Oppressed*, by Paulo Freire (New York: Herder and Herder, 1970), 17.
5 Elizabeth McPherson, Doug Risner, and Karen Schupp, "Why Grade Inflation and Teacher Dispositions Don't Mix," in *Ethical Dilemmas in Dance Educations: Case Studies on Humanizing Dance Pedagogy*, eds. Doug Risner and Karen Schupp (Jefferson, NC: McFarland, 2020), 172.
6 Paulo Freire, *Pedagogy of the Oppressed* (New York: Herder and Herder, 1970), 72.
7 Naomi Jackson, *Dance and Ethics: Moving Towards a More Humane Dance Culture* (Bristol: Intellect, 2022), 79.
8 bell hooks, *Teaching to Transgress: Education as the Practice of Freedom* (New York: Routledge, 1994), 22.
9 Paulo Freire, *Pedagogy of the Oppressed* (New York: Herder and Herder, 1970), 84.
10 Paulo Freire, *Pedagogy of the Oppressed* (New York: Herder and Herder, 1970), 44.
11 Further, politicians are making the case that "the professor's speech is the government's speech," which may affect ballet programs in public education settings; Douglas Soule, "Florida Government Could Censor University Professors in Classrooms, Lawyer for State Says," *Tallahassee Democrat* (Tallahassee, FL), June 14, 2024.
12 Elizabeth Ellsworth, "Why Doesn't This Feel Empowering? Working Through the Repressive Myths of Critical Pedgaogy," *Harvard Educational Review* 59, no. 3 (August 1989): 306–308. https://doi.org/10.17763/haer.59.3.058342114k266250.
13 Nick Stock, "Episode 101: Imagining Education Outside Capitalism," interview with Chris McNutt, *The Human Restoration Project Podcast*, podcast audio, December 27, 2021, https://shows.acast.com/5d546c26ade326bd3b4b47fc/61c8bd1a1c6a7900119b9e67.
14 Elizabeth McPherson, Doug Risner, and Karen Schupp, "Why Grade Inflation and Teacher Dispositions Don't Mix," in *Ethical Dilemmas in Dance Educations: Case Studies on Humanizing Dance Pedagogy*, eds. Doug Risner and Karen Schupp (Jefferson, NC: McFarland, 2020), 172.
15 Naomi Jackson, *Dance and Ethics: Moving Towards a More Humane Dance Culture* (Bristol: Intellect, 2022), 79.
16 Doug Risner and Karen Schupp, eds., *Ethical Dilemmas in Dance Educations: Case Studies on Humanizing Dance Pedagogy* (Jefferson, NC: McFarland, 2020), 6.
17 See Jessica Zeller, "Teaching through Time: Tracing Ballet's Pedagogical Lineage in the Work of Maggie Black," *Dance Chronicle* 32, no. 1 (2009): 57–88. https://doi.org/10.1080/01472520802690283.
18 See Jessica Zeller, "Developing the American Ballet Dancer: The Pedagogical Lineage of Rochelle Zide-Booth," in *Dance on its Own Terms: Histories and Methodologies*, eds. Karen Eliot and Melanie Bales (New York: Oxford University Press, 2013), 283–304. https://doi.org/10.1093/acprof:oso/9780199939985.001.0001.
19 See Jessica Zeller, "Ballet in America: Coming of Age in a Market Economy," in *Shapes of American Ballet: Teachers and Training before Balanchine* (New York: Oxford University Press, 2016), 59–88.
20 Henry A. Giroux, *On Critical Pedagogy*, 2nd ed. (London: Bloomsbury, 2020), 3.
21 Paulo Freire, *Pedagogy of the Oppressed* (New York: Herder and Herder, 1970), 85.

Part 1
Philosophies

1 Ideal-Driven Pedagogies

Ballet is built on ideals. Whether passed down in writing or through the oral and embodied tradition, ideals for how ballet should work in the body and how it should be performed and studied have driven the perpetuation of the form and its pedagogies. Ideals related to ballet's execution and performance can serve as important tools for pedagogues, who might invoke them to inspire and motivate students in their study. Ideals for ballet's form are important for teachers to develop and use—they can help students understand and holistically embrace details of technique, style, and aesthetic. These ideals are why dancers and dance observers fall in love with ballet as an expressive art form. They define ballet.

Inextricable from the ongoing development of technical and stylistic ideals that stipulate how ballet should be danced are both implicit and explicit ideals for *who* should dance it. These include gendered and racialized notions of who and how dancers should *be*: how they should behave and carry themselves, and what their bodies should look like—from internal skeletal structures to more readily visible physical and behavioral attributes. These ideals shape everything from how ballet is viewed in the public imagination; to ballet's labor practices in hiring, casting, and promotions; and further to how ballet is taught, learned, performed, and perpetuated at every level—from the local neighborhood ballet school to the world's most elite ballet companies. It is these ideals, related to dancers themselves, that have come under justifiable scrutiny for their long history of being used for gatekeeping and exclusion.

I examine here what I've labeled "ideal-driven" pedagogies: those philosophical and methodological approaches to teaching that purport to further ballet's traditions by upholding its ideals, first and foremost. I articulate some pedagogical implications of using ideals as a starting place, to differentiate between ballet's defining ideals that constitute the art form and its dehumanizing ideals that have and continue to leave a stain on the profession.[1] I include a discussion, to this end, of blame and accountability. In light of the human harm ballet's ideals have caused,

DOI: 10.4324/9781003332718-3

this is an attempt to offer a modicum of justice and some potential paths forward for those who have experienced the damaging effects of ideal-driven pedagogies—when ballet's ideals are prioritized over dancers' basic humanity.

Evolving Ideals: Definitions and Contexts

As ballet shifts in tandem with social and cultural trends over time, and as it responds to a range of political and economic contexts and events, so too do its ideals. Perhaps most notorious are ballet's bodily ideals or standards for what the dancer should look like, which include their proportions; the shape and size of their limbs, torso, and musculature; their skeletal structures that dictate range of motion; and their outward appearance, including facial features, hair color, and skin tone. Ideals of execution and performance—what a dancer *does*—include adherence to style, form, and technique; a dancer's range of movement qualities and dynamics; their physical clarity and precision; their ability to embody the aesthetic of a work, style, or oeuvre; their musical and rhythmic sensibilities; and their capacity to express through movement or physically interpret an idea. Lastly, ontological ideals related to dancerly *being* establish expectations for a dancer's persona, identities, behaviors, attitudes, and temperament that they bring to the studio, the stage, and the public sphere.

These distinct kinds of ideals function interdependently. In her interpretation of the 1820 dancing manual of Carlo Blasis, dance scholar Merry Lynn Morris notes that:

> Blasis consistently aligned 'good' dance technique with ideals of good behaviour, conduct and integrity. Therefore, certain prescribed forms of the body become associated with more than just good dancing; these forms also led to the dancer becoming a good (and perfect) person.[2]

As Morris considers Blasis's manual to be a significant source "of the ballet technique, as it reflects current day practice," she suggests that associating a student's body with their person continues—that moralizing with regard to the dancer's physical attributes is an ongoing pedagogical practice.[3] Other kinds of interdependencies between ideals exist as well: a dancer's ideal execution of the technique is often predicated on their having an ideal enough body and an ideal enough way of being to gain access to elite institutions for study, for example. A dancer's degree of privilege, in this way, underlies their capacity to participate: such privilege might pertain to their body, their identities and affiliate groups, or their socio-economic class. In practice, the presentational, ontological, and physical ideals associated with ballet dancers are interconnected. Looking at them separately, however, offers a more complete picture of what and how each of these ideals appears in ballet and ballet pedagogies, and how they have evolved over time.

Ideals of Execution and Performance

For centuries, ballet has held idealized expectations for dancers' execution. Any courtier who made a public mistake in their performance was almost certainly, as historian Elizabeth Aldrich describes, "disgraced from court" and obliged to return at the lowest rank to gradually earn back their place in the hierarchy.[4] Ideals for performance have been, historically, the expected outcomes at the most elite levels of the profession. They are embedded in the form—in its documented definitions. It would be impossible to develop a pedagogy of ballet without relying to some degree on ideals of how ballet should be danced; if not made strictly homogenous or one-size-fits-all, these ideals can become important goals for achievement—something to which dancers can aspire and toward which pedagogues can direct their teaching.

Ideals for dancing are often linked to the Schools in which teachers studied and their respective syllabi. Some Schools have national origins or affiliations or are named for their originators, and these foundations have historically driven each School's style. The teaching at the School of American Ballet, for example, idealizes the ability to generate speed and vivacity—qualities George Balanchine believed were uniquely American in nature. Ideals for dancers at the Vaganova Ballet Academy originated in the Soviet-Era commission of Agrippina Vaganova to create a post-Imperial approach representative of Soviet ideology, which lent it a quality that historian Natalia Roslavleva describes as: "space-conquering amplitude of movement."[5] The Bournonville School idealizes a light, buoyant quality in allegro; a quality that famously belonged to August Bournonville himself. Similarly, the Cuban National Ballet School—from its exceedingly high retirés and relevés to its focus on extended balances—is built stylistically on the attributes of its matriarch, Alicia Alonso.[6]

Many longstanding ideals for the execution of ballet technique are written in manual form; most include photographic or hand-drawn images of ballet in what the authors consider ideal bodies, which establish a standard for how they believe ballet should look and be danced. Historically, these texts have allowed the authoring pedagogues "to present their philosophies; provide details of class material, class structure, and musical accompaniment; offer advice; and distinguish themselves from—or align themselves with—their predecessors."[7] The language each manual uses indicates an emphasis on certain qualities over others; this applies similarly to the language teachers choose to use in the ballet class, from the qualities and shapes they emphasize to the very names of the steps they use. The distinction between the Cecchetti Method's battement dégagé (disengaged), the French School's battement glissé (gliding), and the Vaganova School's battement jeté (thrown), for example, indicates distinct movement qualities for a similarly basic step, according to the preferred style and aesthetic value system of each respective School.

When teachers' experience with ballet pedagogy falls outside of any one School or syllabus, as is the case with innumerable dancers and teachers whose ballet background is heterogeneous in nature, their varied experiences become the basis for their understanding of what is ideal in the execution of ballet. While some who would claim purity of School have looked down their noses at teachers without a sole pedagogical pedigree, the pedagogies that emerge from blended ballet heritages are historically just as legitimate.[8] In addition to the multitudes of highly respected teachers worldwide whose individual teaching draws from multiple sources, a prominent and well-respected current example of this is the American Ballet Theatre "National Training Curriculum," which "incorporates elements of the French, Italian and Russian schools of training."[9] During the nineteenth century, the Imperial Russian Ballet School was famously a locale for the meeting of the French, Danish, and Italian ballet techniques.[10] Ballet's overarching ideals for style and execution—for how ballet should be danced—are thus relative, and pedagogies built on the historically erroneous notion that there is only one ideal or "correct" approach should be viewed with great skepticism.

The centrality of bodies to ballet pedagogies refutes the very foundation of ideal-driven pedagogies: that ideals for execution can be objectively "correct." Even if a teacher is associated with a single School or known pedagogical approach, and even if they assert in their teaching that there is only one "correct" way, their expectations for these ideals will be to some degree unique—emerging from their individual embodied knowledge—as will the manifestation of it in the unique bodies of the students they teach.[11] As ballet's various national Schools have all been celebrated precisely because of their differences, as pedagogical approaches continue to expand with increased knowledge and information about the body, and as new choreographies continue to stretch dancers aesthetically, the ballet field will continue to support multiple approaches to idealized manifestations of ballet in the body. Beyond ballet's defining technical elements—a tendu always remains in contact with the floor regardless of School, for example—some ideals for execution are dependent upon each individual teacher's embodied experience and the particulars of their physicalities. The students themselves, similarly, are the most obvious example of why one "correct" way doesn't hold. Insisting on level shoulders as ideal when a student has scoliosis, for example, can be injurious, yet such ideal-driven perspectives have and continue to be enforced. Beyond the embodied work of ballet are the contexts that shape the pedagogies; the amount of

Ideal-Driven Pedagogies 19

studio space and organizing structure of the classes in each school, for example. What is idealized as "correct," once again becomes relative, and ideals of execution, or how one *should do* ballet, are subjective; they shift depending on where or with whom one studies or performs, and they are dependent upon each dancer's and teacher's privilege and context, as much as their bodies and abilities.

Ideal Ways of Being

A number of personal characteristics, from behaviors to demeanors to visible identity markers, have historically constituted the ideal ballet dancer. Most dancing manuals include chapters of instructions or advice for the student, which articulate their responsibilities and how they should *be* if they are to succeed in ballet. Blasis's "first advice is to put yourselves into the hands of an experienced master," while a century later, Luigi Albertieri (a protégé of Enrico Cecchetti) offers a similar insistence: "In the choice of a teacher [students] should exercise special care."[12] Agnes de Mille dedicates the entire volume of *To a Young Dancer* to advising the student in their endeavors, so they can make choices that support their interests in the profession.[13] These writings tend to emphasize the agency and responsibility of the student to determine their own path: to choose a teacher they trust, to be diligent and thorough by asking questions and actively seeking out knowledge, to not retreat or become disheartened when faced with a challenge. Who the student is, how they should be (or appear to be), and what the study of ballet will require of them, are central to these collective articulations of desirable personal qualities of the ideal student.

There is a paradox in play, however, when it comes to the idealizing of dancerly being in the literature. Many of the written requirements for ideal dancers include being self-possessed with agency; having "intelligence, stamina, and dedication," and "courage and tenacity of purpose."[14] Simultaneously, however, they suggest a necessary docility and deference, which dance scholar Brenda Dixon Gottschild criticizes as part of the traditional teacher-student relationship: "Structurally inherent in this relationship is the inferiority of the dancer, in the sense that the approval of the authority and one's willingness to acquiesce to the authority are essential to success."[15] Pedagogue John White supports such a relationship, saying: "Students must learn to trust their teachers, to accept everything the teacher says as the truth. Students should be like sponges, soaking up all the knowledge and information their teachers give them."[16] Likewise, Rory Foster describes his desired one-way student-teacher relationship, saying "When a student begins to argue, misbehave, and resist corrections, it is time for him/her to seek out another teacher, because without complete trust and respect, the training development is breached."[17] These latter descriptions suggest that students should willingly extend trust to the teacher that is not necessarily earned. Karel Shook's imperative for teachers offers important contrast, "The student's confidence has to be won and kept," which supports student agency in its inverse suggestion that the student might indeed *not* feel confident in their teacher—that teachers cannot expect student trust undeservedly.[18]

Approaches that focus on the teacher's total authority expect students to be submissive—to endure any range of teaching methods—from the most useful and supportive to those that may breach personal boundaries or bypass issues of consent for the sake of the work. Gottschild describes her daughter Amel's experience deviating from this ideal:

> My daughter loved dancing, was a hard worker with a lovely, long-limbed, healthy, strong body and an equally strong willpower. She showed promise, but she refused to bend to [Margaret] Craske's demands of old-school manners towards the 'maestra' and suffered for it. [Diana] Byer told me that, following a particularly tense power struggle in class about Amel's demeanor, Craske said to her, 'How do we break that child?' I was taken aback, even after Byer explained to me what Craske meant – namely, Amel's refusal to subordinate herself to authority, as a way of preparing her for a potential life in the hierarchical world of ballet.[19]

The idea that a "strong personality" couldn't possibly coexist with idealized expectations for dancers should be a red flag for the profession. Even the most student-forward texts, those that implore teachers to exhibit kindness and never lose their temper with students, tend to promote similarly authoritarian teaching methods or systems of belief. They imply—incorrectly—that such methods produce agentic, empowered dancers. Rather, as scores of dancers' memoirs and personal accounts demonstrate, the degree of human damage that results from the teacher's expectation of student passivity masquerading as support for student agency is inestimable. Considering the effects of such approaches on teachers, Julia Buckroyd describes the teacher's role as ultimate authority frankly: as "exhausting and a use of the teacher's competence that is wasteful and debilitating."[20]

Some of the written expectations for dancers' behaviors are predicated on privilege. Foster notes: "Adhering to traditional etiquette of the ballet studio is imperative. It involves arriving on time, being properly dressed, following directions, accepting criticism, and being attentive and respectful toward the teacher."[21] A young student is reliant on an available adult to get them to class on time, and proper attire is dependent upon access to financial resources, particularly when students begin pointework or advance in levels differentiated by dress code.

Behaviors, such as Foster's "being attentive" and "following directions" are expectations that privilege neurotypical students because of how they're expected to manifest: often in silence and focused stillness. For neurodivergent dancers—those working with ADHD, dyslexia, or autism, for example, responses to these directives may look different in practice.[22] While such individual differences might not be otherwise visible to or voluntarily shared with ballet teachers, the expectation of idealized behaviors in ballet functions as a barrier to inclusion for these students and any others whose manners or behaviors, for any reason, exist beyond the ideal.

Other ideals for the dancer's being are traditionally gendered and embedded in ballet's pedagogies. Blasis stipulates clear binary conventions for movement quality and dynamics, saying:

> A man's manner of dancing should differ from that of a woman. The pas de vigeur and bold majestic execution of the former is not for the latter, who should shine in graceful supple movements, charming terre-à-terre steps and a becoming voluptuousness and abandon in her poses.[23]

A century later, Pavel Gerdt, who taught at the Russian Imperial School until 1904, "strictly distinguish[ed] between male and female grace. His men-pupils were masculine, while the ballerinas trained by Gerdt for ever retained a feminine softness and poise, coupled with beauty and perfection of *épaulement*."[24] Shook, three-quarters-of-a-century on, goes to even further extremes in support of heteronormativity along a gendered binary, saying:

> ...the eroticism is built in. Both men and women, in a state of near nudity, and an intimate proximity to each other, do the same kind of movements in a defined space. The division between their identities, as male or female, is often obscured, but never obliterated. Indeed, devoid of the contrast of male and female, yin and yang, dance becomes impotent, devoid of meaning, and insupportable as a humanistic demonstration or an art.[25]

While most of these descriptions focus on movement qualities, there are several steps in the danse d'école that have long been designated for either men or women: tours en l'air and bourrées among them. By continuing to code as gendered specific elements of the study, dancers identifying as male or female are restricted in their full range of artistic possibilities, while non-binary dancers are excluded. If the ideal dancer's being is only permissible as male or female, then ballet will miss out on the artistic contributions of innumerable dance artists marginalized by this aspect of the tradition.*

---

* Responding to the limitations of ballet's gender binary for dancers, many teachers and schools have begun allowing all students to learn and practice the entire ballet vocabulary, including traditionally gendered steps and pointework.

These ideals for how—and who—students should *be* in ballet are passed down as part of the pedagogic tradition and become the idealized expectations teachers have for students. They are systemic. They affect whether teachers are willing to teach certain students and how they perceive them, which can affect the duration and quality of a dancer's experience in ballet. Ideals for dancerly being have been integral to the definition and development of what it means to be a ballet dancer over time, and like other ideals, they have enabled gatekeepers to gatekeep; to restrict access to those they believe will not disrupt their efforts to preserve the tradition as they believe it has been and should continue to be.

Ideal Bodies

The ideal body in ballet has a long and complicated history. It has been centered in ballet for so long that, according to Heather Ritenburg, it has become a capital T Truth: "… the discourse producing and reproducing the ideal ballet dancer's body simultaneously produces and reproduces a particular danced aesthetic as the truth – the norm – as 'real' ballet."[26] Like other significant social and cultural constructs, the ideal body has become a Truth because it has been embedded in the work to such an extent that it has shaped the profession's definition and output. In addition, it has affected the selfhood of the dancers who constitute the profession, as Angela Pickard notes: "there is a strong connection between the size, shape and aesthetic of the ballet body and identity as a ballet dancer."[27]

Despite widespread acknowledgment that the ideal body construct is damaging, there is a pervasive belief in the ballet profession and adjacent pedagogical circles that legitimate ballet requires ideal bodies. This belief justifies the tendencies of the field's gatekeepers to exclude those dancers whose bodies are not considered ideal enough. Ritenburg says:

> …the discourse produces a truth about a preferred or an ideal female body shape suitable for ballet. The discourse also produces a truth about a body shape suitable for ballet that invalidates other body shapes. The idealization or truth of a body shape as a 'ballet dancer's body' produces and reproduces an aesthetic in ballet.[28]

She suggests that it is useful, in matters concerning the ideal body, to: "consider a discourse as socially constructed rather than as an enduring 'truth' thereby opening possibilities for resistance to dominant discourses and related practices."[29] This acknowledgment of the subjectivities that lead to an "ideal body" supports the reality that it is a choice—a perception clung to by those in power—that could be countered or dismantled. It also supports the reality that there are many versions of the ideal body—that its characteristics are not the same or consistent over time. Ballet dancers' bodies at the turn of the twenty-first century were decidedly different than those a century, or even 50 years, earlier—a simple photographic comparison would provide strong evidence of the ideal's variability.

Alongside pedagogues and directors, dance arbiters and writers from the nineteenth century played central roles in establishing ideals for bodies. In a review of Romantic Era ballerina Fanny Cerrito, Théophile Gautier wrote:

> Her foot is small, well arched, with a delicate ankle and a well-rounded leg; however, whether because of a belt worn too low or a torso that is actually a little too long, her waist cuts her body into two completely equal parts, which is contrary to the laws of human proportions and particularly unfavorable for a *danseuse*.[30]

Through his assessment of Cerrito's body as central to her performance, Gautier establishes or reinforces that period's physical precedents for female dancers. Male dancers' bodies have been subject to similar scrutiny. Early twentieth-century ballet critic André Levinson remarked on dancer Leonid Leontiev's entrechats by first focusing on his physical attributes: "Leontiev, on the other hand, who is small and disproportionately built with his large head, athletic torso and small, muscular legs, achieves in them genuine lightness and grace."[31] Again, the body is reviewed as a central element of how the dancing is interpreted on the whole; in these writings, the ideal body and the ideals for dance and dancers are inextricable. The critic's aesthetic preferences for the dance become bound up inside their desires to see certain bodies, with certain shapes, identities, and demeanors, on the stage. The rationale for the philosophy behind the ideal body, in this light, is to ensure that the arbiters of the field retain the authority to exclude dancers who do not possess a body they prefer to see; or to at least remind readers of what the ideal dancer's body should look like, even if they're surprised when an unconventional body accomplishes something delightful.

Across more recent ballet pedagogy publications are detailed descriptions of ideal ballet dancers' bodies—typically gendered along a male-female binary. The clear stipulation of physical variables has served as a rationale at all levels of study to exclude dancers whose physiques sit outside its parameters. Gretchen Ward Warren's chapter on the ideal body in her 1989 text, *Classical Ballet Technique*, has drawn frustration and ire behind closed doors—or at least a few raised eyebrows—while the book on the whole has become standard reference material for ballet pedagogues. The chapter in question presents photographs of two specific dancers' bodies, male and female, as "ideal;" points to particular physical characteristics in ways reminiscent of a biology textbook; and describes how such bodies shape dancers' suitability for classical ballet and their career potential. Writing frankly about auditions, Warren says: "The adjudicator's eye is first drawn to, and usually stays with, the dancers with good classical physiques."[32] The clarity in this chapter stings. It also, however, states directly what so many have long understood: that the ideal body is the means by which many are and have been excluded. It affects access to study as well as labor practices: school auditions, school-level promotions, company auditions, contract terms, casting, and promotions in professional rank. While the dancer's capacity to dance ballet at a particular level is certainly part of these determinations, the profession clarifies its commitment to exclusion by demonstrating that the preservation of its traditions is only feasible—only valued—in those bodies deemed acceptable.

In his 1996 text *Teaching Classical Ballet*, White describes bodily characteristics for women and attributes them to the Balanchine aesthetic:

> The new female-dancer look is typified by one who is comparatively tall, long-limbed, pale-skinned, and long-necked. She has a small head with delicate but prominent facial features. And she has boyish hips and an unobtrusive bust. These are the physical features of today's female dancer who, paradoxically, is supposed to combine both femininity and sexlessness.[33]

White's description complicates the relationship of the traditional gender binary in ballet to the ideal Balanchine body while deliberately pointing to whiteness. The effects of the ideal body, then, must be considered through an intersectional lens in which race and gender are interdependent variables.[34] Theresa Ruth Howard, founding curator of Memoirs of Blacks in Ballet (MOBBallet) and a diversity strategist and consultant, takes such an intersectional approach:

> The function of the classical corps de ballet explains why black men do not fall prey to the color barrier: Men never stand in lines as swans, wilis or sylphs, so the depth of their brownness is never an issue in regards to the aesthetic of 'classicism.'[35]

The expectation of homogeneity in the corps de ballet, driven by ideals put forward as objective Truth under the guise of "Classical Ballet," then, makes it harder for Black women—especially those without light skin privilege—to navigate idealized body expectations.

The hegemony of the Balanchine perspective in the United States makes him a pivotal, if not notorious, figure in the development of the ideal body in ballet. The significance of the "Balanchine body" to the larger field has tormented so many dancers over such an extended period that it would be difficult to find a dancer's memoir that didn't include a discussion of their relationship to their own body. Rather, of greater interest given the Balanchine ideal's noted preference for whiteness, is Gottschild quoting Arthur Mitchell's assertion of the irony that Balanchine himself: "described his ideal ballerina as having a short torso, long arms, long legs, and a small head. If that's ideal," Mitchell notes, "then we [black folk] are perfect."†36 Howard is quoted as saying, further, "the Black body is not problematic. 'What's problematic are the implicit biases against the Black body.'"37 Racism in ballet—expressed systemically and in the individual upholding of white supremacist ideologies that maintain the system—is an extra hurdle for even those Black dancers considered to have ideal ballet bodies. It affects whether Black ballet dancers are granted access to ballet by its gatekeepers or treated equitably once inside the gates. The ability of a Black dancer to dance ballet, then, is too often a secondary consideration when up against the racialized prejudices of those at the helm. It is notable, perhaps, that at the time of this writing, Balanchine's New York City Ballet, after 75 years in operation, has not yet promoted a Black woman to the rank of Principal Dancer.

Because ballet cannot be removed from its socio-cultural contexts, its history is an essential lens through which to examine the system of values upon which ballet's ideals are based. Ironically, the ballet ideal has historically defaulted to whiteness, even though dancers of the global majority have legacies and histories in ballet that go back as far and are as significant.38 Kate Mattingly et al. write that "ballet, as an art form, emerges from a multiplicity of people and cultures. In excavating histories of ballet, [Jehbreal] Jackson notices how amplifying the Africanist sources and Islamic influences changes the perspectives and demeanors of Black dancers."39 Returning to Ritenburg's suggestion that ballet's ideal body is a construct whose legacy is built on exclusion, it stands to reason that the choice to change that legacy—to deliberately build more inclusive paradigms as Mitchell, Howard, and Jackson have done—is historically accurate, entirely plausible, and in many places across the field, already underway. Given Warren's description of how the ideal body dictates labor practices, anything less than deliberate efforts toward inclusion is an explicit choice to continue the inequities that emerge from an incomplete history of ballet as solely European in origin.

The body in ballet is scrutinized—judged against this perception-of-the -ideal-that-has-become-Truth, whether by audiences, gatekeepers, or dancers themselves. Everyone contributes to the dialogue, to the creation of this Truth, as ballet's bodily ideals continue to change over time driven by pressing social and cultural forces. A steadily changing cadre of individuals

---

† Gottschild also notes that the "[B]lack dancer's body" is a construct in and of itself; that Black dancers are not a monolith.

participate in determinations of whether arms, legs, and torsos should be considered too long, too short, or mal-aligned; breasts considered too big; musculature considered too pronounced; feet considered too flat. The Truth evolves as more participate in its creation, and over time the change becomes visible; evident in the kinds of bodies—the kinds of people—who are participating in ballet at all levels. This legacy of the ideal body as undergoing continuous transformation provides today's gatekeepers—particularly its teachers who stand guard over the gates of the ballet class and programs of study—with the imperative to once again reshape those ideals toward inclusive and equitable ends.

Ideal-Driven Pedagogies: Enactment and Effects

When levied indiscriminately and framed as the pedagogue's upholding of tradition, ballet's ideals become weaponized to hegemonic and exclusionary ends. Teachers often turn to authoritarian pedagogical approaches as they try to mold individual people into homogenous ideals. They aim to expose discrepancies between students and ideals by pointing to students' deficiencies, while simultaneously pushing students toward ideals in ways that may be physically injurious and, as Maria Papaefstathiou et al. suggest, "emotionally harmful."[40] Students learn by implication that their role is to endure these approaches, and at the very worst, to withstand various abuses as a necessary part of the study of ballet. While ideals for ballet's execution and performance can be important pedagogical objectives, when ideals of any kind take precedence over the health and humanity of each individual dancer, the effects—physically, psychologically, emotionally, and spiritually—can be devastating.

The ability of teachers to prioritize ideals is predicated on the existence of hierarchy—a bestowed pedagogical authority that allows teachers to control how dancers exist in ballet spaces. In her noteworthy 2005 study, Robin Lakes describes a range of authoritarian teaching behaviors through which such control, via ideal-driven pedagogies, has long been enacted. Lakes's study has been widely cited. At the risk of being repetitious or triggering trauma at the re-reading of these behaviors, I am compelled to point out that several twenty-first-century ballet pedagogy publications recommend them as teaching tools. In an attempt to counter such damaging perspectives, I again cite Lakes here.

At their most extreme, authoritarian behaviors used to enforce ideals include: "physical abuse in the form of hitting, slapping, or punching body parts with a hand or stick." Some are psychologically terroristic: "humiliation of students for making errors, screaming, sarcasm, mocking, belittlement, barbed humor, and bullying," "preoccupation with arbitrary behavioral control," "unfair or negative comparisons to other students," "[referring] to adult students as 'girls' and 'boys,' and [using] other forms of infantilization or patronization," and "shaming or denigrating comments about students' weight, build, or body type." Passive aggressively, some teachers rely on "silence or withholding of feedback or responses or, at the least, giving only backhanded compliments," and "rote imitation and repetition over time with unchanging verbal prompts." Lastly, Lakes suggests that: "Teachers exhibit frustration and impatience if there is not immediate and continued mastery of the material presented; some ignore certain students, or storm out of the room in an exasperated rage out of disappointment or anger."[41] I might add to this list the use of tactile feedback without ample opportunity for students to weigh options for consent; displays of various prejudices as microaggressions or more directly; and an unwillingness to take students' individual bodies, proclivities, and interests into account. The list, sadly, could continue.

Lakes situates the root causes for these behaviors in the "authoritarian personality structure" of the teacher, among a number of other cultural, pedagogical, and contextual factors that support these damaging approaches. She suggests that pedagogical authoritarianism derives in part from ballet's tendency to assign guru status to teachers, and some teachers' narcissistic tendencies to welcome it.[42] The establishment of the teacher as one imbued with the power of uncontested authority may result in these kinds of oppressive behaviors that attempt to force student compliance with the teacher's perception of ideals. The teacher's sense of self-importance as enabled by the power of the role they inhabit may magnify the effects of ideals, as it allows them to make the mistaken assertion that their idealized perspective is the only "correct" one.[43] The idea, stated earlier, that ballet could have one objectively correct approach fails to acknowledge the inherent subjectivity of each teacher and the unique bodies involved. It is also historically inaccurate, as it subjugates some of ballet's many honored traditions to others. Students exposed to such ideal-driven pedagogies may begin to perceive ballet as static or finite, which is troubling artistically and insofar as they may begin to see ballet as more or less compatible with certain bodies and certain persons. In addition, students who study with multiple teachers, for example, may struggle to reconcile conflicting approaches if those teachers both insist that their way is the only "correct" way.

In their study on "Child Protection in Ballet," Papaefstathiou et al. offer an explanation as to why the field has been reticent to qualify these behaviors as outright abuse despite their textbook adherence to the definition: "rationalizing discourses are adopted by both teachers and students to deny and normalize harmful practices in ballet that lead to negative emotional consequences."[44] They suggest that because harmful methods are "likely to have a positive impact on [students'] future performance," authoritarian approaches have been considered justifiable in some situations.[45] In an Op-Ed for *Dance Magazine*, authors Rebecca Chaleff, Michelle LaVigne, and Kate Mattingly look to the Duluth

Power and Control Wheel, "used in cases of domestic violence," to identify "approaches similar to those that have been used by some ballet directors."[46] Such approaches as articulated in the wheel include: "playing mind games," "humiliating her," and "making her afraid by using looks, actions, gestures," among others.[47] It is necessary to define these behaviors explicitly as abuse—whether or not they happen in the ballet studio—to at the very least recognize the experiences of innumerable dancers as a most basic first step toward justice.

Complicating these matters is the reality that pedagogies of all kinds tend to self-perpetuate. Teachers tend to teach as they were taught, their experience being the origin of their perspectives in the studio. Those teachers who, as students, were traumatized by pedagogic approaches are likely to teach at least in part with similar approaches, thus continuing the cycle of abuse intentionally or not. These teachers have been hurt by the system they then become, and on and on it goes.

There are external pressures, too, to uphold tradition over all else. I often find myself navigating complicated feelings of being responsible to student wellbeing while also representing the perceived "rigors" of ballet and the profession in my faculty role, for example. In environments that hold examination classes observed by colleagues and school leadership, or in schools that make teachers' graded evaluations of students visible to other faculty, teachers may aim toward ideal-driven outcomes and assessments as proof that they are indeed preserving the tradition and upholding "rigor," even if such outcomes and assessments are holistically mal-aligned with the students.[48]

In the face of ideal-driven pedagogies in ballet classes, students' trauma responses have become rationalized and normalized.[49] The psychological and emotional effects of authoritarian approaches, and of the teachers who use them, can manifest as a range of student behaviors: they might force their turnout or appear to be fighting against their own bodies; self-flagellate in response to failures and frustrations; push through injury or refuse to rest; appear militant in their movement quality, musicality, and approach to class material; try to hide by situating themselves out of the teacher's direct line of sight; withdraw their presence and energy to avoid being seen; watch the teacher while they're dancing in a hypervigilant effort to know if or when they're being watched; or respond to feedback with a too-immediate indication that they understand, even if—perhaps—they don't. It is important to note that these student behaviors are not necessarily indicators of trauma, and no one dancer should be assumed to be traumatized based only on their behavior in ballet class. Additionally, some student conduct around perceived authority figures might be taught and learned culturally, and some behaviors might be the result of neurodivergence or disability. Because of ballet's history of ideal-driven authoritarian methods that result in human trauma, however, it is important to consider how it might manifest.

Some student behaviors—particularly those which demonstrate a forceful physicality or too-eager compliance—might be considered evidence of a strong work ethic, which introduces a significant gray area for ballet educators in interpreting them. Further complicating the issue is the possibility that these behaviors have been both pedagogically reinforced and learned independently—or perhaps they emerge in part from the dancer's constitution or personality. Ballet pedagogies can cause trauma, to be sure, but the relationship is not inherently causal. It is impossible to know the root of a student's trauma—or if trauma even exists—simply by watching them in class. More complex still, according to Alex Shevrin Venet, is the reality that each person's response to trauma is inherently individual: what traumatizes one person may not traumatize another.[50] Rather than trying to diagnose or treat a student—psychologically rooted activities that are decidedly beyond the ballet teacher's expertise and scope of responsibility—an awareness of these and other such behaviors could, rather, inspire teachers to want to get to know the students they teach as whole people; to learn more about their interests and goals; to listen and work to understand each dancer and their individual relationship to ballet.

Pedagogies that privilege the ideal body are known to have prompted dancers to take drastic measures to alter how their bodies look. Warren discusses how plastic surgery has been used to "make oversized bosoms smaller, weak jawlines more definite, and nonexistent arches more shapely."[51] Ritenburg and others describe that disordered eating, as well, can be an outcome of ballet's emphasis on an ideal body:

> The discourse of the ideal female ballet dancer's body produces particular effects; it constitutes other body shapes – other bodies and other dancers – as less than ideal or unacceptable, and contributes to attempts to force unacceptable bodies into body shapes which may support these ideals such as through teaching practices and through self-discipline of food consumption leading to disordered eating.[52]

The effects of dancers being made to believe that they are physically deficient—a result of constant pedagogical comparison to ideals—have the potential take root outside the ballet class in ways that extend into a dancer's daily life and health in a range of quietly insidious ways that go far beyond those I'm able to address here.

The consequences of ideal-driven pedagogies can be especially harmful for dancers in historically excluded groups. Impostor syndrome, for example, can become a silent concern for these dancers, as predominantly white institutions in ballet too often—despite some of their work to become more equitable—placate the biases of those in charge. Gloria Ladson-Billings and William F. Tate assert that when standardized images those in power use to maintain hegemony become internalized by those in marginalized groups, it can lead to a sense of ill-belonging.[53]

When whiteness is communicated as central to the image of ideal ballet dancers via ideal-driven pedagogies, students in the global majority might get the sense that they don't legitimately belong or deserve to participate. Likewise, these students might experience microaggressions or displays of racial superiority from white students, teachers, and directors. Systemic and individualized racism is an ongoing threat to ballet's progress in welcoming a diverse array of dancers and voices into ballet's study and performance. With a basic understanding of the ideal's harmful effects in this light, it is ethically incumbent upon white ballet teachers especially to work toward antiracist pedagogies and systemic change.[54]

In addition to psychological and emotional ramifications of ideal-driven pedagogies, there are outright physically injurious prospects for them as well. While an anatomically well-informed teacher can adapt ballet's technique to a variety of unique structural forms in students' bodies, under a less-well-informed teacher—one whose knowledge of ballet technique is limited by the belief that only certain bodies can accomplish it—the likelihood of student injury is higher. Physical Therapist Dr. Nick Cutri, according to journalist Chloe Angyal, "says that teachers forcing students into positions their bodies can't handle isn't only an 'old-school' problem but one he sees taking a toll on his young patients today."[55] Without additional resources or pedagogic support, these teachers are operating at a loss; their formative assessments of dancers and the feedback they offer in the ballet class can become physically precarious.

White explains the roots of such "typical physical harm" in ballet's ideal body—as derived

> from the teacher's perception that a student is lacking in one of the 'essentials' of classical dance. A list of some of these physical insufficiencies would include turnout, extension, height, weight, general body size and shape, physical proportions, 'pointability' of the foot, demi-plié, etc.

He goes on to note that,

> while some of these physical requirements for classical ballet can be improved upon, most are gifts of birth. No amount of tugging and pulling and forcing will significantly bear fruit in the long run. And many regimens that attempt such improvement are dangerous, leading to long-term joint and muscle injury.[56]

There is widespread agreement in this more recent ballet pedagogy literature that, as Warren says: "it is important for a teacher to recognize those physical 'givens' that cannot be affected by *any* degree of hard work."[57] At the same time, White, Warren, and pedagogue Anna Paskevska also agree that "Very few dancers start off with an ideal body," and that "Many things can be successfully developed and improved in the classroom."[58] The study of ballet can indeed, without injury, enable strengthening, stretching, and postural adjustments in ways that support a healthy dancer. For teachers, this latter perspective is a more inclusive pedagogical stance, in that it prioritizes the possibilities before foreclosing in light of ideals. The concern, of course, is whether teachers have enough information to know when a student reaches their physical limit—when the idea of developing the body goes too far and the work becomes exploitative to bone or connective tissue.

Despite the possibilities for damage and the exclusionary perspective it supports, the historical pedagogical tradition of molding bodies continues today, even with students who appear to have won the "genetic lottery."‡ Teachers engaging in these practices demonstrate their commitment to ideals. The forcing of children's feet into 180 degrees of rotation, for example, with the goal of increasing their innate capacity, is a controversial practice. The torquing of the legs before the bones have ossified deliberately creates "a torsional deformity of the femur" once the bones harden, which Warren suggests "results in a permanently increased degree of rotation."[59] The potential of young bodies to accommodate such forced deformation has famously become woven into the pedagogies in some of the world's most elite ballet academies.[60] Practices at the elite level tend to trickle down via imitation—with potentially fewer resources and support systems—into academies and schools at all levels. Pedagogies reliant upon the ideal body, or which require the presence of bodily ideals for the teacher's understanding of the technique to hold, are dangerous in this light; they have broad implications for dancers' health and wellbeing.

There are also important racialized implications for the ideal body that can become physically injurious. Kehinde Ishangi describes: "Unfortunately, Black dancers – and all dancers of color – often have difficulty studying ballet because they are exposed to prejudices based on what is considered to be an 'ideal' body type."[61] Further, Maurya Kerr notes that "young dancers of the global majority are often told that they, and their bodies, are 'unfit,' the tacit meaning being *unfit according to colonial aesthetics*."[62] The repercussions of these prejudices manifest in how dancers approach their work; Ishangi continues:

> African American students... [compensate] for not having an 'ideal' ballet body, and one of the most often-sighted [*sic*] factors that interferes with attaining that specious standard is their prominent gluteus maximus. Consequently, a dancer might habitually tuck their pelvis during exercise as a way of compensating towards the aesthetic of a body different from their own.[63]

‡ I am grateful to Courtney Harris for sharing this term with me.

The physical and psychological outcomes of pedagogies driven by ballet's bodily and ontological ideals, especially for dancers from historically excluded groups, are thus fraught. In their Foreword to the anthology *(Re:)Claiming Ballet*, Founding Director of Ballez Katy Pyle states:

> Sadly, the thinking used to maintain the racist, cis-heteropatriarchal status quo in ballet that designates the *elite*, standardized technique – what is truly *classical* and *in line with tradition* – makes clear who is inside and who is outside the center. And why should we pay attention to the fringes, to one another, when we all know the *rules* of who belongs and who does not, and why those outsiders don't fit in? We all *know*, from our first ballet classes or performances, what is 'correct' and what is not. This applies to technical standards as much as dress code and classroom decorum. And we carry *this* lineage in our bodies right alongside our technique. These deeply internalized value systems do not just damage us, they also isolate and fractionalize us away from one another.[64]

At the 2022 conference of CORPS de Ballet International, Pyle elaborated on what they called "One of the violences of ballet culture: repetitive enforcement of the singular ideal within a binary (what a man should be, what a woman should be)." Pyle expressed concern for the perception of those in dance studios in small towns across America, asking: "What are the messages that we're passing along? Who gets to belong?"[65]

To wit, Gottschild states that "Bodies are idealized for specific political, economic, and social purposes of inclusion/exclusion, for purposes of figuring out where the Self ends and the Other begins."[66] Ballet's bodily ideal, in this way, has been used to maintain the in-groups and out-groups Pyle references. Adesola Akinleye further suggests that the exclusion of "others" from ballet is used to justify the inclusion of ballet's elites:

> The right to exclude others is assumed as part of the establishment of being identified as part of mainstream ballet: 'I heard you say "ballet" – so where did you train?' I overhear the beginning of the interrogation of a person who has claimed they are a ballet dancer near an established teacher of ballet. The teacher admits laughingly, 'When it comes to ballet I am very protective.' Her attention to who can reference or identify with ballet involves claiming her own place in the *ballet world*, which at the same time tacitly assumes the right of 'use, enjoyment and exclusion.' She feels legitimate in upholding a doctrine that you must *prove* your right to talk about ballet or claim to be a ballet dancer. In claiming the authority to *exclude*, the ballet teacher also upholds her own privileged identity of *inclusion*. The fear of mediocrity is often cited as the reason for such gatekeeping.[67]

This mediocrity, one might assume, would be perpetuated by those who fail to meet gatekeepers' expectations for ideal dancers—those without ideal bodies, without ideal dispositions and behaviors, and without the ideal amount of privilege required to support what gatekeepers would consider the legitimate study of ballet.

Bolstering Akinleye's assertion that ballet's gatekeepers seek to preserve a degree of purity in ballet's lineages, White—following a long line of ballet pedagogues—suggests that some individuals simply aren't born for a career in ballet.[68] He offers no solution, like most authors of ballet pedagogy texts, and seems instead to settle on exclusion as the only option for maintaining the status quo. For teachers, however, excluding or otherwise dismissing students because of physical characteristics tells them they are inherently deficient, and further that they don't have the autonomy to even explore the possibilities. While it is essential in these instances for teachers to make well-informed technical adjustments for certain kinds of bodily restrictions—limited range of motion in the ankles of a student who wishes to dance en pointe, for example—having conversations with students first about how to work with their individual bodies is a more inclusive approach. The preservation of tradition through certain bodies as a noble excuse for gatekeeping is by no means new; it is perhaps the most frequently utilized rationale for continuing to use ideal-driven pedagogies despite the known damage they cause. In using tradition as the reason for dehumanizing practices, teachers shirk their basic responsibilities while revealing a paucity of knowledge and imagination.

From a broader vantage point, authoritarian pedagogies that are driven by ideals sit in stark contrast to the democratic philosophy to which many local and regional ballet schools ascribe, especially in the United States: that everyone is welcome to participate. Driven in part by the economic reality of needing to enroll a critical mass of students for their tuition dollars, in a country with a market economy and limited government support for the arts, many ballet schools in America rely on a democratized approach to enrollment to stay afloat; suggesting that ballet is for everybody and every body. Yet, when those same students—everybody and every body—pay to participate in classes taught by teachers whose pedagogies prioritize ideals, they receive a conflicting message: that they are less-than-ideal for ballet in any number of ways that make them feel deficient, or worse, excluded. The inclusive democratic message, derived from a capitalist financial need, is overridden by the exclusionary perspectives in pedagogies that idealize certain bodies and ways of being.

Broader still is the reality that tradition changes. Whether it happens deliberately or by virtue of changing social, cultural, economic, and political contexts, today's ballet—its techniques, styles, and aesthetics—is far different than it was a century ago, or even just a few decades ago. Bodies change over time as new knowledge about them is developed and becomes part of the study. Entire subfields in dance have emerged, including dance medicine and dance science, which directly support practitioners' needs for more comprehensive knowledge of the body. Cultural aesthetics and trends related to the body and movement arise: ballet's idealized body types take cues from period fitness regimens, as eyes become attuned to certain physical shapes that become normalized in the socio-cultural dialogue. Technological development has revolutionized how ballet is consumed and therefore idealized. Before the Internet and social media, visiting libraries, purchasing VHS tapes, or sitting at home on a Friday night to watch PBS's *Great Performances* were the only ways to see ballet from across the globe, whereas now I can casually scroll past videos of dancers from London's Ballet Black, Ballet Nacional de Cuba, and the displaced United Ukrainian Ballet before I've gotten out of bed in the morning. The prospect of consistent ideals and traditions is a mythology. Across historical time periods and global regions, ballet's ideals have and continue to vary widely, and any pedagogies built on them as static can quickly become relics of an imagined ballet past.

Blame and Accountability

In deference to those who have been hurt by authoritarian ballet pedagogies, it is worth considering how ballet might handle accountability for wrongdoing. Ballet's individual teachers and their individual pedagogies are at fault—yes. There is complexity here, however, as those individual offenses exist inside of the larger ballet system that has historically accepted, if not expected and advocated for, the use of such pedagogies that Lakes describes as "indefensible morally and ethically."[69] More granular still is the issue of those quietly authoritarian elements that have embedded themselves in ballet pedagogies, despite even the most generous teachers' best—albeit perhaps uncritical—intentions.

In a tradition-driven culture like ballet's, teachers continue to be considered unfailingly correct, while the student is viewed as a receptacle for the teacher's knowledge; this dynamic follows critical pedagogy pioneer Paulo Freire's "banking concept of education," in which, "knowledge is a gift bestowed by those who consider themselves knowledgeable upon those whom they consider to know nothing."[70] In this light, teachers may be reluctant to admit their own challenges or gaps in knowledge. As recently as 2010, ballet pedagogy texts tell teachers: "Do not tolerate any differences of opinion"[71] and "Students are expected... to accept the teacher and what is taught unhesitatingly."[72] With support for authoritarian approaches in the literature as evidence of ballet's ongoing orthodoxy, teachers who seek to wield power and perpetuate the tradition as they learned it have ample support and little incentive to change.

Lakes posits a likely reason for why individuals who perpetuate abuses in ballet are rarely challenged in a substantive way: "Perhaps in an art form so steeped in respect for one's elders, there is hesitancy about so bluntly questioning their teaching behaviors, as if such an act would undermine one's heritage."[73] Tradition, in this way, has been used to validate harmful behavior—the profession or larger system of ballet taking more of the blame than any one individual teacher. Scholar Kate Manne issues a word of caution about not laying at least some degree of blame on individual perpetrators of harm; while considering the wider context for their actions. Her subject matter is misogyny, so I have replaced her use of "misogynistic behavior" and "misogynistic social forces" with "ballet's authoritarian pedagogical practices" in the passage below so it speaks directly to the problem at hand:

> There is also a risk of exempting individual agents from blame or responsibility for [ballet's authoritarian pedagogical practices]. I believe blame has its limits here... But if the thought is that we positively ought *not* to consider an individual's actions in an unflattering light, then the result will be predictably politic, even polite, with respect to these agents. In some ways, this would make things easier and less anxiety provoking. And this troubles me. So I spend a fair amount of time here thinking about agents channeling and purveying [ballet's authoritarian pedagogical practices], against the backdrop of and enabled by social institutions.[74]

Manne's perspective suggests that individual teachers should be held responsible, to some degree, for causing harm "against the backdrop of and enabled by" the larger institution of ballet. Mattingly et al. agree: "Disentangling ballet pedagogy and white supremacy means looking at the gatekeepers who continue to prevent dancers and choreographers of color from being supported and elevated."[75]

Those in positions of power are responsible for addressing harm directly with those who perpetuate it. adrienne maree brown offers some complexity here in considering the balance of accountability between individuals and the systems they create and comprise:

> How do I hold a systemic analysis and approach when each system I am critical of is peopled, in part, by the same flawed and complex individuals that I love? This question always leads me to self-reflection. If I can see the ways I am perpetuating systemic oppression, if I can see where I learned the behavior and how hard it is to unlearn it, I start to have more humility as I see the messiness of the communities I am part of, the world I live in.[76]

In my own work, turning inward has become essential; it helps me identify how I uphold systems of oppression and hierarchy. I use reflection to prompt critical examinations of my actions and privileges, while acknowledging where and how I hold power over others. With the explicit understanding that systems are comprised of individuals—myself included—I can begin to change ballet pedagogies on a larger scale by making change to my own pedagogy first. I can work to ensure that damaging pedagogical approaches stop with me, before I consider how I might support accountability measures for others.

Scholar and activist bell hooks offers an approach for moving forward once harm has been done. In my interpretation, her view sits somewhere between Manne's and brown's perspectives:

> We need to speak our shame and our pain courageously in order to recover. Addressing woundedness is not about blaming others; however, it does allow individuals who have been, and are, hurt to insist on accountability and responsibility both from themselves and from those who were the agents of their suffering as well as those who bore witness. Constructive confrontation aids our healing.[77]

hooks has also said, "For me forgiveness and compassion are always linked: how do we hold people accountable for wrongdoing and yet at the same time remain in touch with their humanity enough to believe in their capacity to be transformed?"[78] If those across the ballet field—particularly those with power—could consider this avenue in which abuses could be addressed openly and with compassion for all involved, they could enable the possibility of justice for those who've been hurt and make room for those who've perpetuated harm to grow from a place of humility, care, and greater awareness. They could embrace new approaches through critical pedagogy: balancing a necessary critique of the system with an expansive, unbounded sense of hope that change is possible.[79]

Some abuses in ballet have been flagrant, deliberate, and highly publicized, but most, I suggest, are less so. I suspect that the vast majority of abuses via ideals and authoritarian pedagogies are less visible, less stark, and happening on a smaller scale in ballet studios, while equally as damaging as the notorious and high-profile incidents. Without erring on the side of apologists as Manne cautions, and in an attempt to use self-reflection to better understand the complexity of systemic injustices as brown describes, I recall often those instances in my own teaching when I perpetuated harm, both knowingly and unintentionally: when I was harsh or impatient; when I overlooked or dismissed someone; when I was compassionless. I imagine that most of ballet's pedagogical abuses happen like that—quietly and without much fanfare—as teachers uncritically and with a fair degree of self-justification or self-congratulation pass problematic pedagogies to the next generation. Pyle offers clarity: "Everyone working in Ballet maintains this system – even if it hurts us, and sometimes, especially if it does – and the cycle continues into the future."[80] Teachers without supportive resources, an education in pedagogy, or a reason to actively question tradition are most prone to perpetuating damaging approaches; but even those teachers who regularly interrogate tradition, who do the work of antiracism, and who participate in professional development and seek out new knowledge will make mistakes. As their awareness increases, they may continue to rely on problematic pedagogies, albeit less and less frequently, as they negotiate the learning curve and gradually extract harmful approaches from their teaching. It is in those teachers—the ones who turn inward and make changes to the tradition they received, that ballet can hold out hope for a more productive pedagogical future.

Notes

1 I adapt the term "stain" here from Claire Dederer, *Monsters: A Fan's Dilemma* (New York: Knopf, 2023).
2 Merry Lynn Morris, "Re-thinking Ballet Pedagogy: Approaching a Historiography of Fifth Position," *Research in Dance Education* 16, no.3 (2015): 248.
3 Merry Lynn Morris, "Re-thinking Ballet Pedagogy: Approaching a Historiography of Fifth Position," *Research in Dance Education* 16, no.3 (2015), 247.
4 Elizabeth Aldrich, "French Court Dance," *Dancing: Dance at the Court*, dir. John Hill (ArtHaus Musik, 1993).
5 Natalia Roslavleva, *Era of the Russian Ballet, 1770–1965* (London: Gollancz, 1966), 199.
6 Ramona De Saa, "Distinctive Characteristics of the Cuban National Ballet School Curriculum and its Cultural Traits" (presentation, CORPS de Ballet International annual conference, Sarasota, FL, June 2016).
7 Jessica Zeller, *Shapes of American Ballet: Teachers and Training before Balanchine* (New York: Oxford University Press, 2016), 75.
8 John White coined the derisive term "the Mish-Mash Method," in *Advanced Principles in Teaching Classical Ballet* (Gainesville: University Press of Florida, 2009), 9.
9 "National Training Curriculum," *ABT.org*, American Ballet Theatre, Accessed January 21, 2023, https://www.abt.org/training/teacher-training/national-training-curriculum/.
10 Jessica Zeller, *Shapes of American Ballet: Teachers and Training before Balanchine* (New York: Oxford University Press, 2016), 18–20.
11 See Chapter 2.
12 Carlo Blasis, *An Elementary Treatise Upon the Theory and Practice of the Art of Dancing* (1820; New York: Dover, 1968), 21; Luigi Albertieri, *The Art of Terpsichore* (New York: G. Ricordi, 1923), 5.
13 Agnes De Mille, *To a Young Dancer: A Handbook for Dance Students, Parents, and Teachers* (New York: Little, Brown, 1962).
14 Gretchen Ward Warren, *Classical Ballet Technique* (Tampa: University of South Florida Press, 1989), 82; Carlo Blasis, *An Elementary Treatise Upon the Theory and Practice of the Art of Dancing* (1820; New York: Dover, 1968), 21.
15 Brenda Dixon Gottschild, *The Black Dancing Body: A Geography from Coon to Cool* (New York: Palgrave Macmillan, 2003), 11.
16 John White, *Teaching Classical Ballet* (Gainesville: University Press of Florida, 1996), 75.

17 Rory Foster, *Ballet Pedagogy: The Art of Teaching* (Gainesville: University Press of Florida, 2010), 92.
18 Karel Shook, *Elements of Classical Ballet Technique as Practiced in the School of the Dance Theatre of Harlem* (New York: Dance Horizons, 1977), 34.
19 Brenda Dixon Gottschild, "Ballet beyond Boundaries: A Personal History," in *(Re:) Claiming Ballet*, ed. Adesola Akinleye (Chicago: Intellect, 2021), 107–108.
20 Julia Buckroyd, *The Student Dancer: Emotional Aspects of the Teaching and Learning of Dance* (London: Dance Books, 2000), 117.
21 Rory Foster, *Ballet Pedagogy: The Art of Teaching* (Gainesville: University Press of Florida, 2010), 92.
22 Sophie Bress, "Dancing with ADHD: The Challenges, Surprise Benefits and Tools to Cope," *Pointe Magazine*, November 14, 2022, https://pointemagazine.com/dancing-with-adhd/.
23 Carlo Blasis, *An Elementary Treatise Upon the Theory and Practice of the Art of Dancing* (1820; New York: Dover, 1968), 67.
24 Natalia Roslavleva, *Era of the Russian Ballet, 1770–1965* (London: Gollancz, 1966), 109.
25 Karel Shook, *Elements of Classical Ballet Technique as Practiced in the School of the Dance Theatre of Harlem* (New York: Dance Horizons, 1977), 30.
26 Heather Margaret Ritenburg, "Frozen Landscapes: A Foucauldian Genealogy of the Ideal Ballet Dancer's Body," *Research in Dance Education* 11, no.1 (2010): 72. https://doi.org/10.1080/14647891003671775.
27 Angela Pickard, "Ballet Body Belief: Perceptions of an Ideal Ballet Body from Young Ballet Dancers," *Research in Dance Education* 14, no.1 (2013): 15. https://doi.org/10.1080/14647893.2012.712106.
28 Heather Margaret Ritenburg, "Frozen Landscapes: A Foucauldian Genealogy of the Ideal Ballet Dancer's Body," *Research in Dance Education* 11, no.1 (2010): 72. https://doi.org/10.1080/14647891003671775.
29 Heather Margaret Ritenburg, "Frozen Landscapes: A Foucauldian Genealogy of the Ideal Ballet Dancer's Body," *Research in Dance Education* 11, no.1 (2010): 72. https://doi.org/10.1080/14647891003671775.
30 Théophile Gautier, "Fanny Cerrito in Jules Perrot's LALLA-ROOCK, Marie Guy-Stéphan in Arthur Saint-Léon's LUTIN DE LA VALLÉE," in *Dance as a Theatre Art: Source Readings in Dance History from 1581 to the Present*, 2nd ed., ed. Selma Jeanne Cohen (Princeton: Dance Horizons, 1992), 87.
31 André Levinson, *Ballet Old and New*, trans. Susan Cook Summer (1918; New York: Dance Horizons, 1982), 85–86.
32 Gretchen Ward Warren, *Classical Ballet Technique* (Tampa: University of South Florida Press, 1989), 65.
33 John White, *Teaching Classical Ballet* (Gainesville: University Press of Florida, 1996), 73.
34 Kimberlé Crenshaw originated the term "intersectionality" in "Demarginalizing the Intersection of Race and Sex: A Black Feminist Critique of Antidiscrimination Doctrine, Feminist Theory and Antiracist Politics," *The University of Chicago Legal Forum* (1989): 139–167.
35 Theresa Ruth Howard, "Op-Ed: Is Ballet 'Brown-Bagging' It?" *Dance Magazine*, April 2, 2017, https://www.dancemagazine.com/is-ballet-brown-bagging-it/.
36 Brenda Dixon Gottschild, *The Black Dancing Body: A Geography from Coon to Cool* (New York: Palgrave Macmillan, 2003), 5, 7–8.
37 Theresa Ruth Howard, interview with Chloe Angyal, *Turning Pointe: How a New Generation of Dancers Is Saving Ballet from Itself* (New York: Bold Type Books, 2021), 147.

38 See Sandie Bourne, "Portrayals of Black People from the African Diaspora in Western Narrative Ballets," in *(Re:) Claiming Ballet*, ed. Adesola Akinleye (Chicago: Intellect, 2021), 68–85; Joselli Audain Deans, "Arabesque en Noir: The Persistent Presence of Black Dancers in the American Ballet World," in *(Re:) Claiming Ballet*, ed. Adesola Akinleye (Chicago: Intellect, 2021), 48–67; Melanye White Dixon, *Marion D. Cuyjet and Her Judimar School of Dance: Training Ballerinas in Black Philadelphia 1948–1971* (Lewiston, NY: Mellen Press, 2011); Jehbreal M. Jackson, "Ballet as Artistic and Scientific Inquiry: Incorporating Ballet's Broader History in a Syllabus and in the Studio" (presentation, MOBBallet Symposium/M.I.A. Scholar's Course, Miami, FL and Online, August 2022). See also "Constellation Project," "Roll Call," and "Timeline" at *Memoirs of Blacks in Ballet*, https://mobballet.com.

39 Kate Mattingly, Keesha Beckford, Zena Bibler, Paige Cunningham, Iyun Ashani Harrison, and Jehbreal Muhammad Jackson, "Ballet Pedagogy and a 'Hard Re-Set': Perspectives on Equitable and Inclusive Teaching Practices," *Dance Chronicle* 46, no.1 (2023): 55. https://doi.org/10.1080/01472526.2022.2156747.

40 Maria Papaefstathiou, Daniel Rhind, and Celia Brackenridge, "Child Protection in Ballet: Experiences and Views of Teachers, Administrators, and Ballet Students," *Child Abuse Review* 22 (2013): 136.

41 Robin Lakes, "The Messages behind the Methods: The Authoritarian Pedagogical Legacy in Western Concert Dance Technique Training and Rehearsals," *Arts Education Policy Review* 106, no. 5 (May/June 2005): 4.

42 Robin Lakes, "The Messages behind the Methods: The Authoritarian Pedagogical Legacy in Western Concert Dance Technique Training and Rehearsals," *Arts Education Policy Review* 106, no. 5 (May/June 2005), 4, 9–16.

43 Sanna Nordin-Bates, "S2 E11: The One About Dancer Autonomy," interview with Sarah Scheiwer, *Dance; Better*, Podcast audio, December 16, 2021, https://podcasts.apple.com/us/podcast/s2e11-the-one-about-dancer-autonomy/id1535077862?i=1000545241351.

44 Maria Papaefstathiou, Daniel Rhind, and Celia Brackenridge, "Child Protection in Ballet: Experiences and Views of Teachers, Administrators, and Ballet Students," *Child Abuse Review* 22 (2013), 136.

45 Maria Papaefstathiou, Daniel Rhind, and Celia Brackenridge, "Child Protection in Ballet: Experiences and Views of Teachers, Administrators, and Ballet Students," *Child Abuse Review* 22 (2013), 137.

46 Rebecca Chaleff, Michelle LaVigne, and Kate Mattingly, "Op-Ed: What's Possible in Writing about Ballet?" *Dance Magazine*, May 19, 2023, https://www.dancemagazine.com/op-ed-writing-about-ballet/.

47 "Power and Control Wheel," *Domestic Abuse Intervention Project*, Accessed July 23, 2023, https://www.thehotline.org/identify-abuse/power-and-control/.

48 See Chapter 5 for a discussion of "rigor." John Warner, *Why They Can't Write: Killing the Five-Paragraph Essay and Other Necessities* (Baltimore, MD: Johns Hopkins University Press, 2018), 143.

49 Maria Papaefstathiou, Daniel Rhind, and Celia Brackenridge, "Child Protection in Ballet: Experiences and Views of Teachers, Administrators, and Ballet Students," *Child Abuse Review* 22 (2013), 136, 138; see Fiona Moola and Alixandra Krahn, "A Dance with Many Secrets: The Experience of Emotional Harm from the Perspective of Past Professional Female Ballet Dancers in Canada," *Journal of Aggression, Maltreatment, and Trauma* 27, no.3 (2018): 256–274.

50 Alex Shevrin Venet, *Equity-Centered, Trauma-Informed Education* (New York: Norton, 2021), 7.

51 Gretchen Ward Warren, *Classical Ballet Technique* (Tampa: University of South Florida Press, 1989), 64.
52 Heather Margaret Ritenburg, "Frozen Landscapes: A Foucauldian Genealogy of the Ideal Ballet Dancer's Body," *Research in Dance Education* 11, no.1 (2010): 72. https://doi.org/10.1080/14647891003671775; Maria Papaefstathiou, Daniel Rhind, and Celia Brackenridge, "Child Protection in Ballet: Experiences and Views of Teachers, Administrators, and Ballet Students," *Child Abuse Review* 22 (2013): 128; Fiona Moola and Alixandra Krahn, "A Dance with Many Secrets: The Experience of Emotional Harm from the Perspective of Past Professional Female Ballet Dancers in Canada," *Journal of Aggression, Maltreatment, and Trauma* 27, no.3 (2018), 257.
53 Gloria Ladson-Billings and William F. Tate IV, "Toward a Critical Race Theory of Education," *Teachers College Record* 97, no.1 (Fall 1995): 57.
54 For specific praxis-based methods that support antiracist pedagogies, see Ilana Goldman and Paige Cunningham, "Dear Ballet Teachers, Let's Talk about Race," in *Antiracism in Ballet Teaching*, eds. Kate Mattingly and Iyun Ashani Harrison (Abingdon: Routledge, 2024), 69–77.
55 Theresa Ruth Howard, interview with Chloe Angyal, *Turning Pointe: How a New Generation of Dancers is Saving Ballet from Itself* (New York: Bold Type Books, 2021), 84.
56 John White coined the derisive term "The Mish-Mash Method," in *Advanced Principles in Teaching Classical Ballet* (Gainesville: University Press of Florida, 2009), 17.
57 Gretchen Ward Warren, *Classical Ballet Technique* (Tampa: University of South Florida Press, 1989), 64.
58 Anna Paskevska, *Both Sides of the Mirror: The Science and Art of Ballet* (New York: Dance Horizons, 1981), 9–10; Gretchen Ward Warren, *Classical Ballet Technique* (Tampa: University of South Florida Press, 1989), 64.
59 Gretchen Ward Warren, *Classical Ballet Technique* (Tampa: University of South Florida Press, 1989), 10.
60 Gretchen Ward Warren, *Classical Ballet Technique* (Tampa: University of South Florida Press, 1989), 10–11.
61 Kehinde Ishangi, "Dancing Across Historically Racist Borders," in *(Re:) Claiming Ballet*, ed. Adesola Akinleye (Chicago: Intellect, 2021), 142.
62 Maurya Kerr, "Dismantling Anti-Blackness in ballet: Pedagogies of Freedom," in *Antiracism in Ballet Teaching*, eds. Kate Mattingly and Iyun Ashani Harrison (Abingdon: Routledge, 2024), 87–88.
63 Kehinde Ishangi, "Dancing Across Historically Racist Borders," in *(Re:) Claiming Ballet*, ed. Adesola Akinleye (Chicago: Intellect, 2021), 143.
64 Katy Pyle, "Foreword," in *(Re:) Claiming Ballet*, ed. Adesola Akinleye (Chicago: Intellect, 2021), xi.
65 Katy Pyle and Michael J. Morris, "Radically Re-Imagining the Ballet Canon: A Conversation with Katy Pyle, Founder and Artistic Director of Ballez." (presentation, CORPS de Ballet International annual conference, Richmond, VA, June 2022).
66 Brenda Dixon Gottschild, *The Black Dancing Body: A Geography from Coon to Cool* (New York: Palgrave Macmillan, 2003), 102.
67 Adesola Akinleye, "Ballet, from Property to Art," in *(Re:) Claiming Ballet*, ed. Adesola Akinleye (Chicago: Intellect, 2021), 14.
68 John White coined the derisive term "the Mish-Mash Method," in *Advanced Principles in Teaching Classical Ballet* (Gainesville: University Press of Florida, 2009), 18.

69 Robin Lakes, "The Messages behind the Methods: The Authoritarian Pedagogical Legacy in Western Concert Dance Technique Training and Rehearsals," *Arts Education Policy Review* 106, no. 5 (May/June 2005), 16.
70 Paulo Freire, *Pedagogy of the Oppressed* (New York: Herder and Herder, 1970), 72.
71 John White coined the derisive term "the Mish-Mash Method," in *Advanced Principles in Teaching Classical Ballet* (Gainesville: University Press of Florida, 2009), 16.
72 Rory Foster, *Ballet Pedagogy: The Art of Teaching* (Gainesville: University Press of Florida, 2010), 92.
73 Robin Lakes, "The Messages behind the Methods: The Authoritarian Pedagogical Legacy in Western Concert Dance Technique Training and Rehearsals," *Arts Education Policy Review* 106, no. 5 (May/June 2005): 3.
74 Kate Manne, *Down Girl: The Logic of Misogyny* (New York: Oxford University Press, 2018), xxiii.
75 Kate Mattingly, Keesha Beckford, Zena Bibler, Paige Cunningham, Iyun Ashani Harrison, and Jehbreal Muhammad Jackson, "Ballet Pedagogy and a 'Hard Re-Set': Perspectives on Equitable and Inclusive Teaching Practices," *Dance Chronicle* 46, no.1 (2023): 59.
76 adrienne maree brown, *Emergent Strategy: Shaping Change, Changing Worlds* (AK Press, 2017), 146.
77 bell hooks, *All About Love: New Visions* (New York: Harper, 2000), 232–233.
78 Melvin McLeod, "There's No Place to Go but Up: bell hooks and Maya Angelou in Conversation," *Lion's Roar*, January 1, 1998, https://www.lionsroar.com/theres-no-place-to-go-but-up/.
79 Henry A. Giroux, *On Critical Pedagogy*, 2nd ed., (London: Bloomsbury, 2020), 3.
80 Katy Pyle, "Foreword," in *(Re:) Claiming Ballet*, ed. Adesola Akinleye (Chicago: Intellect, 2021), xi.

2 Student-Driven Pedagogies

In stark contrast to the ideal-driven pedagogies in Chapter 1, the student-driven approaches in this chapter acknowledge the people of students and teachers as the foundation for ballet pedagogies. I call these approaches "student-driven" to situate the historically subjugated student or dancer in an agentic position; as the motivation behind and an active participant in the development of ballet pedagogies. As opposed to ideal-driven, often-authoritarian pedagogies that claim tradition and the false objectivity of textbook ideals to justify gatekeeping, this chapter describes a humanizing pedagogical approach that originates in and develops through the subjectivities of each student and teacher. Embodied knowledge and experience, collaboration and shared inquiry, and pedagogical efforts to build trust are central to student-driven approaches, which actively resist the hegemony of dehumanizing ideals to foreground equity in ballet's study and practice.

Situating ideals and individuals at opposite poles is somewhat of a false dichotomy when it comes to ballet, as no approach to ballet pedagogy can ever be fully divorced from some modicum of ideals or expectations for execution and performance. The danse d'école—the ballet vocabulary—exists; it has forms, definitions, and parameters that even this less-idealized side of the spectrum takes as foundational. While ideal-driven approaches tend to limit who can engage with the material by fitting the dancer into an external, idealized version of ballet, student-driven approaches expand the possibilities by enabling individual dancers, with all their idiosyncrasies, to locate ballet's forms, definitions, and parameters in, with, and through their unique selves. Student-driven pedagogies, to this end, emphasize and value each dancer's person—including their lived experiences, bodies, and identities—as the wellspring for the ballet they learn and dance. They provide foundations for the development of whole dance artists in ballet, rather than upholding documented ideals that have served as exclusionary mechanisms and led to abusive pedagogical practices. These approaches to pedagogy re-envision ideals for bodies and behaviors as only ever sourced from within each dancer,

DOI: 10.4324/9781003332718-4

as self-determined elements of their autonomous participation in ballet. Dancers, then, are in control: of their bodies, their learning, and their personal objectives in ballet. Student-driven pedagogies consider the dancer's experience and embodied knowledge as central not only to their learning and dancing but also to the further development of their own pedagogical voice.

I begin this chapter with a discussion of philosophical perspectives beneath student-driven work. I describe embodied subjectivities as a means through which hierarchies of bodies and knowledges in ballet can be pedagogically reconfigured; and I consider the implications of this work in practice—in body. In acknowledgment that there is no one "correct" way to approach student-driven pedagogies—no "best practices" that will apply to all ballet teaching contexts—I discuss them in the plural to broaden possible points of entry and make space for the development of methodologies that can function inside the many environments in which ballet is taught and learned. These pedagogies are ultimately for individual teachers to devise—the act of pedagogical thinking being central to their manifestations in the ballet class as praxis. This chapter draws from my subjectivities, phenomenologically, through my body and experience; and it engages with field-wide dialogues around developing humanizing, ethical, equitable ballet pedagogies.[1]

Foundations and Definitions

In the tradition of critical pedagogy, student-driven approaches acknowledge systems and institutions as contexts for ballet pedagogies. They are explicit about the historical and ethical reasons for developing humanizing approaches that extend without reservation to all dancers. Student-driven pedagogies ask teachers to acknowledge the histories, knowledges, and experiences students bring with them to the ballet class. They expect teachers to openly rebuff destructive pedagogies that prioritize ideals over individuals and to engage students in critically interrogating those approaches and the systems that enable them—to support students' current work inside the system and to interrupt the further perpetuation of such adverse approaches.

In the tradition of feminist pedagogy, student-driven approaches ask ballet teachers to consider each dancer's whole embodied person as a pedagogical rationale—to be unequivocal in their adapting of ballet to each student as a central, purposeful, and legitimizing feature of the work. These approaches reject a mythical, objective ballet of sameness while embracing the subjectivities that each dancer and teacher brings to ballet's study and practice; they foreground the dialogues between students' and teachers' backgrounds, goals, identities, and bodies. They center the embodied knowledges and lived experiences of everyone involved in pedagogical processes.

Student-driven pedagogies also ascribe to tenets of progressive and democratic education, which overlap with critical and feminist work in and through the teaching praxis, as specific teaching methods can function as the practical application of several related philosophies at once.[2] In this light, student-driven approaches also draw from trauma-informed pedagogies, pedagogies of care, inclusive pedagogies, Engaged Pedagogy, antiracist pedagogies, pedagogies of embodiment, pedagogies of kindness, and liberatory pedagogies, among others. As antithetical to the ideal-driven approaches in Chapter 1, these approaches could also be defined as anti-authoritarian.

The methodologies that emerge from student-driven pedagogies find their ethical center in students as individuals, who motivate both the material and relational elements of the work. Dance scholar Jennifer Jackson, for example, distinguishes between working en dedans—from the outside in, or from ballet's external ideals—and working "from the inside out," or en dehors, which approaches ballet through the individual, subjective people of the dancers.[3] When teachers situate students as rationales for their pedagogies in a student-driven way, the study of ballet originates within each individual dancer, while teachers, from their subjective perspectives, design relevant class material and work with students relationally.

Relatedly, dance scholar Naomi M. Jackson cautions against "assum[ing] a stance that exclusively measures value in terms of final products."[4] While ballet in the moment of performance is dependent upon outcomes, it is vital from an ethical perspective that the pedagogical work to develop those outcomes considers the wholeness of each individual beyond their production capacity—that the process through which students work is as valued in the pedagogy as the outcomes they realize. To this anti-capitalist end, student-driven approaches subvert the hegemony of ideal-driven, or "en dedans" approaches, which privilege the product.[5] They help dancers access an "en dehors" perspective instead—deliberately shifting the pedagogical narrative away from homogenizing ideals and prioritizing each student, with their lived-in bodies and identities that distinguish their dancing.

This is a significant shift in pedagogical drivers: from foundational expectations that each dancer will produce the same external ideal, to commitments to celebrating individual dancers' embodiment of and relationships to ballet. As teachers work to address individual student needs, however, they may find themselves needing more information in areas beyond their expertise as ballet pedagogues. Student-driven pedagogies, then, assume that teachers will continue their own learning as part of their ethical responsibility to the individual; that they will work to complement their existing knowledge with research and practices in education, psychology, sociology, anatomy, kinesiology, dance science, and somatics, the visual and performing arts, and beyond.

Beyond accounting for individual needs and circumstances, student-driven pedagogies are contextual in that they must account for the logistical parameters in which ballet is studied: the length of the classes, the number of class meetings each week, the number of people in each class, the total number of students assigned to each teacher, the available musical accompaniment, the oversight or accountability measures teachers are responsible for, the assessment mechanisms teachers are expected to use, and the degree of control teachers have over those elements in the institution(s) they work for. These administrative contexts, however tedious, have a marked effect on how teaching and learning happen; on how teachers and students engage with ballet. They are systemic factors to be critically considered when developing ballet pedagogies and methodologies, which—in student-driven approaches—are neither monolithic nor static.

Identities play a central role in student-driven pedagogies, for teachers as much as students. The power dynamic in most ballet classes, I suspect, defaults to the traditional hierarchy unless explicitly stated otherwise. When this hierarchy is upset in student-driven pedagogies—when power is redistributed, even in part, to students—it can have social and political implications. While teachers affiliated with dominant identity groups might readily consider sharing power with students, teachers in historically marginalized groups might feel they need to retain some of their given pedagogical power to offset the biases they may encounter in an educational space. This dynamic depends on who teachers and students are, and how they engage: the collection of identities in the ballet studio shapes everyone's experience of ballet—teachers and students alike. The locus of power in these pedagogies is therefore based on whether the teacher feels professionally protected enough to relinquish it; institutional biases—especially in predominantly white institutions—are an essential part of these considerations. Developing approaches that challenge inequitable institutional policies when possible, support a range of identities, and work in dialogue with students to shape the work in humanizing ways are central to the student-driven pedagogical project.

How students see themselves in relationship to ballet will ultimately affect how any pedagogy takes shape. As a result, student-driven approaches must be made fluid; ready to adapt to shifting humanity in the day-to-day work of teaching and learning. What supports one student some of the time will likely not support that same student all of the time, nor will it necessarily support other teachers or other students at any time.* With a range of variables always in play, student-driven methodologies

---

* I am grateful to Nicole Perry for her thinking here.

are built to be pluralistic and heterogeneous: they change in response to shifting stimuli; and they exist in, through, and with the unique people in the room. I want to be careful, however, about allowing this concept to devolve into what Parker J. Palmer calls the "mindless relativism" that he suggests tends to arise in "student-centered" teaching approaches: "One truth for you, another truth for me, and never mind the difference."[6] While there can be innumerable manifestations of student-driven ballet pedagogies, they cohere in practice around the material content of ballet—from the origins of the danse d'école to its more contemporary developments—in terms of material and movement vocabulary. The truths ballet's techniques teach and the wisdom they hold, as embodied by individual dancers, prevent these pedagogies from dissolving into such relativism. The challenge to teachers in student-driven approaches, then, is to not allow traditionally authoritarian ideals to creep into the praxis simply because of ballet's presence as a subject. Rather, the pedagogical objective becomes supporting students materially and relationally as each drives their own study of the form.

Ballet Pedagogies beyond Ideals

Embodied Philosophies

Pedagogue Anna Paskevska describes the process by which ballet pedagogies develop:

> Dance teachers start life as dancers. Their personal experience initially directs them toward certain conclusions, which, in turn, is influenced by a variety of factors: the particular limitations or givens of their physique, emotional response to movement, the happenstance of studying with this and not that mentor, or working with a specific choreographer within a specific repertoire.[7]

Teachers' understandings of and eyes for ballet's function and aesthetics are filtered through their individual bodily lenses and their felt, lived experiences as dancers. Awareness of embodied inquiry is especially critical for pedagogical development: dancers reason with their muscles and infer with their senses; they set parameters, quite literally, with the peculiar shapes of their bones and connective tissues, which—despite ballet's traditional attempts to create uniformity across bodies—are not the same as anyone else's. A dancer's somatic wisdom inspires a cohesive philosophy they can justify in their own body, experience, and movement; their resulting pedagogies are then grounded in what they physically understand. Their unique bodies become the source, the archive, and the channel for their pedagogies. As extensions of their embodied selves, their pedagogies reflect who they are and what they value; they are personal and professional, emotional and intellectual, vulnerable and empowered. The pedagogy evolves with the pedagogue. In the ballet class, then, the fact of the individual—the bodies, identities, and contexts for each teacher and student—is foundational to the teaching, the learning, and the dancing.

Sherry B. Shapiro notes that, "knowledge is always grounded in bodily existence," which helps explain why dancers gravitate toward teachers and coaches whose perspectives make sense in their bodies.[8] These teachers' ways of looking at ballet—including their technical, aesthetic, and stylistic sensibilities—become central to how dancers understand the form and how they come to know their bodies inside of it: their teachers' perspectives become part of their dancing selves. Dancers accept these teachers' work, adapting it to themselves through the physical experimentation, reasoning, and logic that are key to embodied inquiry. The work of pedagogy, then, becomes supporting each student in reconciling the teacher's embodied perspectives with their own unique person and existing knowledge.

Maurice Merleau-Ponty describes this process of embodied learning:

> Whether a system of motor or perceptual powers, our body is not an object for an 'I think,' it is a grouping of lived-through meanings which moves towards its equilibrium. Sometimes a new cluster of meanings is formed: our former movements are integrated into a fresh motor entity, the first visual data into a fresh sensory entity, our natural powers suddenly come together in a richer meaning, which hitherto has been merely foreshadowed in our perceptual or practical field, and which has made itself felt in our experience by no more than a certain lack, and which by its coming suddenly reshuffles the elements of our equilibrium and fulfils [*sic*] our blind expectation.[9]

I read this passage and can feel the physical ecstasy of my first triple pirouette, or the first time I held a sustained balance at the top of a piqué en avant into first arabesque. Merleau-Ponty's words call up the feeling I so vividly remember when a step or phrase came together and *worked* for the first time; offering a new physical sensation around which I could restructure my pursuit. My body became the site for experimentation as I reconciled distinct pedagogical perspectives—even conflicting ones. One teacher said "Up" while another said "Down," for example, and I made these concepts compatible in my body. Sometimes "Down" allowed me to feel more ease than "Up," and sometimes I found that "Up" and "Down" were not mutually exclusive, but worked together as complements, radiating outward in both directions. What began as discrete concepts found new significance and reorganization in my body, as

I conceptualized "Up" and "Down" for myself. I defined and redefined these sensations as I grew as a dancer; situating and re-situating what Shapiro calls the "abstracted-objectified 'thing'" of ballet in, with, and through my body.[10]

Dancers sort through elements of their teachers' pedagogies as they develop their own, using their bodies as the mediums through which they piece together their philosophies. They exercise thorough embodied analysis as they consider elements of their teachers' work that they will maintain, adjust, or reject in their own. Based on their interpersonal experiences and embodied responses, they might choose to perpetuate specific concepts in homage to those who supported their growth. They likely avoid establishing as tenets of their pedagogies those concepts that their teachers may have believed but which were incompatible with their bodies or aesthetic viewpoints. Those concepts could be useful to their broad pedagogical knowledge, so they might stash them away for later use. Despite their discomfort with these perspectives, they can be valuable to the development of pedagogies in that they provide ideas to push against. Incompatible approaches, in this way, can allow teachers to define their pedagogical values inversely; by showing them that they do not align with certain ideas, they can more easily locate their principles. Most likely, though, teachers embrace as pillars of their teaching the concepts they can validate somatically. The body is analytical: it articulates how and why dancers align with or diverge from certain pedagogies. It is because dancers' bodies and their ways of being embodied are different from those of their teachers that they cannot pass down their teachers' work directly or indiscriminately, as might be implied in some of ballet's most patriarchal lineages. Dancers' innate bodily intelligence revises their teachers' ideas and offers new physical renderings of them, and this persistent embodied reinterpretation of ballet leads to its evolution over time.

The locus of ballet is in the soma—the "bodily being."[11] The study of ballet changes dancers' bodies and shapes them affectively, particularly if they begin their studies at a young age. They strengthen and stretch, develop postural markers, and learn to harness their emotions to artistic ends. They come to love their most influential teachers; developing close relationships with those who fostered their development as dancers and individuals—as somas. Because pedagogical perspectives tend to reflect the strongest of those relationships, teachers might try to replicate personality traits of their teachers in an effort to reproduce an environment in which they thrived: if it was meaningful for them, perhaps it will be equally as meaningful for the students they now work with. By that reasoning, the effects of any dysfunctional relationships a dancer had with their teachers could, and often do, seep into their pedagogies, despite their best intentions. If they endured abuse—often disguised as pedagogy or method—they might unconsciously perpetuate, or more insidiously, rationalize this abuse as they develop their own pedagogies. Lineage runs deep: it is ingrained in the soma. In doing the work of keeping ballet lineages alive, teachers pass forward affective elements of pedagogies—the beneficial parts as well as those that might be so entrenched in their experiences that they fail, at first, to see them as harmful or in need of revision.

Particularly for those whose ballet lineages are heterogeneous, articulating a cohesive pedagogy can be a challenge. These approaches may weave together an array of concepts from various syllabi, Schools, somatic practices, or physical regimens into a sound pedagogical approach, yet because it is unnamed, and because of its underlying subjectivity and complexity, it may go unspoken or overlooked as a cogent philosophy. Despite the prevalence of these approaches in the twenty-first century, they are difficult to communicate and have been derided by ballet's purists as less legitimate, which allows national and formalized Schools of ballet to retain a certain authority. Pedagogues' individual embodiment, however, precludes the implication that genres, forms, Schools, and pedagogies—codified or not—are ever monolithic. They may have names, and they may be considered whole entities unto themselves, yet the fact of the soma suggests a substantial degree of variation inside these definitions. Because bodies, identities, and embodied experiences are distinct, and because they are the cornerstones of pedagogical development, it becomes evident that inside of established forms, genres, Schools, or syllabi, there are as many pedagogical philosophies as there are pedagogues. Ballet class is never just ballet class—dancers know implicitly to ask *who* will be teaching.

When teachers engage with pedagogy as an embodied philosophy, they assume the entwined roles of *messenger*: passing down what they have learned; and *progenitor*: originating ideas through the filters of their unique persons and somatic experiences. This understanding—of how teachers' lived experiences and embodiment shape the ballet they received as dancers—allows teachers to begin approaching ballet pedagogies as *praxis*: theoretically informed, systemically transformative practice, or what critical pedagogy pioneer Paulo Freire refers to as "*reflection* and *action* directed at the structures to be transformed."[12] In defiance of the notion that ballet pedagogies can or should be passed down wholesale for the sake of preserving traditions in stasis, a praxis-based approach can allow pedagogies to serve as critical and dynamic homage: to honor the beloved aspects of ballet's traditions while regularly interrogating their value, application, and relevance.

Teaching beyond the Body

When I am in a studio with a class of students, I invite them to help me understand their somatic experiences and what they feel, beyond what my eye perceives they know. I look to the students to teach me how to extend my embodied knowledge to those who don't share my body's structure and understanding—which is to say, all of them. It is the differences between students' bodies and my own that compel me to seek knowledge that originates outside of my body, so I work to learn more about bodies, somas, and pedagogies in supplementary ways. My body might not be the source of this knowledge, but it is my sole framework for understanding it. I cannot learn through a different body, or through my mind without my body's interpretation. My mind and my body are one as I learn new approaches: my mind feels my body's analysis. My pedagogy, then, is my embodied wisdom, which derives from my study of ballet in tandem with sources beyond my study that use my body as a filter. My role is to communicate with each student through my embodied knowledge, while learning about each student's unique way of being embodied—to prompt a bodily dialogue.

Claiming that embodiment is central to the development of ballet pedagogies is not to suggest that as a teacher I am without physical limitations or that my body doesn't change over time. As questions arise in my teaching, I can typically rely on my body's ability to answer them. I demonstrate and analyze concepts—often marked at a lower amplitude—to offer a visual representation during classes, or I try on ideas physically in miniature when in conversation with colleagues or students. If I can feel it in my body, even on a small scale, I can validate it. And when my body changes, after injury, for example—or childbirth, for some—my embodiment changes with it. Aging, likewise, alters my somatic reality: it shows me new ways of harnessing and even deepening my embodiment. I learn to do more—to feel more—with less pliancy and less range. I move more efficiently by necessity. When my body encounters places of resistance or limitation, I can still locate the feeling of the full form in my body, as a phantom limb that I can feel whether or not the full extent of the form is still physically possible. There is emotion in that moment, and acknowledging it reminds me to empathize with where the students might be in their work; how they too are striving to find the fullness of ballet's form in their bodies and their persons. My embodied knowledge is cumulative, and my embodied inquiry is ongoing: I can still feel the full capacities I once had access to, and I continue learning and teaching through my body as I am now.

Emerita Professor Susan Hadley once told me she could tell whose class she was watching by looking only at the students. Watching another teacher work with a class of students I am familiar with offers a similar insight. I appreciate the opportunity to see another's pedagogy—another's body—reflected in the bodies of the dancers who I usually see through the lens of my pedagogy and my body. I see the ways the students respond to a different teacher; how they hear the music, traverse the space, or engage their focus. The context of another pedagogue's embodied philosophy makes clearer to me how the framework of my body shapes my pedagogy.

When I first enter a studio with a new class of students, my knowledge presents itself through my body, while my pedagogy reveals itself more slowly, over time. The first thing students do in a ballet class is to look at how the teacher moves and shapes their body; it makes the expectations clear and serves as evidence of the teacher's experience—a reason to be confident in their knowledge. When I teach, I can feel students' eyes. For better or worse, my body is central to whether students will decide, at first, that they can trust me as a legitimate source of knowledge. My body is also the key to my pedagogy, and by learning to understand my body—as I demonstrate material and exist physically in the studio with them—they learn who I am and what I value. The danger here is that the particularities of teachers' bodies can become ideals of a sort. Vigilance in how teachers use and talk about their own bodies during ballet classes is necessary to avoid comparison, and to support students in seeing the inherent value of their own bodies—and every dancer's body—in their individual physical contexts.

When I am still and quiet in my body, I can be more attuned to the nuances of students' bodies, both as I plan classes and while observing them in class. Sometimes my body—its patterns and preferences that have changed over time—is useful to the work, and sometimes it makes my pedagogy feel myopic or less applicable to the students. Deliberately preparing and teaching classes without stepping inside the dance is not comfortable or easy: actively avoiding my body's movement impulses is a challenge because my embodiment, always and by its nature, affects my choices. Making the attempt to sidestep my patterns, however, helps me expand the range of material I choose and the details my eye perceives. I am always my body and yet I often reach beyond its framework: the students' bodies are their own, and they need to work beyond my body. The further away I get from performing or consistent daily practice, the more important this becomes. Gretchen Ward Warren recommends limiting the amount of physical demonstration teachers offer whenever possible, "In order to discourage the natural tendency of students to imitate the subtle movement mannerisms of their teacher."[13] The teacher's role, in this light, becomes supporting dancers in going beyond what they see in the teacher's body, and further into the function and feeling of their own. When teachers decenter themselves physically in the studio—when they step away from the front-and-center space or avoid drawing attention to their bodies unless there's a specific reason for it—they disrupt the hierarchy of bodies in the ballet studio. Dancers, then, can take the space teachers inhabited; they can literally and metaphorically step forward to locate the feeling of their bodies—themselves—as a rationale for and focus of the work.

A central element of the teacher's charge in the ballet class—to see, analyze, and offer suggestions about a student's dancing that will help that student grow—assumes that they can extend their embodied understanding of ballet to other bodies. Paskevska refers to this phenomenon as: "… the dancer who turns to teaching steps beyond the personal in order to evaluate the technique in a more objective way," and she notes that "personal experience needs to refer to the precepts of the technique in order to be applicable to a broad range of student's [sic] needs."[14] The teacher is responsible, then, for developing a pedagogy that ties together their own bodily knowledge with concepts from the objective, theoretical "ballet" with philosophical consistency. This introduces questions of knowledge acquisition: how and to whom do teachers turn to get this information—these precepts? How thorough should a teacher's continuing education be beyond their own embodied knowledge, and how might they gain access to resources? Ethically, both individual pedagogues and the schools they work for are responsible for first being aware of the breadth and depth of a teacher's knowledge—both physically and intellectually—and for seeking out supplemental educational materials and experiences so teachers can be appropriately resourced with avenues for growth.

There are plenty of teachers who teach material that they've never experienced in their body; a common and often gendered example being those who've never danced en pointe teaching pointe classes. While such a scenario may omit important nuance in the study, once teachers reach a certain level it's possible to judiciously and temporarily teach some things they haven't embodied—ballet's theories can be broadly applied. It's important to distinguish, however, between when a teacher's existing knowledge might work for a group of students even if it's not ideal, and when that knowledge isn't applicable, isn't sufficient, or could be dangerous for a specific age or level. In countries like the United States, where there is no central authority or certifying body for ballet teachers, the realities of the open market combined with limited oversight for ballet education place the responsibility on teachers and the schools that employ them for the safety of the students and the ethical consistency of the teaching. Continued, well-resourced learning about ballet and pedagogies, including information that goes beyond the teacher's own body and experience, is thereby critical to their ability to support a range of students in their individual contexts.

Teaching Ballet Pedagogies: Critical Futures

The purpose of student-driven pedagogies is in part the student's unique embodiment of ballet, as well as the student's agentic capacity to draw on that embodiment as an authority. When teachers acknowledge their own embodied subjectivities as foundational to their pedagogies, they more directly support and facilitate students' development of their own.

Ballet's lineages are built on moments of deep discovery: the instances when dancers somatically understand their experiences enough to articulate and reformulate them; to eventually, as possible future teachers, make them applicable to others. These moments of revision offer a glimpse into how a single pedagogy might look in future incarnations, or how ballet pedagogies on the whole change shape over time. It is each generation's dancers, in this light, who control ballet's legacies of embodied inquiry.

The teacher's body can convey aesthetic and technical perspectives to students and provide valuable inspiration—as guest classes with professional dancers often prove—but a teacher's embodied knowledge of ballet is not enough to comprise a pedagogy on its own, despite the body's central role in pedagogical development. As dialogical in nature, student-driven pedagogies ask teachers to interrogate and communicate their embodied philosophies such that students can interpret them through their own bodies, of their own volition. Key to pedagogies, then, are methodologies and methods: the deliberately designed means by which teachers communicate and help students enact ballet. Methods express pedagogies: they communicate parameters for the relationship between teacher and student; they express a teacher's beliefs about student knowledge and capacities; they ascribe cultural, political, and socio-economic perspectives to bodies; and they reflect worldviews, principles, and standards. These values have historically been part of the "hidden curriculum" in the ballet class rather than being spoken aloud; yet the critical nature of student-driven pedagogies asks teachers to make the system of their ballet class—including their embodied beliefs and ballet's norms and culture—explicit, as a foundation for dialogue.[15]

From the student's vantage point in the ballet class, teachers' pedagogies and methods are one and the same; students interpret a teacher's philosophies through the methods they use to articulate them. As methods cannot be dissociated from pedagogies, they are never value-free, so what a teacher does—the actions they take—can easily be understood as what they believe. Methods, then, have the power to distort pedagogies. Consider, for example, the teacher who repeatedly advises students not to force their rotation because they value physical health and longevity, while at the same time demonstrating with an over-rotated, pronated fifth position themselves—the rubber soles of their black dance sneakers worn down along the inside edges. A teacher's knowledge and beliefs may become more well-informed or critical over time, but they must make an active methodological—and sometimes physical—adjustment in tandem. Without that adjustment, the doing of the teaching continues to communicate a retired belief system. When well-aligned with a teacher's intentions, however, methods can communicate not only pedagogical philosophies but meta-pedagogical processes as well. They can make transparent the complexities of pedagogical development and offer students an entry point for developing their own.

It is not only form and content that is perpetuated in the ballet class but also the mantle of ballet's pedagogical lineage. Teaching ballet means teaching ballet pedagogy. In light of pedagogy's tendency to self-perpetuate, any attempt teachers can make to describe the whys and hows of their teaching will better equip those students who will eventually teach and make the system of study more transparent and accessible to all students. In effect, this is critical pedagogy in action, as the systems and structures of ballet pedagogies are exposed. Dance education scholar Ann Kipling Brown asserts that "discussion of how something is being taught is as important as what is being taught," which suggests that teachers spend time in class demystifying the pedagogical structures and choices that comprise it.[16] This method of teaching communicates the often-undisclosed mechanisms of the ballet class and opens them up for a deeper look, thereby encouraging active inquiry and, potentially, the challenging of tradition.

At the memorial service for renowned pedagogue Maggie Black in 2016, former American Ballet Theatre principal dancer and Artistic Director Kevin McKenzie recalled Black's admonishment when she realized he was becoming overly reliant on her teaching. He explained:

> She very testily came to me one day and said, 'You really don't get the whole point of this whole relationship, do you?' She said, 'Your job is to go take all this work we've done and be able to work with anyone and translate what they have to give you into what you know works for you. I will not call myself a success as a teacher until I know that you don't need me.'[17]

At some point, as Black clearly understood, the teacher's goal for each student must be that they acquire the ability to transcend the teacher; whether in study and performance, teaching, or any other direction the student might choose. This way of looking at the teacher-student relationship shifts the meaningful purpose of ballet pedagogies; it counters the authoritarian ways teachers take ownership over students with language like "my students"; and it illuminates the importance of a collaboration—of being able to call upon "all this work we've done" as a launchpad for the student's autonomous future endeavors.

Toward Equitable Ballet Pedagogies

Subjectivities and Trust

Acknowledging that ballet pedagogies are subjective calls the ballet teacher's traditionally empowered role into question. To be philosophically consistent as they embrace their subjectivity in this position, teachers would have to relinquish their power as arbiters and gatekeepers of an objectively correct ballet: the sole authority at the front of the studio who is always right. Alternatively, teachers could aim to be deeply knowledgeable about ballet while remaining open to continued learning about how ballet might be embodied and understood by others. The care that such a role requires—working in collaboration with whole people, as opposed to the traditional notion of molding acquiescent bodies—is based on teachers' willingness to be open to who students are, who they want to be, and how they think and feel about ballet. It asks teachers to ally themselves with students; to demonstrate care for and trust in them. Earning the trust of students is an open-ended process. The teacher's willingness to extend trust without expectation allows students to determine—to drive—the teacher-student relationship. While the theoretically equal Freirian roles of "teacher-student with students-teachers" might be useful when considering how knowledge is sourced and how it's valued, the inherent imbalances in ballet's hierarchical structures are central to considerations of trust and relationship-building.[18] These power dynamics stipulate that trust aimed upwards—mutual trust, in other words—can never be assumed or expected, because despite teachers' best efforts, mutuality is not the functional reality for students and teachers in most hierarchical twenty-first-century contexts for ballet pedagogies.

The practice of fitting the material aspects of ballet to individual dancers' bodies is not enough on its own to support a student-driven approach, since it is certainly possible to tailor ballet physically to the individual dancer while relying on authoritarian methods to do so. Developing a working relationship with students where trust becomes possible means teachers will necessarily consider more than just students' bodies in the studio; they will consider and treat every student as a whole human with dignity in all facets of the work. Because of the embodied nature of ballet and the bodily dialogue that undergirds the teacher-student relationship, there is a level of intimacy in ballet pedagogies that goes beyond that in a traditional classroom. Given the vulnerability and openness that the study of ballet often asks of dancers—especially during times of plateauing progress, injury, or personal strife, for example—the teacher's extension of trust in a non-transactional way is necessary. It can lay the groundwork for meaningful collaboration.

There seems to be an unspoken assumption in ballet circles that a teacher's prior accomplishments in teaching and performing will, or should, establish sufficient precedent for students to trust them. The legitimacy of a teacher's performing career, however, demonstrates only that a teacher is trustworthy inasmuch as they dance(d) well themselves; that they have connections in the profession, perhaps; or that they have analyzed the art and the technique in their own bodies with significant depth. It suggests nothing of their willingness to acknowledge humanity, their intentions with or for students, their need to fortify their ego, their communication skills, or their desire to help students reach their goals. If a teacher has had a substantial teaching career, potential students might be able to see the effects of their teaching in other students, but this says nothing as to how those results—those dancers—developed; what kind of effect on the dancer the teacher actually had; or whether the teacher used authoritarian means to teach them.

Considering ballet's history of pedagogical abuses driven by ideals, students have far more reason to be skeptical of teachers than to trust them outright. Maurya Kerr suggests that "a classroom immersed in antiracism and pedagogies of freedom... allows space for marginalized students to not trust you—they shouldn't."[19] Those who've spent time learning to navigate authoritarian ballet environments become adept at adjusting to fit in those spaces. Behaviors that might seem to teachers to be an indication of trust, then, might in reality be fear or doubt beneath a well-trained veneer of compliance. Teachers who interpret obedience as evidence of trust or respect thereby miss the mark. Only occasionally, in my experience, have students voluntarily said aloud that they trust me, and to avoid manipulation given teacher-student power dynamics I refrain from asking them. Trust is never for winning. It is not an achievement. The work to earn it continues regardless.

When teachers are as open about their processes of pedagogical inquiry as they hope students might be about their learning processes; when they make explicit their trust in each dancer; and when they assume best intentions, they tilt the hierarchy and lay the groundwork for collaborative working relationships. bell hooks suggests that, "it is often productive if professors take the first risk, linking confessional narratives to academic discussions so as to show how experience can illuminate and enhance our understanding of academic material."[20] The teacher's acknowledgment of their own experiences in various stages of learning, then, is important if dancers are likewise being asked to reflect on their own work. Meeting students in a space of vulnerability by sharing processes, challenges, and histories implies trust in them—trust that they can see the teacher as a human being inside the realm of ballet.

Fostering an environment in which trust is supported is an ongoing process. Teachers' explicit disclosures are important here: stating aloud, repeatedly, that students are experts with the most comprehensive knowledge of their own persons and bodies; and explicitly trusting students to autonomously determine how to best care for themselves and their bodies. Dealing forthrightly with, or even subverting, any policies that might hinder this care is important—attendance, participation, or grading, for example. Teachers might also describe how students' individual perspectives and input contribute to their own pedagogical knowledge; how understanding each student's unique engagement with ballet supports their learning and abilities as a teacher. With a shared belief in the teacher as a learner and the student as holding important knowledge, collaboration becomes possible. This is different, notably, from an expectation of mutuality or equality in a space fundamentally defined by a hierarchical power structure. With collaborative roles intact, teachers and students can co-create approaches that work best for each student in light of their goals. In overtly championing the knowledge and experience students bring to the ballet class—in recognizing that the dancer's interpretation of their own embodiment is central to an effective humanizing pedagogy—teachers make space for students to identify themselves as valuable, and valued, partners in the pedagogic project.

From Homogenized to Differentiated

As a faculty member in a ballet academy, I recall being required to line students up in height order along the barres and in center groups, from shortest to tallest, so that anyone walking by or observing the class would see the illusion of uniformity, as differences in students' height would be less noticeable. The term "objectivity theater" has arisen in educational circles to describe the extraordinary lengths to which teachers will go to demonstrate the look of fairness—each student being held to the same standards, using the same approaches.[21] In its focus on equality, however, this kind of emphasis can lead to inequities, as important differences that affect each student's relationship to ballet are overlooked.

Author and activist adrienne maree brown suggests a need "to create futures in which everyone doesn't have to be the same kind of person."[22] In ballet, this means not just acknowledging or accepting, but celebrating the differences in dancers' bodies, identities, artistic leanings, movement qualities, and ways of learning. Pedagogies rooted in equity honor dancers precisely *for* their individuality rather than in spite of it; they include, and perhaps even highlight, dancers' idiosyncrasies as central to their study of ballet. These approaches ask ballet pedagogues to reject material elements of uniformity in ballet's tradition that have historically been centered in the profession: externalized expectations for 180 degrees of rotation, the 3-o'clock positioning of à la seconde, the devant and derrière positions at 12- and 6-o'clock, respectively. Working with technical approaches that are inclusive of diverse bodily capacities beyond traditionally homogenized expectations is essential; as is supporting and celebrating dancers of all shapes, sizes, identities, and skin tones—whose "looks" may not be the same or aligned with a predetermined or external expectation. It is through the unique people who learn and dance ballet that pedagogies can be imagined and reimagined, and ballet pedagogy made more relevant and meaningful to diverse participants.

It is worth noting that this celebration of individual dancers has, historically, shaped ballet's repertoire. The Petipa classical era work was built around specific dancers' strengths, which has resulted in multiple legitimate versions of nineteenth-century variations. Several twentieth-century choreographers, likewise, cleverly used specific dancers' physical attributes, movement qualities, and personalities to develop bodies of work. Despite the gendered nature of ballet's oft-noted "muses," the concept of individual dancers as oeuvre-defining inspirations stands; Maria Tallchief and Suzanne Farrell shaped Balanchine's ballets, while Lynn Seymour and Margot Fonteyn influenced Frederick Ashton. From Marie Taglioni in *La Sylphide* to Stephanie Dabney in *The Firebird*, to Sylvie Guillem in *In the Middle, Somewhat Elevated*, dancers' unique qualities have changed ballet. The notion that individual dancers can make an imprint on the work they do is thus neither new nor unusual. The differentiation of ballet based on the strengths of individual dancers is, rather, a well-established phenomenon.†

Likewise, pedagogies rooted in the dancer's idiosyncratic context for ballet are not new, rare, or particularly subversive. As early as 1803, Jean-Georges Noverre wrote, "...is it not essential to lead [dancers] to the same end, but by different roads?"[23] While I could tease apart the notion of "the same end," here, Noverre's overarching point stands. Dancers deserve to be supported individually along each of their "different roads," and the practice of doing so falls into a long and revered tradition of pedagogies designed to be applicable to individual dancers. In the twenty-first century, the cadre of ballet educators across the field who extend their pedagogies holistically to individual students continues to grow in new and more radical ways; and the resources that support this work are written, oral, embodied, and transitory. Beyond a burgeoning body of scholarly and trade literature; they are the content of conference presentations, classes, residencies, workshops, podcasts, discussions across social and traditional media, and informal conversations with colleagues and students. While all information about pedagogies should be examined critically, the ballooning of these dialogues alone inspires optimism about the future of the field.

One example of differentiating ballet's material comes from my own teaching. I set aside time during class to work with students—sometimes individually, and sometimes as a group—to refine their arabesques so they become germane to each of their unique bodies. I use a particular barre exercise that has now become standard fare in the material I offer, which emphasizes the oppositional spiral forward on the working side of the back as well as the activity of the supporting hamstring. I often demonstrate it,

---

† I am grateful to Dr. Steven Ha for pointing me in this direction.

and students often have the opportunity to watch others dance it, which necessitates me stating aloud, often, that no two arabesques will look the same in light of students' distinct structures, aesthetic sensibilities, and ways of feeling their bodies. I ask what students feel in their arabesques; how they experience its dynamic architecture; or what they're trying to achieve with it, stylistically. The more each student feels and can articulate how the "abstracted-objectified 'thing'" of arabesque can exist and deepen in their individual body, and the more they see it adapted to others' bodies and perspectives, the better understanding they have of how arabesque works on the whole.[24] Some students use this experience to initiate continued work on arabesques throughout the semester as a focal point of our work together. Hopefully, they begin to perceive arabesque as an embodied concept that can be stylized and adapted to a wide variety of people. A pedagogical approach that originates in both teachers' *and* students' subjective contexts for ballet suggests that ballet's practitioners can—if they choose—make space for a range of individuals to find embodied belonging in ballet's form. This approach relies on subjective knowledge to expand and enliven the ballet tradition; making it more heterogeneous and pluralistic; making it more readily available to dancers with diverse bodies, identities, artistic and technical capacities, and ways of existing in the world.

Relational differentiation, likewise, is important for equity: teachers relating differently to different students. While more slippery, perhaps, than adapting the material to individual bodies, this decided turn away from "fairness" enables more personalized treatment and the development of unique teacher-student relationships that support each dancer's person and needs. In my syllabus, for example, I include a statement—excerpted here—that explains my differentiated approach, which I also make time to read and discuss in class:

> My tone, my choice of language, and my methodology may not be the same from person to person as I learn where you are in your study and how you respond to my feedback.... In my relationships with each of you, I will attempt to honor what makes you an individual: your bodies and approaches to movement, your personalities and ways of being, and the unique histories and contexts that make you, you.

Students respond visibly to my recognition of them as individuals when I read this aloud. Because they then understand that they're not in competition with one another for my favor, community often emerges among them—community being a counterintuitive, even ironic result of emphasizing individuality. As I implemented this practice, I stopped receiving negative feedback about favoritism in my course evaluations. Students have since consistently written anonymous feedback that describes their appreciation of my attempts to see and support each of them differently.

This experience illuminates how an insistence on "fairness," whatever the origin, can become a source of competition between students, who may also, inversely, perceive "unfairness." A focus on differentiating material and relationships in my work seems to reduce this toxicity.

Teaching toward equity requires teachers to reject any homogenizing approaches that they experienced, even if handed down directly from their own teachers or their most beloved mentors. This rejection, or at the very least a reckoning with tradition, is central to the process of productive pedagogic change. As Paskevska notes: "…to seem to doubt one's mentor appears as a disloyalty, yet we must go further and not shy away from asking hard questions."[25] "Hard" these questions may be, but the act of turning away from physically unsound or psychologically fraught approaches teachers experienced during their own study results in the humanizing of ballet pedagogies going forward. These questions, and how teachers rise to answer them, have the potential to shift ballet's tradition toward equity.

From Deficit to Abundance

Student-driven pedagogies have the potential to neutralize "deficit thinking," which education researcher Richard R. Valencia defines as, "an endogenous theory—positing that the student who fails in school does so because of his/her [*sic*] internal deficits or deficiencies."[26] "Internal deficits" in a traditional ballet environment might be considered physical elements that deviate from the ideal body. They could be ways of being that deviate from ideals for behaviors or identities, as in a gender expression that a teacher doesn't understand, or in the outward manifestations of ADHD that seem to flout the rules of decorum. Student-driven pedagogies aim to stop ideals from being deployed as standards against which dancers are considered viable, valuable, or less so. By developing methodologies that support the dancer's individual body as a plentiful source from which their unique embodiment of ballet springs, the authoritarian notion that certain dancers are deficient in comparison to external ideals is diminished. The individual body—and to Jennifer Jackson's point, the individual dancer—becomes the ideal source material for their study of ballet.

Despite teachers' efforts, no amount of pedagogical diligence will preclude the harmful effects of the exclusionary worldview, driven by ideals, that undergirds deficit thinking. Likewise, no pedagogy or teaching methodology will be able to override the damage caused by the latent or unexamined biases at the root of deficit-based approaches. Education scholar Gloria Ladson-Billings asserts: "Not only must teachers encourage academic success and cultural competence, they must help students to recognize, understand, and critique current social inequities. This notion presumes that teachers themselves recognize social inequities and their causes."[27] This requires teachers' dedication to learning about equity in and beyond the studio; it demands critical self-reflection and an ongoing commitment to understanding institutional and systemic racism, unconscious bias, and the workings of privilege, intersectionally, across a range of identities: class, race, age, gender, ability, sexuality, and size among them. Ballet teachers in dominant identity groups—particularly those who possess ballet's idealized bodily attributes—are especially responsible for examining implicit biases, and for considering how the privileges they carry may affect their perception of student deficits.[28]

Journalist Chloe Angyal suggests that "teachers should be willing to reconsider what a 'good' foot—indeed, what a 'good' ballet body—looks like."[29] While I appreciate the overarching thrust of this idea and the desire to find greater abundance at its core, I propose that ballet teachers disengage from such value judgments regarding students' bodies—or anyone else's body, for that matter—as "good" implies the existence of "bad." As they attempt to counter notions of deficit by actively working from a place of abundance, student-driven ballet pedagogies eliminate such comparisons to ideals. They relinquish control over bodies and behaviors—focusing on how each dancer embodies ballet, how they might find expressive capacity through the technique, and how they might be welcomed to lead the pedagogical charge as they work toward individual goals for individual reasons.

Unfortunately, "good" and "bad" have become ubiquitous in describing bodies in ballet, so it is possible, even likely, that students have already engaged with such value judgments about their own bodies. As the relationship between dancers and their own bodies is their purview, despite my desire to change their negative perceptions, my role becomes supporting students in working with their own bodies. It is true that some physical configurations facilitate ballet technique in the body, and it is also true that all students need to learn how to work *with* their bodies no matter what access their physicality offers. In 2006, I spoke with Maggie Black, who expressed concern about the limitations of bodily ideals for this reason:

> The problem with ballet is that people tend to look at specific forms in the body, and I can understand that, because it's helpful in a lot of ways. But also many of the dancers—some of them very famous that I've worked with—didn't have facilities like that at all. If they learn to work physically a certain way, then they have access to their other physical senses and also to the development of their artistry through the physicality.[30]

To this end, I've sought out strategies for working with a range of bodily structures, and I seek support in this area when I do not have sufficient information. I aim to use applicable knowledge to demonstrate that ballet is for everyone, an abundant perspective that emerges in action more than words: when I work analytically, anatomically, and with great care and respect for each student's body and perspective.‡

Students' feelings of deficiency can and do affect their work. Even when exclusionary ideals are not part of the equation, their harmful effects remain—it only takes one irresponsible teacher to instill a self-perception that will devastate a student for the remainder of their dancing years. Teachers working toward equity become responsible, then, for not just discontinuing such practices in their own work, but for offering students strategies for strengthening their self-perception going forward. Critical pedagogy's explicit examination of systems of oppression can support these efforts. A ballet teacher's willingness to dialogue openly with students about institutions, ideals, and the inherent value of individual idiosyncrasies to ballet, can inspire students to reconsider their personal relationships to ballet without demanding they change how they see themselves. hooks's "confessional narratives" can be helpful here as well; if teachers describe how ideals affected their own experiences as dancers, they can identify shared experiences with students and generate compassion and determination around a facet of the system that needs revision.[31]

From Philosophy to Praxis

Ballet educators move from ideal-driven toward student-driven pedagogies as they become more interested in and adept at learning about, with, and from dancers; as they focus on each student's person rather than textbook-prescribed outcomes; and as they become less attached to their role as a gatekeeper. Their awareness of dancers' humanity increases, as does their desire to support their agency fully. Depending on the individual circumstances that inspired a change in perspective, teachers may take more or less time to adjust their teaching.

Two significant events prompted me to develop a student-driven approach based in a humanizing philosophy. First, I misconstrued a student's emotional response to failure as deliberate attention seeking, and after repeatedly dismissing her experience in the moment, I ousted her from the studio and told her to come back when she was ready to work. She returned, shortly thereafter, but her trepidation around me was palpable for her remaining year in the program. Second, the shift to online ballet instruction at the onset of the COVID-19 pandemic put everyone at a physical distance while increasing the collective need for connection and compassion. At the same time, educational institutions were instituting dehumanizing, inequitable, policies and expectations, and this distressing contrast strengthened my commitment to students. For entirely different reasons, both of these instances indicated that I needed to refocus my

‡ I am once again grateful to Dr. Steven Ha for inspiring this line of thinking.

approach—to consider students as whole people first. I needed time to figure out how this would affect my presence and behavior, my underlying assumptions, and my methods. I needed space to flounder and fail, too, as I reworked my pedagogy from its foundation. I still need some of that space today as I continue this work. Teachers' reasons for making pedagogical shifts, in this light, are personal and meaningful. They require as much differentiated support for their pedagogies as students do in their studies.

For these reasons, there is no one way, no step-by-step how-to, for student-driven pedagogies. At their core, these pedagogies are dialogical processes that individual teachers must develop with individual students. They are steeped in the process of inquiry, through which teachers and students consider how their contexts for the study of ballet might support *becoming*. These approaches critically examine systems and institutions while seeking to moderate their effects. They are emergent and spontaneous; with methods often arising in response to moment-to-moment needs that become apparent in the ballet class through all manner of communication. They develop in real time with dancers, as teachers invite them to help determine a working trajectory that the dancers themselves believe is most useful in helping them achieve their goals. In ballet, this process starts not only by treating dancers and students like autonomous people and trusting them to do what's best for themselves and their bodies, but actually believing as much and developing structures that support them through the process. Philosopher Max Van Manen defines pedagogy as: "a fascination with the growth of the other," which situates the teacher's curiosity about the student as central to this work: who they are, how they learn, what they're interested in, how they understand ballet, and what they perceive as aesthetically valuable.[32] A well-trained body alone does not a dance artist make, so the teacher's role becomes listening, observing, and supporting; and making space for students to drive the development of the pedagogy.

Lastly, student-driven pedagogies demand ongoing self-reflexive interrogations of teachers' personal histories with ballet: how they themselves relate to ballet in and through their bodies and lives as dancers-turned-teachers. As teachers reflect on their own relationships to ballet's harmful authoritarian ideals, and as they take action to eliminate any residual effects of these ideals in their teaching, ballet teachers can address—and even begin to undo—some of the damage. This often means acknowledging the harm teachers themselves have experienced in ballet; part of the process hooks refers to as "self-actualization," which requires that teachers "practice being vulnerable in the classroom, being wholly present in mind, body, and spirit."[33] If teachers consider and discuss with students how ideals affect the study of ballet, their own study, and their pedagogical perspectives, they will be drawing on critical and feminist approaches to help tease apart the hegemony of ideals. Likewise, they'll be supporting students negatively impacted by ideals in recognizing a new context for their work, which may enable them to make informed, autonomous choices going forward. The hope, via student-driven pedagogies, is to disrupt the passing down of what Theresa Ruth Howard refers to as "generational trauma" in ballet; to bring teachers and students together to facilitate ballet's sustained growth in ways more meaningful and relevant to more people over time.[34] As dance scholar Paula Salosaari writes: "…furthering a tradition in ballet is not about transferring fixed forms from one generation to another, but rather it is offering the traditional conventions to new persons to experience and live in them, and thereby transcend them."[35]

In my own teaching, moving pedagogy from philosophy to praxis is an ongoing process, full of curiosity, experimentation, and reflection. It is always challenging, quite a bit nerdy, and often—necessarily—joyful. The methodologies (the *how*) and contents (the *what*) of my pedagogy tend to become clearer once I've learned more about the participants (the *for/by/about whom*) who are, essentially, its rationales (the *why*).[36] The next part of this book brings teacher and student perspectives forward in tandem—dialogically. As Part 1 considered philosophies beneath ballet pedagogies, Part 2 considers the people who shape the praxis.

Notes

1. Portions of this chapter were first published in my article: "On Dance Pedagogy and Embodiment," *Conversations across the Field of Dance Studies* 38 (Society of Dance History Scholars, 2017): 17–20. This publication is now under the editorial auspices of the Dance Studies Association, who generously granted their permission for its reuse in this book. https://journals.publishing.umich.edu/conversations/
2. Gretchen Alterowitz, "Toward a Feminist Ballet Pedagogy: Teaching Strategies for Ballet Technique Classes in the Twenty-first Century," *Journal of Dance Education* 14, no.1 (2014): 9.
3. Jennifer Jackson, "My Dance and the Ideal Body: Looking at Ballet Practice from the Inside Out," *Research in Dance Education* 6, no.1/2 (April/December 2005): 25–40.
4. Naomi M. Jackson, *Dance and Ethics: Moving Towards a More Humane Dance Culture* (Bristol: Intellect, 2022), 90.
5. Jennifer Jackson, "My Dance and the Ideal Body: Looking at Ballet Practice from the Inside Out," *Research in Dance Education* 6, no.1/2 (April/December 2005): 26.
6. Parker J. Palmer, *The Courage to Teach: Exploring the Inner Landscape of a Teacher's Life* (San Francisco, CA: Jossey-Bass, 1998), 119.
7. Anna Paskevska, *Ballet Beyond Tradition* (New York: Routledge, 2005), 145.
8. Sherry B. Shapiro, *Pedagogy and the Politics of the Body: A Critical Praxis* (London: Routledge, 1999), 41.
9. Maurice Merleau-Ponty, *Phenomenology of Perception*, trans. Colin Smith (New York: The Humanities Press, 1962), 153.
10. Sherry B. Shapiro, *Pedagogy and the Politics of the Body: A Critical Praxis* (London: Routledge, 1999), 41.
11. Thomas Hanna, *Bodies in Revolt: A Primer in Somatic Thinking* (New York: Holt, Rinehart and Winston, 1970), 35.

12 Paulo Freire, *Pedagogy of the Oppressed* (New York: Herder and Herder, 1970), 126.
13 Gretchen Ward Warren, *Classical Ballet Technique* (Tampa: University of South Florida Press, 1989), 72.
14 Anna Paskevska, *Ballet Beyond Tradition* (New York: Routledge, 2005), 145–146.
15 The term "hidden curriculum" was coined by education scholar Philip W. Jackson in *Life in Classrooms* (1968; New York: Teachers College Press, 1990), and continues to be used across Education and Sociology to describe the implied values and norms in school culture.
16 Ann Kipling Brown, "Provoking Change: Dance Pedagogy and Curriculum Design," in *The Oxford Handbook of Dance and Wellbeing*, eds. Vicky Karkou, Sue Oliver, and Sophia Lycouris (New York: Oxford University Press, 2017), 407.
17 "Remembering Maggie: A Gathering to Celebrate the Life and Legacy of Maggie Black," New York City Center, February 2016.
18 Paulo Freire, *Pedagogy of the Oppressed* (New York: Herder and Herder, 1970), 80.
19 Maurya Kerr, "Dismantling Anti-Blackness in ballet: Pedagogies of Freedom," in *Antiracism in Ballet Teaching*, eds. Kate Mattingly and Iyun Ashani Harrison (Abingdon: Routledge, 2024): 91.
20 bell hooks, *Teaching to Transgress: Education as the Practice of Freedom* (New York: Routledge, 1994), 21.
21 The term "objectivity theater" was coined by Cathie LeBlanc in her blog post "Adventures in Ungrading," cathieleblanc.com, December 22, 2019. https://cathieleblanc.com/2019/12/22/adventures-in-ungrading/.
22 adrienne maree brown, *Emergent Strategy: Shaping Change, Changing Worlds* (AK Press, 2017), 57.
23 Jean Georges Noverre, *Letters on Dancing and Ballets*, trans. Cyril W. Beaumont (1803; Brooklyn, NY: Dance Horizons, 1975), 110.
24 Sherry B. Shapiro, *Pedagogy and the Politics of the Body: A Critical Praxis* (London: Routledge, 1999), 41.
25 Anna Paskevska, *Ballet Beyond Tradition* (New York: Routledge, 2005), 146.
26 Richard R. Valencia, *Dismantling Contemporary Deficit Thinking: Educational Thought and Practice* (New York: Routledge, 2010), 6–7.
27 Gloria Ladson-Billings, *Culturally Relevant Pedagogy: Asking a Different Question* (New York: Teachers College Press, 2021), 28.
28 See Chapter 5 for a discussion of problematic assumptions about students.
29 Chloe Angyal, *Turning Pointe: How a New Generation of Dancers is Saving Ballet from Itself* (New York: Bold Type Books, 2021), 248.
30 Maggie Black in conversation with the author, December 29, 2006.
31 bell hooks, *Teaching to Transgress: Education as the Practice of Freedom* (New York: Routledge, 1994), 21.
32 Max Van Manen, *The Tact of Teaching: The Meaning of Pedagogical Thoughtfulness* (Albany: State University of New York Press, 1991), 13.
33 bell hooks, *Teaching to Transgress: Education as the Practice of Freedom* (New York: Routledge, 1994), 21.
34 Theresa Ruth Howard, panelist, "The State of the Profession," (panel discussion, CORPS de Ballet International annual conference, Online, June 2023).
35 Paula Salosaari, "Multiple Embodiment in Classical Ballet," in *Not Just Any Body: Advancing Health, Well-being and Excellence in Dance and Dancers*, eds. R. Alston, K. Kain, D. Jowitt, J. Kylián and R. Philp (Ontario, Canada: The Ginger Press, 2001), 58.
36 Jessica Zeller, "Pedagogy as Protest: Reimagining the Center," in *Hybrid Teaching: Pedagogy, People, and Politics*, ed. Chris Friend (Washington, DC: Hybrid Pedagogy, Inc., 2021), 120.

Part 2
Perspectives

3 Teacher Presence and Behavior

Who teachers are in the ballet class matters, perhaps more so than is easy or comfortable to acknowledge. Students perceive and interpret pedagogical value systems through teachers' concrete actions and the less tangible elements of the teacher's person. The teacher's presence and behavior—their ways of being and doing—are vehicles through which teachers communicate values and expectations; they give students clues as to how they might safely and productively engage. How teachers exist and function in their positions of power allows students to see their stance on ballet's norms and ideals, on the teacher-student dynamic, and on the relationship between ballet and the people who study it. As the person of the teacher can have a substantial and lasting impact on the student's experience, these deeply subjective elements of pedagogies—of people, really—are important, if a bit thorny, to consider.

While I try to consider multiple perspectives, I approach this complicated discussion from the only vantage point I can accurately represent: my own. As a tenured faculty member in a private, predominantly white, religiously affiliated university, I write from a position of professional security and institutional support. As I work mostly with ballet majors in an audition-based ballet-specific four-year BFA program, my teaching builds on and responds to the efforts of students' previous teachers, as well as the efforts of my colleagues whose dedication to these same students I indirectly benefit from. I am a white, cisgender, heterosexual, able-bodied, middle-class woman, which situates me inside several dominant identity groups that allow me to be easily forthcoming about myself when I teach ballet classes, and to inhabit the space of the ballet studio without fear for or challenge to my person. While my five-feet-tall frame does not proportionately reflect the traditional ideal for classical ballet dancers, I do have a few structural facets that facilitate the form. In my mid-40s, at the time of this writing, I retain enough ongoing capacity to demonstrate with technical and stylistic clarity, although rarely at full physical amplitude.

These often-unspoken gray areas about the teacher's person in the ballet class offer rich territory for the development of pedagogies, so I

DOI: 10.4324/9781003332718-6

spend some time here mucking about in them while reflecting on my own pedagogical history. I question, analyze, and theorize through the lens of my own experience as a student, a dancer, a teacher, a colleague, an observer and researcher, and a participant in field-wide dialogues around ballet pedagogies. Considering the vast possibilities for pedagogical presence and behavior to support the study of ballet for all who participate, the analysis of these complex and deeply human themes in teaching is central to the larger project of humanizing ballet pedagogies. I have few answers in this arena but much curiosity about it, as every ballet class I teach prompts me to delve deeper into the hows and whys of my being and doings.

Teacher Presence: Ways of Being

As a student, the teachers I admired most were those whose very existence in the room prompted a sense of joy, anticipation, or a fire igniting. Their varied presences have become integral to my pedagogy in an aspirational sense, as I try to cause similar effects of their ways of being in my own teaching: how they made me feel, how they inspired me, how they shared their knowledge and love of ballet, and how they showed me what they believed was important—what they valued, and why. Most of it was intangible, subjective, and idiosyncratic: rooted in them as individuals in the world and interpreted by me: as who I was when I studied with them, and as who I am now.

The Teacher Persona

At age 11, I began assisting my beloved childhood teacher with her pre-ballet classes. Photos from that time show me in the studio with a particular posture, tilt of the head, dress code, and smile of approval when in front of students. At such a young age I had clearly embodied what it meant to me, then, to be a teacher. I remember becoming more concretely aware of this later on in my studies, and as I continued my own attempts at teaching. I'd noticed, for example, that some teachers have a formal teacher persona—complete with an air of superiority—that they turn on the instant a student is nearby. I remember walking toward the studio one day as one of my teachers was talking casually with another teacher in the hallway. As I approached, her tone changed, her posture inflated, and she raised her head as though a scent nearby had caught her attention. Looking me right in the eye, her voice dropped down before trailing upward: "Miss Zeller...." I don't remember if I replied—perhaps a "hello"—but I'm certain I smiled dutifully as I walked past her into the studio. I was suspect of her intentions as she paced up and down the barre; intentions she hid beneath her expertly crafted, unflappable exterior, with a gleam in one eye and a dagger in the other. I wasn't afraid of this teacher, but I didn't trust her either—I was cautious about what I shared with her. I held thoughts and questions to myself, I handled injuries quietly, and I eventually developed a persona of my own just so I could engage with her.

There's a gray area between fearing and trusting a teacher that's important to consider from a pedagogical point of view. While teachers must maintain appropriate relationships with students for everyone's safety, adopting an entirely distinct way of being can be both jarring and detrimental—personal façades can interrupt the development of depth and honesty in the work. The formal persona, in this way, becomes a barrier that allows teachers to demonstrate or even flaunt their place atop the ballet hierarchy; it helps teachers protect their power. While some teachers might develop this persona as part of an authoritarian belief system, others may feel the formality is necessary for their own protection; teachers who work in schools where they're surveilled by parents or employers, or where they experience the effects of employer, parent, or student biases. This gray area, too, is important: the existence of a formal persona doesn't always mean that teachers are doing damage—it can be an indication of the teacher's need for personal or professional safety, or their attempt to adhere to what they perceive is expected of them.

The informal teacher persona is likewise complicated. Especially with young teachers—I was no exception—the line between wanting to be a teacher and a friend can become blurred. My insecurities about my ability to establish an environment, to teach a well-loved class, or to garner respect from students resulted early on in a persona that was excessively casual. I didn't understand that making oneself pedagogically trustworthy requires interpersonal and pedagogical skills; including a disciplined interest in learning and caring about others, the ability to listen and support people along their desired path, and a capacity to filter and redirect information so that it reaches someone when and how they need it. Rather, I misinterpreted my desired role as simply being likeable and fun. As I have learned, being a trusted figure means distinguishing between how I am as a friend to my personal friends, and how I am—while being the same core person—to a group of people I may indeed adore, but over whom I hold both implicit and explicit power.

In the next chapter, several student survey participants state that they prefer the teacher-student relationship to be "professional but friendly" in a way that acknowledges power dynamics, protects student privacy and safety, and allows for sincere human connection in an embodied art form.* Perceptive as they are, students can sense the difference between

---

* This research protocol #2022–323 was approved in September 2022 by the Institutional Review Board (IRB) at Texas Christian University.

pretense and genuine, appropriate behavior. As teaching personas are embodied manifestations of pedagogical philosophies, they can affect the teacher-student relationship, as well as student perceptions of ballet on the whole.

Teacher Behavior: Foundations

Behavior, a category as broad as Presence, encompasses all teachers do in the studio. As the task of providing feedback has received the most direct attention in ballet's pedagogical literature and in other areas of this book, I turn my focus here to how teachers observe, listen, and physically conduct themselves during ballet classes; actions that undergird the dialogues and feedback loops in the ballet class.

Seeing

The noted "eye" of the ballet teacher refers to their ability to identify the details of ballet in a dancer—to recognize a physical situation. It is a trait that the most effective teachers possess in unique ways; the mechanism through which teachers understand that the pelvis is retracted, for example, or the spot too slow. Determining what and how to communicate with students based on these observations is a separate pedagogical skill. In my experience teaching student teachers, I've noticed that the act of seeing is harder for them to learn than the communication that follows, in part because the "eye" reflects the teacher's knowledge about ballet's principles beyond the feeling of their own body in the form, with which they've usually had limited experience.

The act of observing students is ripe for consideration. It is a privilege to be given the opportunity to support students in their study of ballet, so acknowledging the intimacy of looking deeply at people—in, with, and through their bodies—is a sacred pedagogical responsibility. Do I observe with curiosity or with judgment; is my aim to inquire or foreclose? What is my default assumption: that they don't want to work hard, or that they're doing their best? Crystal U. Davis suggests that "the observation process is riddled with opportunities for implicit biases to inform the analysis and assessment of human movement and behavior and, by extension, student performance in dance classes."[1] In this light, am I, a teacher with multiple privileges, working to notice and interrupt my biases as I watch? Am I looking from a place of love, having learned enough from bell hooks, who establishes love as necessary and radical ground beneath learning and education?[2] Am I looking to look, or am I looking to see?

From another angle, what do students see in me while I'm observing them? What is my posture doing, and what of my face? What do I allow students to see of my perspective through my act of looking: do I smile at them? Do I grimace? Do I express consternation or displeasure with furrowed brows? While it would be more productive for students to be fully ensconced in their dancing than focused on the teacher's in-the-moment visible response to their work, it would be naïve to think they're somehow unaware of how teachers appear while observing them.

I've noticed that teachers who dance alongside their students seem to scan them more broadly than those who are still while observing—I've experienced this difference with my own teachers and in my own teaching. Despite my desire to move in hopes that my feeling the movement will somehow generate energy in the students' bodies or allow me to communicate a quality or essence, getting out of my own body is important to the acuity of my eye. I am sharper when I stop and watch. I see more of who they are as they move, and I become attuned to where they put their effort—what they're trying to accomplish. I can see the physics in their dancing with individual detail, rather than as a moving whole. I can look in an attempt to empathize—to feel what it might feel like to move as they do, which helps me address issues of alignment, coordination, and musicality with an element of humanity. I can identify what I don't know about them and consider questions I'd like to ask them about their movement choices, patterns, and habits—questions that will help me support them with more specificity and depth of understanding.

Davis notes: "When the authority to observe and evaluate dance performance is based on the viewer's personal familiarity with or similar background to the mover, this raises questions of equity and access."[3] I take it as my responsibility, then, to be cognizant of who I am and what the students allow me to see of themselves—to work to learn about and disrupt my implicit biases; and to speak truthfully and demonstrate curiosity in earnest about that with which I am unfamiliar. I make special efforts to ask students about themselves and their work, particularly when the identities, experiences, and histories they bring to ballet class are different from my own. Nyama McCarthy Brown calls for a self-reflexive approach, saying, "Through reflexivity I can assess a situation, considering power dynamics, my role, and positionality of all parties. I am able to make the needed shifts to my behavior and approach to be a more responsive and effective teacher."[4] This moment-to-moment awareness of the teacher's person can allow them to shape their observations in real time, to suit the context of each teacher-student relationship dynamic.

One of my daily projects is to systematically work my way around the studio so that I see each person in the room repeatedly throughout the class; and to identify who I haven't engaged with enough that day. This disrupts any tendencies I might have to notice some students more than others, for any reason. I am aware that I choose to look at certain students more or less than others for a variety of reasons. Perhaps a student appears to be working hard, or seems removed, or is wearing a bold color, or is making steady progress, or has plateaued, or has a sunburn, or has a longer history with me in the studio. The result is that some students may feel more visible while others may feel less so. If I am unsuccessful, a student might complete a full ballet class with no assurance that I even knew they were there. In an interview with my teacher, Maggie Black, who'd worked with several ballet notables, she told me that it "didn't matter whether they were famous or not famous or whatever. I made the effort to work with everyone because that's the reason they were there."[5] Understanding that seeing is a choice, I follow Black's lead to ensure that I actively observe each student multiple times in each class; because a student's simple presence in the class merits at least that degree of acknowledgment—the feeling of being seen.

While the observation of each student is at the heart of equitable ballet pedagogies, there is an important distinction to be made between seeing and targeting. Some students are used to having adversarial relationships with teachers, whether because of teachers' implicit biases, authoritarian pedagogical approaches, or both. My intention to recognize them or show them I see them will fail if they perceive I am singling them out because of how my presence or behavior intersects with their experience. This is another gray area—how teachers' ways of being and behaving are perceived given students' histories—which calls for teachers to take interest in students, their individual ways of working and learning, and their backgrounds in ballet.

Like so many in education at the onset of the Coronavirus pandemic, I taught my classes online via Zoom during the 2020–2021 academic year. I was quickly thrust into a static position behind my computer screen, where even if I wanted to, I couldn't move with and watch students at the same time. In a failed attempt to record a rehearsal one day, I accidentally recorded the screen with my own face. When I realized what I'd done, I watched the video in horror—as though watching a disaster unfold in slow motion. I remember during that rehearsal thinking about which specific elements of the students' work I'd respond to when they finished the run-through; yet one eyebrow was raised, my hands were often in front of my sometimes slack mouth, and my eyelids were either at half-mast or wide open, staring. My inner monologue and my physical person were telling two entirely different stories. I vowed to be more diligent in aligning my exterior with my interior—not through self-surveillance, which can be counter-productive, but through a greater sense of embodied self-awareness and intentionality.

When I returned to the studio in April of 2021, the students and I were limited in space—to those now-notorious 10′ × 10′ taped-off boxes on the floor. Watching from afar and from behind a mask, I was aware that my body and the top half of my face were the physical elements

I had at my disposal to express my intentions to students. I found myself grateful for my emerging crow's feet, which allowed my smile to be evident from above my mask-line. I smiled at them a lot in earnest, then, since returning to on-site teaching after a year online filled my heart in ways I'd never have expected. I began to watch, too, from a place of love—the simple love of watching students invest themselves in the study of ballet, moving in a space with them, and sharing our mutual love of the work in the face of such turbulence.

I relish what I learned about seeing during that brutally difficult time. The feelings of love I was experiencing for the students and the work had begun to inform my behavior—likely my presence, too—in ways that I hope students could then, and continue now, to feel. Since then, and since becoming more acquainted with how hooks describes the importance of love in pedagogy, I have become more deliberate in how I allow pedagogical love to manifest in my teaching.[6] Love has become a tenet of my pedagogy, which I exercise in part through how I choose to see.

Listening

As with seeing, listening happens before the subsequent action of communicating about it. Early in my career I was so focused as a teacher on my activities and behaviors during class that I rarely gave attention to how I was receiving or understanding information from the students. Learning to listen has been an act of pedagogical maturation—of quieting and decentering myself—so I can work with, rather than talk at, the people in the room.

It seems evident that in order to listen, teachers need to make space for students to speak and express audibly. Inviting students to speak out loud in classes has been an ongoing project in the field of ballet pedagogy for some time, so it becomes important to consider what teachers might do with those voices once they inhabit the space.[7] How teachers engage—carefully or less so—with students' speech can make the difference between humanizing and authoritarian pedagogies. In other words, inviting students to speak up is just the beginning. The actions teachers take once student voices are heard, however, can either confirm or counteract the purpose of inviting them in the first place.

Students in my classes tend to speak up often. I encourage it. Yet I too often don't pause after they come forward; I tend to respond immediately, and sometimes before they can even finish. Time is not a luxury in the classes I teach, and my efforts to be efficient can seem brusque. Lately, I've been trying to make time—to let comments or questions hang in the air for a moment so I can more thoughtfully interpret their words or ask a follow-up question to better understand what's needed in that moment. Occasionally another student will respond before I do—a dynamic I'm interested in fostering further. It reminds me to toss the question to the whole class; to actively support a collaborative working environment in which listening happens in all directions, and listening to one's peers becomes as important as listening to the teacher. I've become aware, too, that how I listen to one student's comment or question indicates to others how I might listen to them—it shows them whether I value student voices. Clarity in how I listen has become paramount in my efforts to show students that I am trustworthy; by validating their contributions and working to better understand their perspectives.

The first pandemic year of teaching through a digital platform taught me a lot about listening. I worked that year with live pianists who played for our classes online, and while these collaborations were wonderful, the technology was set up so I couldn't speak while the students danced: my voice cutting in would make the live music cut out. I had to observe without speaking, which was deeply frustrating at first. I felt that my voice during the dancing was important for students to have sufficient prompting. The more I became used to being deliberately quiet, however, the more my other senses were activated. I learned to see them more clearly—to discern and acknowledge their artistic contributions. I began to notice the choices they made on their own, without my help, and I saw more of their interests appearing in the work. They showed me my voice wasn't always needed in the space. I learned that in ballet pedagogy, listening is part of seeing, and seeing is likewise part of listening. The interpretation through the "ear" in this regard is similar to that of the "eye." Silence, even now, continues to be an important tool in my teaching, particularly when I find myself offering prompts on autopilot, or saying something just to say it—when I realize that I haven't really been listening at all.

Tangentially, I have a fascination with the "mute" function in digital discussion platforms that I have tried to bring to my teaching in the studio. That familiar series of moments when someone is muted but begins to speak, is then alerted to that fact ("you're muted"), unmutes, apologizes, and begins again, is particularly instructive. Once I can hear the contributor or see their captions appear, I find myself actively listening. I often wonder if I would listen more closely if everyone had a mute button in real-time, person-to-person experiences. Taking a moment to unmute would make time and prevent me from responding too quickly or without forethought; just as waiting for others to unmute asks me to be patient in the moment of anticipation. It lessens the potential for an exchange that isn't deliberate, as the act of unmuting is intentional—it tells me if I've been listening.

Embodying

The act of physically engaging, as a teacher, is fraught with questions about bodies—about aging, abilities, self-perceptions, and how teachers' bodies affect students' understanding of ballet. I remember teachers who stared lovingly at themselves in the mirror as they demonstrated so fully they broke a sweat, and I remember those who showed movements with their hands while speaking the steps quietly from a chair. They were all effective at communicating the material and movement qualities they sought, despite the various ways they chose to show them.

The teachers I've watched or worked with over time have used multiple approaches to demonstration based on their evolving bodily situations, and I've experienced the same phenomenon. Regularly using my favorite gesture leg to demonstrate, for example, placated my ego until one persistently aggravated hip flexor convinced me to alternate legs. Now, as I age and experience varying degrees of restriction and personal fitness, I show the material fully only if I'm sufficiently warmed up to avoid injuring myself and to ensure I'm communicating with clarity. Such lessons in humility always prompt me to consider who demonstration is for: myself or the students.

Demonstrations can also raise questions of consistency, as there is philosophical and physical consistency in how teachers embody, model, or somehow physically represent the ideas they emphasize. I've been puzzled to occasionally observe teachers who profess one idea but show something else in their demonstration. In these instances, expectations become unclear and philosophies become suspect; in contrast to those glorious moments when a teacher's ideas become visible in and further illuminated through their body. Practical consistency is likewise important, as teachers might unintentionally demonstrate the same exercise in different ways. As a student in this latter scenario, I recall being chastised for doing the wrong step after guessing incorrectly at which version the teacher wanted. Seeking alignment between what my body communicates and what I aim to emphasize, then, is an ongoing project regardless of whether I'm offering a verbal description or a physical demonstration.

Where teachers situate themselves around the studio establishes an embodied relationship to the students that communicates values and intentions. It is common practice to vary between standing, sitting, pacing, or meandering around the space; to situate oneself front and center, in the downstage corners, on the sides, or upstage behind the dancing. Sometimes I sit in windowsills or stand behind wall-mounted barres, and sometimes I crouch down in the corner or up against the mirror. These places tend to make my presence less central while allowing me to see students' dancing from different vantage points. Watching petit allegro from the side of the studio, I find, can be more instructive than from the front; while standing in upstage corners to watch enchaînements along the diagonal gives me space to talk with individual students as they step off the floor. Both of these configurations take me out of students' direct line of sight while they're dancing, which I like to think allows them some spatial and psychic autonomy, although for some students used to tyrannical authority figures in ballet classes, not being able to see me while they're dancing might be unsettling.

How teachers establish physical proximity to individual students varies widely. I remember having a teacher who paced constantly. I'd watch her walk toward me, stop mere inches away from me at the barre and just hover there for a few moments before adjusting my finger, looking exasperated, expressing mild approval, and moving on. I'd hold my breath through the whole ordeal—my eyebrows rising toward my hairline. In an effort not to repeat what I perceived as a spatial imposition in my own teaching, I used to approach students at the barre from what I thought was a less-terrifying angle—from the side and slightly behind them. The result, however, was startled students and an odd apology as I tried to offer a note on their dancing which then became secondary to them recovering their composure. Less terrifying in some regard, maybe, but more in others. Now I make sure to address students verbally as I approach if I'm not already in their line of sight. Physically situating myself has a twofold purpose: I try to vary the proximity between my body and the students' bodies so they have space to work independently but also know I'm present with them; and I try to ensure at a basic level that I can quite literally see and engage with everyone in consistent and useful ways.

Once teachers have received students' enthusiastic consent to touch and know how to offer tactile feedback safely, how teachers use their own bodies in this process is another consideration.[8] I've observed and experienced taller teachers taking control of a student's body from above, perhaps holding wrists or ankles up in extended positions, while others work from the side or underneath to cue specific muscles or support realignment. Teachers share different kinds of physical information with students depending on what is available to them in terms of height, proportion, and strength. If leverage becomes part of physically supportive feedback—the support of an extended leg, for example—negotiating one's own physical safety while being in constant communication with the student about how they feel that leverage is necessary: the feedback becomes partnering and the student's development of embodied knowledge in those moments can be profound. Generally, however, if I don't have a purpose for being physically in the students' space—for tactile or verbal feedback—I'll get out of their way.

Issues of proximity and distance came into full relief during the early stages of the pandemic. The taped-off boxes on the studio floor meant that I had to remain in the "instructional zone" at the front—a narrow swath that ran along the mirror. From there, I often used my own body to illustrate what I was seeing and how they might adjust. This process put my body in dialogue with students' bodies based on mirroring and modeling, and it reminded me that my body isn't always needed in the space. When the taped boundaries were removed, I resisted offering tactile feedback or walking through the center of the studio for some time, preferring instead to float around the edges and continue communicating from afar. A few students noted their appreciation for the unencumbered space, the fact that I didn't hover around them, and the reduced psychological pressure that can manifest when the teacher is just a few feet away. I reference pandemic-era teaching here again because the experience illuminated my tendencies in seeing, listening, and physically orienting myself. It showed me how I could adjust these actions in new ways—some far more effective than my previous efforts. Physical distancing felt existential at the time, but it has since allowed me to understand how these foundational aspects of teaching can be shaped and reshaped deliberately, in any context, to any end.

Beneath Presence and Behavior

Power and Bias

Elements of a teacher's presence include posture, physical energy and ability, language usage and speech, vocal tone, skin tone, hair style and texture, choice of dress, facial features and expressions, and bodily characteristics. These physical qualities serve as conduits for teachers' behaviors and actions that each student interprets through their own lens. While traditionally top-down power dynamics in ballet classes offer students little authority, recent developments in schools and institutions in the United States—many of which operate as corporations or businesses with a customer-first ethos—allow students to exercise a modicum of power from their otherwise low rung on the systemic hierarchy. Their influence is enabled through student evaluations of teaching, home adults who report student experiences in ballet classes to school authorities, cameras mounted in studios that allow classes to be visible from lobby waiting areas, and video platforms like Zoom that enable class observations by anyone in the room with the student. Most of these structures could be used generatively if they were developed as feedback mechanisms in support of pedagogical dialogues with teachers. Yet, if students or families hold implicit or explicit biases—racism, sexism, gender bias, ageism, ableism, and so on—these mechanisms can instead facilitate the leveraging of these biases over teachers, and particularly teachers in marginalized groups. Such threats to teachers' humanity could understandably shape their presence and behavior in ballet classes, as they attempt to protect themselves from harm.

In higher education, for example, the prejudices encoded in anonymous student evaluations of teaching are remarkable. Researcher

Troy Heffernan suggests these evaluations are "strongly influenced by external factors unrelated to course content or teacher performance" and are "frequently based on student demographics, and students' biases and prejudices based on the teaching academic's gender, sexuality, ethnicity, age or disability as well as other marginalising factors."[9] While student evaluations can allow students to formally register their experiences for the purpose of pedagogical support, if those evaluations hold weight as part of an institution's employment processes, any student biases embedded therein can become powerful enough to influence teachers' livelihoods and concomitant feelings of safety. It follows, then, that teachers who feel they could be endangered by student biases might be less inclined to develop pedagogies that put student humanity first—pedagogies that also ask for some vulnerability from the teacher.

There is substantial complexity here. It is true that students with implicit and explicit biases might hold and exercise power over their teachers, even from the low levels of institutional hierarchies. Yet, I am keen to avoid "both-sides"-ing the issue, as it is wholly inaccurate to suggest that student bias has nearly as much capacity to do large-scale human harm as the biases that originate at the top. When empowered teachers and authority figures enact their prejudices, intentionally or not, they threaten the safety and welfare of multitudes of individuals and their ability to participate in the study of ballet. The influence of their biases on institutional cultures stifles the possibilities for pedagogies, as these skewed perspectives are fundamentally dehumanizing.

As prejudice slung from any direction can cause human damage and lead to inhospitable environments for teaching and learning, institutional accountability is critical. While individual teachers in their positions of power are responsible for interrupting their own biases, ballet's schools and those in leadership positions must also commit to rooting out bias at the systemic level. Currently, significant efforts are underway across the field to support teachers and administrators in identifying and disrupting bias, as those in ballet have begun to acknowledge that authorities with unchecked prejudices continue to inflict direct harm and tarnish opportunities for learning and engagement. Organizations, such as Memoirs of Blacks in Ballet, The Equity Project, Dance Data Project, Final Bow for Yellowface, the Gold Standard Arts Foundation, and others, have been facilitating anti-bias work inside ballet's institutions—making humanizing pedagogies and equitable futures for ballet more possible. Whether in partnership with such organizations or independently, ballet's institutions are responsible for developing cultures and expectations in which antiracist work and practices that disrupt prejudice are implemented in collaborative, meaningful, ongoing, and financially backed ways.[10]

Problematic Assumptions about Students

Even the most well-intentioned pedagogies contain implicit perspectives that can be damaging if they are not critically examined. Teachers' underlying beliefs—including but not limited to identity-related biases—shape every aspect of their presence and behaviors. I've encountered these perspectives most often outside the studio: formally in meetings or conferences; or casually in lounges or the online spaces where teachers gather—around the actual or proverbial water cooler. I've learned to be discerning about these spaces, as they often host a range of viewpoints from the productive and inspiring to the toxic and disturbing.

Some assumptions target students personally and seem to emerge from a general lack of compassion. One teacher I knew accused a student who attended class daily with red eyes and fatigue of being a "party girl" when she was actually plagued with allergies. Another suggested behind closed doors that a student needed "to go lose her virginity" because she struggled to differentiate her legs from her pelvis. More generally, according to a third, "they always try to get away with doing as little as possible." Sweeping assumptions about student intention are also littered throughout ballet pedagogy's extant literature, as teacher-authors who have built approaches around such ungenerous ideas articulate them proudly and with great authority. John White, for example, describes how to teach using what he calls "premeditated pedagogic outbursts":

> If students are bobbling a balance on demi-pointe after a pirouette while holding the barre, ask them why they are hopping or why they are lowering their supporting heel or their working foot to the floor. Then wait for an answer. Of course, there will be none. Then tell them emphatically, 'Do not hop!' And have the students try it again. When they hop again (as they more than likely will), ask once again, even more emphatically, 'Did you understand what I said before? (pause) Do not hop!' When the movement is at last done correctly, remind everyone that overcoming such difficulties often is just a matter of deciding not to commit the error.[11]

I include this here not for those teachers who will push back against such destructive depictions of students—those more concerned with how to help students find stability en relevé, in this example, than playing disparaging mental games. My concern, rather, is for those who seek pedagogic support in earnest from these conversations or texts. Without a critical lens, some may be led to believe that assuming the worst of students is a requirement for legitimate teaching in ballet.

For centuries, ballet pedagogues have upheld notions of ballet's lofty and elusive perfection while assuming human deficit. The out-of-reach physical goal, from this vantage point, should be motivation enough to work to achieve it. In graded or exam-driven ballet environments, this philosophy becomes reality in teachers who are reluctant to give top marks, since there's always more work to do—faster, clearer, higher, stronger. The assumption here is that students can never be enough when compared to the theoretical perfection of ballet. While it is true that ballet offers continuous opportunities for growth even at its most elite levels, expecting students to work and self-motivate in the face of their presumed and persistent deficiency is a damaging pedagogical choice.[12] This perspective can encourage students' perfectionistic tendencies and reward chronic self-flagellation; it can lead to defeatism and burnout.[13] In rethinking this concept in my own teaching, I have adopted an alternative view of the ballet class as a research space, where each student's whole person is their fully stocked laboratory.[14] This has enabled possibilities for students' agentic experimentation and autonomous redirection in ways that subvert traditionally harmful notions of perfection. It welcomes failure as part of the process—as a means for deeper understanding and informed revision.

Another common pedagogical assumption is that teachers can spot a student's "potential." It seems reasonable to suggest that teachers can sometimes see what is physically possible for a student, in that their dancing sometimes reveals glimmers of what their bodies are capable of. What a whole student can do, however, is dependent on multiple and varied factors beyond that student's visible physicality. Their potential includes their goals, mental and emotional states, mind-body connection, economic privilege and access, and personal support system—less visible factors that students might or might not choose to share with teachers. Without taking the student's whole human situation into account, a teacher might further try to leverage the idea of "potential" as motivation. In a 2018 *Dance Teacher* magazine article called "11 Things Every Dance Teacher Wishes Their Students Knew," for example, the first item on the list is: "When I'm hard on you, it's only because I want you to reach your potential."[15] This statement is perilously close to: "I only hurt you because I love you," a phrase and concept associated with domestic abuse. Even if a teacher is well-meaning, telling a student they're not working up to their potential is fundamentally a shaming tactic—different, for example, than a teacher effectively communicating to a student that they believe in them from the outset. The assumptive teacher's inclination to see the student as deficient, or doing less than what the teacher perceives as possible, discounts the student's circumstances and context for studying ballet. It centers the teacher's assumptions rather that supporting the student's realities and wholeness.

As I work to overturn my own assumptions about students' "potential," I have begun sharing with them immediately any glimmers of possibility I see in their dancing, rather than keeping them to myself. If a student shows forward momentum or does something remarkable in a step or exercise, I tell them right away what I saw and ask if they know how they did it. I then suggest they repeat it almost immediately to capture and bolster their actual—no longer "potential"—growth. Whether or not they're able to reproduce that exciting moment, they become more aware of a possible future direction for their work and can develop their own momentum and strategies for how to approach it in later iterations. Acknowledging their competence, rather than pointing out their deficiency, typically results in increased intrinsic motivation to continue the work.

When a student is assumed to not be working up to their potential, a further causal assumption might be that the student is "lazy." Dance teachers and teaching "consultants" across social media platforms complain openly and at length about "lazy dancers," and laziness is cited in ballet pedagogy books as a scourge to be eradicated through authoritarian pedagogical means. To counter such perspectives, Devon Price describes the "Laziness Lie": "a belief system that says hard work is morally superior to relaxation, that people who aren't productive have less innate value than productive people." This construct teaches students that their "worth is [their] productivity," they "cannot trust [their] own feelings and limits," and "there is always more [they] could be doing." Such dangerous moralizing leads students to associate their value with their performance in ballet, and it can lead to injury or worse, as students ignore their own internal bodily signals that they need to rest.[16]

Davis describes how the notion of "laziness" has been attributed specifically to Black students, thereby identifying it as a racist euphemism. She says,

> Another example of implicit biases manifesting in dance classes based on dominant group norms and assumptions occurs when teachers interpret a Black student's body language in between the performance of movement phrases as lazy or immature, even though it may, for some who observe the class, reflect similar the language of White students....[17]

While freely and subjectively interpreting student body language has long been the ballet teacher's purview, a teacher's failure to interrogate their biases while in a position of power may lead to racialized accusations of "laziness." Before acting on such an interpretation, teachers in dominant identity groups especially are responsible for identifying these inclinations and examining—as Davis suggests—how historical perspectives may be affecting their current observations: "In the case of the observation of Black student behavior, the history of minstrel performances and their concomitant interpretations of Black bodies may still influence the unconscious memories of the observer."[18] Bias, in this sense, is intergenerational and can be passed down; it must be interrupted to overturn these deeply embedded assumptions.

Not all assumptions threaten students to the same extent. One of the first assumptions I reconciled in my teaching involved students' facial expressions and dispositions. A young white woman with Balanchine-esque mannerisms arrived in my class and appeared so standoffish—even disdainful in her face during class that I was hesitant to even approach her. When I finally offered her a suggestion at the barre, weeks into the course I'm ashamed to say, she lit up—delighted to be in conversation and curious about what I was asking of her. As I learned more about her, I came to understand that her previous experience had been so harmful that she'd learned to work with a constant inner monologue of self-criticism, which was reflected in how her facial muscles had learned to function during class. Rather than assuming I knew her emotional state and leaving her alone, I could have asked her about herself and taken an interest in her work. While the exterior that students make visible is important to the study of ballet as a visually consumed art form, I learned that instead of foreclosing on a student based on surface-level attributes—unhelpful at best and biased gatekeeping at worst—I could take a curious approach. I now treat facial muscles like any other muscle, capable of taking on excessive tension in a way that skews their desired outcome. Reworking this assumption has resulted in a more fruitful way of negotiating the balance between tension and ease in the body. It has allowed me to enable student agency by supporting their deliberate choice-making about what they wish to portray while they're dancing.

Beyond their effects on a teacher's presence and behavior, assumptions have consequences. They may inversely lead to a lack of support for students who need it: those who display perfectionistic tendencies as they try to reach what their teachers tell them is their "potential;" those who push through injury to demonstrate their dedication to a teacher's unachievable goals for them; or those who engage in overwork to avoid appearing "lazy." Most often, in my experience, it is these students who on the surface seem to be managing well on their own. They may try to avoid appearing to need rest or support, which—particularly in the culture of ballet—tend to carry an unfortunate negative moral connotation. While it is not the teacher's responsibility to diagnose a student's condition, teachers who actively challenge their own internalized assumptions are more inclined to be aware of each student as an individual, to know their baseline attributes, and to perhaps notice when they begin behaving in a way that signals a need for support. They are better equipped to know when and how to intervene, and to be able to work with the student—and perhaps a student's family—to get them the resources and care they need.

In her book, *Equity-Centered Trauma-Informed Education*, Alex Shevrin Venet describes the importance of extending "unconditional positive regard." "The message," Venet says, is "I care about you. You have value. You don't have to do anything to prove it to me, and nothing's going to change my mind."[19] If a student plateaus, then, or if I perceive that a student's effort seems low, or if I read a student's face or body language as disinterested or distracted, "unconditional positive regard" can serve as a generative point of initiation when approaching that student—one which prioritizes care for them as a person over any dance-related concern. More broadly, I prefer to believe that there are reasons students work the way they do, many which will remain unknown to me. I have learned to ask before I assume, which, if a student chooses to share, might help me better understand the student's circumstances so I can tailor my support to the areas in which they express or demonstrate need. Maybe their goals have shifted, or they're working with an injury, or they're frustrated by that pesky triple pirouette on the left. Asking for context first out of an abundance of care supersedes any inclination to find fault. My acknowledgment, in this way, that there is much I don't know about the student's choices and rationales, sets up the possibility for a dialogue around our work and process.

Institutional Contexts

Teachers who try to establish safe and productive learning environments inside systems whose values are fundamentally authoritarian are faced with a paradox. As they consider how their very human presence might affect a group of often younger and less experienced individuals, often inside of institutions whose hierarchies are entrenched and whose inequities run deep, they enact an approach that reconciles their individual pedagogical values with the policies and expectations of their employer. Some may adhere to employer expectations despite disagreeing with them to protect their positions, while others may decide to subvert inequitable school cultures through radical pedagogies despite the possibility that it may endanger their employment. Ultimately, individual teachers are the only ones who can gauge their tolerance for these risks, as each teacher alone can navigate the alignments and tensions between their individual values and the systems in which they labor. While biased or unjust institutional policies are never an excuse for harmful pedagogical practices, they can affect how far teachers are willing to shift toward radical, humanizing, equitable pedagogies.

In my experience in private studios, professional academies, and higher education, the variety of contextual pressures—what I understood to be the expectations and norms in these environments—have affected my presence and work with students. I caved, initially, to the idea that I would be pedagogically illegitimate if I didn't uphold at least some of ballet's notoriously authoritarian perspectives; too often authoritarian pedagogies are considered the only approaches that will elicit a legitimate brand of ballet. How else, the argument goes, will students be prepared to be sufficiently thick-skinned in such a challenging field? The suggestion that teachers who resist authoritarian pedagogies fail to prepare students for the profession or to "produce" dancers—as though they were objects for sale—is the platform upon which ballet's gatekeepers have perpetuated some of the profession's most virulent practices. I feared, for example, that I would not be perceived by colleagues and superiors as "rigorous" enough if I erred on the side of compassion with students, so I made ungenerous assumptions about them instead as I tried to figure out where I fit in those cultures.[20] I didn't offer "unconditional positive regard" out of concern that I would be perceived as too soft. I made snarky comments, and I yelled throughout class to maintain control—getting louder and shooting glances, passive aggressively, if I heard students chatting or saw them unfocused. I became patently unkind to students who did not immediately accept my perspective; I questioned their intentions and made my distrust in them apparent. Authoritarian pedagogies tend to assume that students will try to take advantage of teachers who don't actively demonstrate their power, and I didn't want to be perceived by superiors or colleagues as not savvy enough to notice, even though I didn't hold this assumption myself.

In addition to the implicit expectations in ballet institutions are those woven into school policies and discussed explicitly as part of school culture. I've been horrified, for example, to hear the stated expectation that I would support a school's goals by implementing carceral pedagogic practices: that I would discipline students who didn't adhere to dress codes, who appeared in class late despite perhaps having to rely on others for transportation, who spoke up in class without being invited, and who didn't immediately excel in their work. School authorities thought such approaches were necessary to maintain power and showcase their worth as a school, and they expected teachers to comply. Despite the obvious inequities in these policies given the range of student access and abilities, the school's leadership believed equal treatment for such transgressions was more important than acknowledging or supporting individual student circumstances.

The choices I made as I was negotiating these pressures led to a number of specific events and moments of tension with students that I now deeply regret. I ejected a student from a rehearsal when she became frustrated, I expressed disappointment in a few students after falsely assuming they had lied to me, I ignored students who did not appear to be responsive to my teaching, I regularly received student evaluations that cited favoritism, I dismissed valid student concerns, and I maintained some generally antagonistic relationships with students. I've had the fortunate opportunity to apologize, years later, for some of these behaviors.

On a larger scale, two specific events caused me to understand how far away from my own value system, ethos, and integrity I had wandered while trying to meet institutional expectations. First, I was granted tenure. While the protections of tenure are gradually being eroded by bad faith actors across the landscape of neoliberal academia, there is privilege in having the resources and support, both personally and professionally, to reach such a milestone. It allowed me to reflect on my own philosophy outside of the varied pressures I'd experienced throughout my career to that point—to develop a clear ethical imperative, and to resist systemic pressures or those at the water cooler that seemed regressive in nature. While I'd managed to reject some of the more severe external expectations for nearly two decades before reaching tenured status, I'm distressed, on reflection, that I didn't act on my convictions with more determination before acquiring institutional safety. My individual threshold for risk was lower than I'd have liked; lower than some friends and colleagues who've stood by their pedagogical convictions in the face of institutional demands despite the risk, and sometimes the reality, of dismissal from their positions.

The second event that illuminated numerous systemic inequities and the need for humanizing approaches was the pandemic. Like so many teachers, I began to allow students' health and wellbeing to drive my decision-making, while so many institutions doubled down on surveillance technologies and punitive policies for distance work. Finding my pedagogical values in conflict with the ethos of my institution encouraged my commitment to a more overtly equitable, humanizing approach. At the same time, my way of engaging with people, generally, was changing. I softened and took more time to show care, even with friends and family, and my pedagogy became more clearly aligned with who I was becoming. My course designs, my policies, my methodologies, and my manner of engaging with students all changed in just a few months. My priorities, which I communicate to students every semester, have continued to be their health and safety, and that they have what they need to find meaning and relevance in our work together.

No pedagogy exists in a vacuum. Institutional power dynamics and requirements shape how teachers choose to enact their presence and behavior in ballet classes—a reality that introduces complexity to any discussion of pedagogies. The most privileged, empowered, and secure teachers who fail to resolve any malignant effects of their pedagogies on students are too often protected by the system despite a dire need for accountability. The gray area, however, arises when teachers whose identities or employment status situates them as marginalized or vulnerable in these systems also use damaging pedagogic practices.[21] To be clear, maltreatment of students is never excusable. When it's perpetuated by a teacher without protections in the system, however, any proposed remedy must take the system into account as well as the individual.

Institutional equity, and the creation of institutional cultures that prioritize dignity and humanity, are necessary to enable humanizing pedagogical work. This includes equitable labor practices and security for teachers, to which contract faculty in higher education do not have access. Teachers, as bell hooks suggests, are expected to "provide the necessary conditions where learning can most deeply and intimately begin."[22] Such conditions, however, must be provided for teachers and students, both, and the responsibility for providing and supporting humanizing conditions for labor and learning in ballet environments is shared among the system's constituents: school owners, administrators, faculty, staff, students, families, and—in public education settings for ballet—lawmakers at the local, regional, and national levels. Ballet pedagogies, in this light, are social, cultural, political, and economic issues. They affect everyone who participates in ballet, who are all needed to advocate for and model equity and humanity wherever ballet is taught and danced.

Relishing Complexity

Claire Wootten describes liminality in her feminist ballet class as "chang[ing] *what is expected* and *what is expected of whom*." She defines the liminal space as "a place of 'anti-structure,' where rules, status, and ways of being are shifted from what was previously understood."[23] It is through my ways of being and doing in ballet classes that I attempt to co-create such spaces with students. At their most effective, my presence and behaviors contribute to a fluid, responsive pedagogy, rooted in my whole person's relationship with students as whole people. Growth as a ballet teacher for me, in this light, has happened more in the realm of presence and behavior than in terms of class material. I am consistently aware of how meaningful it is to be in a position—to have the extraordinary privilege—to support student learning and goals through my work with them as dance artists, students, and people in the world. It stands to reason that the more experience I have in teaching, the more predictable my approach becomes; yet I know the opposite to be true. The complexity of navigating my own learning curve while supporting student learning has resulted in behaviors and presence that change as I change and can simultaneously adapt to the students I work with where they are.

This subjective and layered consideration of the human workings of ballet pedagogies is the part of pedagogical development that I relish most. It relates to Parker Palmer's "Subject-Centered Pedagogy," as teachers and students gather around the wisdom of ballet to determine how to approach it together. The shared moments of inquiry and exploration in these experiences make ballet pedagogies necessarily messy and human. I find immense joy in learning about individual students on their own terms and allowing their unique perspectives and contexts to shape and inform my broad knowledge of ballet. It keeps me coming back to class, day after day, as if for the first time—with curiosity about and delight in those I'm working with, and with an ever-deepening love and reverence for ballet.

Notes

1 Crystal U. Davis, *Dance and Belonging: Implicit Bias and Inclusion in Dance Education* (Jefferson, NC: McFarland, 2022), 98.
2 bell hooks, "To Love Again," in *Teaching Critical Thinking: Practical Wisdom* (New York: Routledge, 2010), 159–163; bell hooks, *All About Love: New Visions* (New York: Harper, 2000).
3 Crystal U. Davis, *Dance and Belonging: Implicit Bias and Inclusion in Dance Education* (Jefferson, NC: McFarland, 2022), 83.
4 Nyama McCarthy Brown, "Navigating Anti-racism in an Anti-black Landscape: A Dance Educator's Reflection," *International Journal of Education & the Arts*, 23, no.1 (2022). https://doi.org/10.26209/ijea23n1.
5 Maggie Black, in conversation with the author, December 29, 2006.
6 bell hooks, "To Love Again," in *Teaching Critical Thinking: Practical Wisdom* (New York: Routledge, 2010), 159–163.
7 See Gretchen Alterowitz, "Toward a Feminist Ballet Pedagogy: Teaching Strategies for Ballet Technique Classes in the Twenty-first Century," *Journal of Dance Education* 14, no.1 (2014): 8–17; Susan W. Stinson, Donald Blumenfield-Jones, and Jan van Dyke, "Voices of Young Women Dance Students: An Interpretive Study of Meaning in Dance," *Dance Research Journal* 22, no.2 (Autumn 1990): 13–22; Claire Wootten, "Navigating Liminal Space in the Feminist Ballet Class," *Congress on Research in Dance Proceedings* 41 (Leicester, UK: 2009): 122–129.
8 See Chapters 4 and 5 for discussions of bodily autonomy, tactile feedback, and consent.
9 Troy Heffernan, "Sexism, Racism, Prejudice, and Bias: A Literature Review and Synthesis of Research Surrounding Student Evaluations of Courses and Teaching," *Assessment & Evaluation in Higher Education* 47, no.1 (2022): 150.
10 For more on anti-bias work in pedagogies, see Kate Mattingly and Iyun Ashani Harrison, eds., *Antiracism in Ballet Teaching* (Abingdon: Routledge, 2024); Nyama McCarthy Brown, *Dance Pedagogy for a Diverse World: Culturally Relevant Teaching in Theory, Research and Practice* (Jefferson, NC: McFarland, 2022); Crystal U. Davis, *Dance and Belonging: Implicit Bias and Inclusion in Dance Education* (Jefferson, NC: McFarland, 2022); and Soraya Chemaly, "All Teachers Should Be Trained To Overcome Their Hidden Biases," *Time*, February 12, 2015, https://time.com/3705454/teachers-biases-girls-education/.
11 John White, *Advanced Principles in Teaching Classical Ballet* (Gainesville: University Press of Florida, 2009), 15.
12 See Chapter 2 for a discussion of deficit thinking.
13 See Sanna M. Nordin Bates and Gareth Jowett, "Relationships between Perfectionism, Stress, and Basic Need Support Provision in Dance Teachers and

Aesthetic Sport Coaches," *Journal of Dance Medicine and Science* 26, no.1 (2001): 26–34.
14 I am inspired in this approach by Jennifer Jackson, "My Dance and the Ideal Body: Looking at Ballet Practice from the Inside Out," *Research in Dance Education* 6, no.1/2 (April/December 2005): 34.
15 Haley Hilton, "11 Things Every Dance Teacher Wishes Their Students Knew," *Dance Teacher*, August 13, 2018, https://www.dance-teacher.com/tk-things-every-dance-teacher-wishes-their-students-knew-2593970117.html.
16 Devon Price, *Laziness Does Not Exist* (New York: Atria, 2021), 15.
17 Crystal U. Davis, *Dance and Belonging: Implicit Bias and Inclusion in Dance Education* (Jefferson, NC: McFarland, 2022), 99.
18 Crystal U. Davis, *Dance and Belonging: Implicit Bias and Inclusion in Dance Education* (Jefferson, NC: McFarland, 2022), 99.
19 Alex Shevrin Venet, *Equity-Centered Trauma-Informed Education* (New York: Norton, 2021), 98.
20 See Chapter 5 for a discussion of "rigor."
21 See Chapter 1 for a discussion of accountability.
22 bell hooks, *Teaching to Transgress: Education as the Practice of Freedom* (New York: Routledge, 1994), 13.
23 Claire Wootten, "Navigating Liminal Space in the Feminist Ballet Class," *Congress on Research in Dance Proceedings* 41 (Leicester, UK: 2009): 124.

4 Student Voices

Students' experiences in the ballet class illuminate how pedagogical approaches land: whether they accurately communicate the teacher's philosophy and values; or whether they're effective in supporting students' artistic and technical development. Taking the position that ballet pedagogy as a field is incomplete without student perspectives, I seek out their insights and foreground their voices in this chapter. As authorities on teaching through the lens of their own experiences, students may not be experts on ballet pedagogy on a grand scale, but as the executants and intended beneficiaries of pedagogies, they are not *not* experts in it either. While there are notable distinctions between a student's favorite approach or personal preference and a deliberately designed and effective pedagogical strategy, what a student wishes to share about their experience has great value for teachers. Particularly in a field where the state of studenthood extends through one's professional career, giving time and consideration to how students perceive pedagogies is both warranted and generative.

In early 2023, I conducted 2 anonymous public surveys, to which 54 self-identified ballet students or dancers and 66 self-identified ballet teachers responded. All respondents were over 18 years of age, and they represent a range of demographics with regard to age, gender, race, and sexuality. Participants studied or taught ballet across the United States, some in Europe (mostly the United Kingdom), and a few in Mexico, Cuba, and the Middle East. Nearly 90 percent studied and/or taught ballet for more than ten years. Students described experiences in a variety of contexts for ballet: some studied or are studying ballet in higher education or for enjoyment, and some are dancing professionally or have retired. Teachers, likewise, span the gamut of locales in which one might teach: at colleges and universities, private studios, academies connected to ballet companies, and in ballet companies.

I prioritize the students' and dancers' perspectives throughout this chapter, as they have been historically silenced in ballet spaces and deserve to be heard; and as most ballet pedagogy research centers the

DOI: 10.4324/9781003332718-7

voices of teacher-researchers. I reference the teachers' survey responses on occasion to offer a sense for where teachers and students align or diverge in their thinking. The student survey respondents in this chapter are astute, direct, and present a tall order for teachers to consider, so I try to limit my filtering or paraphrasing of students' precise words through my teacherly lens. Instead, I highlight hundreds of direct quotations from the responses that I've organized thematically and contextualized as they relate to humanizing pedagogies. I also allow the raw survey data to stand on its own at times. As I explicitly intend to emphasize student perspectives, I sometimes use student commentary to conclude a paragraph or section without follow-up. While dangling quotations are unusual in a work of scholarship, making space for students to have the last word on an issue is a pedagogical practice I use in my classes that is applicable here as well.*

These survey responses, generated with Institutional Review Board approval and outside of any specific ballet course or program, offer teachers an opportunity to listen to students without having a personal stake in their perspectives as one might when reading a student evaluation of teaching, for example. Perhaps more so, the density of these perspectives can offer teachers the opportunity to practice believing students—their experiences, intentions, and wishes—as learning to listen and trust in earnest are foundational practices in humanizing pedagogies. If reading this chapter seems like a deluge, which these surveys did to me when I first read the data, I advise readers to prioritize for their own pedagogies those items that are most ethically urgent, relevant to the particular students they work with, and possible inside the parameters of their unique contexts for teaching ballet.

Elizabeth Ellsworth offers a word of caution about listening to students that is important to consider here:

> Although the literature recognizes that teachers have much to learn from their students' experiences, it does not address the ways in which there are things that I as professor could *never know* about the experiences, oppressions, and understandings of other participants in the class.[1]

By recognizing student voices, in this light, it is necessary to avoid any assumption that teachers could understand the full breadth and depth of student experience, or further, that they have a right to know it. Any

---

* I have lightly edited some of the punctuation in these responses for clarity. This research protocol #2022-323 was approved in September 2022 by the Institutional Review Board (IRB) at Texas Christian University.

claim to understand student perspectives, then, must account for student autonomy and respect that which students choose *not* to share. I expect that there is much left unsaid in these pages.

I believe students when they describe their experiences; I trust their intentions in their study and learning of ballet; and I support their individual reasons for participating—their "whys." This perspective is foundational to my pedagogical work and why I chose to seek out student contributions as part of this book. It is also the lens through which I listen, try to understand, and ultimately share the words of these survey respondents who have generously contributed their experiences and perspectives. To this end, this chapter is an invitation to the reader to recognize students as collaborators whose perspectives are essential to equitable futures for ballet pedagogies.

Interpreting Ballet Pedagogies

The first part of this chapter is concerned with experience and interpretation: what students encounter, how certain approaches make them feel, and how they derive meaning from their experiences in ballet classes. Based on the premise I describe in Chapter 2, that practical teaching methods and methodologies communicate both explicit and implicit pedagogical philosophies, I asked students how they might know, from a ballet class, what a teacher believes about technique, bodies, and ballet broadly. I also asked how they might know whether and to what extent a teacher is committed to equity and justice through their teaching.

Respondents interpreted the teacher's values based in part on who they prioritize with their time, attention, and comments during class. "Do they have favorites?" one respondent asked, while another pointed to "who they give the most attention (positive or critical) to in class." Some were likewise concerned with whether "they make a point of talking to everyone" or "give every dancer the same opportunity to get corrections, work in the studio, and be seen and heard." Several participants pointed toward evidence of bodily ideals in value systems, "if only certain body types are given corrections or asked to demonstrate," or as one stated more directly, "always giving feedback to the skinny people." The question one respondent asked: "Do they work with the bodies in front of them?" prompted me to consider that how teachers relate to students' bodies can supersede, from a student's perspective, how or whether they value the whole people in the room—that this respondent referred to "bodies" instead of students, dancers, or people is an indication of such a value system.

Students also understand teachers' beliefs about ballet's ideals by interpreting the subtext of the language teachers use. What teachers say and what they withhold become students' keys to unlocking their pedagogies and ways of thinking. One participant noted, "if teachers correct things you can't change like turnout amount or knees that don't hyperextend, I can tell they have unhealthy expectations for dancers' bodies." An example of such expectations is when teachers say, according to another participant: "'ideally, in the fifth position, both of your feet should be turned out 180°.'" Relatedly, a teacher's commentary indicates to students how they prioritize their concern for ballet's ideals and their concern for student wellbeing. Two respondents noted: "how much they talk about what muscles to use in different combinations shows me how much they care about aesthetics vs. health and safety;" and "I feel supported when offered feedback using anatomical language, not being criticized about my turnout or other limitations I can't control, but being guided on how I can support growth with turnout organization from the pelvis, for example." One respondent reminded me that some disparaging and dangerous age-old adages are still in use: "Telling students that they can 'see their lunch'" is one such platitude, which detracts from the opportunity to teach anatomical realities of abdominal usage, instills unsafe ideas about the ideal body, and implies patently erroneous information about how dancers should—or shouldn't—fuel and maintain their bodies.

Students noted the importance of words, broadly. One made a distinction between "language that explains and guides vs. language that prescribes." Another described that they interpret a teacher's thinking based on "what they say… and don't say." "How they state images (body positive versus not)" and "using descriptive and sophisticated language to critique" were considered evidence of a teacher's beliefs about students and bodies. Students' responses alerted me to just how perceptive they are when it comes to interpreting pedagogical beliefs; they pick them up through "side comments" and "little comments" as much as the more explicit ways these values are expressed—even more, perhaps.

Aside from using contextual clues to decode pedagogies, students describe knowing their teachers' philosophies because "we've had conversations about it" or "my professors have typically been very open in communicating their own beliefs." Such open, explicit discussion of pedagogy indicates that some teachers are employing a critical pedagogic lens—one in which those in power seek to expose the very structures that support that power. This was confirmed by many deeply thoughtful, critically informed responses to the teachers' survey. Talking about various aspects of pedagogy with students—from approaches to technique, to ballet's varied histories, to one's understanding of the body, to beliefs about the teacher-student relationship, to ideas about learning and education—according to nearly half of teacher respondents, is central to bringing critical pedagogy to the ballet class.

Several student respondents noted how teachers use—or don't use—language that indicates how much they've considered equity and inclusion. "Do they use inclusive language for all body types, ethnicities, and economic backgrounds?" one participant asked, while others described that inclusive teachers use "metaphors and references to students that are not gendered unless the teacher knows from the students," and "they provide opportunities to everyone, they don't exclude based on race/ethnicity/body type." Body inclusivity came up repeatedly in the responses, with preference given to teachers who "will give corrections based on anatomy and will not reference body size."

The material of the class—its steps, structure, and movement phrases—also indicates to students what teachers value in ballet technique, particularly as it relates to traditionally gendered steps. One participant suggested that gender-inclusive teachers "allow men and women to try beyond their assigned 'roles'"; and that they "either see what I am limited to or what can expand and challenge me." One respondent described how the teacher's relationship to gendered material is indicative of an overarching system of beliefs: "If they specify that certain steps are for women/men only, or they separate combinations for women/men, it feels exclusionary of all genders – I can tell they are more traditional in their teaching style." Another participant appreciated "when the teacher focuses on how the poses feel in your body instead of what they are 'supposed' to look like," a practice that takes into account the student's full embodiment from the inside as opposed to the reflection of an external ideal.

Similarly, students interpreted teachers' belief systems through their stylistic expectations and the systems of port de bras they adhere to. They saw a teacher's association or self-identification with certain Schools of ballet as innate to and indicative of their beliefs about the body. A few respondents noted that teachers associated with the Balanchine School and the Vaganova School, in particular, had strong preferences "towards some body types" because of the ethos and the aesthetic expectations of those Schools:

> Teachers who conceptualize the foundations of ballet as 'positions' that are 'supposed' to look a certain way often follow a more oppressive and exclusive balletic school of thought. They often, whether explicitly or implicitly, believe that there is a ballet body that is slender, long, hypermobile, etc.

Such responses indicate that some students perceive these Schools and the teachers who come from these lineages to value certain bodies and certain kinds of dancers over others, with one participant noting: "Some prefer a student to force things to fit the standard… others wish their students to work with their natural ability."

When I asked teachers about equitable practices they use, many offered detailed responses that indicate an important trend toward equity-forward approaches, but none mentioned School or class material as a facet of this work. Some of ballet's most exclusionary beliefs, however, manifest directly through the stylistic and technical expectations teachers levy through the class content—as student participants described. No matter how kind or generous a teacher is, if the expectations for a dancer are defined through their knowledge of a School or system of movement predicated on certain bodily attributes, then the pedagogy will maintain a degree of exclusivity, and teachers will serve as gatekeepers, despite any work they do to include all students. This is an area for continued reckoning among ballet pedagogues, who may wish to further these traditions while also prioritizing equitable and inclusive approaches.

Beyond their selection of material, how teachers demonstrate that material, as well as how they talk about their own bodies or experiences with ballet, were indications to some student respondents of teachers' value systems. Students identified a range of ways that teachers make these values evident, from "how they demonstrate," to, further, "how they demonstrate taking care of their own bodies," to "how they talk about their own bodies," to "how they talk about themselves" and "how they present themselves and introduce their work." One participant noted, critically, "If they talk negatively about themselves or how they won't ever look good doing X ballet step because they were born with Y, that tells me they think ballet is restricted to a few body types." The relationship teachers have with their own bodies and the lineages they are a part of, then, are central elements of ballet pedagogies and clear communicators of an ethos.

Beyond the language they use or how they demonstrate the material, students suggested that the teacher's physical presence and bodily actions communicate substantive information. Respondents were attuned to non-verbal cues, or what teachers "don't say." A teacher's "mood," "attitude in general," "body language," "facial expressions," and the "details of the intonation in their voice" were elements students found to be indicative of teachers' perspectives, as well as "the way they look at students," which—for anyone who has ever turned to see a look of disdain on a ballet teacher's face while watching someone make an attempt, contains multitudes.

As these interpretations of teaching are based on the physical presence of the teacher, it is important to consider the potential for students' implicit biases to shape their perspectives. There is ample research, for example, that points to the intersectional prejudices that appear in student evaluations of teaching in higher education—in which Women educators of Color, in particular, are subject to a specific blend of racism and misogyny termed "misogynoir."[2] The ableism and fatphobia that pervade ballet spaces are likewise relevant here, as they may affect the way a student views a ballet teacher. While my intention here is to validate and elevate student perceptions of teaching and ballet pedagogies, it is also important to note the persistent presence of unconscious bias in interpretations of teaching and of teachers as individuals with a range of identities and physical attributes.

While several of the responses above could serve as clear indicators of whether a teacher is dedicated to creating equitable spaces, I specifically asked students how they would know if teachers are committed to equitable, just pedagogies through their teaching in ballet classes. Several respondents noted that they "didn't have exposure," "grew up largely unaware," or believe it "does not affect" them. A few remarked that they weren't sure how to discern this commitment through the teaching in a ballet class. One noted, "Since dance is movement, which is universal, their views on equity and social justice are irrelevant to the class." The fact that this was a lone response in the data set might be an indication that perspectives are shifting away from such universality and its concomitant erasure of difference, and toward a more historically detailed acknowledgment of ballet's varied lineages.

Many respondents, however, were closely attuned to how a teacher's commitment to equity and justice becomes evident in the ballet class. While students noted the importance of language above, many described the work of teachers dedicated to fostering equitable, just pedagogies as moving beyond language into action. One respondent considered the demographics of the students in a class as evidence, saying: "I can tell by the class make up, there should be diversity in class. Lack of diversity means minorities are being kept out or are not comfortable being there." Others focused specifically on a teacher's work to learn about and celebrate students as individuals; that they "make an effort to understand a person's pronouns and their cultural background," or "they don't assume gender." Students' uniquenesses, according to one respondent, include their rationales for dancing: "it's important a teacher acknowledges that each student has their own professional goals of why they chose to be there." Another participant extended the need for individual acknowledgment even further, saying

> a good sign of a teacher having a sense of equity and social justice will come with an acknowledgment that all of our bodies and experiences are different and that this isn't just something that is 'ok' or that we 'have to accept.' This is something that makes us beautiful as individuals and as a group. This enhances the classroom and the art form.

Another theme throughout the student survey data was that of "safe spaces." Many student participants perceive the teacher's ability to create safe learning environments as paramount. Students determine whether a space is "safe" based on "how the teacher enters the space," and whether "students are laughing and enjoying or stressed and anxious." Student respondents consider "how the class starts and ends," and whether the teacher "demonstrates sensitivity towards how the students exist in the world day to day," or if they "encourage a competitive environment where, unless you are a star student, you are not succeeding." One offered the rationale that, "establishing comfort and a safe dance space is important for growth. No one wants to feel unsafe in the space that should be the safest to them." One student respondent noted, "If they demonstrate at least some form of awareness or desire to work towards providing equity and social justice, I feel more protected as I associate that with a safe learning environment." In such spaces, another participant suggested, "the teacher wants to see all their students grow and improve. The teacher works with the student as they are and doesn't discount anyone based on factors they can't control (body type, race, background, etc.)." More broadly, "how they treat students" and "visible attitudes toward all members of class" were common themes, with some suggesting that teachers who "make everyone feel included" might be more attuned to issues of equity in the ballet class; and that "there is an air of fairness, kindness, compassion, and support" in those classes. "The way students are asked to interact with one another as well as the teacher" was part of these considerations as well, which suggests a desire for teachers to actively support community-building and to create or co-create studio cultures in which all students can thrive.

It's notable that the teacher survey respondents shared the students' emphasis on acknowledging individuality as central to equity in ballet pedagogies. They did not, however, go so far as to identify their own person or way of being in the class as part of this equation. While the teachers may have been less attuned to or less explicit about how their own physical presence in the room might affect the students in their classes, the fact that most seem to be trying to support whole individual students is an indication that ballet pedagogies are shifting toward equity. If teachers follow the lead of the students on these matters, based on these responses, they can take this work even further.

A handful of student respondents suggested that teachers' actions toward equity and justice would be obvious beyond the studio, in "how they treat people outside of class." Someone noted, "if this is a cause that someone is passionate about it will flow through every aspect of their lives." While it is not uncommon to hear about ballet teachers—particularly those in higher education, but more and more in the profession as well—participating in antiracist or inclusive pedagogy workshops or research, some student participants suggested that this work doesn't necessarily carry over with consistency into the ballet class. Some took issue when they spotted contradictions between teachers' words and actions: "it really frustrates me when teachers say they are committed to this and do not follow through." One student pointed out a trend along these lines: "I have noticed teachers who have overlooked technique to place dancers in roles to promote the image of equity and social justice. Which is not true equity and social justice." Teachers who are consistent in this regard, according to one participant, "are not afraid to mention and confront issues or take actions that match with the stated beliefs, and follow through with them."

Student participants specifically referenced dress codes as evidence of a teacher's actions to support inclusive environments: "allowing for 'secured' hair vs. bun only," and "if they allow flesh-colored tights, shoes, or costumes that include darker skin tones in class or onstage." One continued this concept beyond the policies themselves into "the way a dress code is enforced," which shifts the focus from the documented policy to its actionable outcomes. Many teachers, in their survey, likewise suggested that expanded dress codes from the traditional expectations of black-and-pink are important foundations for inclusive environments in ballet. While some seemed to indicate that such policies were sufficient, nearly half of the teacher respondents went further into how the policy is implemented. Additionally, some discussed antiracist work and continuing education in implicit bias—well beyond dress codes—that has become integral to their pedagogical development. While there's further to go, there is promise in the cadre of educators in these responses who consider words and policies alone insufficient when it comes to developing equitable, inclusive, just pedagogies.

Along similar lines, how teachers discuss and stage ballet's histories was notable to some students as evidence of pedagogic belief systems. Students identified "making sure to acknowledge the history of ballet and the violence that it has caused certain populations" as important. They were attuned to teachers' implicit messaging in "which ballet figures they teach about," and one participant suggested that "when doing classical works such as Nutcracker, the offensive cultural stereotypes are removed." Some students were in favor of teachers being explicit about their views on equity and inclusion—even stating aloud their positionality as a teacher—and being forthcoming about how they arrived at their belief systems in ballet: "They share their own experiences and explain in their mission statement what their belief is, and how they implement it." One student recalled:

> teachers that I've had often tell personal stories during class to either have the class get to know them, or to give the class encouragement. A teacher who is committed to equity and justice will often tell stories that aren't offensive or will seem like they include everyone.

One student survey participant seemed to suggest that approaches focused on equity would have a deleterious effect on the quality of the teaching. This respondent advised teachers to: "continue to evolve as times evolve but careful to not evolve too much where dilution of content and professionalism are dismissed." Despite the continued presence of perspectives that inaccurately associate inclusive environments with lower standards, the responses from a far greater number of student participants verified the importance of teachers' commitments to equitable, inclusive, just ballet pedagogies; suggesting that it supports their individual work in ballet classes. "I feel more comfortable being honest and open with teachers that are committed to equity and social justice;" "it makes me feel more comfortable trusting them with critiquing my movement," and "these approaches allow students to feel seen and have a sense of belonging. Obvious DEIJ commitment makes me want to learn from that teacher and work hard" were just some of these responses. One respondent went further into detail, explaining that a teacher's demonstrated work toward equity and inclusion will, "inform how open I will be with my identity in a class. This in turn impacts how much I am focusing on the instruction or if my effort is concentrated on staying safe and guarded."

Pedagogies, methodologies, and students' interpretations of them are a complex and persistent—if too often silent—force in any educational setting. If, as Neil Postman and Charles Weingartner suggest, teachers are only ever working with in-the-moment student perceptions, then how students make sense of pedagogies via methodologies is critical for teachers to understand.[3] Necessarily, student interpretations of teaching are individual and malleable, and while trends might emerge, expecting an overarching student perspective to hold for all students is unrealistic. The task for teachers, then, is to avoid conceiving of "student perception," or the students themselves, monolithically. Building a pedagogical process around listening to and learning about individual students—their identities, experiences, knowledges, and ways of learning—is an ongoing and central aspect of humanizing pedagogies.

Envisioning Ballet Pedagogies

The remainder of this chapter is aspirational: it describes what students envision as possible futures for ballet pedagogies; including what they would like to see change, and why. I asked self-identifying students and dancers what made them feel supported in a ballet class, and if they had any advice for ballet teachers. I also asked what their ideal working relationship with their teachers would look like and how it would feel. Reading the responses to these questions as unique takes, rather than speculating on what "students" as a whole might or might not want from a ballet class, is instructive. The subtle distinctions between viewpoints in this data poke holes in any suggestion that "students" are a homogenous group; they once again reinforce the rationale for humanizing ballet pedagogies that acknowledge individuals to equitable ends.

The Teacher-Student Relationship

Participants stressed the need for more balanced, healthy relationships between students and teachers in ballet classes. At the most foundational level, many sought any form of acknowledgment—from their presence in the class to their whole humanity. Many asked for the most basic of greetings from a teacher: "eye contact" or "saying hello." They mentioned a desire for teachers to "acknowledge students by name." Several asked that teachers simply, "know your name," which Maurya Kerr suggests "requires a little extra work outside the classroom," but "is a minimum investment toward making sure that everyone in the room feels seen and held." Kerr notes the inverse as well, saying "The absence of that nominal care is a form of subjection and linguistic violence."[4] To this end, additional students asked for teachers to more specifically "speak directly to me," or "use my name for corrections." One respondent brought nuance to these ideas, stating: "I don't like my name being called out in class, but I do thrive on acknowledgment after class." As there are a range of preferences for how students wish to be acknowledged, any pedagogical approach rooted in students as individuals will try to find a way to support the multiple ways they might optimally engage.

Acknowledgment in ballet classes often takes the shape of a single student, for better or worse, "being asked to demonstrate" some element of class material. Several students sought validation through this practice: "using me as an example," "ask for me to demonstrate something," or more generally receiving "praise in front of the rest of the class." This last response reflects a brand of competitiveness that has long been part of ballet's culture. While this method of highlighting individuals, pedagogically, has legitimate uses in ways that can strengthen community or support teachers who are restricted in their demonstrations, it too often spurs concerns about favoritism and inequity in ballet classes. In these instances, an unhealthy sense of competition can damage peer relationships and erode student self-perceptions, making some who are not highlighted feel inadequate, while putting the selected student in the potentially uncomfortable position of being elevated above their peers. While individual student successes are certainly worth celebrating, the practice of spotlighting a single student is one that requires a nuanced approach.

On a more comprehensive level, participants sought acknowledgment of their whole person and their full sense of identity. This is perhaps in response to the still prevalent "leave it at the door" approach, which has historically asked students to leave aside aspects of themselves that deviate from the teacher's expectations of dancers' beings, bodies, and behaviors. Advice from respondents included: "see your students where they are as who they are;" "see your dancers as whole humans, not just bodies placed in a room;" and "see each person in class as a human being first, with thoughts, emotions, and interests that include dance but also beyond." More broadly, one participant advised teachers to, "try to consider all the possible reasons, influences on students, and factors that go into who they are. Don't assume who your student is, what they go through, or what they need to become." Relatedly, some respondents wanted teachers to acknowledge the fullness of dancer's lives and identities in dance, saying that ideally, "they would never address me by dancer.... I am a human first, and no matter what, there is a life beyond dance. I don't want to be called by only one piece of who I am;" and "I would ask them to be encouraging and to go into class with the mindset that we have lives outside of ballet. That things may be going on in our personal life...."

A desire for "mutual respect" surfaced repeatedly across student responses, with participants sharing a range of views on how this might look and feel in practice. Some focused on what this would ask of the teacher: "the teacher would feel approachable and be able to interact mutually (both the student and teacher learn from each other);" and "I think it's important that a ballet teacher can relate to you or put themselves in your shoes to be more understanding." Some discussed both teacher's and students' responsibilities: "The relationship would be mutual in a way where respect is shared and I as the student can accept feedback humbly and use it to grow. The teacher should treat me with respect in the same way I respect them. It would make me feel seen and make me more excited to learn and to go to class." Another said, "I'd respect the teacher's role as the leader and the teacher would respect my individuality. Both of us would focus on the material.... I'd feel seen and valued, and I'd feel very appreciative of the teacher's knowledge, attention, and time." In spite of suggestions that attempts to level the hierarchy might affect the efficacy of a pedagogical approach, one respondent took a both-and stance in suggesting: "it's very normal and okay to have a very disciplined teaching method, but it's very important to me, as a student, that the teacher is supportive, understanding, as well as respectful for that particular student's beliefs and/or ideas." One participant advised teachers: "you have something to learn from every dancer."

This shared regard would be enacted through what a few respondents referred to as "open communication" between teachers and students, both individually and as a collective. As I've pored over these responses, I've been struck by most students' overarching desire to be seen and heard, and by their hope that teachers might be willing to look and listen. Many participants expressed a desire for their teachers to be "open to questions" and to "answer questions carefully." They sought "a conversation in which both teacher and student experiences were valid and shared" and "a dialogue through both movement and conversation," because "conversation in class is important for concepts to be fully processed and thoroughly communicated." In idealizing their communication with a teacher, one participant said:

> I would like to be able to ask questions, not take myself too seriously if I make a mistake (and not have my teacher criticize me for making a mistake), and be able to communicate if I am struggling. This style of open communication makes me feel seen, heard, and important.

One respondent sought common ground: "Open communication allows me to comment on how I'm feeling/thinking vs. what they are seeing so we can find mutual understanding."

Some participants wanted the teacher to explicitly seek out student perspectives, "asking for feedback" or "asking questions as to what made us feel successful." One said, "I prefer a teacher that encourages feedback, such as when a correction isn't clear or what it makes me feel in the moment physically so we can make better and more efficient progress." Despite the common fear that making room for more open, two-way communication might allow a class to descend into chaos, one participant said:

> I believe there needs to be respect for the teacher and the teacher should say more than the student, otherwise class may not move along very efficiently. However, the teacher should give the student the opportunity to speak sometimes in order to think critically and communicate their thoughts to the teacher when appropriate. This helps me learn from them and their wisdom, but also holds me accountable for my learning and makes me feel like I have some say in the matter.

Likewise, another participant noted:

> It would involve question and answering on both sides, not just a teacher driven class but one that also allows the students to have an influence on their learning. That doesn't necessarily have to mean the students lead the class direction or what happens next, but provides them with the safety to be able to challenge ideas and ask why.

From some participants' perspectives, these efforts toward mutuality would shift the teacher-student relationship to that of mentor–mentee, thereby reconciling the more damaging effects of the traditional hierarchy in the ballet class. Descriptions of this relationship included "friendly," "informal," "respectful," "collaborative," and "like a team." A couple of responses specified that teacher-student relationships should "maintain boundaries." One explained: "The teacher-student relationship can be friendly, but with professionalism. It can make a dancer feel appreciated and safe at the same time." Another agreed, saying "Fostering a positive, openly communicative relationship that still feels safe and professional (i.e. not overly casual…)," was likewise essential. Most specifically, a participant noted: "I prefer a teacher who treats me as a human, as though we are addressing a problem together. I am a professional dancer, and I don't need to be treated like a child."

According to several respondents, this kind of balanced teacher-student relationship would mean that teachers are willing to trust students' knowledge of themselves, their bodies, and their learning processes. Such trust would, in the words of one respondent: "make me feel like a respected dancer who is trusted to grow and improve on my own with the help of a teacher's knowledge." Similarly, some students advised teachers to "let me make the choices I need for my body," and "trust that I know my body."

Several participants shared how they would like their relationship with a ballet teacher to make them feel. Three sought a sense of comfort and support, saying, "I would be able to acknowledge mistakes or fear or nerves or falls. …I would be comfortable enough to give standing consent for minor/supportive touch;" "I would feel comfortable sharing my experience when trying to apply corrections and feel seen as a whole person;" and "Knowing that your teacher is there because they want the best for you and are fully in support of you growing and learning is something that makes me feel comfortable and confident as a dancer." Another was interested in how this relationship could support their approach to their work: "It would make me feel engaged and empowered in my own practice."

In her celebrated book *Teaching to Transgress*, bell hooks notes:

> Since the vast majority of students learn through conservative, traditional educational practices and concern themselves only with the presence of the professor, any radical pedagogy must insist that everyone's presence is acknowledged. That insistence cannot be simply stated. It has to be demonstrated through pedagogical practices. To begin, the professor must genuinely value everyone's presence. There must be an ongoing recognition that everyone influences the classroom dynamic, that everyone contributes.[5]

In my interpretations of these student survey responses, it seems that this valuing of student presence in the ballet class is precisely what participants are seeking when they arrive in the studio: to be seen, heard, acknowledged, and held in high regard by the teachers with whom they wish to collaborate and from whom they wish to learn.

Community in the Ballet Class

Some participants expressed the importance of teachers deliberately and explicitly working with students to build community in the studio.

There were a few outliers, however, who were less interested in the group dynamic and preferred a more traditionally authoritarian approach: "Be more harsh with students that show they want to work hard. Do not put energy into students who clearly do not want to be there." Such perspectives were not the norm, however. Many respondents described how their desired community or class culture would look and feel: "There would be laughter and silliness and community," said one, while another wanted the teacher to focus on student-student interactions; to: "get the students thinking about… how to support their peers." A participant offered some overarching advice to teachers; to "remember that you can develop a strong dancer in a nurturing environment. You don't need to break someone to make them a good dancer and artist." Additional advice was to "ensure that all students are made to feel that they belong."

Several participants suggested that community is dependent on inclusive, equitable dance spaces. These respondents' incisive comments range from admonishments of ballet's culture to the manifold ways equity and inclusion can become part of ballet classes. Students tackled the question of inclusion broadly, through race and gender: "ballet isn't just for thin white women;" and through age and bodily attributes: "include bodies of all shapes and ages, including the quite old and the very fat." One spoke to the diversity of student intentions that they would like to see honored: "please understand that we are there to be better, and even so we all want different things from the experience. Some of us want to be principal dancers, and some of us don't. We both deserve to be there."

A number of participants noted areas for continued work in ballet pedagogies as related to diversity and inclusion, from the overarching "teaching should also include culturally responsive pedagogy," to the more specific, "I would like to see a more rapid integration of mental health resources and awareness in the studio space. I believe diversity in leadership is essential to this process." One suggested that pedagogies that center dancers are important steps toward diversity: "dancers are more than vessels to just fill. I think giving them tools and knowledge while also encouraging their own beliefs and opinions helps push the field to be more diversified." Similarly, one respondent described how the diversification of the ballet style and aesthetic can support diversity in the field:

> Ballet doesn't always need to be perfectly placed and held and so black and white in a way. The gray area holds so much more.... The toxicity and way of teaching, I think most of us have been taught, is that we have to dance a certain way, act a certain way, I look a certain way. That's just not true. I would love to see more diversity in style in Ballet.

Another agreed: "I think that teaching ballet can have a more inclusive and overall be more enjoyable when you take a step away from the 'traditional' teachings of Ballet." Yet another suggested that diversification should extend to hiring practices, music, and repertoire:

> Increasing diversity in the classroom needs to occur. That will only happen by creating a more welcoming environment. Examples: diversity of staff both racial/ethnic and gender; and diversity in the music played in class: much of the music played for ballet is by white composers and it's old; diversity of repertoire in pieces performed.

As might be anticipated, one respondent didn't think the question of equity or inclusion was necessary in ballet, saying "it is too political. At the end of the day it is Ballet.... Ballet has an aesthetic that cannot be changed. To meet this requires hard work. This should not be minimized." Here, again, the historical and profoundly mistaken association of efforts toward inclusion with a lack of "rigor" or legitimacy—assuming it will no longer constitute capital "B" Ballet—is apparent.[6] This trope is at the root, in my view, of so much pedagogic gatekeeping and resistance to change. Another participant offered this counterpoint:

> Ballet education needs to constantly reevaluate itself to fit the new research, understanding, and findings of modern society. It should be inclusive for all who are a part of this generational timeline. It cannot remain historically accurate. The medical field changes, there are different time periods of art, etc. so why can't the dance field also evolve to become something more.

Autonomy and Agency

A number of participants spoke to their desire for greater autonomy and opportunities to use their agency in ballet classes: "ballet teaching needs to focus more on bodily autonomy and choice." Their responses—both in number and voracity—confirm researcher Sanna Nordin-Bates' assertion that one of ballet's most substantive areas of pedagogical deficiency is in providing the kind of autonomy that results in student and dancer wellbeing.[7] Some respondents sought more co-created opportunities for choice, asking "is there flexibility in the classroom?" and "does the teacher create a community with the student that allows student choice, or do they consider themselves the ultimate authority?" Some suggested teachers, "take requests for music and movement choices," and "give options during combinations." Another reflected on not having had choice over their trajectory: "it would have been so valuable to me to have choice earlier about how I engaged with pointe, or rather, whether I did… there should be more than one way for everyone."

Several students were concerned with the traditionally hierarchical power dynamic of the ballet class and how it shapes the possibilities for student autonomy. One advised a degree of pedagogical self-awareness that would support power-sharing: "Be very aware of the power you naturally possess in the classroom, and instead of taking it, shift it to the students. Create space to learn, make mistakes, ask questions, and grow." Others were concerned with issues of ownership; they wanted teachers to be "clear about class being *for* students and our bodies," and idealized that, "they would never… claim this class is 'their class.'" Another participant sought acknowledgment of their individual circumstance as a basis for autonomous treatment:

> As a student, I should still feel that I have a voice in the studio. Just as a teacher plans a class with intention, there should be a recognition that I enter the space with goals for a class. My goals may be predicated on physical injury or mental health. At a certain experience level a teacher should respect a level of student autonomy.

Class Material

While the majority of students offered perspectives on the "how" of teaching, there were a smattering of participants who spoke to the "what," or the material of the class. "Creating engaging classes" was important to one respondent, while "meeting me with their teaching at my level" was a theme across several responses. Two other students likewise suggested that teachers "create a class that feels danceable (e.g. not so difficult as to torture you with steps that the population in the class will never do onstage)," and "take cues from the class for whether something is too hard or too easy." The desires of these participants for teachers to offer class material that addresses the needs of the specific people in the class, rather than teaching content without consideration of individual students, sits in contrast to syllabus-driven classes whose content is developed inside a theoretical framework for a "level" that exists outside the students. Relatedly, participants said that "reading the room when it comes to next steps" is central to the process of "assigning appropriate challenges but not making the students feel overwhelmed and stressed." It is notable that these students wanted to experience a challenge—these responses were not a request to teachers to scale back because of slack student work ethics. To the contrary, these students were clearly aware that building the material of the class based on deep knowledge of ballet's internal progressions, informed by close observations of individual students, is at the core of sound pedagogies.

Student participants expected the content of the ballet class to acknowledge their current abilities while challenging them in productive ways that promote learning and growth. One clarified: "I want to leave feeling encouraged but challenged," while another commented, "I like to be focused and challenged in class but also have a very playful environment." Ideally, according to one respondent, teachers "will guide students through the experience with a casualness that makes the space safe and open to failures, while bringing an excitement and rigor that keep students wanting more from themselves." One participant spoke to the desire for psychological safety when presented with new information: "being able to try new things without risk of discouragement or being made fun of." Another agreed and expanded upon this idea, expressing hope that teachers would help assuage any perfectionistic tendencies, by:

> establishing that failure is all a part of learning, and that it's ok to mess up or fail. As dancers we all know that we want to try to do everything perfectly and sometimes you just have to mess up or fall out of your turn or whatever to actually grow. Perfection does not need to happen to have a good class and knowing that if you don't get as many turns or whatever that's ok too.

Considering these perspectives, creating material opportunities for students to succeed when challenged is critical. This asks teachers to design classes for the actual students who will participate, then, as opposed to designing classes abstractly at a generalizable level of proficiency.

Communication

While each respondent's perspective has implicit value in a qualitative research study, the most quantitatively significant topic to emerge from these surveys was around teacher-student communication—also termed feedback, comments, corrections, and notes here—in the ballet class.[8] This generated the most discussion from question to question across the survey; from how the teacher manages and distributes feedback, to the contents of that feedback, to the ways a teacher's comments would ideally feel when received. Many participants sought "a balance of feedback" between individuals and the whole class:

> I feel supported when ballet teachers balance both individual and collective corrections/notes to the class. I think it allows for there to not be too much pressure on myself or other individuals, while still recognizing us as unique and needing diverse feedback.

More respondents, though, emphasized "personal instruction," "providing individualized feedback," and "occasionally making a comment for me," which participants suggested might result in a sense of "validation," or feeling "seen and celebrated." To facilitate depth of communication with individual students, another participant suggested that teachers "try to have at least one moment with each student at the barre and in centre. Feeling invisible in small classes is not great." In the gray area between individual and group feedback, several asked that teachers "allow for self-correction," and "give an opportunity to 'play'" with material. Self-reflection and experimentation, then—which necessarily include a student's internal monologue—are important parts of the various communications that take place during a ballet class.

Numerous student participants sought confirmation of their efforts balanced with suggestions for improvement and growth. Suggestions for how confirmation might be framed ranged from the broad: "praise," "compliments," "encouragement," and "supportive comments;" to the more specific: "verbalize my success," make "positive comments when warranted," and "recognize progress." One participant offered a rationale for "acknowledging growth": "I feel like it's easy as a student to not see my growth and get bogged down by feeling like I'm not improving." The sheer number of responses that asked teachers to "notice that I'm working on something and state it," or "tell me if I do something well," in addition to non-verbal confirmations such as "nodding," suggests to me that it was not the norm for these participants to receive confirmation of their work. Some asked for communication to be explicitly "constructive," with "gentle direction not correction," while others asked in more detail for "feedback that will help strengthen me in a positive manner" and "feedback that I can implement in ways that help my dancing." The "advice" some participants seek "enforces the idea of progress not perfection," or from a slightly different perspective, "focuses less on perfection and more on the passion."

Despite wanting certain kinds of communication, a few respondents noted how the timing of feedback can affect the feeling of it; one specified that when "time spent on corrections is too long, the student becomes frustrated and embarrassed, but if it's too short the student feels dismissed." Another commented,

> It can be frustrating when every little thing is celebrated because it can slow the class down but when a great amount of effort goes into a correction and it is being applied properly it feels wonderful to be praised, and seen, for genuine work.

A third spoke about the time it takes to implement feedback and make change, in hopes that teachers would "continue to correct me even if I make dumb mistakes, not let a correction go because they give up, encourage me, but not give compliments just to give compliments – being authentic but kind." This student—as did many others across this survey—seems to be seeking an acknowledgment of their effort and their humanity, which they suggest is possible inside a challenge.

A balance between tactile and verbal feedback arose in the responses, along with some deeply individual preferences. Some participants asked for "verbal compliments or corrections," or "words of affirmation." Some found explanations of technical details useful, to avoid excess reliance on imitation, with one advising teachers to "explain the why/how of body mechanics, not just having dancers parrot moves," and one looking for "explanations of why and how something works." One expressed concern over how verbal feedback is offered: "Some practices used by some teachers are more like verbal abuse than anything else."

Tactile feedback was also a common theme; some respondents asked teachers to "give physical one on one corrections that require touch," use "hands-on corrections," and "physically assist with placement." More than half of those mentioning tactile feedback noted the importance of "asking permission to touch you," or "asking for consent before touching," as "not all bodies have the same experiences." One participant elaborated on the challenge of tactile communication in ballet classes: "I've generally had positive experiences with quick/minor touch-based correction, but I know how wrong it can go." Another cautioned: "ballet teachers should pay attention to physical corrections, they need to make sure they are not pushing the student so far past their limit they become injured," and, one urged teachers to "stop forcing turnout," an anatomically unsound practice, tactile or otherwise, which according to one participant demonstrates a need for "more awareness of the physiological aspects of ballet." In this light, another respondent suggested that teachers use touch only when necessary; and that they prefer studying with teachers for whom the "touching of students is not their first instinct."

"Remember that words are impactful, and to make corrections in a non-diminishing way," one respondent advised. A substantial number of participants described having negative experiences with teacher-student communications in ballet classes. Several advised teachers to use "corrections that are not belittling," to offer "feedback in class without making me feel embarrassed," and to avoid "denigrating people as a teaching tool." Some made appeals to teachers to cease making remarks about students' bodies—practices that they called "archaic and outdated:" "Please, no weight comments. Help me find ways to work with my body, not against it." One participant was necessarily direct: "stop body shaming." Another suggests that comments on the body that might be construed as positive or complementary are just as problematic as those that are less so: "please do not comment on a student's body ever. Or overly comment on someone's feet or lines that you like." One participant referenced the harm that can result from such communications: "ballet itself can be extremely traumatic. Scaring students, embarrassing them, commenting on their bodies – this will never work. Even the students who excel in their craft will carry the weight of these traumas for the rest of their life." Another student urged: "Never comment on the students' weight or body structure. Never give dieting advice. Check in and provide support if there are issues, but leave those evaluations to professional nutritionists, therapists, etc." This response asks teachers to know the extent of their expertise and will take action when a student's needs exceed their capacity.

Attending to Individuals

A teacher's recognition of individual students' identities and bodily contexts was important to most respondents. One student shared: "My current ballet instructors are adamant that every body is different and will have different struggles and strengths." With regard to individual identity, and gender in particular, some sought spaces in which they would be fully recognized. One made an appeal to this end: "please provide a space where identity is not assumed;" while another asserted: "no gender should be told how to wear their hair or clothes. No gender should be there solely to be strong or solely to be the 'flower.' No child should be told to change their body just to dance."

The teacher's awareness of individual students' ways of knowing and learning, and their ability to support specific individual needs, was a major theme across responses. Ideally, according to one participant, "the teacher would know what I'm working on, what's hard for me but getting better because I'm working at it, and would acknowledge that work whether (or not) the result is 'good' compared to others." In a similar vein, another wanted "the teacher to know my level and help me work to the next level.... the class would not just be taught to the highest level dancer in the class." A third sought "instruction that demonstrates an understanding of my habits and general way of moving. That makes it much easier to get helpful instruction as opposed to 'try harder.'" Another added a layer of complexity to a long-held pedagogical perspective: "the idea that students can be their best by being pushed beyond what they were previously capable of is not inherently bad, but should be changed to recognize that everyone moves at a different speed."

Several respondents asked for teachers to "pay attention to" a number of items with regard to the individual: "each student's strengths, and what is difficult or painful for them;" "students' reactions and feedback throughout class;" "how we're feeling, how our bodies are doing, and how we think the class is going." To this end, one participant noted the need for "more emphasis on dance science and taking care of the mental and physical wellbeing of each individual dancer," and another offered the following suggestion based on their own individual experience: "try to see if the obvious error or misalignment might have an underlying cause. I'm often aware of the issue and I'm trying to correct it, but don't realize something else is preventing that." One student explained: "please understand that people learn in different ways, and if a student isn't doing your correction, it's not because they don't want to or don't trust you. It's a sign you need to adjust your approach." This seems to suggest that teachers not take it personally or wield their authority if a student doesn't respond to feedback as anticipated—a decidedly teacher-centered reaction to student work. Instead, as this participant notes, a willingness to adapt one's approach—to exercise curiosity about the student and seek out new resources in support of student needs—may be warranted.

As a caveat to the call for individual attention as the primary focus of feedback inside a class, one respondent cautioned teachers not to become so individualistic that the study of ballet becomes competitive or isolating:

> Another thing I've thought about often since stepping away from the ballet world and witnessing the camaraderie of dancers in other styles of dance... is how isolating classical ballet can be. I never felt like I was part of a team – it was always one against one, me vs. myself (but also me against everyone else in trying to get solo or principal roles in pieces).

More plainly, another participant suggested to "avoid comparison," which is likewise critical to the ballet class community that several student participants expressed a desire for.

The Teacher's Qualities

Several respondents offered perspectives on the human qualities that ballet teachers bring to classes. Some were interested in teachers who bring humor to classes or are willing to "let loose": "Are they willing to be playful, or do they take ballet more seriously than necessary at all times?" One suggested: "Maintain a sense of humor and generosity of spirit. Ballet is serious, but doesn't have to be somber or solemn." Others advised teachers to let love and kindness guide their work: "be patient with students;" "give all corrections with kindness and operate with a genuine desire to see dancers learn and improve;" "love your students well and cultivate a love for dance and ballet;" and "teach with care, joy, and love." Inversely, a participant noted: "negative language or attitude towards a student will not help them learn, nor will fear."

Respondents sought teachers who are engaging and enthusiastic, who offer positive encouragement, and who teach from a foundation of integrity and a belief that students are fundamentally capable. One said: "I like when a teacher is positive and prepared because that motivates me and helps me believe in myself and my abilities." Terms and phrases students used to describe those teachers included: "warm" and "comfortable," and they described their teaching as including: "joy and knowledge and encouragement," and "with corrections given in a kind manner." To allay any concerns that students' requests for "positivity" might equate to a diminished desire for instruction or challenge, one participant noted that "critiquing is necessary, but never degrading." Some asked for frankness, with "honest corrections and honest validations," and implored teachers to: "please be honest with us. Please do not be passive aggressive." In addition to honesty, a teacher's ability and willingness to be ethical, or to "practice what you preach," was important to several student respondents.

Some students mentioned a preference for teachers who demonstrate a quality of self-reflection and a willingness to continue in their own learning—to know what they know and what they don't, and to take action when they need additional information. Two said they learn best from teachers who are "constantly growing and learning in their pedagogical practices and are open-minded/flexible," and who "know how to properly challenge each class." Suggestions for teachers included: "take each class as a learning opportunity," "figure out how technique can be adapted to the body;" "learn anatomy and physiology! Understand structural differences;" and "get some continuing education on how athletes need to fuel their bodies." "Conversations about strength and how to think about your anatomy in a functional way," according to one respondent, "might help dancers of differing builds find their way in a professional world that is changing."

Taking the idea of continuing teacher education further, one participant noted:

> The way teachers are trained to teach ballet needs to be more rigorous and requires standards of practice for even private studio teachers. Teachers should understand the developmental and cognitive level of the students they teach better and work in feedback and instruction around that information.

This was a common theme in the teacher's survey as well; that pedagogical oversight in the form of licensure, along with ongoing formal training for teachers of ballet regardless of sector, would mediate some of these issues—particularly regarding physical safety and knowledge of the learning process. To this point, one student respondent shared: "I have great teachers right now. One is a better teacher than the other. The one with lesser teaching skills needs some consultation, but one would not dare tell him."

114 *Humanizing Ballet Pedagogies*

Compassion

For as much compassion as students ask of teachers, they offered a fair degree of reciprocal compassion for those teachers they believe are trying. One provided reassurance: "don't beat yourself up if you feel like you weren't perfect – teachers have a lot to think about during class." Two respondents expressed real understanding in the face of uncritical pedagogies that have historically harmed students. One said: "I don't find it to be a sufficient excuse, but I understand that many teachers are only teaching how they were taught, and the vast majority truly believe that it is the right way;" while the other framed it as less deliberate, or perhaps ignorant: "I have to have a lot of grace, because I believe most teachers are just not aware and doing it because of the generations of teachers they learned from, and carrying things subconsciously."

According to most of these respondents—both students and teachers—changes to ballet pedagogies are happening, but more change is needed; these were common themes that appeared across the survey data. Several students said: "it's changed a lot since I've left the professional world but there's always more work;" "it is already becoming more accepting, but there is still a lot of work to do to break certain stereotypes;" "it already is… more sensitive to diversity and moving away from negative reinforcement and damaging comments about bodies;" and "it seems to be heading in the right direction." One shared: "I am fortunate enough to have teachers who are actively rebelling against the way they were taught, and the way they were treated when they danced in professional companies." Some student participants, however, were less enthusiastic about the degree of change happening, saying: "it is already starting to change, though slowly. Ballet technique should be rooted more in science and anatomy, instead of just 'this is how we've always done it;'" "too much is emphasized on lines and slenderness. Change is being made, but it is still evident in the subconscious of every teacher I have had;" and "we need to treat dancers as professionals, not children. And they shouldn't have to suffer for their art."

Some student respondents suggested that ballet pedagogies in educational contexts are changing more quickly than in the profession: one was a college graduate who went on to dance professionally: "it has evolved in the educational scenes, such as college. But many in the professional scene do not have a ballet pedagogy background, and it can sometimes be hard to adjust back to those settings after now being aware how much certain actions and words impact how I feel in class." Another respondent had similar concerns:

> I think it already is in higher education and open classes. I am worried about K-12 training in preprofessional ballet schools… Ballet at

young ages needs to be both technically correct, but also not scarring psychologically to children. It is hard to find a school that does both, especially one affiliated with a ballet company.

Yet another noted the distinction: "Dance as an art form has the ability to impart so much natural confidence in its students when the cultural norms aren't weaponized against them!"

Without generalizing or considering "students" or "dancers" monolithically, the vast majority of responses to these surveys indicate that students and dancers from across ballet backgrounds are hungry for effective, humanizing pedagogies that consider each and all students to be autonomous collaborators in their study of ballet. Optimistically, surveys indicated that while there are still some teachers engaging in damaging authoritarian practices, many are now actively experimenting with approaches that attempt to honor individual students in renegade fashion. Students deserve nothing less.

Notes

1 Elizabeth Ellsworth, "Why Doesn't This Feel Empowering? Working through the Repressive Myths of Critical Pedgaogy," *Harvard Educational Review* 59, no.3 (August 1989): 310.
2 Moya Bailey, *Misogynoir Transformed: Black Women's Digital Resistance* (New York: New York University Press, 2021); Troy Heffernan, "Sexism, Racism, Prejudice, and Bias: A Literature Review and Synthesis of Research Surrounding Student Evaluations of Courses and Teaching," *Assessment & Evaluation in Higher Education* 47, no.1 (2022): 144–154.
3 Neil Postman and Charles Weingartner, *Teaching as a Subversive Activity* (New York: Delacorte Press, 1969), 97.
4 Maurya Kerr, "Dismantling Anti-Blackness in ballet: Pedagogies of Freedom," in *Antiracism in Ballet Teaching*, eds. Kate Mattingly and Iyun Ashani Harrison (Abingdon: Routledge, 2024), 90–91.
5 bell hooks, *Teaching to Transgress: Education as the Practice of Freedom* (New York: Routledge, 1994), 8.
6 See Chapter 5 for a discussion of "rigor."
7 Sanna Nordin-Bates, "S2 E11: The One about Dancer Autonomy," interview with Sarah Scheiwer, *Dance; Better*, Podcast audio, December 16, 2021, https://podcasts.apple.com/us/podcast/s2e11-the-one-about-dancer-autonomy/id1535077862?i=1000545241351.
8 The Rambert School faculty and staff use the term "feedforward" as a generative concept and counterpoint to "feedback," while Nancy Romita and Allegra Romita prefer "clarifications" to "corrections," as they are a source of clarification about a teacher's aesthetic and technical perspectives. Jessica Zeller, "Ungrading/Unmarking: Philosophies and Practices," (workshop with Rambert School faculty and staff, Online, September 8, 2022); Nancy Romita and Allegra Romita, "Equity-informed Alignment Cueing for External Rotation and Pelvic Stability in the Ballet Aesthetic through Functional Awareness®" (presentation, CORPS de Ballet International annual conference, Online, June 2024).

Part 3
Praxis

5 Student Agency and Autonomy

The ethical treatment of human beings has not always been ballet's strong suit. Ethics, however, are perhaps the most basic yet important rationale for prioritizing student agency and autonomy in the ballet class. While changes in the current ballet landscape are encouraging, it remains necessary to state outright that dancers and students of all ages, abilities, bodily contexts, and identities deserve the dignity of having their agency acknowledged and autonomy supported, especially in the environments where they learn and develop as embodied artists—where trust and vulnerability are central to the process. Critical pedagogue and feminist theorist bell hooks describes: "a space where we're all in power in different ways."[1] This notion of differentiated power among "all" asks teachers to consider the ethical implications of who is in control of what—when, how, and why. Such an anti-hierarchical approach lays the ground upon which students can learn to harness their power in historically authoritarian ballet spaces. It is the primary responsibility of ballet teachers and institutions, then, to develop and support pedagogies that regard students and dancers as whole people; respect each student's de facto agency over themselves and their engagement with ballet; and offer students spaces in which to practice autonomy and develop as agentic individuals.

Dance psychology researcher Sanna Nordin-Bates asserts that many dance pedagogies continue to diminish the degree to which dancers can access their agency or operate with a sense of autonomy, and many of the survey responses in Chapter 4 confirm as much.[2] More optimistic, however, are the contributions of some survey participants who described experiences with pedagogies that affirmed their autonomy. Recent scholarship also provides evidence of progress in this area: pedagogical researchers in ballet investigate relationships between student agency and somatic practices; draw from autonomy-forward pedagogical praxis in dance studies and education to apply to ballet classes; develop antiracist approaches that challenge hegemonic, hierarchical power structures; link autonomy to the development of skills in creativity, collaboration, and artistry; and

DOI: 10.4324/9781003332718-9

harness their own lived experiences across ballet environments to justify the need for further work to this end.[3]

To contribute to this burgeoning dialogue, I begin this chapter by considering how researchers in psychology and education define both *agency* and *autonomy*, as "agency" in particular has become what Nordin-Bates describes as a "buzzword" that requires further interrogation.[4] I describe a methodology I refer to as *yielding*, which helps me enable student agency and autonomy in my own teaching. Lastly, I consider how uncritical notions of "rigor" can complicate the process of facilitating student agency and autonomy in ballet environments.

Agency and Autonomy Defined

Psychologist Albert Bandura links agency to the construction of the self and the development of one's own identity. He suggests that personal identity is defined through the creation and persistent re-creation of the self through experience.[5] As bodies and identities are indelibly entwined, the importance of making space for agency in an educational environment in which bodies are central to the work cannot be overstated. If ballet educators can develop contexts in which students can feel and use their agency as part of their embodied experience, they are supporting students' holistic growth; allowing the study of ballet to support the development of the self through its physicality.

Trauma researcher Bessel A. van der Kolk describes agency as "the feeling of being in charge of your life: knowing where you stand, knowing that you have a say in what happens to you, knowing that you have some ability to shape your circumstances."[6] Education researchers Gert Biesta and Michael Tedder take a more active approach, defining agency "as something that is *achieved*, rather than possessed, through the active engagement of individuals with aspects of their contexts-for-action."[7] These dual perspectives—that agency is both a feeling and an achievement—are connected. The feeling of agency can prompt its use and vice versa; the enacting of agency can elicit the feeling of it. Ballet teachers are uniquely poised to bring these perspectives together: they might facilitate a dancer's agency by focusing on their active engagement with ballet—their dancing—while emphasizing the feeling of agency through their growing competence.

The notion of "giving students agency" appears in ballet's pedagogical literature and scholarship, in the responses to the teachers' surveys that undergird the previous chapter, and, anecdotally, in my conversations with ballet teachers. It describes the prospect that teachers can distribute agency to a student through pedagogical means and is often stated with honorable intentions. While my quibble with this phrase might be partially semantic, the language educators use to describe this work matters.

Well-meaning educators seeking to support students rely on this idea, which ironically ascribes the power over a student's inherent agency to the teacher. It situates the teacher in a position of total control—a decidedly authoritarian stance. Biesta and Tedder's description challenges this concept. The authors explicitly note that agency is not something possessed for bestowing, rather it is actively achieved through engagement.[8] This suggests that the task for educators is to devise conditions, develop methodologies, and initiate experiences in which students can feel, identify, and enact their agency; to support them in using it to their own desired ends.

The concept of agency implies that one can, themselves, take action. A degree of social power underscores this capacity, as one might use their agency to take action that affects others as much as themselves. Autonomy, likewise, implies and acknowledges the power of independent action, but it further considers the availability of the circumstances for that action. In their development of Self-Determination Theory that includes autonomy as a central tenet, psychologists Richard M. Ryan and Edward L. Deci define autonomy as: "acting according to our own wishes and goals; having input and choice."[9] This suggests that the larger systemic context makes space for that action; that it offers the freedom to choose. Ryan and Deci consider autonomy—alongside "relatedness" and "competence"—as "essential for facilitating optimal functioning of the natural propensities for growth and integration, as well as for constructive social development and personal well-being."[10] They describe it as "a basic need," and call it "an energizing state that, if satisfied, conduces toward health and well-being but, if not satisfied, contributes to pathology and ill-being."[11] This rationale for supporting autonomy in ballet pedagogies is significant, then, as it associates a lack of autonomy with active harm. If teachers develop conditions in which students can exercise autonomy in the study of ballet, possibilities for harm can be reduced pedagogically.

Bandura offers some nuance to the idea that agency or autonomy could ever be fully exercised: "People do not operate as autonomous agents. Nor is their behavior wholly determined by situational influences. Rather, human functioning is a product of a reciprocal interplay of intrapersonal, behavioral, and environmental determinants."[12] The pedagogical objective, then, is to enable ballet's most beloved traditions and those who participate in ballet to grow and develop together; to honor both traditions and individuals simultaneously. This is possible, I propose, without uprooting important elements of ballet traditions or diluting the depth of study. Rather, supporting the individual's need for agency and autonomy in and through the work of the ballet class incorporates ethical, equitable, humanizing approaches into the ballet traditions most worth perpetuating.

Yielding: A Methodology

When teachers relinquish the role of indisputable arbiter and recognize that their knowledge of ballet is shaped by their own experiences, identities, and biases, they are ready to develop circumstances that facilitate student agency and autonomy. The concept of *yielding* offers a methodological basis for tipping the hierarchy—for developing a collaborative approach with students. Yielding has innumerable possibilities: it might be interpreted literally as surrendering the physical space—moving away from the teacher's traditional headquarters at the front of the studio. It might refer to turning over the aural space by being quiet while students are dancing an exercise. With regard to class content, yielding the authority of a single approach would mean allowing various stylistic and technical ideas to come forward; either in the material of the class or the discussion around what is or isn't "correct." The notion of yielding might be invoked to help students eliminate excessive tension; to allow movement to happen, rather than forcing it. More broadly, yielding suggests that teachers initiate a psychologically and emotionally open environment in the ballet class—one in which the teacher's mental or emotional state doesn't dominate the energy in the room or become a concern for students.

As a methodology, yielding leads to a generous pedagogical stance—a sharing of power. When teachers yield, they respect students' knowledge and choices about ballet and about themselves. They create possibilities for students to practice determining their own paths and they respect the outcomes; even, or perhaps especially, if the decisions students make don't reflect the teacher's view. Yielding, then, asks teachers to be prepared to negotiate a range of perspectives that might arise in a class where students' prior knowledge and experience are valued. Claire Wootten describes such approaches in ballet as resulting in "a distinct, if unsettling, shift of status."[13] There is uncertainty here, as teachers are no longer in control of all aspects of the class and students' participation. For teachers, a sense of security in one's self and knowledge is paramount in this effort. Nordin-Bates describes how ballet teachers' insistence upon a single correct approach "because I said so," "masks a lack of competence or confidence on the part of the instructor, because it takes guts to say, 'I don't know.'"[14] A teacher's willingness to work with multitudes and unknowns is therefore central to yielding; it includes being open to the individual ways of being, learning, and dancing that each student brings to the ballet class.

Despite the reality that many students are eager for agency and autonomy, some students may require support in their process of stepping forward when teachers step back and yield power to them. Having studied and learned in ballet environments that include a wide range of authoritarian practices, these students have learned how to work while being silenced. While some students will easily embrace the practices of choice-making or speaking up, others may require specific support to this end. Like their teachers, these students may need time to adjust when presented with a new power dynamic. They may need simple reassurances to help them unlearn their conditioned responses to oppressive environments, as well as opportunities to develop the critical and analytical skills needed to make choices. Maurya Kerr suggests that "we can strive to teach in such a way that students understand that everything they do in class is within their purview and agency; that everything is a choice; that not making a choice is a de facto choice...."[15] which introduces the prospect that a student may enact their agency to opt out of what teachers perceive to be an agentic stance. Additionally, some students may hold a cultural or familial reverence for authority figures, a perspective rooted in a value system that doesn't prioritize individual agency. As agency cannot be given, neither can it be forced. For teachers, offering spaces to learn agency and autonomy is as important as respecting how a student chooses to engage with it.

Yielding affects teachers as much as students. When teachers yield power to students, it suggests that they are reckoning with their own lineages. They're not content to pass down tradition for its own sake; they do not conceive of their responsibility as only to ballet or their branch of ballet's family tree. Rather, they acknowledge their responsibility to students—those engaging with ballet's traditions on their own terms. These teachers critically adjust the teachings they themselves experienced, and they seek out new information to supplement their knowledge: on various styles and approaches to ballet technique, implicit biases and antiracist pedagogies, somatic practices, anatomy and dance science, student development and psychology, philosophies of education, and beyond. As teachers work to expand their knowledge base in support of the choice-making that is central to student agency and autonomy, they accept the vulnerability that comes with not being the sole possessor of knowledge; they develop the humility that allows them to learn with and from students as they would with any other partner or collaborator.

While the responsibility for developing pedagogical approaches rests largely with teachers, a sense of professional security is critical: teachers may feel freer to share power with students if they feel institutionally safe; if they can be assured that a student's surprise or dismay at an authority figure not assuming complete control or asserting an all-knowing stance won't have a negative effect on their employment. In higher education, for example, the crisis of contingency combined with the race- and gender-driven biases in student evaluations of teaching might dissuade teachers in contingent positions—the majority of the professoriate in the United States—from taking some of the risks yielding requires.[16] Systemic issues, including policies, cultures, and an institution's ability to remedy inequities, will similarly affect whether teachers feel safe enough to yield power in their pedagogies. If institutions for ballet seek to support students, they will likewise commit to being in dialogue about how best to support teachers' agency and autonomy, as teaching and learning conditions are one and the same. In higher education, this dialogue includes outright support for academic freedom. In ballet institutions at large, such support includes regular communication with teachers as to their challenges, successes, and needs; as well as underwriting and providing opportunities for meaningful and ongoing pedagogical development.

Yielding: In Practice

Foundationally, yielding requires interest in learning about individual students and their tendencies, in and through the work of the ballet class. This dynamic, improvisatory practice asks teachers to be of the moment, curious, and open in their communication with students. In my own teaching, I use inquiry and observation to learn from students how they think about and approach various elements of the class; as well as how they feel, physically or otherwise, while dancing. I then make proposals—a range of approaches for them to experiment with and choose from—based on what they have shared with me and what I understand of their aesthetic leanings, professional goals, physical capacities, and ways of learning and embodying movement. They then try on various options—they experiment—with my support, and we work together to develop language around what they find most useful. I describe this approach here as I use it with BFA dance majors in a private, four-year, predominantly white institution. Many of these students seek professional careers in ballet, while some have professional interests in related fields. Our classes are 80 minutes in length and we often have the privilege of working with a pianist. For the duration of an academic semester, I work with the same group of fewer than twenty students three consecutive days each week, and they study with my colleagues on the remaining two days.

Inquiry and Observation

Asking questions of students can be a loaded proposition. Being asked a question by the person in charge may land differently from student to student, depending on their relationship to authority. Given ballet's notorious pedagogical reliance on rhetorical questions used to disparage or humiliate students, I watch my tone and often explain my purpose when I ask questions. I state explicitly that I'm asking in earnest so I can better understand their approach, and that their answers will help me shape my knowledge to suit their specific needs. Through this rationale, students tend to become less suspect of me as a possible interrogator, and more aware that I value their participation as a pedagogical partner. This process looks different for each student. Some students, I get the sense, remain skeptical of me as an authority figure asking questions, while others are more immediately open to the idea of working together. I have learned not to expect anyone's trust or willingness to participate in these ways, and I've learned that I need to seek out collaborative relationships differently with each student. Asking questions and taking them seriously when they respond, though, demonstrates my interest in them and my belief in their knowledge; it is central to how I yield power in ballet classes.

The questions I ask help me understand why a student might be approaching a step or phrase in a particular way—they help me get to the root of how a student conceives of ballet. I first try to grasp their intention and to do so without judgment through open-ended questions. I might ask, "How are you thinking about that?" for example, to ascertain where a student is with a step or movement sequence. I can then either confirm that I see them working in that way and offer new or complementary information, or I can ask them to describe further, which often sheds light on their previous experience and existing knowledge. If another teacher had instructed them in the approach they're using, for example, or if they had deduced it from years of practice, I try not to invalidate that knowledge unless it's unsafe or anatomically unsound, at which point we analyze it together. If I don't dismiss the approaches students bring or those I'm less familiar with as "incorrect," my experience suggests that students become more open to and curious about trying new approaches—qualities that will serve them as professionals in any field.

Sometimes I share my observations to clarify my perception before asking: "I see you anticipating the timing of the takeoff. Is that deliberate?" This encourages the ever-elusive critical thinking and metacognition, as it asks the student to analyze their work and contextualize it among other possibilities: they could, in this example, delay the takeoff to different ends. This gives me information about students' histories and perspectives that helps me understand their work. A related approach with the whole class works similarly: I tell them some of the things I'm seeing as they do an exercise in groups, and then I ask students to offer their strategies or ways of approaching it to everyone. This rounding up of ideas sometimes prompts questions or necessitates clarification, but most students find their peers' ideas to be useful. I typically confirm these perspectives for those students who might be less inclined to trust another student's knowledge—to model the perspective that even the traditional authority figure values student knowledge and expertise. I like to think that this approach supports community-building, but I'd have to ask the students to confirm this suspicion before claiming as much.

I tend to inquire about students' successes as much as I do about the moments that challenge them—to reinforce what worked or encourage continued attempts. I might ask: "What did you do to make that happen?" or, often excitedly, "How did you do that?!" Understanding why a step was successful can have just as much value as understanding why it wasn't: it provides information to press further into or apply to other areas of the class. When a student shares their process, I often encourage them to focus on what they felt, and to "chase that feeling" when they repeat it, which validates their execution and their embodied analysis. Keesha Beckford notes that she is "always in search of discovering a student's often individualized kernel of technical enlightenment," which this process has supported in my teaching.[17] At its most basic, an understanding of a successful outcome constitutes confirmation of their work that dancers can feel good about. Sometimes, an earnest congratulation without any additional commentary is enough.

Proposals, Rationales, and Experimentation

Once I understand their intentions, I can propose relevant options. What if they try it *this* way to see what's possible? Or, might they consider *this* school of thought? Sometimes I'll offer more than one approach—stylistically, anatomically, or musically, for example. As we work, we clarify objectives and rationales: what feels sound or secure in their bodies, what do they identify as progress, what seems more efficient or artistically informed, and why? Oftentimes, students will note that something I suggest is different than what they think is "correct," so we parse the distinctions and acknowledge multiple legitimate approaches. The loosening of rigid perceptions around "correct"-ness often creates space for experimentation—for students to find validity in both tinkering with new ideas and pressing further into what they know and understand.

In the material, I often leave spaces for them to fill: the fourth eight-bar phrase in an adagio, for example, or the balance at the end of a barre exercise. I might ask more advanced students to design their own plié exercise or a long phrase of cambrés, balances, and stretches after a rond de jambe. When I offer material choices, I try to offer help with decision-making for those less inclined to exercise their own agency or who need more context to make an informed decision. Some dive in headfirst, whether or not I offer support. Others, especially those raised in authoritarian ballet environments, might find the prospect of making their own choices foreign and need a place to practice. I've also worked with neurodivergent students—those with ADHD, for example—who find too much flexibility or too many options challenging to navigate.[18] To provide some structure and rationales, I might say, for example, "The option with the consecutive relevés would be useful for strengthening, while the option with the extended balance offers an alignment challenge." If a student is having a particularly tough class, I might suggest they choose options that will bring them the most joy in their dancing—an emphasis that supports intrinsic motivation.

Offering two established stylistic approaches to a step can also be useful: asking students to choose between preparing for a pirouette en dehors with a fourth position demi plié on both legs or with a stretched back leg, for example. As I'm more versed in the version with the demi plié on both legs, I might ask students who have more experience with the stretched back leg to share their knowledge of that coordination. I try to support student choice-making by asking whether they are more interested in deepening their understanding of the more familiar option in today's class, or is today the day to try the one they're less acquainted with to broaden their individual repertoire? I typically note that these choices are both valid and valuable—both are represented in ballet's styles and repertoire.

Offering steps from the traditionally male and female vocabularies to all dancers—making the study of ballet more equitable—is gradually becoming more common in ballet classes, even at the most elite levels of the field.[19] The presentation of gender through ballet's movement can be made an option as well, as choosing how to embody and present traditionally masculinized or feminized carriage allows for engagement with ballet beyond the binary.* Likewise, if students are working on a specific style or aesthetic sensibility for upcoming performances, I encourage them to bring it into their class work, or to make choices in class that support their work holistically. It is true that consistency is essential to the study of ballet, but so too in the twenty-first century is versatility and exploration inside the form, particularly at the advanced, pre-professional, and professional levels. In this sense, it is up to teachers in all levels of ballet to determine which elements of class to open up for student choice, with sound anatomical options always taking precedence.

Sometimes there is an approach or a step that I think would be useful for the class or a specific student to use, so I don't offer options. In these moments, I might explain why I've made this determination on their behalf, which Nordin-Bates suggests is an effective alternative to offering choices.[20] The need to justify my choices makes me more purposeful in my class design. Such rationales also allow me to model pedagogical decision-making so that when students have the space to make choices

---

* I am grateful to Dr. Fen Kennedy for alerting me to this possibility.

of their own, either as dancers or future teachers, they understand how pedagogical values and intentions can shape the material. Rationales, too, help students see that the construction of a ballet class and the details of how ballet can be embodied aren't secrets—that teachers aren't the only ones permitted access to a comprehensive understanding.

The Language of Feedback

Once the choices are made and students are working on material, I might ask them to help me develop cues that resonate for them so I can direct my response toward how they conceive of the work. I might ask students to share some words or phrases they associate with certain elements or physical sensations, which I can then use to prompt them. One student I worked with, for example, sustained a balance in the center for such a long time that it surprised them, and when I asked how it felt they responded with uncertainty. I asked them to try the balance again and share what they thought about when trying to replicate it, and they replied, "down the leg;" explaining that they stabilized the balance by sending energy down into the floor through their standing leg.[†] After that, I often used a "down the leg" cue for them in technically related steps—pirouettes and allegro, in this instance, where sending energy into the floor is likewise useful. Knowing that this student understood the cue because they'd developed it made our communication in class efficient and individualized—well worth the brief moment it took for me to seek out their perspective and assistance.

Bodily Autonomy

Regard for students' bodily autonomy is a core tenet of yielding—or any humanizing approach—as authoritarian ballet pedagogies have historically and continue today to cause significant harm through the violation of personal physical boundaries. The persistent global, political, and legal onslaught against bodily autonomy, however, has compelled me to go beyond yielding; beyond sharing power, and rather turning it over completely. I aim to establish spaces where students' rights to determine parameters for their own physical participation are fiercely protected, and to offer opportunities for them to practice developing and communicating those parameters to others. By constructing spaces for students to practice considering whether and how to seek, give, deny, or withdraw consent to touch or be touched, teachers can diminish harm

---

[†] Thank you, JW.

in ballet classes and support students in their lives beyond the ballet studio. Consent-forward environments are not foreign to dance; Contact Improvisation communities, for example, have long worked with consent-based practices, and ballet has thankfully begun to take note. A surge of recent activity among ballet companies in hiring Intimacy Coordinators—experts in consent-based practices who can mediate hierarchical power dynamics—is underway as well, perhaps in response to the emerging ethical imperative to support dancers' bodily autonomy in their places of work and study.

As touch and physical feedback are legitimate methods for providing useful information in ballet classes, seeking consent to use these tools allows teachers to support individual students' bodily autonomy. In ballet classes, I use a three-tiered approach to consent practices. First, I meet with students individually outside of class at the beginning of the term to discuss their overall comfort level with touch-based correction, and whether or how they would prefer I incorporate it into our work together. I invite them to change their mind at any time without providing a reason, and I try to assure them that their response will not have a negative effect on my perception of them or my work with them in the studio—that all possible choices with regard to touch are choices I deeply respect. Then, at the beginning of each class, I ask all students to close their eyes and for those who would like me to use tactile feedback that day to please raise their hands. As class continues, if I see that touch-based feedback might benefit a student whose hand was raised, I approach them and ask again if I have permission to cue them physically, with information about how and where I would touch them. I also try to express as little urgency as possible—hardly ever in the middle of a movement phrase or without warning. Tema Okun describes urgency as a tool of white supremacy that "perpetuate[s] power imbalance," so pressing students to make quick decisions might result in them making choices that uphold racialized and authoritarian power dynamics—the very antithesis of autonomy.[21] Providing time for consideration, then, is critical. I may not be able to fully eradicate the power differential in ballet classes, but these consent-based practices help me mitigate them.

While most often students respond to this approach in the affirmative, actively supporting students who decline my request for consent is essential to this work. Particularly if they have declined in front of other students, my response shows others how I would respond to them in a similar situation and can open the door for students to take on what Dr. Fen Kennedy has called "the agency of refusal."[22] Particularly when students are injured, ill, or generally need space to say "no" or "not today," I might thank them for taking care of themselves first, before reiterating the space they have to continue doing so. Students often feel the need to explain themselves, because making the choices they need to make for their bodies can seem daunting in a field that prioritizes deference, "rigor" and the perceptions of authority figures. I do everything I can to reassure students that their choice-making is important, and their choices won't negatively affect my perception of them. While I never expect students to accept this given my position, I continue to make the effort. Similarly, overarching institutional policies, especially punitive ones like attendance and grading, can make these choices challenging for students, so I often find myself mediating inequities in my application of these policies to individual student circumstances. The process of supporting bodily autonomy is evolving in my work as I continue to learn about it, but students have already confirmed its value in their anonymous evaluations of my teaching.[23]

The result of my approach to yielding is that students have become more driven and enthusiastic about their work, likely because they experience a sense of ownership and authority in the work they helped create parameters for. Nordin-Bates notes that autonomy "helps us grow intrinsic motivation," which my experience supports.[24] Students tend to be less concerned about what is "right" or "wrong," and more curious about the lineage or derivatives of certain steps or ideas. As a teacher, I find my own autonomy in this: I never have to engage in the false objectivity of trying to represent all of ballet. Rather, by honoring what each person brings to the ballet class, everyone's subjective knowledge and experience becomes valuable. As a group of people with a shared interest in ballet, yielding allows us to explore the subject matter together, as collaborators.

A Challenge to Yielding: Perceptions of Rigor

In reading the literature and participating in dialogues around ballet pedagogies over the last 20 years, I've noticed that "rigor" is often considered a desirable and necessary trait. While the trend is moving quickly toward approaches that center students and tilt hierarchies, I notice both a righteous challenge from traditionalists and an underlying anxiety among more progressive ballet teachers as to whether humanizing approaches can elicit the same results—the same quality of dancers—as traditionally authoritarian pedagogies. "Rigor" has become a dog whistle of sorts for both groups and most who fall somewhere in between: a term often invoked uncritically to prove that one's chosen pedagogy is effective and legitimate. With such a range of uses, "rigor," needs further examination.

When ballet teachers step out of the sole position of authority to yield to student agency and autonomy, they risk having their work criticized for not being "rigorous" enough. When the teacher doesn't drive the work, the foremost concern is that these pedagogies somehow fail to uphold The Ballet Ideal, The Tradition, or The Expectations of The Field. Questions tend to arise as to whether students can possibly meet expected outcomes or reach their full "potential" if they are permitted too much of a voice in their own work; if they will be prepared to enter a sometimes-brutal profession if they are not accustomed to brutality; or if the teaching they experienced was too "feel-good," as though feeling good about studying ballet is somehow a problem.[25] These same critics tend to use "rigor" as a covert justification for authoritarian pedagogies, or as a euphemism for a teacher's refusal to reflect on how their teaching may cause harm. To rebut these challenges, forward-thinking pedagogues have unfortunately taken to using the same harsh language as their critics to substantiate their far more student-driven approaches. The kind of "rigor" that acknowledges students' humanity, offers them relevant challenges, and enables them to reach their goals in the field is rooted in a value system that acknowledges process as much as product, and holistic development as much as sparkling technique and expansive artistry. The words teachers use may be the same when it comes to "rigor," but they are not participating in the same conversation.

Ballet is not the only field where this terminology presents a problem. The "rigor wars" have raged on for some time across education; they have prompted renegade Alfie Kohn to coin the phrase "the cult of rigor."[26] Clarissa Sorensen-Unruh, a STEM professor, notes that "rigor is a gatekeeping mechanism," and John Warner, a writing professor, notes in his discussion of rigor that "when students say a class was 'hard,' they often mean 'confusing' or 'arbitrary,' rather than stimulating and challenging."[27] Their collective point is significant: work that is hard for hard's sake is evidence of an exclusionary approach designed to test students to determine whether they are worth educating. "Rigor" for its own sake establishes in groups and out groups; it is a means by which to rank individuals, invoke competition, and maintain hierarchical power dynamics. Aspirationally and more equitably, however, educational developer and historian Kevin Gannon refers to "intellectual rigor" as based in content as opposed to policy; it is appropriately challenging and achievable, as well as purpose-driven and fulfilling.[28]

If "rigor" is to continue to be used to describe ballet pedagogies, it's important to define the term—to consider how it's enacted and how it appears in the ballet class. Is sweating evidence of a pedagogy's rigor? Is injury? Does the size or shape of a dancer's body, or other visible identity markers, affect whether their work is perceived as rigorous? Is regular class attendance or adherence to policies evidence of rigor? Is rigor qualitative or quantitative: is it in how many pirouettes a dancer does; or is it in the speed, shape, or musicality of the spot? What of extension or rotation? Is there rigor in the measurable quantities or in how they become part of the movement? Is student self-flagellation required for a ballet class to be considered rigorous? Or sycophancy? Or a lack of joy, as Kohn suggests?[29] If a dancer feels good about or satisfied with the work they've been doing, has the teaching been sufficiently rigorous? Alternately, if a teacher reprimands a student, are they upholding rigor? Plagued with such vagaries, "rigor" is necessarily subjective: whether a pedagogy is sufficiently "rigorous" will depend on who is asking, who is teaching, who is dancing, and in what context.

Yielding to student agency and autonomy can be challenging when those who believe such anti-hierarchical approaches lack "rigor" are in power in a ballet organization with the ability to establish policy, precedent, and culture. The pressure some teachers are under—in authoritarian terms—to "create" dancers is significant, and this perception coming from a supervisor or administrator can put a damper on their willingness to try approaches that encourage student autonomy. Pressing upwards for further definition of "rigor" is critical, then, for ballet educators in this position. For ballet educators at large, however, pressing inward is necessary: reflecting on and determining one's own pedagogical relationship to "rigor"—perhaps even creating a definition of one's own—will bring critical clarity to these field-wide dialogues.

In my use of yielding, I reframe "rigor" as *depth*. It appears in the critical processes students develop, which translates to their embodied work. They step forward into the spaces I vacate; they deepen their capacities for self-direction and self-motivation. They find language and context through which to analyze their embodied experiences, and they engage with curiosity and inquiry. Most develop greater self-sufficiency and become more self-possessed: as agents of their own work, they self-evaluate and experiment to make changes on their own, without always needing my prompting. When students develop these processes, they tend to invest more deeply in the outcomes—their dancing—which grows exponentially to their desired ends. In this light, my responsibility has become encouraging depth rather than pushing for "rigor;" sharing my power with students so they can develop their own critical praxis of asserting their agency and exercising their autonomy.

Notes

1 bell hooks, *Teaching to Transgress: Education as the Practice of Freedom* (New York: Routledge, 1994), 152.
2 Sanna Nordin-Bates, "S2 E11: The One about Dancer Autonomy," interview with Sarah Scheiwer, *Dance; Better*, Podcast audio, December 16, 2021, https://podcasts.apple.com/us/podcast/s2e11-the-one-about-dancer-autonomy/id1535077862?i=1000545241351.
3 See Tanya Berg, "Ballet as Somatic Practice: A Case Study Exploring the Integration of Somatic Practices in Ballet Pedagogy," *Journal of Dance Education*, 17, no.4 (2017): 147–157; Alana Isiguen, "Making Space: Inclusive and Equitable Teaching Practices for Ballet in Higher Education," in *Antiracism in Ballet Teaching*, eds. Kate Mattingly and Iyun Ashani Harrison (Abingdon: Routledge, 2024), 78–84; Kate Mattingly and Kristin Marrs, "Searching for

the Yet Unknown: Writing and Dancing as Incantatory Practices," *Journal of University Teaching & Learning Practice* 18, no.7 (2021): 195–213; Sanna M. Nordin-Bates, "Striving for Perfection or for Creativity? A Dancer's Dilemma," *Journal of Dance Education* 20, no.1 (2020): 23–34; Casey L. Thorne, "Practicing Choice: Progressive Pedagogy in Contemporary Ballet Training," (doctoral dissertation, Mills College, 2018).
4 Sanna Nordin-Bates, "S2 E11: The One about Dancer Autonomy," interview with Sarah Scheiwer, *Dance; Better*, Podcast audio, December 16, 2021, https://podcasts.apple.com/us/podcast/s2e11-the-one-about-dancer-autonomy/id1535077862?i=1000545241351.
5 Albert Bandura, "Toward a Psychology of Human Agency," *Perspectives on Psychological Science* 1, no.2 (2006): 170.
6 Bessel A. van der Kolk, *The Body Keeps the Score: Brain, Mind, and Body in the Healing of Trauma* (New York: Penguin Books, 2014), 97.
7 Gert Biesta and Michael Tedder, "Agency and Learning in the Lifecourse: Towards an Ecological Perspective," *Studies in the Education of Adults* 39, no.2 (Autumn 2007): 132.
8 Gert Biesta and Michael Tedder, "Agency and Learning in the Lifecourse: Towards an Ecological Perspective," *Studies in the Education of Adults* 39, no.2 (Autumn 2007): 132.
9 Richard M. Ryan and Edward L. Deci, "Self-Determination Theory and the Facilitation of Intrinsic Motivation, Social Development, and Well-Being," *American Psychologist* 55, no.1 (January 2000): 74.
10 Richard M. Ryan and Edward L. Deci, "Self-Determination Theory and the Facilitation of Intrinsic Motivation, Social Development, and Well-Being," *American Psychologist* 55, no.1 (January 2000): 68.
11 Richard M. Ryan and Edward L. Deci, "Self-Determination Theory and the Facilitation of Intrinsic Motivation, Social Development, and Well-Being," *American Psychologist* 55, no.1 (January 2000):74.
12 Albert Bandura, "Toward a Psychology of Human Agency," *Perspectives on Psychological Science* 1, no.2 (2006): 165.
13 Claire Wootten, "Navigating Liminal Space in the Feminist Ballet Class," *Congress on Research in Dance Proceedings* 41 (Leicester, UK: 2009): 125.
14 Sanna Nordin-Bates, "S2 E11: The One about Dancer Autonomy," interview with Sarah Scheiwer, *Dance; Better*, Podcast audio, December 16, 2021, https://podcasts.apple.com/us/podcast/s2e11-the-one-about-dancer-autonomy/id1535077862?i=1000545241351.
15 Maurya Kerr, "Dismantling Anti-Blackness in ballet: Pedagogies of Freedom," in *Antiracism in Ballet Teaching*, eds. Kate Mattingly and Iyun Ashani Harrison (Abingdon: Routledge, 2024), 90.
16 See Troy Heffernan, "Sexism, Racism, Prejudice, and Bias: A Literature Review and Synthesis of Research Surrounding Student Evaluations of Courses and Teaching," *Assessment & Evaluation in Higher Education* 47, no.1 (2022): 144–154; Glenn Colby, "Data Snapshot: Tenure and Contingency in US Higher Education," *Academe*, Spring 2023.
17 Keesha Beckford, "Dive In," in *Antiracism in Ballet Teaching*, eds. Kate Mattingly and Iyun Ashani Harrison (Abingdon: Routledge, 2024), 133.
18 Karen Costa, "Systems Aren't Scary," October 31, 2022, https://karenraycosta.medium.com/systems-arent-scary-e55d8ac63bc7
19 Peter Boal, in conversation with Nancy Dobbs Owen and Steven Ha, "Guest Artist Conversation with Peter Boal, Artistic Director, Pacific Northwest Ballet," (panel discussion, CORPS de Ballet International annual conference, Online, June 2024).

20 Sanna Nordin-Bates, "Ballet: Dancing Under the Weight of Preconceived Ideas?" in *Ballet, Why and How? On the Role of Classical Ballet in Dance Education*, ed. A. Alten (Amsterdam: ArtEZ Press, 2014), 56.
21 I was made aware of this aspect of Okun's work in the course, "Foundations of Intimacy," offered by Intimacy Directors and Coordinators (IDC). Tema Okun, "Sense of Urgency," *White Supremacy Culture*, August 2023, https://www.whitesupremacyculture.info/urgency.html.
22 Fen Kennedy, email to the author, May 24, 2024.
23 I have used resources from Whistle and Intimacy Directors and Coordinators (IDC) in developing this approach in my ballet classes. See https://disruptingdance.com and https://www.idcprofessionals.com.
24 Sanna Nordin-Bates, "S2 E11: The One about Dancer Autonomy," interview with Sarah Scheiwer, *Dance; Better*, Podcast audio, December 16, 2021, https://podcasts.apple.com/us/podcast/s2e11-the-one-about-dancer-autonomy/id1535077862?i=1000545241351.
25 See Chapter 3 for a discussion of the problematic concept of "potential." John White, *Advanced Principles in Teaching Classical Ballet* (Gainesville: University Press of Florida, 2009), 135.
26 Jamiella Brooks, "Evolving beyond Crisis: Connecting to the Future," (presentation, POD Network Conference, Online, November 9, 2021); Alfie Kohn, "The Cult of Rigor and the Loss of Joy," in *Feel-Bad Education: And Other Contrarian Essays on Children and Schooling* (Boston: Beacon Press, 2011), 147–151.
27 Beckie Supiano, "The Redefinition of Rigor," *Chronicle of Higher Education*, March 30, 2022, https://www.chronicle.com/article/the-redefinition-of-rigor; John Warner, *Why They Can't Write: Killing the Five-Paragraph Essay and Other Necessities* (Baltimore, MD: Johns Hopkins University Press, 2018), 143.
28 Beckie Supiano, "The Redefinition of Rigor," *Chronicle of Higher Education*, March 30, 2022, https://www.chronicle.com/article/the-redefinition-of-rigor;
29 Alfie Kohn, "The Cult of Rigor and the Loss of Joy," in *Feel-Bad Education: And Other Contrarian Essays on Children and Schooling* (Boston: Beacon Press, 2011), 147–151.

6 Evaluation and (Un)Grading

One of the most significant distinctions between ballet in higher education and ballet in private studio, company, or academy settings is the use of letter grades as a means for evaluation. When these two historic institutions merge their evaluative processes, the nested hierarchy that results presents double the challenge to equity for those developing humanizing pedagogies in ballet in higher education. In this chapter, I consider the histories and contexts of ballet, academia, and grades in examining the effects of academic grading systems on the ballet class in higher education. I propose that the principles of ungrading, a growing movement that challenges the hegemony of grades, can support teachers in advancing equity through policy and in re-imagining ballet pedagogies toward humanizing ends. I share my own experience designing and implementing an approach to ungrading in the ballet classes I teach, and I describe the substantive changes it continues to inspire for my pedagogy on the whole, beyond just the evaluative elements. Lastly, I reflect on the systemic and pedagogical challenges of alternative approaches to grading for teachers and students alike.

Evaluation in Ballet

As an academic institution, ballet has developed and maintained an approach to evaluation, outside the walls of higher education, for centuries. Historically, the qualitative criteria for ballet's performance and execution were carefully scripted into lofty and often political treatises written by mostly white, usually male ballet choreographers, directors, and critics—those seeking to establish themselves as arbiters. Alongside these discourses on ballet's aesthetic expectations, teachers published practical dancing manuals that documented ballet technique; these books outline the material, structure, and vocabulary of the ballet class (the danse d'école), including elements of style, musicality, and relevant pedagogical approaches in step-by-step detail. Even when written by or derived from the work of a specific person, like Agrippina Vaganova or Enrico Cecchetti, many of these writings and the syllabi associated with them have become effectively objective standards and curricula—the backbones for schools of ballet worldwide. Whether or not a school adheres to a specific syllabus, these scaffolded skills and structures that constitute ballet as a practice and a form undergird evaluative processes in every environment where ballet is taught and danced.

Teachers' perspectives enliven these documents. Their unique views are often sought after—they are typically understood as valid at the very least, if not authoritative beyond question. By virtue of the experience and knowledge that makes them credible, they support students' embodiment of documented standards, and their subjectivities, in this light, are important to their evaluations of individual students. In the day-to-day work of the ballet class, the teacher-as-evaluator is tasked with formative assessment, which helps them determine when and how to escalate material challenges; adding beats to allegro steps or additional revolutions to pirouettes, for example. Teachers also design summative evaluations, which may include examinations or demonstrations that require students to reach a benchmark before they are permitted entry into the next level of study; a model forged by some of ballet's most historically significant schools and widely adopted across ballet academies and programs. As teachers' embodied and accumulated knowledges filter their perceptions of how a student dances, evaluation happens from body to body inside of ballet's documented structures.[1] The fully embodied perspectives of individual dance-artists-turned-teachers don't just have credence in these settings; they are deeply valued knowledges that are mined as part of the evaluative process.

It is notable that while ballet's documented vocabulary is not inherently exclusionary, it can easily become so depending upon how the teacher interprets it and expects it to look vis à vis their own embodied lens, their relationship to ideals, and any unexamined biases they may hold. Evaluation in ballet has thus been ripe for gatekeeping. As authorities in part because of the unique perspectives they hold, teachers and their evaluative approaches are central to how dancers perceive themselves, their abilities, and their future possibilities in the profession. Teachers are thus responsible for understanding their own subjectivities and biases, and for mitigating the potential for harm to occur in and through subjective evaluative practices.

Ballet in Higher Education

In the early twentieth century, when dance was first making its way into academe, the progressive education movement was well underway. Early progressives like Booker T. Washington, W.E.B. Du Bois, Anna Julia Cooper, and John and Evelyn Dewey theorized experience and discovery as central to learning—the opposite, broadly speaking, of today's emphasis on outcome-driven course design.[2] According to historian Janice Ross, higher education dance matriarch Margaret N. H'Doubler was "looking for... a form of dance that could be made to fit into the institutional frames that [she] already knew would surround it."[3] Her experience with ballet was limited to some observations of classes in the 19-teens, where she found the pedagogy overly prescriptive and reliant on rote methods, as opposed to the Deweyan discovery-based learning that she was keen to use as the basis for bringing dance into higher education.[4] John Dewey's work emphasized process and product, or the formative and summative, as interconnected in arts-based education. As an ardent follower of his ideas, H'Doubler's rejection of ballet was in part because it was so focused on the performance—the outcome. She was more interested in the process of problem-solving that took place in the studio, which she didn't believe ballet could facilitate.[5]

As H'Doubler's mentor sent her off to find a movement form "worthy of a college woman's time" to bring into the academic setting, H'Doubler's perception of ballet as an "un-intellectual outlier" resulted in her rejection of ballet as a form well-suited to higher education.[6] As co-authors Kate Mattingly, Keesha Beckford, Zena Bibler, Paige Cunningham, Iyun Ashani Harrison, and Jehbreal Muhammad Jackson point out, H'Doubler's belief in the white modern dance tradition formed the foundation for dance programs in higher education and resulted in a "racially segregated realm where white dancers were valued as artists and educators."[7] Despite not being H'Doubler's chosen form, ballet eventually entered this realm when the first BFA program in Ballet was established at Texas Christian University in 1949, followed by the emergence of several other ballet programs across U.S. higher education in the ensuing decades. While it continues to encounter and push against the stigma of anti-intellectualism in higher education, ballet's historical privileging of whiteness allowed it to easily assimilate into the values already embedded in H'Doubler's model of dance in higher education.

Grades and Grading

Letter grades have been in use in the United States for more than a century. The now-ubiquitous system of A-F letter grades was first used at the end of the nineteenth century at Mount Holyoke College and intermittently throughout most of the early twentieth century, before coming into widespread use in the 1970s.[8] Susan D. Blum describes that the increasing focus on assessment in the twentieth and twenty-first centuries emerged from the "scientific management views of schooling," which were based on early prejudiced efforts to evaluate human intelligence. Blum writes,

> IQ and even the notion of *general intelligence*, or *g*, have been criticized as being racist, classist, sexist, ableist, and more. They derive from the notion that there is a single, fixed amount of intelligence... and that every individual can be arrayed against all others in an objective distribution.[9]

Like IQ, standardized tests have an exclusionary history, with the development of the Scholastic Aptitude Test (SAT) by Carl C. Brigham, a psychologist and noted eugenicist, in 1926.[10] Standardized tests—standardization and "objective distribution" also being central aims of a graded system—were first intended to and continue, today, to reinforce inequity. The system of grades works to similarly slanted ends; stratifying students without taking access or privilege into account. As Blum notes, "Grades and success in school and out of school correlate almost completely with prior advantage."[11] The harm grades do will therefore be exacerbated among historically disenfranchised groups: Black and Brown students, Indigenous students, students of Asian heritages, LGBTQ+ students, nonbinary students, neurodivergent students, and disabled students; the very groups that early advocates for standardization sought to subjugate.

Steeped in Skinnerian behaviorist principles, letter grades, point systems, and GPA (Grade Point Average) scales that rank and rate students have since become so deeply embedded in the education system that their value is assumed, not proven. Higher education pedagogy scholar Jesse Stommel writes that "they are an institutional instrument of compliance that works exactly because they have been so effectively naturalized."[12] There is a startling lack of research that suggests the use of letter grades to be effective for learning, despite the time, energy, and consternation of typically well-meaning faculty given to creating detailed graded paradigms for evaluating student work with numbers and letters. A growing body of work, however, demonstrates the harms of grading; the earliest essays pointing out the detriment of grades to learning were written in the 1930s, followed by a boom in the 1980s and 1990s in research on grades' adverse psychological effects, and a more recent expansion of these ideas in the pandemic era.[13] In spite of these ongoing efforts, the hegemony of grades and grading persists. Much of today's research on evaluation, well into the twenty-first century, examines grades through the lenses of critical pedagogy and Critical Race Theory. As Education scholar Gloria Ladson-Billings suggests, when "student 'success' is represented in achievement within the current social structures extant in schools," we are at risk of "reproduc[ing] the current inequities" in the system.[14] For students who are already subjected to bias in schools, then grading processes, by Ladson-Billings's logic, have the potential to double down on that bias.

Taking the implications of systemic injustices a step further, Asao B. Inoue references Bourdieu's concept of *habitus* to explain how the very practice of grading functions in education:

> We may care deeply about not perpetuating white supremacy, and about not being racist in our judgments and grading practices, but the paradox in educational systems is that those systems that we have to work in set limits and exert pressure on us to grade, and to grade by quality, quality that is determined by white racial *habitus* that structure our disciplines and social settings, which hold the most economic and cultural power.

Inoue goes on to describe how educators' internalized understanding of grading obscures their abilities to see this racialized hegemony of graded systems, saying: "The carrot of success, which is a euphemism for taking on a White racial *habitus*, keeps us from realizing just how internally colonized by grades and the hegemonic White racial *habitus* we all are."[15] Considering that ballet has historically privileged whiteness via its ideals and that whiteness was valued in H'Doubler's design for dance in academia that persists today; and understanding the relationship of letter grades to early twentieth-century standardization efforts shaped by eugenics, it is reasonable to suggest that white supremacy—to Inoue's point—is endemic to grading ballet in higher education on all fronts.

Grades and Grading in the Higher Ed Ballet Class

When ballet's reverence for teachers as gatekeepers meets the system of grades in academia, the hegemony of evaluation becomes twofold. Ballet doesn't need numeric or letter grades for evaluative purposes given the credence the pedagogue's individual qualitative evaluation holds. Ballet has plenty to contend with in terms of acknowledging and disrupting the biases that can emerge from such subjectivities, and grades serve only to complicate that work. As deeply entrenched institutional structures, however, grades are most often required for evaluating ballet classes in higher education. Further complicating the merging of evaluative practices in these arenas is the entwined nature of the relationships between dancers, dancing, and the body. Dance scholar Sherry B. Shapiro asks, for example, "When the dance no longer exists, where does the dancer reside?" which implies that if dancing is graded, so too are dancers; the fact of the body suggests that teachers cannot separate dancers from their dancing in order to evaluate it.[16] As students' bodies—the locus of their identities, histories, and persons—are at the center of this ranked, quantitative evaluation, some healthy skepticism and further examination into the effects of grading ballet are warranted.

Grades matter. They stratify and sort students into categories to determine who is and who is not deserving: of scholarship consideration, future endeavors like internships or graduate school, the esteem of families, peers, and teachers, and beyond. On a more personal scale, however, grades become a narrative students hear about themselves. As Joshua R. Eyler notes, "grades consistently communicate to students that they fall short of an ideal, regardless of the degree to which they may have improved over the course of a semester, a year, or an academic career."[17] Students may hear teachers communicating through grades about their bodies, behaviors, and abilities in comparison to ballet's ideals, or they may understand their grades to be a moral judgment on themselves and their bodies as right or wrong, good or bad. Students may interpret grades as an indication of whether teachers "like" or value them as people, or whether they think students have "potential."[18] Elizabeth McPherson, Doug Risner, and Karen Schupp suggest that "students may also internalize grades in ways that they become the grade they repeatedly receive."[19] Grades that students interpret as a reflection of their person or identity in this way can affect wellbeing, mental health, learning, and beyond. Neil Postman and Charles Weingartner's suggestion that "all you ever have to work with, as a teacher, are the perceptions of learners at a particular time,"[20] makes a teacher's intentions for what grades mean largely irrelevant in the face of a student's perception of them. The implications of a grade's perceived narrative are thus significant—for students' senses of self, safety, and belonging.

Professor of educational psychology Ruth Butler's studies from the 1980s reveal that grades harm intrinsic motivation.[21] As a form of extrinsic motivation, grades tend to dampen students' interest in work that may have previously held great fascination for them. When a student becomes motivated to learn something like ballet—an interest they perhaps discovered by seeing a performance, participating in a community dance event, or following in their family's footsteps—and grades are introduced as an extrinsic evaluative measure, their desire may be diminished as the purpose and meaning behind their participation shifts. In higher education, this waning interest is often most visible during a student's first year of enrollment in a dance program, when most attrition takes place. While there may be several factors involved in a student's decision to discontinue their study, their disillusionment or loss of enjoyment over time might be attributed in part to the fact that they're being extrinsically compelled to participate in something that needs to be, and perhaps has previously been, intrinsically nourished.

Teachers often develop slippery moral and ethical justifications for grading, perhaps to make the institutional requirement palatable or consistent with their pedagogies. The idea, for example, that students could be graded on their individual progress implies that teachers have developed a method of scaling, quantitatively, each student's unique qualitative work on the A-F or parallel numeric spectrum, in a distinct manner than that of their peers yet on the same standardized system of measurement. The prospect that teachers could grade students against their own "potential" is equally implausible: according to Eyler, it suggests teachers can know with certainty the full extent of "students' vast potential" such that they could use it as a benchmark.[22] The most insidious such justification, perhaps, is that grades are earned, not given. This rationale is a form of gaslighting that obscures the hegemony of grades in the institution and the weight of the teacher's power and perspective in levying them. The notion that the student is solely responsible for their grade eliminates any acknowledgment of biases on the part of the grader, despite students' likely awareness of it. Similarly, it ignores the inequities at the root of the system of grades on the whole. In practice, to Eyler's earlier point, grades reinforce a model of deficit thinking—that the problem is with the student not measuring up, rather than the system trying to feign objectivity by measuring the immeasurable.

To make the case that the grading process is unbiased and trustworthy, educators design rubrics that reify the academic insistence on objectivity and quantifiability. They work to standardize and communicate "fairness." Educational theorist and advocate Alfie Kohn describes rubrics as an "attempt to deny the subjectivity of human judgment," which, in ballet, is contradicted by the field's high regard for individual dance artists as teachers and evaluators—their histories, embodied knowledges, and aesthetic choices.[23] In my 15 years of experience grading with rubrics in ballet classes, I often felt a profound sense of unease; the choice between an A- or B+, for example, seemed to mean something different for each student despite the standardized system's definitions of those strata for broad, "fair" applicability. Too often I couldn't substantively articulate why I chose one grade or another, as the letters didn't allow me to take into account that perhaps a student was working with a slow-to-recover injury, an assistive device, or a family tragedy. Maybe one student's spine was more flexible than another's, or one student's available rotation facilitated ballet's ideals more than another's. Perhaps there was a global pandemic.* Or perhaps I, as the subjective evaluator, hadn't gotten enough sleep that week. The context matters, because not all students begin with

---

* Consider that when facing a global pandemic in March of 2020, many institutions of higher education "pivoted" to a Pass/Fail grading policy for the purpose of assuring greater equity. Despite their quick return to A-F grading later that same year, this extraordinary moment showed institutions' hands: this shift was an apparent acknowledgment that the A-F scale poses the threat of inequity by too often failing to consider issues of privilege, access, or unique circumstances of any kind.

the same privileges or proclivities as rubrics would suggest, and all evaluators hold implicit biases. When students push back, challenge a grade, or levy accusations of favoritism in response to evaluation, it feels heated and personal—because it is.

In their respective work, Crystal U. Davis and Nyama McCarthy Brown support the use of rubrics as disruptors of bias in grading, to make standards and expectations more explicit and objective. Rubrics, in this light, articulate the expectations for how students will be evaluated so students can feel secure that the evaluation of their work is not based on biased views.[24] Davis even offers a mechanism for identifying educators' biases through an analysis of their rubrics.[25] These disparate interpretations of rubrics as part of grading are worth further examination, as this is a significant gray area for educators—one shaped by privileges and positionality. To be sure, identifying and interrupting biases is essential for equity in evaluation. I am uneasy, however, about the implications of distributing rubrics to students as objective documents, especially in spaces that aspire to be humanizing—those that foreground teacher's and students' subjectivities as important to the study of ballet. In this light, I am thinking about some both-and possibilities, so students could better understand the person doing the evaluating, while being made aware of or even participating in the development of expectations for their work. To this end, teachers might include a positionality statement in their rubrics for ethical transparency, while including at least some expectations for students that can be tailored to each student equitably, for example. This could also look like teachers offering teacher-designed rubrics as a choice for students to opt into as part of their evaluation in a course; or even as a disclosure and description of the teacher's subjective views and values that wouldn't necessarily be connected to grades. Teachers could ask students to collaborate on the design of individualized or overarching rubrics for the class, or students could develop rubrics on their own or using the teacher's rubric as a template or springboard. The process of developing rubrics would necessarily include the teacher's communication of their background and perspective as part of the evaluation process—something that is prevalent in dance scholarship but not necessarily in studio-based work—and would be predicated on teachers' work with individual students, so it would necessitate student input. There are innumerable creative possibilities. This range of perspectives regarding rubrics, however, illuminates how identities and teaching contexts shape pedagogies, and it suggests the importance of developing evaluative mechanisms that can support individuals in equitable, ethical, and contextually meaningful ways.

There are some students, in my experience, who appreciate being graded for any range of reasons. Students who thrive with extrinsic motivators like grades are most often comfortable not deviating from the rules, ideals, or standards as given—they rely on the perspectives of teachers to illuminate their progress and place. In the context of twenty-first-century ballet, however, too much rule-following and adherence to ideals, authorities, and existing standards may hinder students' development as whole dance artists. Susan Crow and Jennifer Jackson suggest that ballet educators

> Consider the psychological impact on the artist of an education which concentrates on re-producing existing images, where identity is defined by an external image without real exploration of the internal movement logic of the language or with no release of a personal 'dance' voice in which to 'speak' ballet?[26]

The prospect of exploring and self-directing beyond established paradigms for achievement, ideals, or what is "correct" might seem too risky for students who are seeking a particular grade; they may fear being poorly evaluated and thus guard their degree of engagement, doing only what they're told or what they're shown will allow them to elicit high marks. The punitive potential of grades threatens the kind of bold choice-making that the profession has long touted in its most celebrated artists, both as contributors to collaborative choreographic processes and as autonomous drivers of their own artistic development.

Perhaps the most significant problem with grades in ballet pedagogies is that they are layered atop the evaluative dynamics already present in the ballet class. If ballet's notorious authoritarianism is present—if a teacher's motivations are in question and student competition is fierce—then grades will likely spark additional mistrust and antagonism. Students may compare grades once they're distributed, for example, as they might seek to discover where they are in the pecking order. As students perceive what their grade means for their relationship with the teacher, their behavior in the studio may change; they may adopt a more competitive approach to try to gain approval, among innumerable other troubling responses. Even in progressive ballet spaces, grades can make students suspicious of their most trusted teachers. I remember many a telling moment at the end of each semester, when I'd submit grades through the online portal and wait for an inevitable handful of heated emails in response. The feeling of antagonism in those messages, and the subsequent conversations I'd have with those students, was always a departure from my experience of them during the semester, where I'd perceived we'd built a working relationship based on mutual respect and care. There is dissonance in the teacher's paradox of advocate-arbiter to be sure, and once I understood that it made manifest, largely, through graded evaluations, I began to seek out alternative approaches.†[27]

---

† While I only address ungrading in this chapter, there are numerous approaches to alternative grading that can help mediate this issue, including labor-based grading contracts, portfolios, and process letters, among others.

Ungrading: Policies and Practices for Equitable Evaluation

In acknowledging that grades are so deeply embedded as to be inextricable from educational institutions, ungrading offers possibilities for providing institutions with the grades they require without relying on hierarchical graded assessments; rather it dismantles those hierarchical structures through power sharing. There is no one "correct" way to ungrade. Course designs are typically based on student self-reflection and shared authority over the grade between teacher and students; two core tenets that individual instructors can apply in creative and context-specific ways. Despite what its name suggests, ungrading most often does include grades by necessity, but as an action—a "present participle," as Jesse Stommel notes—it is an ongoing process of questioning and subverting the hierarchical tradition in which the teacher must determine those grades "unilaterally."[28] The sharing of authority over the grade gives the student some, if not total control over their policy-driven outcome; it thereby minimizes the inequities endemic to the system of grades. In practice, this might look like the student and teacher each providing half of the grade at the end of the term based on co-developed objectives; or it might go so far as to leave the full authority over the course letter grade with the student, with opportunities for student self-reflection and teacher-student dialogue around the *whats*, *hows*, and *whys* that comprise the evaluation process. At their core, ungrading approaches support the development of a collaborative relationship between teacher and student, and they can help students find intrinsic motivation while building metacognitive self-awareness about their work. While it may manifest through a shift in policy, ungrading inspires a critical pedagogical function that decouples grades from learning and situates them as two distinct entities with two distinct aims.

Ibram X. Kendi suggests that policy, and those who have the power to write it, are central to the exclusion and racism that institutions at large have long perpetuated.[29] Because I am in the fortunate position to create grading policies as part of my course designs and determine how I will work with any existing grading policies required by my program and institution, enshrining equity into these policies has become the focus of my work. The principles of ungrading support the design of more equitable grading policies because they interrupt the effects of instructors' biases on student outcomes. An adjustment to policy alone, however, as Sara N. Ahmed describes, is insufficient: "You can change policies without changing anything. You can change policies in order not to change anything."[30] Alex Shevrin Venet clarifies this distinction, saying: "The existence of equitable policy doesn't guarantee equitable practice."[31] In other words, disrupting the status quo through policy design is only a textual shift. It's easy to replace one inequitable system with another under the guise of change; avoiding such performative efforts means both writing equitable policies and following through by making resolute changes to deeply ingrained perspectives and behaviors.

In their "Equity-Care Matrix," Maha Bali and Mia Zamora assert that care-based approaches can help teachers make equitable policies—what they term "contractual equity"—more just in practice: "to ensure it goes beyond words and documents and becomes the lived experience within a social space."[32] Ungrading, in this light, is not a policy substitute for teachers in dominant identity groups to use in lieu of doing the work of unlearning racism and disrupting implicit biases—this must happen in tandem with policy change. As I describe throughout the rest of this chapter, my experience designing and working with an ungrading policy in my ballet classes was just the start of a much more extensive process of re-envisioning and re-engaging my pedagogical praxis in ballet comprehensively: in thought, design, and action.

While teachers might be quick to wonder how their designs for ungrading might enable equity for students, it is important to consider as well how the instructor's identity shapes this work. Equity for teachers, in humanizing pedagogies, is just as integral to the design and implementation of these policies. Chavella Pittman and Thomas J. Tobin encourage consideration of "classroom power dynamics," asking:

> What if you have neither the institutional authority (a full-time or tenure-track job) nor the dominant-culture identity (by virtue of your race, gender, and/or ability) that usually go hand in hand with being treated as a respected, powerful presence in the college classroom?[33]

Ceding full power over the grade, then, might be too risky or vulnerable for faculty who do not feel institutionally well-supported or secure. Faculty whose employment is based in any part on student evaluations may likewise have concerns about trying something new, especially considering the potential for bias to contaminate anonymous student evaluations of faculty in marginalized groups.[34] To mitigate the institutional inequities for teachers that Pittman and Tobin describe, ungrading can be implemented incrementally: faculty can choose to retain some control over the grade. Students could be asked, for example, to reflect on and grade one element or assignment in a course rather than the course as a whole. Or, teachers and students could co-grade, splitting the grade's total value between them. As higher education has become a socio-cultural and political target in the United States, and as trust between educational institutions and employees has been significantly eroded since the pandemic's onset, the balance of job security and personal wellbeing with ungrading and other non-traditional or otherwise subversive pedagogical approaches are important for teachers to navigate in their individual contexts.

Ungrading in the Ballet Class: One Approach

How I choose to release my power over students' grades is based largely on who I am in the academic ballet studio. As a tenured, white, cisgender, heterosexual, able-bodied woman teaching ballet for over a decade in a four-year, private and predominantly white institution, I have ample privilege to test out non-traditional pedagogical models, while being largely protected from retribution or backlash. It is a degree of autonomy that I do not take for granted. These advantages allow me to push the boundaries of power dynamics in ways that may make less privileged teachers feel uncomfortable or unsafe. Laila I. McCloud states: "the discourse around ungrading as a liberatory pedagogical practice has ignored the ways that white supremacy and whiteness impact its implementation."[35] In this light, as I describe my experience bringing ungrading into university ballet classes, my positionality is important to consider; it has allowed me to take significant professional risks—to benefit in particular from the whiteness historically privileged in both ballet and academia. This risk assessment will necessarily be different for each individual teacher in light of the changing and sometimes volatile political, socioeconomic, and cultural backdrop for higher education.

My approach to ungrading in the ballet class has been evolving since 2017, when I first experimented with it in my traditionally academic dance courses in history, theory, and teaching methods. The students I work with in ballet, notably, are BFA undergraduate dance majors—many specifically ballet majors, and many of those with professional aspirations. I see the same class of fewer than 20 students 3 times each week, which allows us to develop a strong rapport over the 15-week semester. I offer these students full authority over the portion of the grade I am responsible for, while also engaging them in a structured reflective practice and a dialogical process around their work.‡

---

‡ Several faculty members contribute to the evaluation of each student in such courses. I give students my percentage of the grade's total while explicitly acknowledging that each faculty member has a rationale for their evaluative practices. I aim to support my colleagues' approaches when in conversation with students, even if we disagree. This is a gray area that I continue to wrestle with from an ethical perspective.

Over the course of two weeks early in the semester, I meet with each student outside of class for 15 minutes so we can establish some trajectories and themes for their dancing and our work together.[§] I use these meetings as an opportunity to get to know students better—to learn about their interests and histories in ballet, and to make space for them to establish parameters around feedback, touch, and consent in class. I take notes during these meetings that I reference throughout the semester to remind myself of these individual details. The themes we choose to focus on are often based on concepts and skills they've been working on, or they pertain to their creative interests and professional goals. If a student has a minor in Kinesiology or Movement Science, for example, it's likely that their trajectory will include an anatomical focus; while if a fourth-year student will be attending ballet company auditions throughout the year, we'll likely work toward a more polished, performance-esque style of taking class, emphasizing their quick apprehension of material and deliberate artistic choices.

At mid-term, students provide me with a process grade and a loosely prompted written reflection; I ask them to discuss their learning process and how they feel about their dancing at that point, as well as any changes they'd like to make. Mid-term grades are required in my institution for the purposes of communicating to students their quantitative progress at the midway point, so I use this as an opportunity for students to practice grading themselves in preparation for the final course grading process, as the grades they assign themselves at the midway point are replaced by the grades they provide at the end of the course. If I have questions or concerns based on their graded submissions or their reflections, I might ask for a quick check-in outside of class, and I encourage the students to do the same.

At the end of the term, students participate in a jury class that comprises a separate graded element. They select a single letter grade for my percentage of their daily work in the course and for the jury class, and they write a self-reflective essay—what I call a Learning Narrative—that describes their work and their choice of grades. The prompts I provide for the Learning Narrative ask them to reflect on their process of learning or how they worked, as well as on the skills or outcomes of learning they demonstrated as a result. I also ask students to reflect metacognitively on what they learned about themselves as dance artists and learners in

---

§ Regular meetings with students at the beginning and end of the semester and the establishment of individual goals are also part of the TCU School for Classical & Contemporary Dance's regular assessment mechanism in ballet technique courses, which I designed with my colleagues. I am particularly grateful to Elizabeth Gillaspy for her thoughtful contributions to this process.

ballet, and what they intend to carry forward into future study.** Once they submit these reflections, I meet with each student again during exam week to discuss their work and confirm their final grades.

In this approach, every student's choice of grade stands, and I accept it as their outcome. By doing so, I interrupt the possibility that any latent biases I hold might affect a student's quantifiable outcome in the course in a way that could affect their future options. My accepting the grade outright also allows students to take a stance on what grades mean to them: whether they believe grades can accurately represent or reflect their learning and dancing, or whether they see grades as an institutional requirement divorced from their work. As critical pedagogy in action, this element of my ungrading design puts the student in the position to think critically about the system they're in—something we discuss as a class in preparation for their grading process.[36]

This approach could be adapted by holding meetings during class time or in small groups. It could incorporate peer feedback if class sizes are prohibitive. It could include offering a class a buffet of foci to choose from, rather than fully individualizing the trajectories. In these and other ways, it could be creatively re-designed to suit students in studio and K-12 environments, and the reflective process of qualitative self-evaluation could be used in pre-professional and even professional settings.[37]

Student Perspectives

During 2019 and 2020, I conducted a study across four studio-based and classroom-based courses.†† I used my course design for ungrading and added a prompt in the Learning Narrative which asked students to describe the effects of ungrading on their work and their experience. In these responses, one student wrote: "I felt more agency in my work, a greater sense of professionalism, and in turn more room to push past my boundaries in new ways – without fear." This comment suggests that grades hamper risk-taking, and that removing them offers students an opportunity to practice working in a way that more directly replicates the expectations for professional dancers. Another noted, "I can honestly say my mental/emotional health took a huge turn for the better this semester through my work in ballet class." In pandemic-era higher education, institutions are asking faculty to support student mental health, often without providing adequate resources or strategies to faculty for offering

---

** This course design is inextricable from my work with student reflective practices. I describe the structures and prompts I use throughout this process in Chapter 7.

†† This research protocol #1920-114 was approved in December 2019 by the Institutional Review Board (IRB) at Texas Christian University.

that support. In my interpretation of this response, ungrading becomes a pedagogical strategy that can function to this end, as it diminishes the pressure associated with grades and allows students to find intrinsically motivated fulfillment in the daily work.

Another student acknowledged a challenge of ungrading, saying that the structure "allowed me to check out at times. A better way to say that is that *I* have allowed *myself* to check out at times." I see this statement as a net positive. At first, it points to the potential for students to *lose* motivation when top-down evaluation isn't there to push them—a challenge to ungrading. But the second part of this statement makes me optimistic: that this student can now recognize the difference between being extrinsically and intrinsically motivated, and that they've learned to metacognitively analyze how they're working, and why. They're also identifying their own role in the learning process, as they seem aware in the subtext that they're the one ultimately responsible for finding ways to intrinsically motivate even when they might otherwise want to "check out." While this is just one challenge to ungrading—I address others below—this approach can support teachers in helping students strategize for intrinsic motivation over time, learn to take responsibility for their work, and develop the metacognitive capacity to identify their work habits that need attention—all necessary skills for professionals in any field.

Teaching beyond Grades

The most exciting aspect of ungrading for me is how it has touched every corner of my teaching. It was grounded in a policy change at first, but once I took that first step, I've watched it radiate into how I engage with students and how I perceive my responsibilities as a teacher. When I am no longer in the position of judge and the constant low hum of "how will I grade this?" disappears, I am free to focus on supporting students in the moment, on their own terms. This paradigm has helped me become a more useful resource—not a guru to follow—as students show me where they're most in need of my expertise and support. My objective, then, is to help students find ways to feel proud of their work, and themselves, in ways that will be reflected in their self-evaluation. Removing the grade from my purview, in this way, has had a fundamentally humanizing effect on my work; it has allowed me to develop collaborative, care-forward working relationships with students. As the context-specific nature of pedagogies suggests that ungrading will affect each teacher differently, I offer here several of the effects this approach has had on my pedagogy in ballet.

As long as I've been teaching, I've tried to provide every student with balanced amounts of individualized feedback multiple times in every class—an approach inspired by my teacher, Maggie Black.[38] The collaborations that emerge through the process of ungrading, though, have helped me develop more expansive approaches to this simple top-down distribution of my ideas and critiques. As I am no longer responsible for tracking students' progress to graded ends, I can spend my time being more inquisitive about their process, knowledge, experience, and intentions—from what they're trying to accomplish to how they're thinking about it. I am less beholden to the traditional approach of offering comments based solely on my observation and assessing whether they "take" my "correction." The concept of "meeting the student where they are" is often bandied about in pedagogy circles, but this approach allows me to deliberately enact that metaphor. I find myself working to understand each of them with a level of depth I hadn't before; not only to figure out how ballet can work for their individual bodies as I've always done, but to learn from them how they understand ballet, which then shows me where my knowledge and support might be most useful.

My methodology for *yielding*, which I describe in Chapter 5, emerged from my approach to ungrading. As part of that work to support student agency and autonomy, I ask questions in earnest to better understand students' intentions and existing knowledge of a step or a sequence, and to demonstrate my interest in them as people. This then helps me tailor my feedback to their individual needs, while building rapport. When I decentered my own perspective because I would no longer be the sole evaluator, I began to try understanding their intentions with a step or phrase first, and to then consider how it relates to my perspective. If we seem to disagree about a step's execution or how they might clarify it in their body, for example, I acknowledge the disparity and the reality that there are multiple valid schools of thought in ballet. If I don't have to levy a grade, my perspective serves as a resource rather than the standard. In addition to diminishing the inequities of grades on the whole, this aspect of ungrading also allows me to subvert the gatekeeping that ballet's internal model of evaluation promotes. It is challenging to actively calm my ego when the moment calls for me to stop insisting upon my preference. If the very notion of what is "correct" is context-specific, though, then without the need to grade my major responsibility becomes helping students understand how or why they might approach a step a certain way; stylistically, anatomically, or musically, for example. Sometimes I suggest they try both of our preferred versions as a way to understand the breadth and range of valid approaches to the step; sometimes I ask them to work with the version they use less often to gain greater aptitude in it; sometimes I explicitly state the value I see in one version and suggest that they try it; and sometimes I leave the choice to them. This more open approach helps me navigate the differences between their various backgrounds of study and anatomical idiosyncrasies, and it supports the range of styles a dancer may need in their professional toolbox. If I were still grading, perhaps based on a rubric

I'd designed, I might have limited the possibilities to my own embodied perspective or to those elements I aesthetically value most. Ungrading, in this light, has expanded the possibilities for course content and my dialogical processes with students.

As I let go of the power of the grade, I can no longer assume the deference that comes with it. In this light, ungrading keeps me honest. It asks me to regularly acknowledge my subjectivities—my leanings toward or away from certain Schools of thought in ballet, as well as the roots of those leanings in my own body, experience, privileges, and position. Without a mechanism for maintaining control or compelling student consideration of my perspective, I am forthright when I don't have a concrete answer; I admit when I need students' input to understand how best to advise them. As a result, students have been more likely to engage with my feedback because it reciprocally engages with their perspectives. They often seek out additional opportunities to dig deeper, asking questions and engaging in generative conversation. An unexpected benefit of this policy change, this shift from the traditional role of the ballet authority via relationship-building has since become a core focus of my teaching. It requires that I acknowledge and push against my own privileged position at ballet's gates, and likewise that I ethically interrogate my given authority to evaluate another person's embodied knowledge without their voice and participation.

This approach has shown me how to work from a place of plenty. As I no longer feel pressure to focus only on "fixing" or specifically tracking those items I will eventually need to rate along the A-F scale, I can watch and appreciate students' holistic efforts in class and allow that appreciation to steer my feedback. I try to bring a joyous sense of congratulation to moments when something works particularly well; I ask how it felt and check in about whether the student understands what they did to make it happen. In trying to reinforce their successes rather than only attending to what doesn't measure up, I attempt to help them see the full breadth of their work—to appreciate and understand their strengths and their challenges in a balanced, useful way.

Ungrading has helped me avoid using praise as a reward, as evaluative praise tends to stoke competition between students for attention and approval. Functioning similarly to grades as an extrinsic motivator, Kohn suggests praise "may impede performance" as students may seek out more praise rather than attending to the work for its own sake.[39] In place of approval, I aim to fully acknowledge students for their work in every respect—to use what Kohn calls "encouraging words."[40] I try to acknowledge students' work analytically, without imposing up or down judgment, using phrases like: "That works well for you because..." which allows me to address the details of their efforts while confirming individual choices and contexts.

An unexpected but welcome result of ungrading is the sense of community that often emerges in classes. While I cannot speak to students' experiences, since I've started using this approach, I've noticed students expressing more support for one another, and even for me, than I'd experienced before. Most of the time, the group dynamic in classes feels vital and encouraging; students champion one another's attempts and cheer on (with snaps) their successes. This was not deliberate on my part, but I estimate that this community sensibility may arise because students are less concerned about how I might evaluate their work in comparison to others'—they can use the space and time to work as they work best, or perhaps more importantly to learn what is most effective for them. The removal of grades as a ranking system, and the focus on their individual study, deemphasizes the competitive element that can so easily manifest as students seek approval from the source of the rankings. Knowing they all have my support as whole individuals, students instead develop increased competence and, it seems, a level of confidence in themselves that makes them more available to both support and take interest in others' work.

Challenges and Further Considerations

The chief challenge to ungrading is related to the question of "rigor:" concerns with the quality of students' dancing, abilities, and performance, when grades are not part of the evaluation process.[41] The more I work with ungrading paradigms in ballet, the more I believe it prompts significant progress in most students' performance. Student goals for their dancing have been substantial, ranging from easing excessive tension; to increasing extension, magnitude, strength, or power in specific ways; to refining certain positions or movements; and to developing certain movement qualities. Knowing they will be evaluating their own work and knowing that they know better than anyone else the scope of their own "potential" seems to motivate most students to hold themselves to exceedingly high standards. Their danced outcomes are strong evidence of this: some run toward what they consider big or important challenges with enthusiasm; some become more analytical and deliberate; and others experiment with new ideas more easily and frequently. I attribute their demonstrable progress to their work inside the ungrading paradigm; to reflect and self-evaluate, to metacognitively understand how their work reflects their larger goals and associated expectations, and to motivate themselves to achieve those goals. I've begun to understand that the challenge students give themselves is often more meaningful, in this light, than the challenge I or other authority figures can provide.

Like any pedagogical approach, ungrading is not without challenges when it comes to implementation. It can be difficult, for example, to make the case early on to students that I will actually—15 weeks later, when it counts—let go of my power over their grade. The system has shown students their place at the bottom of the hierarchy for the entirety of their educational careers, so my attempt to rectify that in a concrete, quantifiable way might seem suspect at first. While my assurances and reassurances that I won't change the policy at the last minute in a punitive power grab can be helpful, students either trust me or are skeptical until that moment of truth. I have found that asking students about their experiences being graded, talking explicitly about grades as systemic constructs with a history, and sharing my pedagogical philosophy with them more broadly has helped me mediate some of the student discomfort around this substantial paradigm shift.

There is legitimate concern among those in the ungrading and alternative grading communities that students in historically excluded groups who are asked to self-evaluate may do so through the lens of "impostor syndrome," or having internalized the structural prejudices in both the ballet and academic hierarchies. In both of these institutions, the effects of exclusionary policies and practices are magnified intersectionally; often resulting in female-identifying Students of Color being most susceptible to feeling a lack of belonging or that success is out of reach.[42] My anecdotal experience, in a predominantly white institution, supports this dynamic. Ladson-Billings and William F. Tate describe this phenomenon, saying:

> Members of minority groups internalize the stereotypic images that certain elements of society have constructed in order to maintain their power. Historically, storytelling has been a kind of medicine to heal the wounds of pain caused by racial oppression. The story of one's condition leads to the realization of how one came to be oppressed and subjugated and allows one to stop inflicting mental violence on oneself.[43]

Making a space for students to talk through the "story of their condition" as part of end-of-semester meetings, in this regard, can be useful. In other words, teachers can express curiosity about why these students have selected a certain grade for themselves, and ask whose criteria or lens these students are using to self-evaluate? I have occasionally suggested a rethinking when I believed a student's grade for themselves might have been affected in this way; I have proposed a higher grade to acknowledge their work inside this systemic context while being explicit that I ultimately trust their judgment. Many have happily agreed, while some have insisted I accept their choice of grade. Ungrading alone, then, cannot heal the damage of racism, sexism, or impostor syndrome, but the framework—which relies in part on individual goal-setting—can help students learn to trust their own perspectives as valid inside an exclusionary system. By offering students more power over their circumstances in the ballet class, teachers can demonstrate that their identities, knowledges, and contributions are valued. Explicitly communicating trust in students' abilities to evaluate their own work and belief in their best intentions as they do so, is central to this process. As these conversations necessarily ask teachers to negotiate their own identities with those of the students, they must become well equipped to identify and address the possible effects of their own implicit biases on students via pedagogies and policies.

Those already engaging with ungrading processes know it can be difficult to pin down the meaning of the teacher's role and its related responsibilities once the power to use the grade as a motivator or a disciplinary tool is diminished. Choosing not to wield the grade may at first feel like a blow to the pedagogic ego; a demotion; or a somehow diminished version of the teacherly identity. It may feel disorganized or like a loss of control, or perhaps even a loss of the perceived "respect" that could be assumed just by walking into the studio. It may, however, feel liberating, or too simple to be academic enough, or—hopefully—joyous and generative. Introducing ungrading practices gradually, to ascertain what feels possible and secure in one's teaching context, can help teachers negotiate the discomfort that may arise as they step out of a historical gatekeeping role and consider their own value in the ballet class without the grade. Likewise, being in dialogue with fellow educators and students around these practices—talking through the shift as it happens—can allow teachers to consider the many implications of an inequitable institutional practice too long taken for granted.

It is inside the doubly hegemonic environment of ballet in higher education that teachers and students engage in the ultimately optimistic acts of teaching, learning, and dancing. There are many inequities at the institutional level in both ballet and higher education, to be sure, and small-scale policy shifts will not be able to eradicate all of them. Letting go of the power over the grade, however, constitutes immediate action that can help mediate systemic inequities and contribute to humanizing ballet pedagogies.

Notes

1 See Chapter 2 for a discussion of ballet pedagogies as embodied philosophies.
2 Michael Hines and Thomas Fallace, "Pedagogical Progressivism and Black Education: A Historiographical Review, 1880–1957," *Review of Educational Research* 93, no.3 (2023): 457–463.
3 Janice Ross, *Moving Lessons: Margaret H'Doubler and the Beginning of Dance in American Education* (Madison: University of Wisconsin Press, 2000), 115.
4 Janice Ross, *Moving Lessons: Margaret H'Doubler and the Beginning of Dance in American Education* (Madison: University of Wisconsin Press, 2000), 114–115.

5 Janice Ross, *Moving Lessons: Margaret H'Doubler and the Beginning of Dance in American Education* (Madison: University of Wisconsin Press, 2000), 129.
6 Melonie B. Murray, "The Uneasy, Unexplored, and Under-examined Existence of Ballet in American Higher Education," *Research in Dance Education* (2021): 4–5. Also quoted in Janice Ross, *Moving Lessons: Margaret H'Doubler and the Beginning of Dance in American Education* (Madison: University of Wisconsin Press, 2000), 112.
7 Kate Mattingly, Keesha Beckford, Zena Bibler, Paige Cunningham, Iyun Ashani Harrison, and Jehbreal Muhammad Jackson, "Ballet Pedagogy and a 'Hard Re-Set': Perspectives on Equitable and Inclusive Teaching Practices," *Dance Chronicle* 46, no.1 (2023): 42.
8 Susan D. Blum, ed., "Introduction: Why Ungrade? Why Grade?" in *Ungrading: Why Rating Students Undermines Learning* (Morgantown: West Virginia University Press, 2020), 6–7; Jesse Stommel, "How to Ungrade," in *Ungrading: Why Rating Students Undermines Learning*, ed. Susan D. Blum (Morgantown: West Virginia University Press, 2020), 25.
9 Susan D. Blum, ed., "Introduction: Why Ungrade? Why Grade?" in *Ungrading: Why Rating Students Undermines Learning* (Morgantown: West Virginia University Press, 2020), 7–8.
10 Ibram X. Kendi, *How to Be an Antiracist* (New York: One World, 2019), 102.
11 Beckie Supiano, "The Unintended Consequences of 'Ungrading,'" *Chronicle of Higher Education*, April 29, 2022, https://www.chronicle.com/article/the-unintended-consequences-of-ungrading.
12 Jesse Stommel, "How to Ungrade," in *Ungrading: Why Rating Students Undermines Learning*, ed. Susan D. Blum (Morgantown: West Virginia University Press, 2020), 28.
13 See Susan D. Blum, ed., *Ungrading: Why Rating Students Undermines Learning* (Morgantown: West Virginia University Press, 2020); Ruth Butler, "Task-Involving and Ego-Involving Properties of Evaluation: Effects of Different Feedback Conditions on Motivational Perceptions, Interest, and Performance," *Journal of Educational Psychology* 79, no.4 (1987): 474–482; Ruth Butler, "Information Seeking and Achievement Motivation in Middle Childhood and Adolescence. The Role of Conceptions of Ability," *Developmental Psychology* 35, no.1 (1999): 146–163; Joshua R. Eyler, *Failing Our Future: How Grades Harm Students, and What We Can Do about It* (Johns Hopkins University Press, 2024); Alfie Kohn, *Punished by Rewards: The Trouble with Gold Stars, Incentive Plans, A's, Praise, and Other Bribes* (Boston: Houghton Mifflin, 1993); Alfie Kohn, "The Case Against Grades," *Educational Leadership* 69, no.3 (November 2011): 28–33; Jesse Stommel, *Undoing the Grade: Why We Grade, and How to Stop* (Denver: Hybrid Pedagogy, 2023). See also the work of the Human Restoration Project, https://www.humanrestorationproject.org and Hybrid Pedagogy, https://hybridpedagogy.org.
14 Gloria Ladson-Billings, *Culturally Relevant Pedagogy: Asking a Different Question* (New York: Teachers College Press, 2021), 17.
15 Asao B. Inoue, *Labor-Based Grading Contracts: Building Equity and Inclusion in the Compassionate Writing Classroom* (Fort Collins, CO: The WAC Clearinghouse; Boulder: University Press of Colorado, 2019), 27, 48.
16 Sherry B. Shapiro, *Pedagogy and the Politics of the Body: A Critical Praxis* (London: Routledge, 1999), 118.
17 Joshua R. Eyler, *How Humans Learn: The Science and Stories behind Effective College Teaching* (Morgantown: West Virginia University Press, 2018), 212.
18 See Chapter 3 for a discussion of "potential."

19 Elizabeth McPherson, Doug Risner, and Karen Schupp, "Why Grade Inflation and Teacher Dispositions Don't Mix," in *Ethical Dilemmas in Dance Educations: Case Studies on Humanizing Dance* Pedagogy, eds. Doug Risner and Karen Schupp (Jefferson, NC: McFarland, 2020): 171.
20 Neil Postman and Charles Weingartner, *Teaching as a Subversive Activity* (New York: Delacorte Press, 1969), 97.
21 See Ruth Butler, "Task-Involving and Ego-Involving Properties of Evaluation: Effects of Different Feedback Conditions on Motivational Perceptions, Interest, and Performance," *Journal of Educational Psychology* 79, no.4 (1987): 474–482; Ruth Butler, "Enhancing and Undermining Intrinsic Motivation: The Effects of Task-Involving and Ego-Involving Evaluation on Interest and Performance," *British Journal of Educational Psychology* 58 (1988): 1–14; Alfie Kohn, *Punished by Rewards: The Trouble with Gold Stars, Incentive Plans, A's, Praise, and Other Bribes* (Boston: Houghton Mifflin, 1993).
22 Joshua R. Eyler, *How Humans Learn: The Science and Stories behind Effective College Teaching* (Morgantown: West Virginia University Press, 2018), 80–81.
23 Alfie Kohn, "Speaking My Mind: The Trouble with Rubrics," *The English Journal* 95, no.4 (March 2006): 13.
24 Crystal U. Davis, *Dance and Belonging: Implicit Bias and Inclusion in Dance Education* (Jefferson, NC: McFarland, 2022): 120–121; Nyama McCarthy Brown, *Dance Pedagogy for a Diverse World: Culturally Relevant Teaching in Theory, Research and Practice* (Jefferson, NC: McFarland, 2022): 82–84.
25 Crystal U. Davis, *Dance and Belonging: Implicit Bias and Inclusion in Dance Education* (Jefferson, NC: McFarland, 2022), 84.
26 Susan Crow and Jennifer Jackson, "Balancing the Books," *Dance Theatre Journal* 14–15 (1998/2000): 39. See Paula Salosaari, "Multiple Embodiment in Classical Ballet," in *Not Just Any Body: Advancing Health, Well-being and Excellence in Dance and Dancers*, eds. R. Alston, K. Kain, D. Jowitt, J. Kylian and R. Philp (Ontario, Canada: The Ginger Press, 2001), 58.
27 See the Introduction for more on the "advocate-arbiter."
28 Jesse Stommel, *Undoing the Grade: Why We Grade, and How to Stop* (Denver: Hybrid Pedagogy, 2023), 6; Alfie Kohn, "The Case against Grades," *Educational Leadership* 69, no.3 (November 2011): 32.
29 Ibram X. Kendi, *How to Be an Antiracist* (New York: One World, 2019), 18–20.
30 Sara N. Ahmed, "Resignation is a Feminist Issue," *feministkilljoys.com*, August 27, 2016, https://feministkilljoys.com/2016/08/27/resignation-is-a-feminist-issue/comment-page-1/.
31 Alex Shevrin Venet, *Equity-Centered Trauma-Informed Education* (New York: Norton, 2021), 154.
32 Maha Bali and Mia Zamora, "The Equity-Care Matrix: Theory and Practice," *Italian Journal of Educational Technology* 30, no.1 (2022): 100.
33 Chavella Pittman and Thomas J. Tobin, "Academe Has a Lot to Learn about How Inclusive Teaching Affects Instructors," *Chronicle of Higher Education*, February 7, 2022. https://www.chronicle.com/article/academe-has-a-lot-to-learn-about-how-inclusive-teaching-affects-instructors.
34 Troy Heffernan, "Sexism, Racism, Prejudice, and Bias: A Literature Review and Synthesis of Research Surrounding Student Evaluations of Courses and Teaching," *Assessment & Evaluation in Higher Education* 47, no.1 (2022): 144–154.
35 Laila I. McCloud, "Keeping Receipts: Thoughts on Ungrading from a Black Woman Professor," *Zeal: A Journal for the Liberal Arts* 1, no.2 (2023): 101.
36 See Jessica Zeller, "The Meanings of Grades," in *Crowdsourcing Ungrading*, ed. David Buck, https://pressbooks.howardcc.edu/ungrading/chapter/the-meaning-of-grades/.

37 See Chapter 7 for the reflective prompts I use in Learning Narratives.
38 See Chapter 3 and Jessica Zeller, "Teaching through Time: Tracing Ballet's Pedagogical Lineage in the Work of Maggie Black." *Dance Chronicle* 32, no.1 (2009): 57–88.
39 Alfie Kohn, *Punished by Rewards: The Trouble with Gold Stars, Incentive Plans, A's, Praise, and Other Bribes* (Boston: Houghton Mifflin, 1993), 101.
40 Alfie Kohn, *Punished by Rewards: The Trouble with Gold Stars, Incentive Plans, A's, Praise, and Other Bribes* (Boston: Houghton Mifflin, 1993), 106–110.
41 See Chapter 5 for a discussion of "rigor."
42 See the origin of this term in Kimberlé Crenshaw, "Demarginalizing the Intersection of Race and Sex: A Black Feminist Critique of Antidiscrimination Doctrine, Feminist Theory and Antiracist Politics," *The University of Chicago Legal Forum* (1989): 139–167.
43 Gloria Ladson-Billings and William F. Tate IV, "Toward a Critical Race Theory of Education," *Teachers College Record* 97, no.1 (1995): 57.

7 Reflective Practices

Reflection enables growth. When reflection is a deliberate and structured element of ballet pedagogies, teachers and students alike stand to benefit. For teachers, regular reflection supports pedagogical development: it allows for the identification and revision of damaging elements of ballet's ideal-driven, authoritarian pedagogies and the emergence of new or bespoke approaches that foster student growth. For students, reflective practices can offer insight into the processes and outcomes of their embodied learning, while contributing to their broader knowledge of both self and systems. Contextually relevant, thoughtfully designed reflective practices, to these ends, can bring teachers and students together in the study of ballet as a critical praxis.[1]

I begin this chapter by grounding reflective practice in educational philosophies. I describe an approach from my own teaching that has been effective for student learning, relationship-building, and my ongoing development of a humanizing pedagogical praxis in ballet. I then address reflective practices for students that have become central to my work with them as I seek to nurture student-driven competence and metacognition, and student agency and autonomy through the study of ballet. While I specifically refer to my work with BFA dance majors here, all of the approaches in this chapter can be—with some creative pedagogical thinking, perhaps—adapted to any ballet environment or group of dancers, from established professionals to pre-ballet dancers, and everyone in between.

Definitions and Contexts

Reflection is a necessary function in the development of equitable and humanizing pedagogies. Philosopher Max Van Manen describes reflection as "a fundamental concept in educational theory"; "in some sense... just another word for 'thinking.' To reflect is to think. But reflection in the field of education carries the connotation of deliberation, of making choices, of coming to decisions about alternative courses of action."[2] This definition of reflection as an intentional act entrusts pedagogues with the responsibility of determining what is valuable in an educational setting. Progressive pedagogy forebear John Dewey similarly defines "reflective thought" as "active, persistent, and careful consideration of any belief or supposed form of knowledge in the light of the grounds that support it, and the further conclusions to which it tends."[3] He endows reflection with a certain ongoingness—"active, persistent"—that requires a deep understanding of a phenomenon's context and a willingness to follow its tendencies without prescribing an external end or goal. Likewise, dance education scholar Doug Risner notes that reflective practice's "aim is not absolute certainty, statistical predictability, or law-like, fixed solutions...."[4] This living practice of reflection challenges pedagogues to continuously consider prior knowledge, current contexts, and future implications, without expectations for specific results.

This open-ended nature of reflection for the pedagogue is philosophically aligned with progressive education's attention to open-ended learning, in which students' individual knowledge and experiences are vital.[5] The current education system's emphasis on outcome-based instruction hampers such open-ended efforts, as it asserts the outcomes of the learning process before it can begin in earnest. In this restrictive environment, spontaneous associative ideas that organically emerge from students' independent critical thinking or embodied analysis are often deemphasized—if given the opportunity to emerge at all—as they are peripheral to the expected outcomes for which teachers are often held responsible. In these contexts, curiosity-driven thinking or experimental approaches might be given less time or import in classes, despite the need for these qualities to be actively developed in creative fields. In addition, measurable outcomes are more highly valued in schools than qualitative outgrowths, which might be more difficult to define or quantify at the outset. The possibilities for unforced, unplanned, ruminative learning are thus devalued and diminished. Ballet in higher education, in the age of accreditation, is similarly affected.

As quantifiable outcomes are sometimes attached to overarching syllabi or program-level materials, it is reasonable to suggest that they most often do not take the proclivities or challenges of actual students into account. It has become more and more common for educational institutions to stipulate the expected outcomes for various courses and class levels as separate from the persons or interests of either teachers or students. Rather, advocates for neoliberal education focus on what they want the course to produce irrespective of those who will engage with it, which is anathema to humanizing perspectives on education. As Kevin M. Gannon notes, "outcomes are not self-actualizing."[6] This is a troubling development, given the self-actualization and work toward becoming at the core of humanizing pedagogies, and given the reality that teachers need the ability to move flexibly and with agency over course content in response to students and student work. The increasing emphasis on school-determined pre-meditated outcomes is a signal that those in leadership positions believe the educator's role to be that of a delivery vehicle for said outcomes, rather than an autonomous champion and facilitator of meaningful, relevant student learning. I point this out to illuminate this challenging trend as both context and rationale for the deliberate use of reflective practices, rather than to suggest that pre-determined learning outcomes and reflective practices are mutually exclusive. To the contrary, reflective practice is a tool that can support teachers and students in navigating such outcome-oriented expectations when a full-scale overhaul of the system is implausible.

As ballet pedagogy is traditionally outcome-oriented—the study typically culminates in performance, after all—it presents a similar challenge to the prospect of pedagogical open-endedness. Ballet's established vocabulary and theories of the body are documented as outcomes in national or program syllabi, which, directly or abstractly, undergird the classes teachers design. To eliminate ballet's outcomes would be to push against its very identity as ballet, as its ideals for performance and execution constitute the form.[7] The challenge for teachers becomes honoring both ballet as a beloved art form and the unique dancers who dedicate themselves to it, which reflective practices in ballet classes aim to facilitate.

Aligned with the traditionalist argument for "rigor" is the notion that approaches driven by students instead of outcomes or ideals are insufficient preparation for a ballet career.[8] I propose in this chapter that it is entirely possible to support students as whole individuals while supporting their engagement with ballet's embodied traditions at every level. More generatively, even, reflective practice allows pedagogues to balance ballet's aesthetic and technical elements with individual students' embodied knowledge, tendencies as learners, and career aspirations; it offers a means for teachers to advance humanizing pedagogical philosophies inside the highest quality study in ballet. By offering students strategies for reflecting on their work metacognitively and determining their future efforts accordingly, reflective practices prepare them directly for the demands of professional life in ballet or any field they may choose.

Reflective Practices for Teachers

The approach to reflective practice I describe here is theoretically aligned with Van Manen's four forms of reflection, which take place in the intervals of time before, during, and after an educational experience.[9] Van Manen references Donald Schön's theories of "reflection-in-action" and "reflection-on-action," which establish the temporal relationship between an activity and the consideration of that activity.[10] Risner, similarly, articulates the fundamental questions reflective practitioners ask themselves in both present and past tense: "What do/did I do? Why do/did I do that?"[11] In my teaching, these time-based frameworks offer me tools for reconciling the tensions between humanizing pedagogies, ballet's traditions, and any opportunities or limitations I might encounter in my teaching context. They support me in regularly engaging with students as whole people—including their identities, behavioral qualities, aesthetic preferences, physical tendencies, and individual goals.

Before Class

Van Manen calls his first form of reflection "anticipatory reflection," or the pedagogue's preparation for an educational experience.[12] In ballet, this pre-class reflection can be considered in part from a material perspective, in that ballet comes equipped with level-appropriate vocabulary or program syllabi that establish benchmarks for progress. Reflection on ballet's material is not a new phenomenon, nor is it unique to my work, in that the basic act of planning a class is a central aspect of teachers' work. Even the most authoritarian teachers reflect as they choose the material content of their classes. Teachers working toward equitable, humanizing pedagogies, though, understand that students will necessarily advance through material elements in unique ways. In my preparation for ballet classes, then, I construct a logical progression of steps and concepts that balance my program's standards for each level with my perception of the current needs, interests, and abilities of the specific students I'll be working with.

Anticipating the students' need for flexibility with material is critical: Van Manen notes the importance of trying to imagine how students will engage with and respond to material.[13] I prepare a thorough plan while preparing for the likelihood that I'll abandon some or all of it as needed on a given day. To enable fluidity with class content, I might construct a few possibilities for a step or a phrase, or I might prepare options based on ballet's built-in degrees of difficulty: building from à terre to en relevé, en pointe, or en l'air, for example. I don't adjust the content for each student unless there's a situation that calls for it—a student recovering from injury, for example—but I prepare to facilitate individual students' agency and progress by considering which exercises might be more challenging for some than others, and by recalling what they have shared with me of their goals. Sometimes I ask students for material requests—their favorite steps, for example—and weave them into the material that day or in upcoming classes. My class, then, supports and challenges these students in accordance with their objectives and ballet's traditional progressions; I endeavor to meet each student where they are in their work, while considering where they want to be.

In anticipation of teaching, I also prepare a behavioral approach as I work to be a source of inspiration and encouragement. In the moments—however few—before each class, I reaffirm my confidence in the students' intentions: I remind myself that they are motivated, want to enjoy their work, and want to do their best. I check my ego and note that each class is about and for the students—the *why* and *for whom* that guide my work—and I prepare to offer what Alex Shevrin Venet refers to as "unconditional positive regard."[14] My intention is for optimism, enthusiasm, and good humor to shape my genuine presence in the studio and manifest authentically in my physical body, tone of voice, and personal energy. If students can rely on the consistency of my temperament and actions, they may become freer to focus on themselves and their dancing without concern about my thoughts or behaviors.

Anticipating, as well, that students are sometimes challenged in the contexts of their own lives outside the studio, I prompt myself to engage them with compassion and avoid making assumptions. Asking them to dissociate from their world outside the studio—the authoritarian "leave it at the door" approach—derives from what bell hooks describes as "fear that the conditions of the self would interfere with the [learning] process."[15] This age-old tactic, while perhaps intended to heighten students' capacity to focus on the work, in practice expresses an unwillingness to engage with dance artists as whole people, in that it asks them to separate their embodied, lived experience in one environment from a likewise embodied, lived experience in another. I question, frankly, whether such disconnection is possible. In this light, I endeavor to find balance between acknowledging the fullness of students' life experiences and offering support whether or not they choose to work through moments of adversity.

While my teaching has always acknowledged student health and wellbeing, the onset of the pandemic in 2020 gave me ample cause to go further in that direction. Rather than trying to seek out the details of students' situations in a way that might violate privacy, my approach has been to unequivocally express support for students' bodily autonomy and believe in their abilities to care for themselves: I have learned to trust students. I include in my syllabus materials and repeatedly state out loud in class that I trust them to make decisions that support their overall wellness—that I believe they know themselves best. This perspective is honest; I've come to it upon seeing that it's detrimental to my relationships with students and to student growth, overall, for me to assume anything but their best intentions. These anticipatory reflective methods typically allow me to bring open, thoughtful, joyful, generous energy into the studio—to appreciate students as authorities over themselves and their work.

During Class

Van Manen's second form of reflection, "active or interactive," is related to Schön's reflection-in-action.[16] Van Manen describes it as a "stop-and-think type of reflection" that enables on-the-spot decision-making and illuminates the "interactive reality of the pedagogical moment or situation."[17] Such active reflection during a ballet class can be challenging from a material perspective. Despite my efforts to plan for student needs within ballet's systematic design and program standards, I occasionally observe that I over- or under-anticipated what they needed on a particular day. I reflect in the moment to determine whether it's safe and worthwhile for the class to work through the material as I configured it. If not, I respond: I change a step, a transition, or an element of timing. Sometimes, after they dance the exercise, I turn the reflective process over to the students and inquire about their experience with it. If it felt simple to them, I might challenge them to be more specific or more artistically present when we repeat it, or I might add a layer of complexity: a faster tempo, a reversal, a longer balance, an extra pirouette, or with battu, for example. Whichever direction I choose to go with the material, I aim to be supportive of all student attempts, particularly the less successful ones. This support is not the same as telling students their work is accurate if it isn't, but it acknowledges the fact that they didn't select the content and engaged with material that may not align with their proclivities, interests, or physical preferences. Humility and flexibility on my part, then, are central to active reflection, which asks me to make continuous decisions that balance my aims for the class with how I see individual students responding.

Dewey considers "a state of perplexity, hesitation, doubt" to be part of the reflective process.[18] This state of uncertainty is part of Van Manen's "stop-and-think" moment.[19] Authoritarian pedagogues who wish to appear infallible might deny having this experience during class; they often express to students that theirs is the only correct way despite the inaccuracy of such a hard line. While I might insist on a certain particularity in a step, style, or movement phrase for a pedagogical purpose—often accompanied by an explanation of that purpose—I balance my insistence by thinking aloud through moments of ambivalence. In my experience, most students are quick to learn that a teacher who freely questions or exhibits doubt is both knowledgeable and interested: I might notice students tilting sideways or backing up into their standing legs in a first arabesque penchée, for example, and consider changing it to second arabesque to (re)introduce oppositional forward support. When I encounter such hesitation or doubt during a class, I might explain my thought process and, sometimes, ask students to weigh in and discuss. Perhaps they express readiness, despite my hesitation, to try first arabesque again, making a concerted effort to support the standing side and standing leg; at which point I applaud their motivation and we continue with that specific challenge. Or, perhaps some students wish to try second arabesque for extra support, which differentiates the material among class participants.

My willingness to allow students to see my consideration of what's most useful for them at that moment, and to incorporate their perspectives as we move forward, demonstrates my trust in them; it supports our collaboration and their learning. Reflection-in-action becomes visible in ballet when teachers are transparent about the pedagogic choices they make based on philosophical, aesthetic, and anatomical perspectives, and on their knowledge of the students they're working with. Particularly for dancers in the United States whose training might not derive from a single School in theory or approach, clarity about a teacher's choices can validate and stretch students' range of experiences and enable them to make informed technical and stylistic decisions given the options available.

"[T]he interactive pedagogical moment" is Van Manen's third form of reflection, and another interpretation of Schön's reflection-in-action that involves "a certain mindfulness."[20] Van Manen states:

> Living the pedagogical moment is a total personal response or thoughtful action in a particular situation. Thoughtful action differs from reflective action in that it is thinkingly attentive to what it does without reflectively distancing itself from the situation by considering or experimenting with possible alternatives and consequences of action.[21]

This metacognitive process of listening, then choosing and hearing my words in the moment as I speak them aloud allows me to be deliberate and thoughtful in my communication with students. The immediacy of these moments—how I listen and speak, and how or why I provide cues and feedback, for example—is part of my larger reflexive context for teaching. These moments of introspection around my presence and behaviors are central to my pedagogy in that they establish the core of my interactions and relationships with students; they are the intra- and interpersonal moments that inspire my deepest reflection after class.

The interactive pedagogical moment asks pedagogues to—as if out of body—listen to the sounds of their own voices, attend to their use of language, and see their own postures and facial expressions. Despite my before-class anticipatory reflection, or if I have less time to dedicate to this preparation, I sometimes notice my tone slip or my choice of words become vague. I adjust accordingly if I notice this loss of awareness in myself or if I see a change in how students respond to me. Sometimes I outwardly acknowledge a poor choice of words, perhaps going so far as to explain why it was a problem. I try to be alert to individual students who seem to be favoring a body part or withdrawing, and I might check in with them quietly on the side of the room. Likewise, if a student has a success, I try to celebrate it with them in the moment. If students are focused and specific about their work I commend them in earnest;

brightening and amplifying my voice and physical energy to encourage them further. My eye must go beyond identifying technical details: it must be attuned to the students' energies and the back corners of the studio, where so much goes on beneath the surface of the class. I try to spot when a student repeatedly leaves the room or when they seem to be having trouble, and I carefully consider my language and the space we're in as I approach them about it. Particularly since the beginning of the pandemic era, I have used a simple "how are you," or other such broad entry point to demonstrate care first—to express concern for their wellbeing as part of a check-in, rather than making assumptions. This inquiry also allows them to direct our interaction—perhaps they are struggling in some way but don't want to share it with me; or maybe they need some kind of support and wouldn't have asked for it if I hadn't reached out. Their response dictates my next move. As developing dance artists with autonomy, they deserve my thoughtful engagement with them in the moment as well as the space to manage their daily relationship to ballet—and to me—in the way they determine is best. Our collaborations and their dancing, then, develop with respect, care, and compassion.

After Class

Van Manen's "recollective reflection," like Schön's reflection-on-action, enables teachers to derive meaning from their experiences because of temporal distance, and to shape their future actions in response.[22] In the few minutes that follow any class, ideally, I reflect on it as Dewey describes reflection: "turning a topic over in various aspects and in various lights so that nothing significant about it shall be overlooked—almost as one might turn a stone over to see what its hidden side is like or what is covered by it."[23] My unidealized reflection, in this light, is critical; I must be able to look honestly at my work and the students' work. Perhaps I question my choice of material, or recall an individual student's learning: did someone make a discovery that I could re-emphasize in tomorrow's class, or did someone struggle with a concept or step that I could revisit? Perhaps an injury affected someone's work, or maybe a student seemed unusually distressed or resigned. I might have made a language choice that I would like to reconsider, I might have offered an analogy that I would like to remember, or I might have unintentionally overlooked a student who was trying to disappear by dancing in the back corner. Perhaps I was too firm with a student who was having a difficult time, or maybe I could be more insistent about a certain detail. The replaying of such moments is necessary, but not for their own sake: reflection-on-action is only useful if it elicits change—what Van Manen refers to as using "the thoughtfulness that I have been able to acquire in recollective reflection" to determine "possible actions."[24] I ask why and seek a remedy when

I see in hindsight that I made an unfortunate choice; I am not above apologizing to students or acknowledging my mistakes. I might have said just the right thing at the right time, so I think back through that moment to glean insight. I use these reflections to keep myself open and listening to the students—to maximize their opportunities for development in our next class.

As I delve further into learning about and interrupting my own biases, I have begun to revisit my behaviors—actions and interactions—after class. I ask myself which students I spent the most or least time with, and why. Are there certain bodies, behaviors, aesthetic approaches, or ways of learning that I find myself gravitating toward? How am I interpreting the range of energies in the studio, and am I making assumptions that I need to interrogate? Why do some classes seem fruitful and joyful while others are frustrating or energetically low? Whose experience and perspectives have I not made a concerted effort to understand, and whose perspectives can I be more open to and curious about? Reflection, in this light, includes regularly reflecting on how my biases manifest in the ballet class—from biases around race, gender, and ability, to biases around bodies, behaviors, and ideals.

Persistent Reflective Practice

Beyond the temporal approaches that Van Manen and Schön theorize is an overarching point of reflective inquiry that can be structured in a number of ways: it asks teachers to consider whether the pedagogical philosophies they articulate coincide with their actions in the ballet class. In other words: Are teachers actually doing what they say they're doing? It's a challenge, certainly, to envision and generate a teaching philosophy; but the challenge of enacting it as stated is far greater. It is likewise challenging—and humbling—to look honestly at the teaching after the fact, at what's already happened, to determine if the pedagogy-in-practice is in alignment with its proposed theoretical foundations.

I've used a few sources of information to gather outside views on my teaching: students' perspectives, colleagues' perspectives, and recordings. Hierarchical power dynamics stipulate that students be offered anonymity in feedback on teaching, which supports them in speaking freely without fear of retribution. Anonymous student evaluations—as distinguished from requests for anonymous student feedback—can contain gendered and racialized biases and are sometimes used in hiring and promotion, so these tools should be used with care and caution to protect teachers' rights and wellbeing; particularly for teachers in historically marginalized groups.[25] Equitable labor practices aside, student feedback can be exceedingly valuable for teachers; offering individual perspectives from those who've experienced their teaching firsthand. While students cannot be expected to offer pedagogical solutions to the issues they might describe, these mechanisms can permit teachers a glimpse into what it's like to participate in their classes so they can determine if changes are needed and which changes to make.[26]

Pedagogical communities can be a generative source of support through dialogical reflection. Groups of teachers who gather either on site or virtually to discuss pedagogies can be fortifying and educative. Collegial feedback is valuable as well, whether written or discussed. Inviting colleagues—both in dance and beyond—to observe and discuss a class can offer deep insight. In my experience, this outside perspective on how I am relating to students has been most helpful; it has offered me insight into the more ineffable elements of my ballet classes that I can only otherwise see from my own perspective; including the tone, the pacing, the energy, the relevance of the material, and the apparent quality of the human relationships in the room.

While video recordings have often been used as a tool for students to track their own progress, both video and audio recordings can likewise offer teachers a realistic look at their teaching.[27] Recordings show me my own pedagogic patterns, for better or worse. Audio recordings alert me to the language and tone I tend toward, while videos show me the areas of the studio I'm in most, the students with whom I spend the most time, and how my physical presence affects the energy in the room. Having come of age before the ubiquity of smartphone cameras, the prospect of watching or listening to myself teach is a daunting one. I don't record myself often, in this light, but when I do, it helps me identify whether my teaching, in practice, aligns with the pedagogies I espouse in theory.

This ongoing process of meta-reflection includes important questions of lineage: how are teachers' own histories and experiences affecting their teaching; what elements are they bringing forward from their own teachers, and how have they adjusted or reshaped the teaching of those predecessors? If teachers are drawing from the work of those whose approaches were authoritarian in nature, they must consider if it's possible to keep the material or conceptual elements while relinquishing the damaging relational aspects of those approaches; they are subsequently responsible for determining if they're separating them effectively in their own teaching. While students, colleagues, and technology can help, a reflective writing approach might also be useful here: journaling or even researching their ballet family tree can help teachers more deeply engage with the pedagogies they're perpetuating. In my graduate research and subsequent publications, for example, I interviewed and studied the work of Maggie Black and Rochelle Zide-Booth, whose perspectives are both central to my own.[28] By delving into my own pedagogical lineage, I developed a sense of being connected to the people and elements of the tradition I choose to perpetuate, which helps confirm and sometimes challenge my choices.

Lastly, dancing, to the extent teachers can, supports embodied pedagogical reflection. While giving myself a barre, for example, I can often hear echoes of certain teachers offering me specific comments or directives, from Maggie's "UP, Jess!" to Rochelle's "Let me hear the *brush*." I can feel their presence around me in these moments in a deeply poignant way that is useful and instructive to me as both a dancer and a teacher. This process helps me connect back to the ethos and philosophies of the approaches I'm passing forward—those I trust and understand through my body, and those I work to honor in my pedagogy.

Reflective Practices for Students

Workshopping

I work with models of Schön's "refletion-in-action" and "reflection-on-action," to support students in thinking deliberately about their work in the very moment that they're doing it as well as after the fact. In almost every class I teach, I spend concentrated time on a few areas of the technique. These workshops ask students to tackle a step or sequence that requires complexity in coordination or alignment, while giving me time outside of a full phrase of movement to actively reflect on that element in their dancing. We workshop *pirouettes* often, because they require time and an individualized understanding of coordination. The students spread out around the studio to "play," as I suggest, with their turns, while I orbit the space and work with as many students as possible. The low hum of interactions—sometimes not so low—tends to make the space feel vibrant and charged in an experimental way. Ballet class, in these moments, becomes a science lab.*[29]

If a student succeeds but cannot identify why, I might ask that student to think back and articulate—in words, sounds, or gestures—what the attempt felt like physically so they can identify it from the inside and pursue that same feeling when they try it again. Alternatively, if a student can readily identify what they were aiming for, I'll ask them to immediately repeat it—to apply their reflection—so they can reinforce the feeling of the concept and their success. Other students then benefit from their colleagues' embodied research and reflection, and I learn just as much: hearing the student describe their physical approach and sensation provides me with information to use as I cue them in subsequent attempts. Often, others in the class will spontaneously begin experimenting with what they see working for their peer; they might start sharing insights on

---

* Van Manen refers to Schön's work on reflection as "suspiciously similar to the process of scientific inquiry itself."

their own or I'll prompt them to do so, which centers student-generated knowledge as valuable.

In an example of "reflection-in-action," I often ask students to get inside the feeling of turning to determine elements they can control in the step, whether chaînés, pirouettes en dehors from fourth position, grand pirouettes en dedans in attitude, or any other turn we're working on in class that day. How does the alignment of their pelvis during the turn affect the landing? How does the timing of the spot relate to the music? What kind of activity do they need in the supporting leg to enable a clear finish? In asking them to attend to the in-the-moment feeling of the step, they are reflecting in-action at the very moment it's needed to control the outcome. Similarly, with allegro, I ask them to focus on the feeling of the fully stretched position in the air, so they can control the landing despite gravity being at the helm. Adjusting in the moment is a skill necessary in performance—one that ballet tends to teach by default, but also one which structured opportunities for reflection can help build more deliberately, to emphasize student capacity and a greater sense of embodied authority.

The workshop process also promotes curiosity and problem solving; it allows students to engage in their own analytical process. It offers students time to experiment—to have multiple attempts with low stakes—so that failure might begin to seem less discouraging and more a necessary part of learning. Likewise, it allows space for students to work together if they choose, to collaborate rather than compete, and to hone their own pedagogical eye in real time. It emboldens students to handle complex movements independently and gives us both space to identify how ballet can be adapted to their individual bodies and movement inclinations.[30] Lastly, the knowledge I take away from observing their self-directed integration of reflection into their process allows me to better support their efforts—it helps me understand how they learn.

Semester-Long Reflective Practice

As my classes take place in the context of a 15-week university semester, I structure student reflections using temporal approaches similar to those I describe for teachers, yet spread out across the duration of the semester: early in the term, at mid-term, and at the end of the term. These opportunities for reflection initially emerged from my approach to ungrading in my ballet classes, which I describe in the previous chapter, as ungrading and reflective processes are inextricable in my work. Beyond the benefits of a reflective process for students, this approach, in a very basic way, allows me to learn more about each student so I can be useful to them: how they understand ballet, how they think about themselves in ballet class, and their individual goals and interests.

Early Term

In the first few weeks of the semester, I meet with each student outside of class, and outside of the studio. I use these meetings to get to know students or catch up with those I've known previously, and to learn where they are in their study at that point. My aim is to better understand their experience to that point in terms of style and approach. I ask about the specific technical elements they've been focusing on in class and what's important to them, and I try to get a sense for how they think about ballet. The simple act of asking students about their previous work is an invitation for them to reflect on it, even if they don't disclose all the details. Based on their suggestions, we develop a trajectory for their work that semester that builds on where they've been and feeds their longer-term interests in ballet. I might make suggestions based on what I've seen in our first few classes together, but many have a clear sense for what they'd like to work on, and I tend to follow their lead.

I also use these early term meetings to gather student consent for tactile feedback, which—based on my initial foray into the tenets of intimacy direction and coordination—includes a conversation about the kinds of feedback that work best for them and if or how they prefer tactile feedback to work in daily classes.† This question asks them to reflect on their relationship to feedback, to me as their teacher, and to their bodies in ballet classes, which some students aren't ready to address at that moment. Given ballet's historically problematic assumption that teachers have the right to place hands on student bodies as part of the teaching, this question—depending on their experience—might introduce to students the prospect that their body in the studio is their own, and that they have the right to determine whether and how they are touched as part of the work. If they offer a preference, I note it and I invite them to update it at any time throughout the semester with no justification needed. If they don't make a choice at that time, I refrain from using tactile feedback in class until we have another chance to check in.

I take notes during these meetings and review them frequently, as I work to build a relationship with each student. In light of the traditional power dynamics between teachers and students in ballet, I find that my own openness about my own history and experiences is helpful in these meetings when relevant, along the lines of bell hooks's analysis:

---

† I completed the initial course, "Foundations of Intimacy," through Intimacy Directors and Coordinators, Inc., and I intend to pursue this work further.

"professors who expect students to share confessional narratives, but who are themselves unwilling to share are exercising power in a manner that could be coercive."[31] When I meet with students, then, I might share my own related experiences and how I understand certain elements of ballet, if the conversation warrants it. I am also understanding of the choices students make in terms of what information they are or are not comfortable sharing: "you don't have to answer that" is a phrase I use when I see even slight hesitation. This degree of openness as part of reflective conversations has become important to my process of developing collaborative relationships with students.

Mid-Term

Having set up some trajectories with students during our early term meeting, I ask students to reflect on their work by responding to the following questions in writing several weeks later:

- Please discuss how you approach ballet class. What processes do you use to learn new information or expand your knowledge?
- Please discuss your dancing. Consider the outcomes or results of your work in ballet class.
- What is working, and/or what needs adjustment? What will you change or emphasize going forward?
- Please share anything else you'd like to add about your work or learning in this course.

Depending on how they respond to these questions, I might respond to their reflections in real time during classes, which mostly looks like acknowledgment—short comments that let them know I've read their reflections and support the direction they're going. Or, if they express concern about an element of their work in their writing, I'll focus on that element specifically during our next few classes. Alternatively, if they seem unsettled or somehow dissatisfied with their work, I might reach out for a short check-in meeting outside of class. Sometimes a mid-term change in trajectory is needed, based on new information like an injury, or in light of new discoveries that seem more compelling to focus on than what we'd originally laid out. I've had experiences in which I thought I understood where a student wanted to go based on our early term meeting, but the mid-term check-in offered clarity. Vice versa, these check-ins have also been useful for dancers to seek clarity from me on something we'd been working on that we weren't able to fully explore during class. Either way, their reflection leads us forward and supports the development of our work as collaborators.

End-Of-Term

At the end of each semester, as part of the ungrading paradigm I discuss in Chapter 6, I ask students to write what I call Learning Narratives, which emerge from the following prompts:

- Discuss your *process*: evaluate your engagement with course content by reflecting on how you handled all aspects of this course, including but not limited to how you managed feedback, how you made choices and self-directed, how you participated in the class community, how you approached your wellbeing, and how you navigated your inner monologue. Consider how your process worked this semester and note any adjustments you would like to make in the future.
- Discuss your *dancing*: evaluate how your work has changed from the beginning of the semester until now. Consider: did certain elements improve more than others, and why? Could you have gone further? What elements of your work are you proud of? Please describe.
- What have you learned about yourself—as a dancer, an artist, a collaborator, and a learner—in this course?
- What will you do with this knowledge in the future? Make a commitment to yourself and/or give yourself a charge for next semester or the road ahead.

These prompts expand on the ideas in the mid-term reflection. The first three questions ask students to reflect in depth on several facets of their work across the semester. The fourth question activates the reflection—it puts it to work as the beginning of a new reflection cycle. Its future-casting nature supports students in moving forward into whatever environment they'll encounter next, whether it's a break in which they'll study elsewhere, another semester with me or my colleagues, or the start of a career. While there is no required length for this reflection, and while I do not require students to address all of the ideas in each prompt, I am consistently moved by the depth of meaning and relevance students choose to discuss. While the point of these assignments is for students to reflect, they support my reflective process as well: showing me what students are capable of, how my teaching supported their work, or where I could perhaps have done things differently. These narratives remind me that student learning and knowledge is vast—it goes well beyond the limitations of learning outcomes, which seem trivial in light of the immeasurable and unpredictable learning that students experience. Most importantly, reading students' insights consistently reaffirms my choice to trust them as autonomous agents in their own work.

Student-Driven Reflective Practice

Beyond these three temporal periods of reflection that I offer, some students choose to make reflection a daily practice, keeping journals or diaries of their work. Others use informal, periodic chats with me as a means for regular reflection, sharing important moments of insight or realization they have along the way that I can then highlight in our work together. Sometimes these chats take place during my office hours or in a hallway between classes. If a student takes the time to tell me what struck them, formally or less so, I am thankful they chose to share it with me, I commit to supporting that work in class, and I request that they keep in communication with me as they continue their investigations. Since these reflections are the result of a student's self-generated achievements and interest, I use our time in class together to that end; redirecting my feedback to these ideas whenever possible in support of their goals.

Paulo Freire considers reflection part of praxis when paired with action and "directed at the structures to be transformed."[32] Establishing reflective practices for teachers and students alike, in this sense, builds a foundation for developing critical, praxis-based pedagogies that can actively reconfigure the oppressive, authoritarian aspects of ballet's pedagogical traditions in humanizing ways. Reflection asks those perhaps younger or less experienced to identify their perspectives, use their voices, and educate upward, while teachers work to listen rather than speak, to collaborate rather than dictate, and to tilt hierarchies. Choreographer Alonzo King suggests:

> if the goal of your work is to help change the world, it means that we have to first change ourselves. Anything that we recognize as harmful, whether it be systems, or individual behaviors, we have to examine our own lives to see if it exists within us.[‡33]

The exercise of reflection makes space for teachers to turn inward and develop value systems as pedagogues beyond the bounds of authoritarianism's limitations; a praxis-based approach that supports students and teachers, both, in their work toward becoming in ballet.

---

‡ I am grateful to Kate Mattingly for alerting me to this quote.

Notes

1 Portions of this chapter were initially published in my 2017 article: "Reflective Practice in the Ballet Class: Bringing Progressive Pedagogy to the Classical Tradition," *Journal of Dance Education* 17, no.3 (2017): 99–105.
2 Max Van Manen, *The Tact of Teaching: The Meaning of Pedagogical Thoughtfulness* (Albany: State University of New York Press, 1991), 98.
3 John Dewey, *How We Think* (Boston: D.C. Heath, 1910), 6. http://www.gutenberg.org/files/37423/37423-h/37423-h.htm
4 Doug Risner, "Motion and Marking in Reflective Practice: Artifacts, Autobiographical Narrative, and Sexuality," *Journal of Dance Education* 17, no.3 (2017): 92.
5 See John Dewey, *Experience and Education* (New York: Simon & Schuster, 1938); See also Michael Hines and Thomas Fallace, "Pedagogical Progressivism and Black Education: A Historiographical Review, 1880–1957," *Review of Educational Research* 93, no.3 (2023): 454–486.
6 Kevin M. Gannon, *Radical Hope: A Teaching Manifesto* (Morgantown: West Virginia University Press), 137.
7 See Chapter 1 for a discussion of ideals.
8 See Chapter 5 for a discussion of "rigor." Rory Foster, *Ballet Pedagogy: The Art of Teaching* (Gainesville: University Press of Florida, 2010), 92; John White, *Advanced Principles in Teaching Classical Ballet* (Gainesville: University Press of Florida, 2009), 135–137; Jessica Zeller, *Shapes of American Ballet: Teachers and Training before Balanchine* (New York: Oxford University Press, 2016), 91–120.
9 Max Van Manen, *The Tact of Teaching: The Meaning of Pedagogical Thoughtfulness* (Albany: State University of New York Press, 1991), 101–118.
10 Donald A. Schön, *The Reflective Practitioner: How Professionals Think in Action* (New York: Basic Books, 1983); Donald A. Schön, *Educating the Reflective Practitioner: Toward a New Design for Teaching and Learning in the Professions* (San Francisco: Jossey-Bass, 1987).
11 Doug Risner, "Motion and Marking in Reflective Practice: Artifacts, Autobiographical Narrative, and Sexuality," *Journal of Dance Education* 17, no.3 (2017): 93.
12 Max Van Manen, *The Tact of Teaching: The Meaning of Pedagogical Thoughtfulness* (Albany: State University of New York Press, 1991), 101–105.
13 Max Van Manen, *The Tact of Teaching: The Meaning of Pedagogical Thoughtfulness* (Albany: State University of New York Press, 1991), 103.
14 Alex Shevrin Venet, *Equity-Centered Trauma-Informed Education* (New York: Norton, 2021), 98.
15 bell hooks, *Teaching to Transgress: Education as the Practice of Freedom* (New York: Routledge, 1994), 17.
16 Max Van Manen, *The Tact of Teaching: The Meaning of Pedagogical Thoughtfulness* (Albany: State University of New York Press, 1991), 101.
17 Max Van Manen, *The Tact of Teaching: The Meaning of Pedagogical Thoughtfulness* (Albany: State University of New York Press, 1991), 101, 107.
18 John Dewey, *How We Think* (Boston: D.C. Heath, 1910), 9.
19 Max Van Manen, *The Tact of Teaching: The Meaning of Pedagogical Thoughtfulness* (Albany: State University of New York Press, 1991), 101.
20 Max Van Manen, *The Tact of Teaching: The Meaning of Pedagogical Thoughtfulness* (Albany: State University of New York Press, 1991), 101.
21 Max Van Manen, *The Tact of Teaching: The Meaning of Pedagogical Thoughtfulness* (Albany: State University of New York Press, 1991), 109.

22 Max Van Manen, *The Tact of Teaching: The Meaning of Pedagogical Thoughtfulness* (Albany: State University of New York Press, 1991), 101.
23 John Dewey, *How We Think* (Boston: D.C. Heath, 1910), 57.
24 Max Van Manen, *The Tact of Teaching: The Meaning of Pedagogical Thoughtfulness* (Albany: State University of New York Press, 1991), 116.
25 Troy Heffernan, "Sexism, Racism, Prejudice, and Bias: A Literature Review and Synthesis of Research Surrounding Student Evaluations of Courses and Teaching," *Assessment & Evaluation in Higher Education*, 47, no.1 (2022): 144–154.
26 See Chapter 4 for student perspectives on teaching.
27 Gretchen Ward Warren, *Classical Ballet Technique* (Tampa: University of South Florida Press, 1989), 81–82; Rory Foster, *Ballet Pedagogy: The Art of Teaching* (Gainesville: University Press of Florida, 2010), 113.
28 See Jessica Zeller, "Teaching through Time: Tracing Ballet's Pedagogical Lineage in the Work of Maggie Black," *Dance Chronicle* 32, no.1 (2009): 57–88; and Jessica Zeller, "Developing the American Ballet Dancer: The Pedagogical Lineage of Rochelle Zide-Booth," in *Dance on Its Own Terms: Histories and Methodologies*, eds. Karen Eliot and Melanie Bales (New York: Oxford University Press, 2013), 283–304.
29 Max Van Manen, *The Tact of Teaching: The Meaning of Pedagogical Thoughtfulness* (Albany: State University of New York Press, 1991), 225n48.
30 Carrie Gaiser Casey, "Being the Authority of Your Own Body: Pedagogy and Agency," *Ballet Geekout!* 2017.
31 bell hooks, *Teaching to Transgress: Education as the Practice of Freedom* (New York: Routledge, 1994), 21.
32 Paulo Freire, *Pedagogy of the Oppressed* (New York: Herder and Herder, 1970), 126.
33 Kate Mattingly and Iyun Ashani Harrison, eds., *Antiracism in Ballet Teaching* (Abingdon: Routledge, 2024), 181.

Conclusion
Reflections on Becoming

It is well within the profound imagination and creativity of those in power across the ballet field to envision pedagogies that not only do not cause harm but actively support growth and becoming. It is likewise ethically necessary and entirely possible to teach ballet in a way that considers the perspectives of the people who participate in it. Approaching the development of ballet pedagogies from these perspectives is not abandoning tradition as purists might suggest, but precisely the opposite: it is an honoring of ballet and its histories by supporting its contemporary relevance, meaning, and development, as well as its ethical, equitable futures. Humanizing pedagogies, in this sense, can allow ballet to have a becoming of its own. In this concluding chapter, I offer a distilled series of takeaways based on my ongoing experience with humanizing pedagogies: what I've learned and how my work is changing as I shift my approach.

Ballet pedagogies do not develop in a vacuum. Much of the joy and fulfillment I experience as a ballet teacher comes from the people who enrich my daily work of teaching; they challenge my thinking and offer new ways to consider that which I think I know. Being in dialogue with colleagues broadens my context as I draw from and am inspired by their expertise, while being in dialogue with students reminds me why I teach ballet. I have become fascinated by how and why different people embody and think about ballet differently, and my resulting process of learning about people has been foundational to my own becoming, which—like humanizing pedagogies—is always in process. While this work has happened for me largely inside the walls of higher education, teachers in any ballet context can pursue relevant pedagogical dialogues. Curiosity, or the simple act of asking people about their experiences with ballet pedagogies, can begin a whole new line of thinking—a whole new level of understanding.

These interactions allow me to locate myself in the larger scheme of ballet pedagogies; to contextualize and validate the knowledge I hold. While this can be satisfying, it also reminds me that I'm not done, I haven't arrived, and there's further to go. Elizabeth Ellsworth points to the reality that there is a fundamentally "unknowable" nature to pedagogy, in that among class participants there are "multiple knowledges" that are each, themselves, "contradictory, partial, and irreducible."[1] After decades of teaching, finding myself among these unknowns is refreshing, as it frees me from the most unrealistic and pressure-filled expectation of ballet teachers: omniscience. It situates me as one of many people in the studio who knows and who sees, and it identifies me as one of many who could contribute meaningfully to someone's study of ballet. Teaching in this context has begun to feel less encumbered and fraught, and more about developing generative processes of collaborative inquiry.

As I've spent time exploring this approach, I've developed a greater sense of excitement—and lessening fear—around these unknown elements; a sense of open anticipation every time I walk into the studio. What will I learn today, about ballet, or students, or myself? What knowledges will appear? What will we discover and create, together? This shift has altered my perspective about my role and responsibilities. It makes my ballet pedagogy more optimistic: I find myself trusting that something meaningful will happen each time I walk into a studio. I find myself trusting that the students will show me how to begin each day, which deepens my interest in how they as people might intersect with ballet's unlimited possibilities from one day to the next. I also find myself trusting myself more and more; to be open and responsive to what I can't plan for and what I don't know.

The more I work with humanizing approaches, the more I see how many students have been conditioned by the hegemonic notion that, as students, they somehow deserve less esteem than other classifications of people. As I've learned to extend "unconditional positive regard" to students in a non-transactional way, to acknowledge them as whole people, and to assume their best intentions, I often notice their surprise or uncertainty at first, as they may be unfamiliar with what it means to interact with an authority figure who both believes them and believes in them.[2] I also notice students extending me a similar kind of regard organically: if I ask students how they're doing during a particularly dense mid-semester week, for example, someone will typically chime in and ask how I'm doing too. This may seem like a basic, care-forward exchange between people, and that's the point. Approaching the work from this foundation of personal consideration simplifies our interactions and facilitates the study of ballet from a humanizing perspective.

Structures are everywhere in ballet. I am reminded in this work that structures are not antithetical to humanizing pedagogies but are deeply compatible with the call to develop them—this work is not without form or clear design. An acknowledgment of humanity in ballet does not equate to a free-for-all or an abandonment of histories, rules, or depth of study; rather it enables the parameters of the work to account for who we are, in our contexts. The structures and formats I teach with are relatively traditional, and at the same time flexible and responsive. Ballet's frameworks, and I, breathe more easily during ballet classes now: I adjust the structures when the needs or objectives of the people in the room—including my own—call for it.

My skills have developed because I talk with and hear from students more often. Aside from feeling gratified to know more about who I'm working with each day, my eye has become sharper because I can consider the whole person I'm seeing and can better grasp why or how something is or isn't happening in their work. In part, asking them to help me understand what they're experiencing and what they're trying to do allows me to respond to their needs directly, so my suggestions have become more applicable. The range of information I have to draw from is broader, as I've been challenged to ask questions and seek pedagogical support for specific anatomical, artistic, or technical situations as they arise. I've also become a better facilitator of learning through an experimental approach that welcomes failure; it is as instructive for me as it is for the students. Extending an invitation to this process through my actions rather than my words has been important. I find that demonstrating and embodying my interest and receptivity is a more genuine way of inviting student perspectives than the current pedagogical language trend of "I invite you to...," which starts to feel diminished or distorted in meaning after enough repetitions.

I've learned through this work that I both benefit from and reflect the power and ethos of the systems I operate within, and that this demands my work to change oppressive systems. The privilege of job security allows me to push upward against systemic issues that dehumanize—against punitive or exclusionary policies, for example—without too much fear of retribution. I try to use that privilege whenever possible. I can also use that power locally, by reflecting on my work and my position, to make changes that will benefit the people around me. If I am honest with myself about my own perceptions and behaviors, the change I can make in myself and my ballet pedagogy can be as immediate as I want it to be. I have learned that the more I practice change, the better I get at changing.

Leveraging my tenured privilege to deviate from carceral pedagogies required by the program or institution—grades, absence penalties, and otherwise punitive policies—has resulted in other authoritarian practices that lingered in my work becoming obvious and irrelevant. I've stopped grading, for example, so I've been able to release the implication that growth should be linear—that students should theoretically be able to improve from C to B to A inside an arbitrary timeframe of 15 weeks, as though the reality of learning doesn't also include plateaus and backtracking and failure as necessary and useful. I've stopped policing students who don't follow institutional policies to the letter and started conversations with them about themselves, as people, from a simple place of care. I've stopped concerning myself with whether students are being and doing according to idealized field-wide expectations, or if they're dancing in accordance with my stylistic and technical preferences. I stop assuming I know why they're there, or why they're not. I've started asking what they want for themselves, and I feel freer to extend my support for the work they want to do. I've begun to see that most students' love for ballet will appear more readily when the study aligns with their goals, and most will happily nerd out with me about it if I show them that I love it too. We begin to share ballet, then. It becomes our common ground.

Because I turned over the power of the grade to the students, my responsibility changed. I had to find ways to compel the work without the carrot of a grade—to make it meaningful, relevant, and accessible, and to figure out what would be intrinsically motivating, even joyous, for all of us. My new role is much more varied and exciting: I can be a novice as I try to understand and learn about each new student I work with, and I can be a sounding board and thought partner for those I've known a bit longer. The opportunity to learn new things alongside students feels decadent; and it's balanced by the opportunity to support students' work with my existing knowledge.

When I first started teaching, I'd hear my teachers coming out in my work. I'd use their phrases, give their exercises, and look through my approximation of their eyes. As I continued, I saw what other teachers were doing and folded some of their perspectives into my work as well. By looking deeply and extracting my own perspectives from this tangle of voices as part of the humanizing process, I've begun to hone and validate my own pedagogy as consistent with my lived experience and identities. Having the space to consider how my relationship to ballet shapes my pedagogical values has been key to my process of becoming—it is a privilege. As a result, I have begun explicitly validating students' perspectives and relationships to ballet, as I seek to communicate the value of identifying one's own voice in the context of many voices.

Along those lines, finding joy in ballet class is a value I learned from Rochelle Zide-Booth, which humanizing work helps me enact. Dancers dance most often because they love it, and there are few things more thrilling than a class where that joy has space to be felt and relished. The physical exhilaration of grand allegro, the sumptuous reach of the balancé, or the preposterous energy that's generated when chaîné turns are just the tiniest bit too fast are the euphoric moments rooted in the very thing of ballet itself. I like to think that students can still take ballet seriously even when we take time to appreciate those moments of delight—to linger in and chase after the moments that feel physically delicious. Humor has become a big part of my communications, to this end. As a highly effective intrinsic motivator when not used at anyone's expense, humor can support finding enjoyment in the work. I've learned to acknowledge the ridiculous things that ballet asks people to do and to normalize the sometimes equally ridiculous ways it can feel to try those things for the first or fiftieth time, because sometimes pointing out the silliness in learning ballet can create space for ease and levity to complement the gravitas of the work. Most importantly, perhaps, the joy of dancing offers an essential and exciting avenue for artistic expression. I believe in students' capacities to hold these multitudes, and I believe earnest laughter in a ballet class is a most special sound.

The counterpoint here is accepting that failures are an important part of my process. Some of my desired changes have taken years to make in spite of my want to adjust my approach more immediately. I find I can't reach every single student; there seem always to be some students who I communicate more easily with and others who I struggle to understand or support. Despite my best intentions, I've made mistakes. I've found myself apologizing to students for behaving thoughtlessly: for saying the wrong thing, in the wrong way, at the wrong time; for causing hurt or embarrassment. These instances always prompt deep reflection, and I learn for the next time. I'm certain I'll continue bumping into my own developing understanding about people and identities, and I'll keep working to identify and address my biases. In this light, I try to approach my own failures as I encourage the students to—with humility, an honest apology, and action to make things right—before returning to try again.

Working toward a humanizing approach with and for students has enabled and propelled my own self-actualization. The approaches I describe throughout this book have supported me in this process; they have resulted in a remarkable feeling of simplicity, and of doing less more effectively. I plan a ballet class as a flexible framework, and I try my best to treat people well. The world won't end if we don't get to the medium allegro or the grand pirouette one day, but it might if the people in the room are chronically disempowered to create the circumstances they need to be whole. By streamlining my priorities in this way, I have also made space for myself, as a person in the world who teaches ballet, among other things. Embracing my own growth while trying to support students in doing the same has humanized my pedagogy nearly as much as all that exists in these pages.

One of humanizing ballet pedagogy's most thrilling features is its heterogeneity: the very fact that it is driven by and aims to support a wide range of people's experiences, bodies, identities, and knowledges. Its facility for change—its ability to be responsive, and to adapt to people and contexts—is an exhilarating core element of the work. Ballet's subjective nature, which embraces teachers' and dancers' wonderfully idiosyncratic qualities, is what keeps its traditions relevant and meaningful over time, and this approach to pedagogy actively values those subjectivities. At heart, then, humanizing ballet pedagogies support and honor the people who embody and enliven ballet's evolving traditions—those who will shepherd ballet pedagogies into the future.

Notes

1 Elizabeth Ellsworth, "Why Doesn't This Feel Empowering? Working Through the Repressive Myths of Critical Pedgaogy," *Harvard Educational Review* 59, no.3 (August 1989): 318–321.
2 Alex Shevrin Venet, *Equity-Centered Trauma-Informed Education* (New York: Norton, 2021), 98.

Selected Bibliography

Ahmed, Sara N. "Resignation Is a Feminist Issue." *feministkilljoys.com*. August 27, 2016. https://feministkilljoys.com/2016/08/27/resignation-is-a-feminist-issue/comment-page-1/.
Akinleye, Adesola, ed. *(Re:) Claiming Ballet*. Chicago: Intellect, 2021.
Akinleye, Adesola. "Ballet, from Property to Art." In *(Re:) Claiming Ballet*, edited by Adesola Akinleye, 10–28. Chicago: Intellect, 2021.
Alterowitz, Gretchen. "Toward a Feminist Ballet Pedagogy: Teaching Strategies for Ballet Technique Classes in the Twenty-first Century." *Journal of Dance Education* 14, no.1 (2014): 8–17. https://doi.org/10.1080/15290824.2013.824579
Bailey, Moya. *Misogynoir Transformed: Black Women's Digital Resistance*. New York: New York University Press, 2021.
Bali, Maha, and Mia Zamora. "The Equity-Care Matrix: Theory and Practice." *Italian Journal of Educational Technology* 30, no.1 (2022): 92–115. https://doi.org/10.17471/2499-4324/1241
Bandura, Albert. "Toward a Psychology of Human Agency." *Perspectives on Psychological Science* 1, no.2 (2006): 164–180.
Beckford, Keesha. "Dive In." In *Antiracism in Ballet Teaching*, edited by Kate Mattingly and Iyun Ashani Harrison, 129–134. Abingdon: Routledge, 2024.
Berg, Tanya. "Ballet as Somatic Practice: A Case Study Exploring the Integration of Somatic Practices in Ballet Pedagogy. *Journal of Dance Education* 17, no.4 (2017): 147–157. https://doi.org/10.1080/15290824.2017.1310382
Biesta, Gert, and Michael Tedder. "Agency and Learning in the Lifecourse: Towards an Ecological Perspective." *Studies in the Education of Adults* 39, no.2 (Autumn 2007): 132–148.
Blum, Susan D. ed. *Ungrading: Why Rating Students Undermines Learning*. Morgantown: West Virginia University Press, 2020.
Bress, Sophie. "Dancing with ADHD: The Challenges, Surprise Benefits and Tools to Cope." *Pointe Magazine*. November 14, 2022. https://pointemagazine.com/dancing-with-adhd/.
brown, adrienne maree. *Emergent Strategy: Shaping Change, Changing Worlds*. Chico, CA: AK Press, 2017.
Brown, Ann Kipling. "Provoking Change: Dance Pedagogy and Curriculum Design." In *The Oxford Handbook of Dance and Wellbeing*, edited by Vicky Karkou, Sue Oliver, and Sophia Lycouris, 399–414. New York: Oxford University Press, 2017.

Brown, Nyama McCarthy. *Dance Pedagogy for a Diverse World: Culturally Relevant Teaching in Theory, Research and Practice.* Jefferson, NC: McFarland, 2022.

Brown, Nyama McCarthy. "Navigating Anti-racism in an Anti-black Landscape: A Dance Educator's Reflection." *International Journal of Education & the Arts* 23, no.1 (2022). https://doi.org/10.26209/ijea23n1.

Buckroyd, Julia. *The Student Dancer: Emotional Aspects of the Teaching and Learning of Dance.* London: Dance Books, 2000.

Butler, Ruth. "Task-Involving and Ego-Involving Properties of Evaluation: Effects of Different Feedback Conditions on Motivational Perceptions, Interest, and Performance." *Journal of Educational Psychology* 79, no.4 (1987): 474–482.

Butler, Ruth. "Enhancing and Undermining Intrinsic Motivation: The Effects of Task-Involving and Ego-Involving Evaluation on Interest and Performance." *British Journal of Educational Psychology* 58 (1988): 1–14.

Casey, Carrie Gaiser. "Being the Authority of Your Own Body: Pedagogy and Agency." *Ballet Geekout!* 2017.

Chaleff, Rebecca, Michelle LaVigne, and Kate Mattingly, "Op-Ed: What's Possible in Writing about Ballet?" *Dance Magazine.* May 19, 2023. https://www.dancemagazine.com/op-ed-writing-about-ballet/.

Chemaly, Soraya. "All Teachers Should Be Trained to Overcome Their Hidden Biases." *Time.* February 12, 2015. https://time.com/3705454/teachers-biases-girls-education/.

Costa, Karen. "Systems Aren't Scary." October 31, 2022. https://karenraycosta.medium.com/systems-arent-scary-e55d8ac63bc7

Crow, Susan, and Jennifer Jackson, "Balancing the Books," *Dance Theatre Journal* 14–15 (1998/2000): 36–40.

Davis, Crystal U. *Dance and Belonging: Implicit Bias and Inclusion in Dance Education.* Jefferson, NC: McFarland, 2022.

De Mille, Agnes. *To a Young Dancer: A Handbook for Dance Students, Parents, and Teachers.* New York: Little, Brown, 1962.

De Saa, Ramona. "Distinctive Characteristics of the Cuban National Ballet School Curriculum and its Cultural Traits." Presented at the CORPS de Ballet International annual conference, Sarasota, FL, June 2016.

Dederer, Claire. *Monsters: A Fan's Dilemma.* New York: Knopf, 2023.

Dewey, John. *How We Think.* Boston: D.C. Heath, 1910. https://www.gutenberg.org/files/37423/37423-h/37423-h.htm

Dewey, John. *Experience and Education.* New York: Simon & Schuster, 1938.

Ellsworth, Elizabeth. "Why Doesn't This Feel Empowering? Working Through the Repressive Myths of Critical Pedgaogy." *Harvard Educational Review* 59, no. 3 (August 1989): 297–324. https://doi.org/10.17763/haer.59.3.058342114k266250

Eyler, Joshua R. *How Humans Learn: The Science and Stories behind Effective College Teaching.* Morgantown: West Virginia University Press, 2018.

Eyler, Joshua R. *Failing Our Future: How Grades Harm Students, and What We Can Do about It.* Baltimore, MD: Johns Hopkins University Press, 2024.

Foster, Rory. *Ballet Pedagogy: The Art of Teaching.* Gainesville: University Press of Florida, 2010.

Freire, Paulo. *Pedagogy of the Oppressed.* New York: Herder and Herder, 1970.

Gannon, Kevin M. *Radical Hope: A Teaching Manifesto*. Morgantown: West Virginia University Press.

Giroux, Henry A. *On Critical Pedagogy*. 2nd ed. London: Bloomsbury, 2020.

Gottschild, Brenda Dixon. *The Black Dancing Body: A Geography from Coon to Cool*. New York: Palgrave Macmillan, 2003.

Gottschild, Brenda Dixon. "Ballet beyond Boundaries: A Personal History." In *(Re:) Claiming Ballet*, edited by Adesola Akinleye, 99–115. Chicago: Intellect, 2021.

Hanna, Thomas. *Bodies in Revolt: A Primer in Somatic Thinking*. New York: Holt, Rinehart and Winston, 1970.

Heffernan, Troy. "Sexism, Racism, Prejudice, and Bias: A Literature Review and Synthesis of Research Surrounding Student Evaluations of Courses and Teaching." *Assessment & Evaluation in Higher Education* 47, no.1 (2022): 144–154. https://doi.org/10.1080/02602938.2021.1888075

Hines, Michael, and Thomas Fallace. "Pedagogical Progressivism and Black Education: A Historiographical Review, 1880–1957." *Review of Educational Research* 93, no.3 (2023): 457–463. https://doi.org/10.3102/00346543221105549

hooks, bell. *Teaching to Transgress: Education as the Practice of Freedom*. New York: Routledge, 1994.

hooks, bell. *All About Love: New Visions*. New York: Harper, 2000.

hooks, bell. *Teaching Critical Thinking: Practical Wisdom*. New York: Routledge, 2010.

Howard, Theresa Ruth. "Op-Ed: Is Ballet 'Brown-Bagging' It?" *Dance Magazine*. April 2, 2017. https://www.dancemagazine.com/is-ballet-brown-bagging-it/.

Howard, Theresa Ruth. "The State of the Profession." Panel discussion, CORPS de Ballet International annual conference, Online, June 2023.

Inoue, Asao B. *Labor-Based Grading Contracts: Building Equity and Inclusion in the Compassionate Writing Classroom*. Fort Collins, CO: The WAC Clearinghouse; Boulder, CO: University Press of Colorado, 2019.

Ishangi, Kehinde. "Dancing Across Historically Racist Borders." In *(Re:) Claiming Ballet*, edited by Adesola Akinleye, 129–145. Chicago: Intellect, 2021.

Isiguen, Alana. "Making Space: Inclusive and Equitable Teaching Practices for Ballet in Higher Education." In *Antiracism in Ballet Teaching*, edited by Kate Mattingly and Iyun Ashani Harrison, 78–84. Abingdon: Routledge, 2024.

Jackson, Jehbreal M. "Ballet as Artistic and Scientific Inquiry: Incorporating Ballet's Broader History in a Syllabus and in the Studio." Presented at the MOBBallet Symposium/M.I.A. Scholar's Course, Miami, FL and Online, August 2022.

Jackson, Jennifer. "My Dance and the Ideal Body: Looking at Ballet Practice from the Inside Out." *Research in Dance Education* 6, no.1/2 (April/December 2005): 25–40. https://doi.org/10.1080/14617890500373089

Jackson, Naomi. *Dance and Ethics: Moving Towards a More Humane Dance Culture*. Bristol: Intellect, 2022.

Kendi, Ibram X. *How to Be an Antiracist*. New York: One World, 2019.

Kerr, Maurya. "Dismantling Anti-blackness in Ballet: Pedagogies of Freedom." In *Antiracism in Ballet Teaching*, edited by Kate Mattingly and Iyun Ashani Harrison, 85–94. Abingdon: Routledge, 2024.

Kohn, Alfie. *Punished by Rewards: The Trouble with Gold Stars, Incentive Plans, A's, Praise, and Other Bribes*. Boston: Houghton Mifflin, 1993.

Kohn, Alfie. "Speaking My Mind: The Trouble with Rubrics." *The English Journal* 95, no.4 (March 2006): 12–15.

Kohn, Alfie. "The Case Against Grades." *Educational Leadership* 69, no.3 (November 2011): 28–33.

Kohn, Alfie. "The Cult of Rigor and the Loss of Joy." In *Feel-Bad Education: And Other Contrarian Essays on Children and Schooling*, 147–151. Boston: Beacon Press, 2011.

Ladson-Billings, Gloria. *Culturally Relevant Pedagogy: Asking a Different Question*. New York: Teachers College Press, 2021.

Ladson-Billings, Gloria, and William F. Tate IV. "Toward a Critical Race Theory of Education." *Teachers College Record* 97, no.1 (Fall 1995): 47–68.

Lakes, Robin. "The Messages behind the Methods: The Authoritarian Pedagogical Legacy in Western Concert Dance Technique Training and Rehearsals." *Arts Education Policy Review* 106, no.5 (May/June 2005): 3–18. https://dx.doi.org/10.3200/AEPR.106.5.3-20

Manne, Kate. *Down Girl: The Logic of Misogyny*. New York: Oxford University Press, 2018.

Mattingly, Kate, Keesha Beckford, Zena Bibler, Paige Cunningham, Iyun Ashani Harrison and Jehbreal Muhammad Jackson, "Ballet Pedagogy and a 'Hard Re-Set': Perspectives on Equitable and Inclusive Teaching Practices," *Dance Chronicle* 46, no.1 (2023): 40–65. https://doi.org/10.1080/01472526.2022.2156747

Mattingly, Kate, and Iyun Ashani Harrison, eds. *Antiracism in Ballet Teaching*. Abingdon: Routledge, 2024.

Mattingly, Kate, and Kristin Marrs. "Searching for the Yet Unknown: Writing and Dancing as Incantatory Practices." *Journal of University Teaching & Learning Practice* 18, no.7 (2021): 195–213.

McCloud, Laila I. "Keeping Receipts: Thoughts on Ungrading from a Black Woman Professor." *Zeal: A Journal for the Liberal Arts* 1, no.2 (2023): 101–105.

McLeod, Melvin. "There's No Place to Go but Up: bell hooks and Maya Angelou in Conversation." *Lion's Roar*. January 1, 1998. https://www.lionsroar.com/theres-no-place-to-go-but-up/.

McPherson, Elizabeth, Doug Risner, and Karen Schupp. "Why Grade Inflation and Teacher Dispositions Don't Mix." In *Ethical Dilemmas in Dance Educations: Case Studies on Humanizing Dance Pedagogy*, edited by Doug Risner and Karen Schupp, 163–175. Jefferson, NC: McFarland, 2020.

Merleau-Ponty, Maurice. *Phenomenology of Perception*. Translated by Colin Smith. New York: The Humanities Press, 1962.

Moola, Fiona, and Alixandra Krahn. "A Dance with Many Secrets: The Experience of Emotional Harm from the Perspective of Past Professional Female Ballet Dancers in Canada." *Journal of Aggression, Maltreatment, and Trauma* 27, no.3 (2018): 256–274.

Morris, Merry Lynn. "Re-thinking Ballet Pedagogy: Approaching a Historiography of Fifth Position." *Research in Dance Education* 16, no.3 (2015): 245–258. https://doi.org/10.1080/14647893.2015.1036019

Murray, Melonie B. "The Uneasy, Unexplored, and Under-examined Existence of Ballet in American Higher Education." *Research in Dance Education* (2021). https://doi.org/10.1080/14647893.2021.1960300

Nordin-Bates, Sanna. "Ballet: Dancing Under the Weight of Preconceived Ideas?" In *Ballet, Why and How? On the Role of Classical Ballet in Dance Education*, edited by A. Alten, 53–57. Amsterdam: ArtEZ Press, 2014.

Nordin-Bates, Sanna M. "Striving for Perfection or for Creativity? A Dancer's Dilemma." *Journal of Dance Education* 20, no.1 (2020): 23–34. https://doi.org/10.1080/15290824.2018.1546050

Nordin-Bates, Sanna. "S2 E11: The One About Dancer Autonomy." Interview with Sarah Scheiwer. *Dance; Better*. Podcast audio. December 16, 2021. https://podcasts.apple.com/us/podcast/s2e11-the-one-about-dancer-autonomy/id1535077862?i=1000545241351.

Nordin-Bates, Sanna M., and Gareth Jowett. "Relationships Between Perfectionism, Stress, and Basic Need Support Provision in Dance Teachers and Aesthetic Sport Coaches." *Journal of Dance Medicine and Science* 26, no.1 (2001): 26–34. https://doi.org/10.12678/1089-313X.031522d

Okun, Tema. "Sense of Urgency." *White Supremacy Culture*. August 2023. https://www.whitesupremacyculture.info/urgency.html.

Palmer, Parker J. *The Courage to Teach: Exploring the Inner Landscape of a Teacher's Life*. San Francisco, CA: Jossey-Bass, 1998.

Papaefstathiou, Maria, Daniel Rhind, and Celia Brackenridge. "Child Protection in Ballet: Experiences and Views of Teachers, Administrators, and Ballet Students." *Child Abuse Review* 22 (2013): 127–141. https://doi.org/10.1002/car.2228

Paskevska, Anna. *Both Sides of the Mirror: The Science and Art of Ballet*. New York: Dance Horizons, 1981.

Paskevska, Anna. *Ballet Beyond Tradition*. New York: Routledge, 2005.

Pickard, Angela. "Ballet Body Belief: Perceptions of an Ideal Ballet Body from Young Ballet Dancers." *Research in Dance Education* 14, no.1 (2013): 3–19. https://doi.org/10.1080/14647893.2012.712106.

Pittman, Chavella, and Thomas J. Tobin. "Academe Has a Lot to Learn about How Inclusive Teaching Affects Instructors." *Chronicle of Higher Education*. February 7, 2022. https://www.chronicle.com/article/academe-has-a-lot-to-learn-about-how-inclusive-teaching-affects-instructors.

Postman, Neil, and Charles Weingartner. *Teaching as a Subversive Activity*. New York: Delacorte Press, 1969.

Price, Devon. *Laziness Does Not Exist*. New York: Atria, 2021.

Pyle, Katy, and Michael J. Morris. "Radically Re-Imagining the Ballet Canon: A Conversation with Katy Pyle, Founder and Artistic Director of Ballez." Presentation at the CORPS de Ballet International annual conference, Richmond, VA, June 2022.

Risner, Doug. "Motion and Marking in Reflective Practice: Artifacts, Autobiographical Narrative, and Sexuality." *Journal of Dance Education* 17, no.3 (2017): 91–98. https://doi.org/10.1080/15290824.2017.1286880

Risner, Doug, and Karen Schupp, eds. *Ethical Dilemmas in Dance Educations: Case Studies on Humanizing Dance Pedagogy*. Jefferson, NC: McFarland, 2020.

Ritenburg, Heather Margaret. "Frozen Landscapes: A Foucauldian Genealogy of the Ideal Ballet Dancer's Body." *Research in Dance Education* 11, no.1 (2010): 71–85. https://doi.org/10.1080/14647891003671775.

Romita, Nancy, and Allegra Romita. "Equity-Informed Alignment Cueing for External Rotation and Pelvic Stability in the Ballet Aesthetic through Functional

Awareness." Presented at the CORPS de Ballet International annual conference, Online, June 2024.

Ross, Janice. *Moving Lessons: Margaret H'Doubler and the Beginning of Dance in American Education.* Madison: University of Wisconsin Press, 2000.

Ryan, Richard M. and Edward L. Deci. "Self-Determination Theory and the Facilitation of Intrinsic Motivation, Social Development, and Well-Being." *American Psychologist* 55, no.1 (January 2000): 68–78.

Salosaari, Paula. "Multiple Embodiment in Classical Ballet." In *Not Just Any Body: Advancing Health, Well-being and Excellence in Dance and Dancers,* edited by R. Alston, K. Kain, D. Jowitt, J. Kylián and R. Philp, 58. Ontario, Canada: The Ginger Press, 2001.

Schön, Donald A. *The Reflective Practitioner: How Professionals Think in Action.* New York: Basic Books, 1983.

Schön, Donald A. *Educating the Reflective Practitioner: Toward a New Design for Teaching and Learning in the Professions.* San Francisco, CA: Jossey-Bass, 1987.

Shapiro, Sherry B. *Pedagogy and the Politics of the Body: A Critical Praxis.* London: Routledge, 1999.

Shook, Karel. *Elements of Classical Ballet Technique as Practiced in the School of the Dance Theatre of Harlem.* New York: Dance Horizons, 1977.

Stinson, Susan W., Donald Blumenfield-Jones, and Jan van Dyke, "Voices of Young Women Dance Students: An Interpretive Study of Meaning in Dance," *Dance Research Journal* 22, no.2 (Autumn 1990): 13–22.

Stock, Nick. "Episode 101: Imagining Education Outside Capitalism." Interview with Chris McNutt. *The Human Restoration Project Podcast.* Podcast audio. December 27, 2021. https://shows.acast.com/5d546c26ade326bd3b4b47fc/61c8bd1a1c6a7900119b9e67.

Stommel, Jesse. "How to Ungrade." In *Ungrading: Why Rating Students Undermines Learning,* edited by Susan D. Blum, 25–41. Morgantown: West Virginia University Press, 2020.

Stommel, Jesse. *Undoing the Grade: Why We Grade, and How to Stop.* Denver: Hybrid Pedagogy, 2023.

Supiano, Beckie. "The Redefinition of Rigor." *Chronicle of Higher Education.* March 30, 2022. https://www.chronicle.com/article/the-redefinition-of-rigor.

Supiano, Beckie. "The Unintended Consequences of 'Ungrading.'" *Chronicle of Higher Education.* April 29, 2022. https://www.chronicle.com/article/the-unintended-consequences-of-ungrading.

Thorne, Casey L. "Practicing Choice: Progressive Pedagogy in Contemporary Ballet Training." Doctoral dissertation, Mills College, 2018.

Valencia, Richard R. *Dismantling Contemporary Deficit Thinking: Educational Thought and Practice.* New York: Routledge, 2010.

Van der Kolk, Bessel A. *The Body Keeps the Score: Brain, Mind, and Body in the Healing of Trauma.* New York: Penguin Books, 2014.

Van Manen, Max. *The Tact of Teaching: The Meaning of Pedagogical Thoughtfulness.* Albany: State University of New York Press, 1991.

Venet, Alex Shevrin. *Equity-Centered, Trauma-Informed Education.* New York: Norton, 2021.

Warner, John. *Why They Can't Write: Killing the Five-Paragraph Essay and Other Necessities.* Baltimore, MD: Johns Hopkins University Press, 2018.

Warren, Gretchen Ward. *Classical Ballet Technique*. Tampa: University of South Florida Press, 1989.

White, John. *Teaching Classical Ballet*. Gainesville: University Press of Florida, 1996.

White, John. *Advanced Principles in Teaching Classical Ballet*. Gainesville: University Press of Florida, 2009.

Wootten, Claire. "Navigating Liminal Space in the Feminist Ballet Class." *Congress on Research in Dance Proceedings* 41 (Leicester, UK: 2009): 122–129.

Zeller, Jessica. "Teaching through Time: Tracing Ballet's Pedagogical Lineage in the Work of Maggie Black." *Dance Chronicle* 32, no.1 (2009): 57–88. https://doi.org/10.1080/01472520802690283

Zeller, Jessica. "Developing the American Ballet Dancer: The Pedagogical Lineage of Rochelle Zide-Booth." In *Dance on its Own Terms: Histories and Methodologies*, edited by Karen Eliot and Melanie Bales, 283–304. New York: Oxford University Press, 2013. https://doi.org/10.1093/acprof:oso/9780199939985.001.0001

Zeller, Jessica. *Shapes of American Ballet: Teachers and Training before Balanchine*. New York: Oxford University Press, 2016.

Zeller, Jessica. "Reflective Practice in the Ballet Class: Bringing Progressive Pedagogy to the Classical Tradition." *Journal of Dance Education* 17, no.3 (2017): 99–105. https://doi.org/10.1080/15290824.2017.1326052

Zeller, Jessica. "On Dance Pedagogy and Embodiment." *Conversations Across the Field of Dance Studies* 38 (Society of Dance History Scholars, 2017): 17–20.

Zeller, Jessica. "Pedagogy as Protest: Reimagining the Center," In *Hybrid Teaching: Pedagogy, People, and Politics*, edited by Chris Friend, 117–120. Washington, D.C.: Hybrid Pedagogy, Inc., 2021.

Zeller, Jessica. "The Meanings of Grades." In *Crowdsourcing Ungrading*, edited by David Buck. May 25, 2023. https://pressbooks.howardcc.edu/ungrading/chapter/the-meaning-of-grades/.

Index

abuses, in ballet 34, 36
adrienne maree brown 35, 57
agency 19, 106, 119–124, 126, 129, 132, 159, 161; defined 120–121
Ahmed, Sara N. 145
Akinleye, Adesola 32, 33
Albertieri, Luigi 19
Aldrich, Elizabeth 17
Alonso, Alicia 17
American Ballet Theatre 18, 54; National Training Curriculum 18
American Capitalism 8
Angyal, Chloe 30, 61
antiracist pedagogies 6, 30, 44
Ashton, Frederick 58
authoritarian approaches 27, 28, 105
authoritarian ballet environments 56, 126
authoritarian pedagogies 33, 36, 42, 75, 86, 131, 158
authoritarian practices 123, 178
autonomy 6, 9, 93, 106, 107, 119–125, 127, 129–132; defined 120–121

Balanchine, George 17
Bali, Maha 145
ballet: abuses in 34, 36; academies 57, 136; educators 5, 29, 58, 62, 120, 132, 143; environments 82, 88, 120, 122, 158; forms 2, 15, 42, 50, 59; ideals 9, 16, 25, 26, 34, 93, 94, 140; institutions 86, 124; pedagogues 23, 44, 57, 81, 96; schools 4, 7, 10, 33, 95, 136; teachers 1, 3–5, 32, 61, 63, 96, 98, 100, 102, 104, 119, 120, 176, 177; technique 16, 17, 30, 61, 95, 114, 123

ballet classes 9, 28, 50, 51, 53, 54, 70, 72, 75, 79, 84, 93, 97–104, 107, 108, 110–112, 122, 127, 129, 131, 135, 161–163, 165, 170, 171; ungrading in 146–149
BalletMet 8
ballet pedagogies 2, 4, 5, 9–10, 17, 18, 42, 46–55, 88, 98, 100, 114, 176, 178; attending to individuals 111–112; autonomy and agency 106–107; class material 107–108; communication 108–111; community, ballet class 104–106; compassion 114–115; embodied philosophies 46–49; envisioning 100–115; interpreting 93–100; teacher's qualities 112–113; teacher-student relationship 101–104; teaching, critical futures 52–54; teaching beyond body 49–52; *see also individual entries*
Ballet Russe de Monte Carlo 7
Bandura, Albert 120, 121
Beckford, Keesha 137
becoming 2–6, 70, 75, 173, 176–179, 181
bias: and power 79–80; *see also individual entries*
Bibler, Zena 137
Biesta, Gert 120, 121
Black, Maggie 7, 61, 74, 149, 167
Blasis, Carlo 16, 19, 21
Blum, Susan D. 137, 138
bodily autonomy 106, 128, 129, 162
Bourdieu 139
Brigham, Carl C. 138
Brown, Ann Kipling 54
Brown, Nyama McCarthy 73, 142

Index

Buckroyd, Julia 20
Butler, Ruth 140

Cecchetti Method 18
Chaleff, Rebecca 27
"Child Protection in Ballet" (Papaefstathiou) 27
classical ballet 24, 30
Classical Ballet Technique (Warren) 23
class material 17, 28, 44, 88, 96, 101, 107
collaborative approach 122
collaborative choreographic processes 143
collaborative working environment 76
collaborative working relationships 56
complexity, relishing 88–89
contemporary American culture 8
"contractual equity" (Bali and Zamora) 145
critical co-investigators 3
critical pedagogy 2–4, 6, 10, 36, 43, 54, 62, 138, 148
Crow, Susan 143
Cuban National Ballet School 17
Cunningham, Paige 137
Cutri, Dr. Nick 30

Dabney, Stephanie 58
dance classes 72, 83
Dance Magazine 27
dancers 15–17, 20, 21, 23, 24, 29, 31, 42, 43, 46, 48, 56, 58, 60–63, 139
Davis, Crystal U. 72, 83, 142
Deci, Edward L. 121
Dewey, John 137, 159, 163, 165
diversity 6, 7, 97, 105, 106, 114

education 3, 4, 10, 72, 74, 113, 119, 120, 123, 139, 143, 158, 159
educational institutions 62, 144, 159
Ellsworth, Elizabeth 92, 176
embodied inquiry 46, 47, 50, 53
embodied knowledge 43, 50, 52, 53, 141, 151, 160
embodied learning 47, 158
embodied philosophies 46, 49, 51, 53
"en dedans" approaches 44
equitable ballet pedagogies 43, 54–62, 74; deficit to abundance 60–62; homogenized to differentiated 57–60; subjectivities and trust 54–57

equitable evaluation 144–146
equitable labor practices 88, 166
equitable pedagogies 85
equitable policies 145
equitable practices 95, 145
equity 59–62, 93–95, 97–100, 105, 106, 135, 145
"Equity-Care Matrix" (Bali and Zamora) 145
Equity-Centered Trauma-Informed Education (Venet) 85
evaluation 80, 135–157; in ballet 135–136
evaluative practices 139, 146
explicit biases 79, 80
Eyler, Joshua R. 140, 141

Farrell, Suzanne 58
feminist ballet class 88
Fonteyn, Margot 58
Forsyth, Sondra 7
Foster, Rory 19
Freire, Paulo 2–4, 10, 34, 49, 173; *Pedagogy of the Oppressed* 3

Gannon, Kevin M. 131, 159
Gautier, Théophile 23
general intelligence 138
Gerdt, Pavel 21
Giroux, Henry A. 10
Goetz, Jan Hanniford 7
Gottschild, Brenda Dixon 19, 20, 32
graded systems 138, 139
grades 135, 137–154, 179; in higher ed ballet class 139–144
grading 137–139; ballet 139, 140; in higher ed ballet class 139–144; policies 144

habitus 139
Hadley, Susan 50
Harrison, Iyun Ashani 137
H'Doubler, Margaret N. 137, 139
Heffernan, Troy 80
hierarchical power dynamics 4, 107, 131
hierarchical power structures 57, 119
higher education 85, 88, 91, 96, 98, 135–137, 139, 141, 146, 148, 154; ballet in 136–137
hooks, bell 3, 56, 62, 72, 88, 104, 119, 162, 170; *Teaching to Transgress* 104

Howard, Theresa Ruth 24, 64
humanity 3, 5, 6, 26, 55, 62, 73, 79, 88, 101, 110
humanizing approaches 87, 121, 128, 130, 177, 180
humanizing pedagogies 2, 3, 5, 6, 92, 100, 158, 159, 161, 176, 177; *see also individual entries*
humanness 2, 3, 5
humor 179, 180

ideal ballet body 25, 31
ideal ballet dancers 19, 23, 29
ideal bodies 17, 22–26, 29–31, 33, 60
ideal-driven pedagogies 17, 19, 21, 23, 25, 27, 29, 31, 33, 35, 37
ideal-driven pedagogies 15–41; blame and accountability 34–37; definitions and contexts 16–17; enactment and effects 26–34; execution and performance 17–19; ways of being 19–22
Imperial Russian Ballet School 18
implicit biases 10, 25, 61, 72–74, 83, 96, 99, 123, 142, 145, 154
inclusion 6, 21, 25, 32, 95, 99, 100, 105, 106
individual bodies 27, 33, 59, 60, 150, 169
individual dancers 26, 42, 44, 46, 55, 58, 60, 112
Inoue, Asao B. 139
institutional equity 88
intentions 70, 74, 75, 77, 86, 92, 93, 96, 125, 126, 128, 150, 162
interactions 164–166, 168, 176, 177
intrinsic motivation 127, 140, 144, 149
Ishangi, Kehinde 31

Jackson, Jehbreal Muhammad 25, 137
Jackson, Jennifer 44, 60, 143
Jackson, Naomi M. 3, 6, 44
Joffrey Ballet 7

Kendi, Ibram X. 144
Kennedy, Dr. Fen 129
Kerr, Maurya 31, 56, 101, 123
King, Alonzo 173
knowledge 6, 7, 19, 33, 34, 43, 47, 50, 51, 55, 113, 122, 125, 150, 172
Kohn, Alfie 131, 141, 151

Ladson-Billings, Gloria 29, 60, 138, 139, 153
Lakes, Robin 26, 27, 34
language of critique 10
LaVigne, Michelle 27
laziness 83
Leontiev, Leonid 23
letter grades 135, 137–139, 144
Levinson, André 23
liberatory pedagogies 4, 44
liminality 88

Macedo, Donaldo 3
Manne, Kate 35
Mattingly, Kate 25, 27, 35, 137
McCloud, Laila I. 146
McKenzie, Kevin 54
McPherson, Elizabeth 2, 3, 140
Merleau-Ponty, Maurice 47
Mille, Agnes de 19; *To a Young Dancer* 19
"mindless relativism" (Palmer) 46
misogyny 96
Mitchell, Arthur 25
Morris, Merry Lynn 16
movement qualities 16, 21, 28, 58, 77, 152

neoliberalism 4
Netherlands Dance Theatre 7
neurodivergent students 126, 138
Nordin-Bates, Sanna 106, 119, 122, 127, 130
Noverre, Jean-Georges 58

objectivity theater 57
Okun, Tema 129
open communication 102, 103

Palmer, Parker J. 46, 88
Papaefstathiou, Maria 26, 27; "Child Protection in Ballet" 27
Paskevska, Anna 30, 46, 52, 60
pedagogical/pedagogies 9, 15, 18, 29, 36, 43–53, 58, 63, 80, 87; abuses 36, 56; approaches 18, 26, 42, 49, 59, 74, 101, 102, 135, 152; development 7, 46, 49, 53, 88, 99, 124, 158; of freedom 56; inquiry 10, 56; perspectives 48, 63, 111; philosophies 49, 72, 153, 160, 166; practices 3, 16, 35, 92, 104, 113, 146; praxis 2, 145, 158;

skills 71, 72; values 48, 87, 128, 179; work 8, 44, 88, 93; see also individual entries
Pedagogy of the Oppressed (Freire) 3
Pickard, Angela 22
Pittman, Chavella 145
pluralism 8
Postman, Neil 100, 140
power 4, 27, 35, 45, 79, 86, 94, 119, 121, 122, 132, 144, 153, 154, 178; and bias 79–80; imbalance 129
practice grading 139, 147
Price, Devon 83
professional dancers 104, 148
Pyle, Katy 32, 36

racism 30, 61, 96, 144
radical pedagogies 85, 104
recollective reflection 165
reflective practices 148, 158–175; definitions and contexts 158–160; for students 168–173; teachers 160–168
reflective practices, students 168–173; early term 170–171; end-of-term 172–173; mid-term 171; semester-long reflective practice 169; student-driven reflective practice 173; workshopping 168–169
reflective practices, teachers 160–168; after class 165–166; before class 161–162; during class 162–165; persistent reflective practice 166–168
reflective process 148, 163, 169, 172
responsive pedagogy 88, 105
rigor 9, 28, 106, 108, 113, 120, 130–132, 160
Risner, Doug 2, 3, 140, 159
Ritenburg, Heather Margaret 22, 25, 29
Roslavleva, Natalia 17
Ross, Janice 137
Ryan, Richard M. 121

Salosaari, Paula 64
Scholastic Aptitude Test (SAT) 138
Schön, Donald A. 160, 164, 166, 168
Schupp, Karen 2, 3, 140
self-actualization 63, 180
self-determination theory 121

Seymour, Lynn 58
Shapiro, Sherry B. 47, 139
Shook, Karel 20, 21
social inequities 60
social justice 97–100
somatic practice 49, 119, 123
Sorensen-Unruh, Clarissa 131
Stommel, Jesse 144
student agency 6, 20, 84, 119
student agency and autonomy 119–134; yielding 122–130
student behaviors 28, 29
student biases 71, 80
student-driven pedagogies 42–65; ballet pedagogies 46–54; equitable ballet pedagogies 54–60; foundations and definitions 43–46; philosophy to praxis 62–64
student evaluations 79, 80, 87, 92, 123
student learning 158, 160, 172
student participants 96–100, 108, 109, 112, 114
student relationship 19, 55, 59, 71–73, 94, 101, 103, 104
student respondents 94, 96, 98, 113, 114
students, reflective practices 168–173
student trust 20, 55
student voices 91–115; ballet pedagogies, envisioning 100–115; ballet pedagogies, interpreting 93–100

Taglioni, Marie 58
Tallchief, Maria 58
Tate, William F. 29, 153
teacher behavior 69–89; embodying 76–79; foundations 72–79; listening 75–76; seeing 72–75
teacher presence 69–89; teacher persona 70–72; ways of being 70–72
teachers: institutional contexts 85–88; intentions 53, 140; knowledge 34, 52, 53, 102, 104; power and bias 79–80; problematic assumptions, students 81–85; reflective practices for 160–168
teaching ballet 3, 6, 7, 9, 10, 92, 106
Teaching Classical Ballet (White) 24
Teaching to Transgress (hooks) 104
Tedder, Michael 120, 121
Thalia Mara company 7

To a Young Dancer (de Mille) 19
Tobin, Thomas J. 145
training 6, 113, 114
trust 19, 20, 51, 54–56, 92, 93, 125, 153, 154, 162, 164

ungrading 135–157, 169; in ballet class 146–149; challenges and considerations 152–154; paradigms 152, 172; policies and practices, equitable evaluation 144–146; practices 9, 154; student perspectives 148–149; teaching beyond grades 149–152

Vaganova, Agrippina 17
Vaganova Ballet Academy 17
Valencia, Richard R. 60
van der Kolk, Bessel A. 120
Van Manen, Max 63, 158, 160–166, 168
Venet, Alex Shevrin 29, 85, 145, 162; *Equity-Centered Trauma-Informed Education* 85

Warner, John 131
Warren, Gretchen Ward 23, 24, 29–31, 51; *Classical Ballet Technique* 23
Weingartner, Charles 100, 140
White, John 19, 81; *Teaching Classical Ballet* 24
white racial habitus 139
white supremacy 129, 146
Wootten, Claire 88, 122
working relationship 55, 143

yielding 120, 122–124, 128, 130, 132, 150; bodily autonomy 128–130; challenge to 130–132; feedback, language of 128; inquiry and observation 124–126; methodology 122–124; perceptions of rigor 130–132; in practice 124; proposals, rationales, and experimentation 126–128

Zamora, Mia 145
Zide-Booth, Rochelle 7, 167, 179

For Product Safety Concerns and Information please contact our EU representative GPSR@taylorandfrancis.com
Taylor & Francis Verlag GmbH, Kaufingerstraße 24, 80331 München, Germany

www.ingramcontent.com/pod-product-compliance
Lightning Source LLC
Chambersburg PA
CBHW070609300426
44113CB00010B/1468